T. R. Wilson was ░░░░░░ borough on the edge of the Fens. He attended the University of East Anglia, and his love of East Anglia – its landscape, people and history – has always been central to his life and work. He submitted his first novel, *Master of Morholm*, at the age of twenty-three, at which time he was a student on the University of East Anglia MA course in Creative Writing, under Malcolm Bradbury and Angela Carter. His MA submission was part of the novel which was later published in 1989 as *Treading on Shadows*. His most recent novel, *Roses in December*, is also available from Headline. He lives with a word processor in a small flat.

*Also by T. R. Wilson from Headline*

Roses in December

# Hester Verney

## T. R. Wilson

HEADLINE

First published in 1993
by HEADLINE BOOK PUBLISHING PLC

First published in paperback in 1993
by HEADLINE BOOK PUBLISHING PLC

10 9 8 7 6 5 4 3 2 1

ISBN 0 7472 4115 5

Printed and bound in Great Britain by
HarperCollins Manufacturing, Glasgow

HEADLINE BOOK PUBLISHING PLC
Headline House
79 Great Titchfield Street
London W1P 7FN

For Dave Marzy

The romance growing up in the interstices of a mass of hard prosaic reality.

THOMAS HARDY

# Part One
## 1895

# Chapter One

Hester Verney was fifteen when she made the first important decision of her life. She made it in the chill dead middle of a spring night, sitting on the settle by the empty hearth, and sipping herself awake with cold black tea. Her father had made that settle with his own hands, from bog-oak dug up out of the fen fields; and as was the way with bog-oak, the settle had warped, so that the polished seat sloped at an angle along its length. To sit on it for more than a moment was to feel oneself sliding, slowly, gradually, steadily, from one end to the other; and by the time Hester had completed this progress, she had made her decision.

Her father had woken her a few minutes before, coming with an oil-lamp into the bedroom she shared with her sister and brothers and urging her in a whisper to shake a leg; and while the younger ones slept on above, she had dressed and come downstairs to find the family's few possessions wrapped up in bundles, her father's old horse standing in the shafts of the cart outside the open door, and all the signs of a flitting, familiar to her from earliest memory.

'I'm got to go, gel,' her father said, still in a whisper, though there was half a mile of bare pitch-black fen between them and the next house. 'There's rent owing summat cruel. If they'd just be patient, then they'd git it, sooner or later; but they wun't be patient – so they wun't git it at all, and that ain't my fault.'

Hester was used to her father's fractured logic, and she only said: 'Where to this time?'

Her father rolled up the pegged rug from the floor and tied it with string; then stood pensively contemplating a crate that contained a dozen fish-kettles, packed in straw. 'I still reckon I could find a use for these,' he said. He had bought them from a market trader in Whittlesey and had been unable to sell a single one: they did not fit over the turf fires of fen cottages.

'They're no good,' Hester said. 'Anyway, the handles come off.'

'Detach-able,' her father said mysteriously.

She was properly awake now: she finished the tea. 'Father, where are you going to go?'

'I'm finished here. I don't seem to git a run o'luck here.' Her father picked up the oil-lamp, tried to pick up the crate as well, needed both hands, set down the oil-lamp on the floor. 'I reckon I need to mek a clean break. A clean sweep. A new broom.' The metaphors entangled him for a moment, and he went and, uncertainly, picked up the broom from the hearth. 'No,' he said, putting it back, 'what I mean is, I'm gitting off the fen altogether. I shall try me luck over Leicester, where your aunt Netty is.'

Hester stared for a long moment into the dregs of her tea. Then she stood, picking up the oil-lamp before her father kicked it over, and looked at him in its pasty light. A smile came and went on his face.

'Your aunt Netty's a good woman, Hester,' he said. 'She's been pressing me to go over there for long enough. I know you don't git along with her all that special—'

'I'm not coming, Father. No, not on account of Aunt Netty. Even though she looks at me like summat that crawled out of a drain. And she always smells of tar-water. And even though,' she added, warming to her theme, 'she carries on like she's the Queen just because she's got a skerrick of old Nottingham lace on her table and some pretend flowers under a glass bowl what look like they come off a gravestone—'

'Not to everybody's liking,' her father said, shaking his head.

'But anyhow, it's not her. I said to meself last time we had to flit that I weren't going to do it any more; and I'm decided.'

Her father reached up to scratch his head, found he was wearing his hat, and scratched that instead. 'I know it's not been much of a life for you lately, gel,' he said. 'Racketing about from pillar to post. I just don't seem to be able to hold

4

on to money these days. But once we git over to Leicester, mek a fresh start—'

'It ain't that. Father, I'm got friends here,' Hester said. 'I'm been gitting good work at Langtoft's farm. Mrs Langtoft's been teaching me dairying and everything. I don't want to chuck it all up again.'

'I know, gel. I know. I'm been thinking of that. But I'm got to go, you see. There's Artie Gill an' all, carrying on all unreasonable reckoning I owe him money. Well,' he added, conceding a minor point, 'I do owe him money. But the point is, I seem to have lost all me reputation round 'ere.'

Hester could have told him that his reputation was all too intact; but she was too fond of him for that and, even leaving aside loyalty, she was like him in several ways. She did not think much the worse of him for being chronically unreliable: while he was hopelessly improvident, he was also affectionate; and if there was no god but the one god, Respectability, then she was quite as much a pagan as he.

'And then there's Mrs Puddock, you see,' her father said, 'gitting the wrong idea'; and he coughed delicately and took down the brass candlesticks from the mantelpiece.

Mrs Puddock was a widow who kept a good table and, it was said, had no objection to men getting their feet under it. She was the latest in a series of single or widowed women of a certain age with whom, in the course of several years' flitting from place to place around the fens, Hester's father had become tenderly involved. It was never his intention to begin these decorous affairs. He was a man of susceptible temperament and natural gallantry; and though he was a vague and ungainly creature, there was still a sort of distressed handsomeness about his perenially hopeful face and blue eyes, which these ladies seemed to take to; and one widow at Chatteris, from whom he had beaten a hurried retreat, had evinced a startling tendency to lay hold of him by his side-whiskers, and call him a Saucebox.

'She's a charming woman, Mrs Puddock,' her father said, 'but I do think our association will have to come to an end.' For he never meant anything by these entanglements: they were born of the same airy romanticism of spirit that had made him

5

lease an osier-bed and try his hand at making baskets, because he said his French Huguenot ancestors had done so, or set up a cart selling lemonade to the Irish navvies working on the new railway cut, because he thought some of them might be Temperance. And besides, in that same spirit he was faithful to the memory of Hester's mother, dead seven years since. 'You see why I'm got to go, don't you, gel?'

She nodded. 'And you see why I'm had enough of the flitting, don't you, Father? You know how Mrs Langtoft is always asking me to go and live in at the farm. With a room and everything – she's always right kind to me – it'd not be like going into service. And that's what most gels of my age are done by now.'

'They're very good sort of people, the Langtofts,' her father said. He was still absently holding the candlesticks. She took them from him, and packed them in a box. 'Ah, I suppose it had to come sooner or later. The young 'uns'll miss you, Hester.'

'Well, I hope so. I mean – you know what I mean. But there's Becca twelve now, and starting to earn soon, and Georgie and Arnold able to shift for theirselves. Besides, Father – I know you won't say it, so I will – I'm another mouth to feed, ain't I?'

'Thass never been a consideration wi' me, gel,' her father said solemnly. And with some truth, for his children were always hungry. 'Well! Your aunt Netty'll be sorry not to see you. I know that'll be better for the young 'uns, being close to her – she's a rare hand wi' children, my sister Netty.'

Hester held her tongue. She knew about Aunt Netty's hand: it was large, hard and red, and always seemed to be descending on your ears. If she had any uneasiness about separating herself from her family at last, it was at the thought of the young 'uns coming into that rather slapping orbit of Aunt Netty. But at least they stood more chance of being fed, and of being turned out smartly. Hester had never been one for playing the little mother – that was for story-books – the young 'uns being accustomed to setting out for school with no more than a cat-lick and a slice of bread-and-seam in their hands. She would miss them – there was a lump like a potato in her throat

6

at the thought of saying goodbye – but her mind was made up. She had truly had enough of the moonlight flits, the shifting and bolting and hiding under the table at the bailiff's knock. They had been nearly a year now at the cottage on Hinching Fen: she had friends, good work at Langtoft's farm, a feeling of home. The fen was her place.

'Now you're sure the Langtofts'll tek you in?'

'I'm sure. Mr Langtoft'll likely be astir soon, he's usually up at five. I can git a bed at Lizzie Gosling's if they're not ready for me.'

She helped her father carry the bundles out to the cart. The old horse turned his neck to watch them, indifferently, as if nothing could surprise him any more. The fen night was a great void around them, punctured here and there with stars.

'Better wake them young 'uns, and lay the bed in the bottom of the cart. We should git as far as Peterborough by daybreak.' Her father was whispering again, as if the silent blackness teemed with lurking creditors. 'Don't really like to flit without saying goodbye to folks. Tell the truth, I'm afraid they'd be asking me not to goo. They'll find they miss having a good higgler about the place – you'll see.' He adjusted the halter and went on, as if speaking into the horse's ragged ear: 'Funny, saying goodbye to you like this, gel. I s'pose it means you're growed up – and I can't quite believe it somehow.'

Hester smiled, gave him a kiss, and refrained from saying that living with him, she had had to grow up well before time, and this only set the seal on the process.

The young 'uns, in various states of sleepiness and protest, were roused from bed: the oat-flight mattress was placed in the cart, and Georgie and Arnold, after sitting up and blinking like two bewildered owls for a few minutes, had burrowed down and gone to sleep again by the time the cart was moving. The fen-drove that led to the high road was in an atrocious state after spring rains, but they had been through all this before and slept soundly despite the lurches and bumps; and Becca sat beside Hester with a look of resignation at this familiar reality and of having just been roused from some very different dreams.

Dawn was the merest phosphorescent presence, like some vast ghost haunting the eastern horizon, when her father pulled

7

up the cart at the corner of a drove. 'I'll let you down here then, gel. You give my best to the Langtofts, and tell 'em I'm sorry I didn't git chance to say goodbye to 'em proper-like.'

Hester climbed down. Her father handed her the carpet-bag containing her worldly goods.

'Be a credit to me, now. And any trouble at all, you know where we are. I s'll write you, though you know I ain't much of a penman. Your mother were always the one for writing. She could spell any word you cared to name. Excepting cottage, I seem to remember. That one always seemed to trip her up. And I tell you what – as soon as I git set up, and mek a bit o' money, I s'll send you the train fare, so's you can come and visit. That'll be summat to look forward to, wun't it?'

She was glad at the last to see her father floundering back to his old, hopeless optimism; even though its effect was to make the tears that had been standing in her eyes fall at last. She kissed her sister, promised to write, and watched the cart go creaking away. Colour was leaking into the sky; and all around, out of the formless dimness, fields and dykes and trees were stealing into view, as if they had been away somewhere in the empty night, and had just that moment come stealthily back. Abruptly, Hester was a little frightened: by nothing physical, but by an idea; the idea that she was alone. All at once she saw her life as a thing belonging only to her: as something precious that was being thrust into her hands. She picked up her bag and began to walk down the long drove to Langtoft's farm, with the world of the wide fens taking on shape around her, as if she were just that moment being born into it.

# Chapter Two

1

Hinching Fen covered half a thousand acres of the great flat basin known as the Bedford Level. It was a place sufficient of itself. The towns of Huntingdon, Peterborough and Ely were all at a distance that would have been accounted convenient in a district less poor, isolated and elemental: as it was, the fount of such amenities as the folk of Hinching Fen enjoyed was Stokeley, a diminutive market town a couple of miles down the river, consisting of a ruined abbey, an enormously wide High Street, and a nest of houses with deep roofs and long dormer windows that gave them the look of having low foreheads, and of glowering at each other in suspicion. For the rest, the land was all, and the land was low, black, peaty, strange, and precious; and given half a chance the water would take it back.

Such were the horizons of Hester's world for the next three years. Langtoft's farm lay in the middle of the fen: a geographically imprecise expression, but one readily comprehensible to any fen-dweller – for to live in the fens is always to live in the middle of them. The farmhouse was a square building of brick and tile, not large, with a crow-stepped gable-end facing the east wind that came like a battering-ram over the fields. The farm was worked for the most part by the Langtofts alone; and while Hester earned her keep, with an allowance of pin-money when times were good enough, and was trained up much as any female farm-servant would be, she was from the beginning encouraged to count herself part of the family. No one in that part of the country was rich; and those few big farmers who did go in for ceremony, and

9

yellow gig-wheels, and lace curtains, elicited more contempt than respect.

Mrs Langtoft took Hester under her wing. There were three sons in the house, but Mrs Langtoft's only daughter Mary had died from diphtheria in infancy and, as she confided to Hester, she missed having a girl about the place. Often she spoke of her 'Meery', and what a shame it was they never raised her.

'Ah! I could just picture my Meery looking like you now, gel,' Mrs Langtoft would say, as Hester came into the kitchen glowing from the winter's morning. 'She'd have been just your age – and just your colouring too, I reckon, if she'd ha' lived.'

This colouring of Hester's was one which her father would no doubt have attributed to the Verneys' French blood, of which he was so proud: others – in a land where the plough turned up the paved causeways of Caesar's legions, and the 'ole Romans' were spoken of as familiarly as great-grandparents – might have harked back further. In fact it was a complexion not uncommon in the fens: and whether or not she had inherited the blue eyes from the Danes who had sacked Stokeley Abbey, the very fair, almost waxen white skin from the free-born Saxons who had made their last stand here against the Norman tide, and the pure black hair, blue-black in sunlight, from the French Protestants who had sought refuge from persecution in this watery land, in Hester the ensemble was both peculiarly native and striking.

She came into her looks late. The needy, harum-scarum life with her father had meant that the physique of a child had persisted into her sixteenth year, and it was the influence of Langtoft's farm that effected a transformation, rapid as the forcing of a hothouse flower. Poverty at such small family farms was held at a distance only by unremitting labour, but held it was, and the food that came to Mrs Langtoft's scrubbed deal table, while plain, was substantial. There was home-cured bacon and ham, there was home-baked bread, there was fresh milk, there were potatoes and greenstuff in plenty, and there were also Mrs Langtoft's formidable puddings, known as water-wallopers, which could take the edge off the keenest appetite. When the winter weather was raw and savage, and the fen, as Mr Langtoft said, was 'as blea as nowhere on God's earth, not excepting Roosia', you always came indoors to the blaze of a good turf fire; and when the rain drenched those naked shelterless fields, there were always clean dry clothes to change into, stitched by Mrs Langtoft and herself in the evenings by the light of the oil-lamp. Merely the absence of those deprivations to which she had long been accustomed was enough to send Hester's body shooting from girlhood to young womanhood, and seeming to omit adolescence in between – a pleasant enough omission, indeed, though perhaps as a consequence a certain healthy element of self-doubt was lacking in a nature otherwise open, generous and tolerant.

It would have taken a more saintly girl than Hester – emerging thus from a gawky and harassed youth, schooling constantly interrupted by the vagaries of a father who was a large child himself – not to feel a newly satisfying sense of self. 'I see you, gel,' Mrs Langtoft would say, as Hester hovered before the polished milk-pan hanging on the dairy wall, 'admiring yourself there. You'll see the devil over your shoulder one of these days!'

But it was a feigned sternness: Mrs Langtoft liked to regard the girl as her protégée, and it rather comforted her than otherwise to witness the flourishing promise that 'her Meery' would have enjoyed in her place. And Hester examined her image with perhaps as much genuine pleased surprise as outright vanity. The reflection showed her an oval face, high-cheekboned, and dominated by a pair of eyes large and limpid enough for the cloister, the force of which was partly disarmed by dark slanting brows, expressive of scepticism: whilst, in strong contrast, the tilt of her nose and upward curve of her lips might have come from a portrait of one of Charles II's lazily humorous mistresses. With her dark hair bound up to reveal small ears and a fair neck, she had something of the erect shapeliness of a flower – no exotic bloom, but a country flower as English as Chaucer. Hester gazed, and was what the Chapel called ensnared by the flesh; but in spite of Mrs Langtoft's warning she did not see the devil over her shoulder. What she did begin to notice, after she turned eighteen, was the face of the Langtofts' eldest son Chad observing her. But when

11

she turned round, he would always be walking away, or busy with something. Beyond those odd covert stares there was no alteration in his manner towards her; and as hers was a mind very much at ease, and never inclined to burden itself with unnecessary reflection, she scarcely gave the circumstance a second thought.

It was the more natural that Chad should remain in the background of her consciousness, in that it was Mrs Langtoft around whom life at the farm revolved. Everyone worked hard: Hester; Mr Langtoft whose name was Charles and was therefore known as Wag; Chad who was twenty and Jacob and Will who were in their early teens; but Mrs Langtoft was the oil in the engine. She was a small, neat, round, black-eyed woman, sturdy as a Shetland pony, utterly tireless, and deft and quick in everything: she even had a habit of rapid blinking, as if there were a lot of blinks to get through, and not much time to do them. Her square red hands were never still: they wound wool or worked stitches while she waddled from place to place or waited for a pot to boil; and when the cat jumped on her lap of an evening, her fingers would stroke and scratch to such an alarming degree that it was almost as if she had half a mind to unpick him, and start him all over again. The work of the farm was unceasing, and at times like harvest it rose to frenetic pitch, and in Mrs Langtoft there was a fear that if they let up for a moment, everything would collapse. She had burning memories of the terrible distress of '79, when some on the fen had survived on potato peelings and turnip-tops.

'Git on!' she would say. 'Git on, will yer – you want to end up on turnip-tops?' She was fond of her menfolk, but she confided to Hester that they were useless articles, and needed driving: and if they showed signs of lingering at the breakfast-table, and reluctance to turn out, Mrs Langtoft would charge amongst them as if she were a ball and they were so many skittles, and scatter them off to work.

With her Hester learned all the tasks of the distaff side of the farm. She milked, she made butter, she baked bread, she tended the pigs; she scrubbed the brick floor of the big kitchen, she black-leaded the range and scoured the hearth with red ochre, she heaped the laundry into the great boiler on washing-days when the house ran with steam that made it more damp than ever; and at harvest she worked with the others in the fields, tying the sheaves that Mrs Langtoft raked. Always at these times Mrs Langtoft seemed to be far ahead of her, clad despite the heat in the invariable black high-collared dress, wielding the rake with her short arms that never tired. 'Come on, git on!' she would say, if the men leaned on their scythes for a few moments. 'Never git done at this rate. Tek us a month o' Sundays at this rate.'

The work was exhausting, but Hester – while she would gladly do nothing and lie in the sun all day given a chance – found she thrived on it. She became supple as a young tree. Her legs, from the awkward stalks of neglected girlhood, grew long, straight and strong by dint of walking about the sprawling distances of the fen: her arms were as firm as apples. Her skin, subject to that East Anglian climate of sustained sunlight tempered with cool wind, was infused with colour sufficient to ripen but not coarsen it. Between rough twill sheets she slept the profound satisfying sleep of those who trouble not in the least about what the next day will bring; and to a disposition already conditioned, by life with her father, to taking nothing very seriously, was added a cheerful sense of the ridiculous and a readiness to laugh. 'You'll see, my gel,' Mrs Langtoft would say, 'the wind'll change one o' these days and your face'll get stuck like it!' But again it was a severity she did not mean, for she could not deny that laughter suited the girl's face, and that there was a peculiar charm in the way that a little glimpse of pink tongue showed against her white teeth.

Hester's wants were few; but as she turned eighteen, and the reflection in the milk-pan began to arrest her attention more strangely and pleasingly, they seemed to sharpen, and to pierce her in the form of sudden wishes for some item of adornment beyond the capability of her needle. A silk ribbon, a strip of lace, a feather to trim her Sunday straw hat, some mother-of-pearl buttons that she had seen on a blouse at chapel – such things appealed to her with an absurd urgency. Stokeley was where they were to be had, but that meant a four-mile walk across the fen, or waiting until Mr Langtoft went over to market in his waggon, and both of these were contingent on the farm

13

being able to spare her. The easiest way to procure luxuries was by the tallyman.

Mrs Langtoft did not approve of the tallyman. He was known as 'Rob' Risby, from the abbreviation of his name painted on the tailboard of his cart, though some said the epithet had a more sinister significance. He came regularly out from Stokeley to tour the widely scattered fen cottages, offering for sale a variety of goods from clothes to trinkets to crockery, all to be paid for on an 'easy' instalment basis which made them the more tempting to folk who lived always on the margins of poverty. Hester limited herself to combs and beads, and once a bangle that produced a bright green stain on her wrist; but many women on the fen were inveigled into buying things on the tally that they could not afford, and this roused Mrs Langtoft to fury.

'Silly davils!' she snorted. 'Putting theirselves in debt for a bit o' trumpery! They ain't got the sense they were born with. It meks my blood boil.'

But the real reason she was so vigilant against Rob Risby was her husband. Mr Langtoft was sadly susceptible to the tallyman. If Mrs Langtoft were the first to spot Risby's cart coming up the drove, all was well: she would go running out of the house, flapping and shooing as if he were some species of large despoiling bird, and crying: 'You git away! You'll do no good here! We don't want no kickshaws!' But if for some reason she was not at hand, then Mr Langtoft was helpless, a fly to the tallyman's web.

'He's got me again, gel,' Mr Langtoft would say to Hester, coming into the house bearing an umbrella, a shoe-tree, or a bed-valance with huge purple roses on it. 'I dunno how it is. It's summat about the way he talks. I go all sort of weak-like.'

It was not that Rob Risby dazzled him with patter: far from it. Hester watched and listened from the kitchen window one day, when Mrs Langtoft had gone to call on a sick neighbour (only a mile's walk), and the tallyman's cart drew up outside the yard where Mr Langtoft was working. She saw the farmer straighten up and frown, and then march up to the gate as if he were resolved to be firm.

'We don't want nothing off you,' he said, in quite a

14

stalwart voice. 'So you're wasting your time, thanks all the same.'

Rob Risby got down from the cart, throwing the reins over the pony's head. 'Morning, Mr L. How're you keeping?'

'I'm all right enough,' Mr Langtoft said suspiciously, keeping his hands on the latch of the gate. 'But like I say, we don't want nothing today.'

The tallyman nodded. 'Just as you say, Mr L. If you don't want nothink, you don't want nothink. I thought as I'd pass the time o' day, any road.' He was a thin, hollow-chested, worn-looking man, with sparse pale hair, a feeble whisker, and a voice of reedy timbre that drooped off into a frequent sigh. 'I won't deny I'm got a little trifle here as I thought you might want to look at, at least: I brought it out special on account o' you; but it don't matter.'

'Why, what's that, then?' Mr Langtoft said, still gruff.

'We-ell,' the tallyman said, with great reluctance, pulling a small parcel from his pocket, 'it's rather a nice thing, you know; a pair of sewing scissors, very dainty, Sheffield steel, and in their own little case of morocco leather, with spaces an' all for needles. Soon as I saw it, I thought of Mrs L, her being such a smart needlewoman as everybody knows, and likely to appreciate such a thing, which there's not everybody would. I like things to go where they're appreciated, you see, and so I was even thinking of letting it go for two-and-sixpence, which is doing myself down summat chronic.'

The little case was held out, negligently, and Hester saw a sort of paralysis creep over Mr Langtoft's face as he gazed at it. Then he seemed to rally, and shook his head. 'No,' he said stoutly, 'not interested.'

Rob Risby's forehead wrinkled in pain. 'Have I made a mistake, d'you think, Mr L? Does it seem a little shoddy? I try never to buy shoddy – not that there's some who wouldn't notice either way – but there's some folks whose judgement I rely on – and I'd hate to think I'd offered summat in the way of an insult—'

'No, no,' Mr Langtoft said, uncomfortable now, 'I didn't mean that, you know. But –' he bit his lip – 'we can't afford it.'

'Well, Mr L,' Rob Risby said, 'you're got me. Two shillings it is.'

'Eh—?'

'Oh! I know it's worth more than that. But I can't fight you, Mr L. You're too strong for me, and thass a fact. You might as well tek it for one and ninepence –' here the tallyman's gloom deepened terribly, and he fetched a great sigh – 'and just kill my poor ole wife off altogether.'

This imputation of murderous designs against Mrs Risby threw Mr Langtoft into alarm. 'Why, whatever do you mean?' he said. 'What's the matter?'

'It's the stomach, poor soul,' Rob Risby said, 'it's always been her trouble, and this time . . .' and his weak voice faded completely.

Mr Langtoft, in a tone of dismay, hoped it was not very bad?

'It *is* bad,' the other said, judicially, 'I wish I could deny it. There's only certain foods as she can tek at all. I says to her last night: Mother, could you fancy a bit o' fish? I could, Robert, she says – but we ain't got the money to buy it, have we? And I had to say no. Ah, that would be nice, she says, a bit o' fish – say whiting, or hake, nothing fancy – and you know, Robert, I feel better just a-thinking on it. Thass a little harmless fancy we go through, you see, Mr L: sometimes we pretend kidneys, and sometimes we make-believe bacon – and so we bear up.' He swallowed, and fixed his eyes on the distance.

'Well, now, look here,' Mr Langtoft said, 'I didn't say I wouldn't tek it for two shillings, you know.'

'Now thass a funny thing. I says to my poor ole wife the smorning: Mother, bear up, I says, because I'm gooing to see Farmer Langtoft today, and if there's one man on the fen as has got a reputation for fair dealing, and sense, and recognising the value of independent tradesmen with a living to make, then he's that man.' Rob Risby shook Mr Langtoft's hand, with an appearance of deep humility. In a moment the transaction was done, and Mr Langtoft was in possession of the scissors-case, and actually looking as if he felt he had come out of it rather well. The tallyman began to put up the tailboard of his cart; then paused, and turning back to the farmer with renewed dejection, took something else from his pocket.

'I don't suppose for a moment, Mr L,' he said, 'you'd consider investing in a couple o' these?'

'Smelling-salts?' Mr Langtoft laughed: he was confident again. 'What would I want with them?'

The tallyman seemed to wince at the laughter, and shook his head. 'Well! I promised our Nelly I'd try. I can't do no more . . . I suppose it won't be long now.'

This mention of Nelly threw Mr Langtoft again into discomfiture. 'Why, who's Nelly?'

'Our youngest, Mr L. Sick abed now. It's the lights, you see. Rising. Mother reckons it's on account of how she were frightened by a balloon going up at Pete'borough Fair when she were carrying her. Anyhow, I'm afraid we shan't raise her. Oh! bless you, Mr L,' he went on sympathetically, as Mr Langtoft showed great agitation of mind, 'it's nothink as can't be cured. Don't think that. But it's a question of paying for the medicine, you see. Afore I come out the smorning, Nelly sat up in her little bed, leaning on one hand – the other hand was holding her doll, you see – leastways it's nearly a doll – it only lacks the head – and she makes shift to sort of imagine the head there, if you follow me – and so she bears up. There's a lot of imagination in our family, Mr L . . . if nothink else . . . She sat up, and she says to me, Daddy, shall you git the medicine today? And I says, not wishing to lie to her: Nelly, that depends on me mekking a bit o' money – and that all depends on the customers, you see. And she says, Daddy, why wun't them customers give you a bit o' money – are they very bad men? And I says no, Nelly – they ain't bad. I won't believe that of 'em . . .'

A few minutes later Mr Langtoft was standing, crestfallen, on the threshold of the kitchen. Besides the scissors-case and the smelling-salts, he was holding a cigar-box and something dusty in felt and wool which he explained to Hester, dubiously, as a 'pen-wiper'.

'D'you think Bess'll be awk'ud with me?' he asked, without hope.

Hester, struggling to maintain an expression of the utmost seriousness, said she was afraid so.

'Beggared if I don't think he plays on me, that one,' Mr Langtoft said. 'Well, I s'll git a dusting-off for this.' It was a curiously appropriate phrase, for Mr Langtoft being a loose, baggy, shapeless sort of man, and his grizzled hair and bedraggled moustache seeming to trap everything from corn-chaff to wood-shavings, he was a standing affront to the neat habits of his wife, who was unable to come near him without dusting him down, and plumping him up, and generally rearranging him.

At the scullery door Hester listened to Mrs Langtoft's lamentations on her return; and when Mr Langtoft made a despairing effort to justify the smelling-salts, saying they might rouse the old horse when he was sluggish of a morning, she had to cram her apron into her mouth to stop herself bursting out laughing. It was just then that a shadow fell across the doorway to the yard, and she saw Chad standing there.

'What you laughing at?' he said.

His expression was so mistrustful that she sobered a little. She explained.

'Oh! that,' he said. He continued to stand in the doorway, tapping his muddied boots on the step, looking at her and not quite looking at her. Hester swallowed another laugh, and began to work the pump.

'Should you like it if somebody bought you things?' Chad said abruptly.

'I don't know – nobody ever has,' Hester said.

'But would you though?' Chad said, in his dogged way.

'Well – not smelling-salts.'

'Not smelling-salts. I don't mean nothink like that.'

'Well, I should like it, of course,' she said; but as she turned from the pump Chad was already gone.

She did not think anything of this at the time; nor did she recall the small indications of a shifting in Chad's manner during the last few months. They touched her consciousness like breath on glass, condensing and evaporating in a moment. There seemed nothing remarkable in the fact that he often appeared suspicious of her laughter, as if fearing it was directed at him. Chad had always been the slowest to laugh of the household, seldom sharing the high spirits of his younger brothers, moving quietly about the farm somewhat in a circuit of his own, and often inclined to be touchy. If she had been observant, she might have detected a note of intensity in what she took to be his normal silences and stares; his fastening, terrier-like, on the most trivial remarks and not letting them go. But to Hester's spontaneous nature was added the characteristic egotism of youth, which arranges other people into a mere concomitant pattern, like so many planets to the sun of self: and it was not until the long frost which began after Christmas of her nineteenth year, that she was forced to review the pattern, and confront its disruption.


2


It was Uncle Bevis who started it.

He came out to the farm in his dashing little gig, on a bitter bright February morning, when there was cat-ice at the edges of the dykes, and the ploughed fields sparkled as if they had been sugared. Hester was in the kitchen boiling up pig-taters, and Mrs Langtoft was mixing the pudden, when they heard the smart clop of hooves and the crunch of wheels, followed by a familiar voice roaring out: 'Whup, Chaddy, bor! Mind when you tek 'old on her – she's as lively as a cricket the smorning!'

Mrs Langtoft snatched off her hessian apron. 'There's Uncle Bevis – pass me my clean apron, Hester gel – and goo and call in Wag and them boys. And fetch out the nodding-cake we made yis'dy – I'm sure Uncle Bevis will tek a slice.'

It was notable that whilst the family were always at some pains to receive Uncle Bevis properly, none of them looked forward to his visits with much pleasure. He was a relation of Mrs Langtoft's, who had done well for himself as a butcher, and had a bay-windowed house in Stokeley, with its own set of railings. He liked to present himself in the character of a sportsman, and to speed off in his gig to the races at Huntingdon, and to clink tankards with horsey persons in the bar-parlours of inns hung with hunting-prints; and there was a hint of breezy condescension in his periodic descents on the Langtofts' farm to, as he put it, 'gee them up'. He had an apparent compulsion never to call anyone by their plain name, but always to lend it a jolly and, as it were, sporting aspect; and while 'Hester' had defeated him for a while, he had at last triumphantly modified it to Hetty – which made her want to scream every time.

But, he was a person of consequence: and so Hester called in Mr Langtoft and his sons, who were dyke-roding at a small distance from the house; and she was just fetching out the nodding-cake, a confection of pastry, sugar and currants of which Uncle Bevis was known to be fond, when Mrs Langtoft cried: 'There! I knew I should ha' laid a fire in the Room. Goo and mek it up, Hester – there's turves enough.'

The big, warm and cheerful kitchen was where the family lived: the Room was an icy parlour, a small square frigidarium where a row of upholstered chairs were preserved, as if they were of fresh composition, and liable to go off. But just then Uncle Bevis came in, stamping and blowing, and hallooed out: 'No, no, Hetty, not for me! Don't trouble for me – a comfortable kitchen fire suits me – no pampering. Well, Bessy, and how do I find you?'

He was a big man, this uncle Bevis, made bigger by a suit of eye-catching check, with a great close-cropped ginger head, a fox-coloured moustache, plump red ears, hands like hams, and a substantial seat which he turned to the fire. Everything about him was large, ruddy, and obtrusive; and even when he was not talking, there was a continual noise about him, from the jingling of watch, watch-chain, seals, buttons, studs, and silver and copper money in all his pockets. He threw down his stiff bowler hat, which left a red weal round his forehead, and clapped his hands at the old dog lying in the corner. 'Come here, then, Towser! Come here, you old davil!'

The dog (whose name was Dan, not Towser) tried to slink away, but was forced to submit to the jovial mauling that Uncle Bevis, who boasted of a way with animals, thought all dogs rejoiced in – just as all horses were to be heartily slapped, and cats picked up by the scruff with a facetious shout of 'Meow!' 'Ha ha, you rascal!' he said, rolling Dan about on the floor, whilst the dog, who was gentle and not at all rascally, looked

20

as if he wished he were elsewhere. 'You would, would you? I know you, you davil.'

The dog was saved at last by the entrance of Mr Langtoft and his sons. 'Whup, Jakey! Whup, Billo!' Uncle Bevis cried, and proceeded to his usual greeting of the boys, which was to punch them on their upper arms, laughing the while, and making boxer's feints. 'The old fellow keeps you at it, eh? No rest for the wicked – and they don't come much wickeder, I'll be bound. Eh?' For he considered he had a rapport with boys too; and after a further series of playful cuffs, head-butts, and shoulder-slappings, he squeezed his rump at last into the Windsor chair, and regaled them with accounts of fist-fights and ratting, until the tea was made.

'So, Waggy, and how do you get along?' Uncle Bevis said, between mouthfuls of nodding-cake.

'Not so very bad,' Mr·Langtoft said with caution. 'But I wish this here frost would goo. It's the davil to plough, and there's gret old cracks forming in the dykesides.'

'You're at the mercy of the elements – thass your trouble out here. Always fighting the elements. Thass what's good about setting up in town. Not that I couldn't put up with it here meself,' Uncle Bevis added, for fear of seeming unmanly. 'Why, I thrive on it – I can spend a day up to me knees in snow and think nothing of it—'

(Mr Langtoft stirred, as if he did not think much of it either.)

'It'd be no hardship for me – but there's my wife to consider.' Uncle Bevis's wife was a shadowy figure, who never went out, but had headaches in a darkened room full of caged birds.

'And how do you go along, Uncle Bevis?' Mrs Langtoft said.

'I can't complain, Bessy – I can't complain,' Uncle Bevis said, jingling excessively, and throwing out his stomach. 'I'm thinking of setting up another gig – nothing fancy. Old Chancy Lowe, who keeps the livery stables, gives me a fair bargain. I wonder you don't trade in that old cart of yours, Wag, for summat a bit sprucer.'

'I'm thought about it,' said Mr Langtoft, though he had not,

21

'but it don't seem practical, with the droves the way they are in winter.'

'True – true. But bless you, while there's a long frost there's skating – ain't you seen it? It's froz all across Milney Wash. I see a whole issue of folk skating there just yis'dy. Why, where's the point in living on the fen, without going skating? Chaddy, bor –' Chad had just come in from seeing to the pony – 'you can skate a bit, can't you?'

'Ah,' Chad said. 'I ain't been this year, though. Don't seem to git time.'

'You want to mek time – frost most likely wun't last much longer. What about you, Hetty? Ain't you ever skated?'

'No,' Hester said. 'I never learned.' The peripatetic life with her father meant she had missed out on such things.

'Why, you can't call yourself a fenlander if you ain't skated,' Uncle Bevis said. 'I was a beggar for the skating-matches when I were a lad – maister used to box me ears for sloping off to 'em –'cos, you know, I were only a 'prentice then: no bigger than Billo here –' here Will came in for a few more cuffs, and had his hair rubbed the wrong way – 'and twice as skinny. I used to go to Bury Fen where the races were – and I remember tekking part once, and beating the chap who were reckoned to be champion – only they disqualified me, on account of I were too young.'

'Perhaps you could teach me, then, Uncle Bevis,' Hester said, not without mischief.

'Wehrr, I'd like to, gel, but I ain't kept it up these last few years – my wife, you see, she reckons it ain't safe, so I left off for the sake of her nerves.'

'I know I'm got an old pair o' skating-pattens what'd fit the gel, somewhere,' Mrs Langtoft said. 'We used to go when we were courting, Wag – d'you remember? – and you had to hold me up the whole time.' She patted her husband's arm affectionately – for she was fond of him, albeit he was a useless article – and even with this gesture she was unable to resist giving him a prod and a dust, and rearranging his waistcoat.

'There you are then!' Uncle Bevis said. 'Chaddy bor, you could teach Hetty here skating. Why, it puts Blood in you – there's no exercise like it!' And he made a pair of great fists,

22

and performed a mime, expressive of skating into a head wind, at an unlikely speed.

'Ah, that'd be nice for you, gel,' Mr Langtoft said. 'You don't git a lot of outings. Should you like that?'

'All right, then,' Hester said, for she was willing to try anything once.

'What d'you say, Chad?'

'I don't mind,' Chad said.

'Let's see,' Mr Langtoft said, 'you could go tomorrer—'

'Not tomorrer!' Mrs Langtoft said, in a pouncing way. 'Sunday tomorrer – not on a Sunday.' For Mrs Langtoft, as was usual on the fen, was Chapel, and embraced that subtle interpretation of the Day of Rest, which precluded doing anything on it that might be nicer than working. 'Besides, we're got the preacher coming to dinner tomorrer. We're got a missioner coming all the way from Spalding to our chapel, Uncle Bevis, and it's our turn to give him dinner.'

'That'll be a treat for him, Bessy, as ought to inspire him to highest eloquence,' Uncle Bevis said; while Mr Langtoft looked at the fire, and seemed to suffer a temporary lowering of spirits. 'But any road, what's against this evening? The moon's near full, and there'll be folk galore there, and bonfires on the ice, I shouldn't wonder.'

There was nothing against that evening; and before Uncle Bevis left, he treated them to balletic demonstrations (on the kitchen floor) of how to bend the knees, and how to turn, and how to stop, and how to figure-of-eight – all of which manoeuvres apparently involved treading on people's toes, and elbowing them in the face. 'Ah, you'll tek to it like a natural, gel!' he assured Hester; and having already punched the boys goodbye, he modified the gesture in deference to her sex in the usual way, by digging his hands in his pockets, and bumping her sideways, as if he were trying to break down a door.

'Poor ole lot – I reckon they wouldn't do nothing if I didn't goo and gee 'em up now and then,' Uncle Bevis said to himself as he rattled away in his gig.

'Uppity ole fool – I bet he never skated in his life,' Mr Langtoft said to himself as he went back to work.

Chad Langtoft was a fair-haired young man, with light eye-brows and eyelashes, and that fairness of skin that tends at times almost to a tender rawness, and on which a flush of embarrassment or anger shows up like blood on snow. His frame was a light, fine-boned one, though wiry and strong; and with pronounced cheekbones where the skin seemed thinner than ever, and very transparent blue eyes: altogether he gave the impression of lacking a layer somewhere, and of going too naked into the world.

Whether or not as a direct consequence of this, an extreme caution marked his manner. He would never give an opinion: 'I don't mind,' he would say: 'Whatever you like,' or ''S all right enough'; yet it was a kind of indifference that did not suggest equanimity or self-possession. It was almost, Hester thought, as if an opinion, a thought or a feeling were a secret thing, and might betray him if it were let out.

So it was no surprise to her when Chad said, that afternoon as they were getting ready to go skating: 'You don't have to go if you don't want.'

'No, I want to,' she said. 'I don't know how I shall get on, but I'll have a go. Don't you want to go?'

'Oh! I don't mind.'

So as the afternoon darkened, she changed in her small attic room, putting on woollen stockings and a knitted scarf, which constituted all her winter wear; and pinned her hat with a long silver pin, which had been sent to her as a present by her father a year or so ago. Since then he had faded further from sight: her sister and brothers were all earning their keep in Leicester, at shoe-factories, and living with Aunt Netty, while her father had disappeared north, apparently with some quixotic scheme of becoming a fellmonger, though he never could bear the sight of a dead animal. More and more her life before Langtoft's farm seemed like an incoherent dream, in which her own identity was as vague as a phantom. She looked at the plain little room and thought, 'I've been happy here': and at the same time the thought was flavoured with a little unaccustomed dissatisfaction – for to pass from a state of happiness, to an exterior perception of it, is to render it finite and conceive its end. Pessimism was no part of Hester's character, for the simple reason that she never thought of the future at all; but just for a moment, rather as she had done at that moment when she had said goodbye to her father at the corner of the drove, she glimpsed a large space about the contours of her life, and wondered how it was to be filled.

The sun was low when she and Chad walked to Milney Wash, traversing the bone-hard fields, and crossing the dykes by the narrow bridges made of railway sleepers. Chad, with a muffler added to his usual outfit of white duck trousers, jacket over sleeved waistcoat, and neckerchief, seemed sunk in a great shyness of her – as if they had not been living and working side by side for three years.

'Chad, what's Uncle Bevis's wife like?' she asked him, uncomfortable at the silence. 'You ever seen her?'

'I'm seen her in Stokeley once,' Chad said. 'Not to speak to.'

'It'd be funny if he were frit on her, though, wouldn't it? I mean, him mekking out he's so manly and all – it meks you wonder. I'll bet thass what it is. I bet when he gits home he has to knuckle under, and do everything she says, and she teks a broomstick to him.'

It pleased her to find she had made Chad laugh: he looked better when he laughed.

'Father says there's a chap like that lives over at Forty Feet Bridge,' he said. 'Goes down the Labour In Vain and sups hisself silly and talks big all night 'bout how he's the master in his house and then when he gits home his wife's waiting for him wi' the coal-shovel.'

It was a long speech for Chad, and again she was pleased at having drawn him out. 'Shall you be master in your own house when you git married, Chad?'

His guard came up again. 'How d'you mean?'

'Well . . .' She hadn't meant anything really. 'You know – wear the trousers.'

'Oh! I don't know.'

25

It was a subject, in fact, on which she herself had views both decided and cloudy. Decided, because she was never going to call any man 'maister', as some women on the fen still referred to their husbands; and as far as she could see, once it got to broomsticks and coal-shovels, you might as well give in and each go your ways. Cloudy, because at the core of her practical nature she was intensely romantic, and conceived of love as transforming prosaic reality, not merely overlapping it, and certainly not emerging from it.

The noise of exhilarated voices reached them before they were in sight of Milney Wash, such is the carrying power of sound on the fens; and when they arrived they found several score of people, skating on the expanse of water-meadow which was frozen to an even smoothness, lined here and there with cracks which showed that the ice would bear safely. The sun was close to the horizon, and in its declension had scored a great brazen trail in the sky, deepening to fiery orange where it traced the ribs of cloud, and shedding over the scene a biting metallic radiance. There was a pure cold suspension in the air, which seemed to lend its quality to visual perception, so that the very shadows on the ice were crystalline in their definition, and the figures of the skaters were outlined with an aura, like silhouettes beaten out of copper.

There were a lot of people there whom they knew, from the scattered cottages and the odd hamlets, scarcely rising to the status of villages, around the fen. On the edge of the field someone had lit a brazier and, dotted about on the ice, incongruously, were a few chairs, both for sitting on to fasten your skates and for beginners to hold on to. The sound of the skates, now deep and grumbling, now shrill, was exciting, and Hester thought it looked very easy.

Her friend Lizzie Gosling, whose father kept the Hinching Fen mill, came gliding over as she was putting on her skates.

'Hester Verney – I'm never seen you skating before.'

'I'm never done it before. Chad's going to teach me.'

Lizzie Gosling was a plump, dark, deceptively sleepy-looking girl, with a pretty sceptical mouth, who could give such sharp answers that the boys did not quite know what to make of her. She blinked her heavy lids at Hester and then at Chad, and nearly-smiling as always said: 'I shall have to see this. Didn't you bring a cushion to stick on your behind?'

'I'm sure I can do it if you can, you ole haybag,' Hester said, in the affectionate terms which they always used with each other. 'Come on, Chad. Let's show her.'

She teetered upright and Chad took her hands crosswise. She went about a yard before she fell down.

'Graceful,' Lizzie said, in her dry way. 'Very pretty, that.'

For some time after that Hester remembered only getting up and falling down, with a few wildly wobbling upright interludes. After the first few falls it ceased to hurt and, what with the relentless inevitability with which her bottom hit the ice, and the deadpan comments of Lizzie, she could not stop laughing.

'Go again,' Chad said. 'Try again.'

'It looked so easy!' Hester said, and the frost-smoky horizon wavered in her tears of laughter, and then swooped as she fell down again.

All around them other people were laughing as they slipped and overbalanced and collided; but Chad did not laugh. All the time he went doggedly on, skating with competent strokes, and helping her up; until at last she staggered, exhausted, to a chair.

'I reckon it's harder work than lifting taters!' she gasped, wiping her eyes. 'Never mind Uncle Bevis's fancy turns – I can't even stand up!'

Chad crouched down, with his arms on his knees, his eyes on the other skaters.

'S'll we go home now, then?' he said after a moment.

She looked at him in surprise.

'Well,' he said, seeming to study the composition of the ice at his feet, 'if you're only going to laugh, and not do it properly.'

'I can't help it,' she said. 'It don't matter, does it?'

'I don't like being laughed at, thass all.'

'Chad, I weren't laughing at you! I was laughing because o' falling down.' She did not know what to say to him: his hostility smote her like a wave. In the rich apricot rays of the setting sun, streaming level now across the ice, his cheeks were stinging red: while conversely, all colour seemed to have left his pale eyes.

'Evening to you, Hester. Evening to you, Chad.'

The voice belonged to Henry Wake, who came skating over to them with his hands behind his back. He did this with great dignity, as befitted a man who was superintendent of the chapel Sunday School, and had no doubts that everyone shared his good opinion of himself.

'Not seen you here afore, Hester,' Henry Wake said. 'Correct me if I'm wrong.'

'It's my first time,' Hester said. 'I'm not gitting on very well!'

'Ah, it'll come – it'll come. I think you'll find that you're keeping your feet too far apart. Bring 'em together as soon as you feel you git your balance, as it were. I think you'll find this is where you're going wrong.' Henry was a man approaching forty, rather lacking in height and length of limb and breadth of shoulders, and with little sharp features curiously crammed in the middle of his face, so that there was something about him suggestive of the last loaf in the baker's oven, made with such dough as was left over. He was only an ordinary one-hoss farmer, but his work for the chapel and a smattering of education which made him talk, as folk said, like a newspaper, gave him at least in his own eyes a certain prominence on the fen. 'Ain't that right, Chad? By-the-by, you'll be having the missioner for dinner at yourn tomorrer, I believe? Ah, I reckon he'll do us proud, this one. He's got a high reputation for a sermon, straight from the heart, as it were. He used to be the drunkenest man in Spalding – I think you'll find my information's correct on this point – till one day the spirit moved in him, and he were plucked as a brand from the burning. They say he wrestled with himself for two days and a night, not excepting mealtimes. Now, Hester! Don't say you're give up already.'

'No,' Hester said, getting up. 'I'm going to have another go. Come on, Chad. I want to try.'

Chad, after a moment, took her hands again. She wobbled forward, trying to think of unhappy things so as not to laugh.

'That's the way,' Henry Wake said. 'I'd advise you to keep

your head well forward – I'm been skating for thirty years, and I think I can speak with some authority on this point. Knees bent, knees bent!'

This time she kept her balance for some thirty yards, and all at once her legs seemed to stop their wild juddering and to relax. Chad swung her round in a wide arc, and then held her just by one hand as they glided back towards Henry Wake.

'I did it, I did it!' she cried.

'Better – much better,' Henry said. 'A word of advice from the right quarter, you see. If I might be allowed one more suggestion – as skating is summat I know about, as it happens, there's no point in pretending it's not – keep the back straight as you lean forward, and then I think you'll find you git on a lot better.'

Lizzie Gosling rejoined them as Henry lifted his hat and skated away. 'Yes, I saw you,' she said, 'wonders'll never cease. Henry giving you lessons, an' all.'

'Oh, ole Henry Wake. It's Chad here who's taught me. Come on, Chad – let's go again.'

She said this out of a simple desire to please Chad, who had seemed hurt at her not trying, and also because she was beginning to enjoy it now. It seemed however to startle him, and to bury him in abstraction again, so much so that he lost his own balance and fell.

She went down with him, laughing. 'There, now we're even,' she said: and at last got him to laugh too.

'I can never tell whether you're mekking fun or not,' he said, as they skated again.

'Well, you want to just mek fun of me back,' she said.

He frowned. 'I can't, though.'

The sun had gone down. A crisp turquoise twilight hovered over the flat levels, and there was the first breath of wind, like the twanging of a great cold string in the air. They skated on for some time, as Hester's confidence grew. At last one of her skates needed oiling, and they went over to the brazier, where a man named 'Sunny' Daintree was mending and oiling skates for coppers. He was a molecatcher, and a gravedigger besides, and anything else he could turn his hand to, and was known as Sunny because of his gloomy disposition.

29

'Mekking a few bob, Sunny,' Chad said.

'It's summat, I suppose,' Sunny said. He was bald, pink, smooth, and ageless, like a cherub who had fallen and known great woe; and, incongruously, he had a chirping voice that seemed made for cheerfulness. 'I can't see it lasting, meself.'

'Think we're in for a thaw, then?' Hester said.

'It wouldn't surprise me,' Sunny said.

'Well! it'll be nice to have a bit of warm weather, any road.'

'I don't know.' Sunny shook his head. 'Last time I remember a frost like this, there was terrible flood after it. You couldn't go to bed for fear of waking up drownded. It wouldn't surprise me if that happened again. I wouldn't be a bit surprised.' He turned the skating-patten over in his seamed hands, as if it were a poignant relic prompting reflections too deep for tears. 'Well, thass the best I can do wi' that.'

It was quite late when they made ready to go home at last, and stars, like small chips of frost themselves, were breaking out in the sky. They walked slowly back across the fields. The exercise, the tension and relaxation, the pure cold air, had left Hester feeling both tired and exhilarated; and when she remembered that tomorrow the preacher was coming to dinner, she exclaimed aloud in sudden despondency.

'It's always so stiff,' she said. 'I hate sitting all stiff and formal like that.' The members of the chapel took turns in having the travelling preachers to dinner, and it was a great event in the Langtoft household, marked with unaccustomed formality. While it was this that chiefly repelled Hester, she was also something of an unregenerate spiritually. If she would not exactly go so far as to say all religion was just cant and hypocrisy – her particular hates – it was only because Mrs Langtoft was devout, and she liked Mrs Langtoft. It was typical of her to thus make the personal the arbiter of her judgements. 'After all, the preacher's only an ordinary chap like anybody else,' said she. 'Thass the point of going to chapel and not church, ain't it?'

'Well,' Chad said, 'you'd never have the vicar to dinner, anyway.'

'Thass true,' she said. Nobody, saint or sinner, liked the vicar of the scattered parish, who lived in a big house on the edge of the upland, and always spoke to you as if he were breaking bad news to an exceptionally dim-witted foreigner. 'Do you believe in it all, though, Chad? You know – when they go on about the flames burning for ever more, and how we're all going down there, every one on us, unless we repent.'

'Yes,' Chad said, with unusual promptness and conviction. 'I believe it.'

'What, even if we're just sort of ordinary sinners – you know, haven't done any murders or thievings – just swearing and missing chapel and things like that?'

'I believe it,' Chad said again. And then, shortly: 'It's what's in your head.'

She thought of what had been in her head lately that might consign her to the flames: wishing nosey old Mrs Onyett who had called her flighty would fall in the dyke, envying Lizzie Gosling that lace-fronted blouse that would look so much better on her, watching with interest that handsome young carter stripping himself down to wash at the pump . . . Well, after all, if you couldn't call your thoughts your own . . .

'You did enjoy it, didn't you?' Chad said.

'Enjoy what?' she said, with a guilty start.

'The skating. It was good, weren't it?'

'Oh! yes. It was lovely. Mind you, I shall have a few bruises in the morning where I shan't be able to see 'em. Shall we go again?'

'If you like,' he said. 'If you want to. I mean, you did enjoy it, didn't you?'

'Course I did.'

'Good. We'll go again some time then. If you'd like to.'

He was an odd one, she thought: she would have to tell Lizzie about this. But she had a suspicion of what Lizzie, in her dry way, would say. She would say Chad was sweet on her; and at the same time she remembered the glances in the milk-pan, the silences . . . But Chad? – Chad who had scarcely ever spoken to her, who had barely paid more attention to her than to any other fixture of the farm? She disbelieved it, and was obscurely flattered in the same moment.

Hester at this time had two trivial characteristics that were

31

yet indicative of much: she could fall fast asleep in a matter of seconds in any place and at any time of the day, and she could dismiss an uncomfortable thought from her mind and genuinely forget about it. The latter was a kind of mental double-jointedness, and she exercised it now, as she walked down the drove with Chad. It was an ability that a worrier might have sorely envied; and it had never occurred to Hester that it might be anything but an unmixed blessing.

4

A bird's-eye view of Hinching Fen on Sunday morning would have disclosed a multitude of little processions, marching out from cottages and along droves, and all appearing to converge on an insignificant little brick building fronting the high road that crossed the flat land like a line drawn on a map. A short flight away, north and south, the same bird might have observed the sublime ruins of two great abbeys, which (supposing the bird to have been alive to such impressions) rendered the brick building even more insignificant, and its attraction more inexplicable.

To the people of Hinching Fen, however, the Wesleyan chapel was 'their' place. It was on a manageable and human scale; and in that landscape, where there were no hills, not many animals, few trees, and fewer houses, the human figure bulked large and important in the unobstructed view, and was genuinely the measure of all things. An experience familiar to fen-dwellers on foggy days was the apparent spectacle of giants walking towards them across the fields: an optical illusion in which a person of normal stature appeared to loom hugely, by some strange distortion of perspective produced by the misty air and the level distances. But it was a distortion appropriate to life on the fen, and to that intensely individual character perhaps expressed by Andrew Surfleet, the oldest man in Hinching Fen (and some said the silliest), when he described his one visit to Cambridge thus: 'Ah, I couldn't abide it, bor. There was so many people I couldn't look at 'em all.'

The opportunity it presented for having a good look at

each other was, of course, one of the secondary attractions of the chapel. Turn-outs were impeccable. Dresses spoke of the tremendous labour of flat-irons heated on turf fires: children looked as unhappy as only stiff collars and tight boots could make them; and about the heads of the men there was a sort of a general righteous ache of hard hats pressed down like lids on oiled hair. And busying himself everywhere was Henry Wake, nodding, greeting, patting children's heads, and drawing attention – by means of coughing and rubbing it with his handkerchief – to the brilliance of the brass pulpit rail, which he had spent the morning polishing.

Mrs Langtoft too had been devout since dawn, and through breakfast had practised hymns in her ardent contralto: it was odd to hear that sturdy bright little woman asserting, as she raked out the oven, that she Thirsted, she Pined, and she Died. But when the chapel congregation threw themselves into the hymns, it was always old Andrew Surfleet whose voice could be heard lifted in a quavering falsetto above everybody else. He was an ancient peering pippin of a man, with an innocent dewy face framed by a white beard, and, as the saying went, not much oil in his lamp; but he dearly loved a good sing, and he allowed for his shortness of breath by a novel system of punctuation. "'Hide me. O. My Saviour. Hide. Till the. Storm of. Life is past.'"

Hester, even with her ability to fall asleep virtually at will, had been thwarted at first by the hardness and uprightness of the pine pews, and by one's extreme visibility; but she had evolved a method whereby, when the time for the sermon came, she placed her chin on her chest and clasped her hands as if she were absorbed in the profoundest spiritual meditations, and was thus able to snooze quite comfortably. On this occasion, however, the sight of the visiting preacher arrested her. He was an elderly man with a dead white face, black eyebrows, a sharp red nose, and gappy teeth, so that on looking up at the pulpit she had the bizarre impression of being harangued by a snowman. But what was most transfixing about him was the way he could not keep still. It was plainly true, as Henry Wake had said, that this reformed sinner had once been the drunkenest man in Spalding; and if salvation had sobered him, set his feet upon a rock, and washed him in the blood of the Lamb, it had done nothing for his DTs. His hands did not simply tremble. They were a blur. When he gave the psalm the Bible capered in his fingers as if it were alive, and nearly went flying over the pulpit on to Henry Wake's reverent head. Hester knew she was done for if she did not control herself now: she took a pin from the collar of her blouse and prepared to jab herself with it if the laughter threatened to burst out.

The sermon, without notes and straight from the heart just the way folk liked them, contained the expected references to the preacher's former iniquities. 'I were a boozer,' the preacher cried. 'I testify to it. I looked on the wine when it was red, I were a brawler, I were raging. I did reel to and fro, and stagger like a drunken man, which I was, and I lifted up my hand against my old woman, and I did clobber her. And I dwelled in the tents of wickedness.' He was able now to steady his hands on the edges of the pulpit; but this did nothing to moderate the twitching, the convulsive wink, the ticking cheek, and a motion of the head as if he were continually seeing something startling over his left shoulder. 'The heat of the flames was already on me, and the fiend's hands were already clawin' hold of me. And the heat of them flames is terrible, the heat of them flames is like a burning fiery furnace, like the burning fiery furnace where them three men were thrown, in the Book of Daniel. And them three were Shad-hat, Meese-hat, and a Dibnibo.'

Hester jabbed the pin in her finger, while to her right an expression of perplexity formed on Mr Langtoft's face. The preacher himself hesitated, but then casting his wandering eye over the heads of the congregation, and perhaps fortified by the pervasive atmosphere of Hats around him, repeated the names. 'Shad-hat, Meese-hat, and a Dibnibo. And what happened to Shad-hat, Meese-hat, and a Dibnibo, when they was chucked in the burning fiery furnace? Did they burn? Did they swelter, and roast, and frizzle? No. They was saved.'

'Ah!' said Andrew Surfleet, who was given to pious interjections, though sometimes they were only twinges of rheumatism.

'And why was Shad-hat, Meese-hat, and a Dibnibo saved? Because they served the Lord, thass why. And can you say the same, all on yer? When the time comes, shall you be saved like Shad-hat, Meese-hat, and a Dibnibo, or will the flames tek you, and burn you up to ashes, except they won't, see, cos you'll just go on burning for ever, and never gitting any less?'

'Ah!' said Andrew Surfleet again, rather uncertainly; and began chewing his beard.

'There's only one way,' the preacher said, fixing them, as far as he was able, with a steady gaze. 'There's only one way to avoid the flames what's waiting for you. There's only one way to be saved, I tell yer. And that is –' he stretched out his arms, and in a paroxysm of shakes reached his peroration – '*to put yourself in the safe hands of the Lord.*'

Hester stuck the pin in her finger till it drew blood, and managed to convert the yelp into an 'Amen!' that made Mrs Langtoft smile on her, and think the spirit had moved in that heathen girl at last.

The preacher was not a man for small talk. He came stumping back to the farm in a stern silence, as if still brooding on the word of the Lord. Mr Langtoft, in his friendly way, inquired of him: 'Had much snow over Spalding this year?'

'There wun't be no snow in the next world, brother,' the preacher said, knitting his black brows. 'Nor ice neither, nor hail . . . Nor slush,' he added grimly.

'There now!' Mrs Langtoft said with satisfaction, and seemed to think so poorly of her husband for lowering the uplifted tone, that she dusted him down in quite a bitter manner.

After that Mr Langtoft's spirits visibly sank. He was a temperate man, and preferred to take his religion in moderation. He was well aware that his wife preferred it in stronger doses: but he did not mind that, as long as it stayed in the chapel and did not come home with them. The preacher, however, had other ideas. He was fired up with salvation; and in expressing it, he still had all the boozer's belligerence.

They sat down to dinner – pudden first, meat after, in the old fen way – and Mr Langtoft had just picked up his knife and fork when the preacher burst with a groan into a long extempore Grace.

'Look down on us, Lord, seated at this board all set about

35

wi' food and the fruits of the earth what come from out of your bounty and what we don't deserve, none on us, poor wretched sinners, full as we are of fancies, and greed and sloth and worldliness, and thinkin' on our stomachs instead of your blessed mercy . . .'

It was perhaps an unfortunate chance that the preacher was seated directly opposite Mr Langtoft, so that the prayers seemed to have him as their especial object. Certainly Mr Langtoft appeared disconcerted at this great volley of sinfulness coming straight at him, especially when his own stomach, stimulated by the smell of pork, gave a great growl.

The Amen came at last, when even Mrs Langtoft had begun to reach out a finger to see if the pudden were still hot; and after that things went better for a time. The preacher was fully occupied with his knife and fork, which in his unsteady hands made a clashing like a fencing-match, and then with getting the food to his mouth without that recurring urge to look over his shoulder. Mrs Langtoft said what a nice job Henry Wake had made of the chapel, and Hester chipped in with a remark about Henry Wake's old horse not having the farcy after all, and gradually the conversation seemed to be moving away from the holy at last; when all of a sudden the preacher, facing Mr Langtoft, and with the righteous light in his sunken eyes, exclaimed:

'Do you know what it's like to have Nails driven through your hands and feet?'

Mr Langtoft hastily swallowed a lump of pudden. 'Well,' he said with an air of being helpful, 'I got a tin-tack in me thumb once.'

This was clearly not the right answer, and Mr Langtoft intercepted a crushing glare from his wife.

'Our Lord knew them pains,' the preacher said.

'Ah, so He did, so He did!' sighed Mrs Langtoft.

She and Hester began to clear the plates, and Hester went to draw the pork and the tater-net out of the pot.

'That was for us He bore them pains,' the preacher continued, while they dished up. 'And do we care!'

'Hark at him!' Mrs Langtoft said to Hester in an admiring undertone.

The addition of gravy to the meal was unfortunate. Jacob and Will, seated on either side of the preacher, came in for most of his. Jacob, a stoic at fifteen, carried on gravely eating in spite of the brown rain showering on him, but Will, the youngest, began to look more discontented at each splash, and seemed about to protest when the preacher paused again, and demanded,

'Have you ever had a Spear thrust in your side?'

Mr Langtoft, who could hardly have been expected to suffer such a mishap, still looked uncomfortable at the omission.

'Our Lord did,' the preacher said, exhibiting mashed greens between his teeth. 'He knew what it were like. But do we care? Do we think on it? No! We laugh, we carouse, we frolic about, and kick up our heels!'

Mr Langtoft looked as guilty as if he had been doing all those things at that very moment.

'And what about the scourging! Think o' that! The laying on of whips!'

'Well, after all,' Hester said, with some idea of protecting Mr Langtoft, 'you can't be thinking of such things all the time. It ain't natural.'

Across the table Chad lifted his eyes to her in surprise at her daring.

'Ah! I was such a one as you once, my gel,' the preacher cried. 'I was defiled with my own works, and went a-whoring with my own inventions. I warn you. You'll be chastised with scorpions.'

'Why, I don't even know what a scorpion looks like,' Hester said.

'Summat like a spider, I reckon,' Mr Langtoft said. 'With a sting.'

The preacher's eloquence, thus challenged, seemed to falter. He applied himself to his dinner, contenting himself with a truculent stare all round the table at intervals, until his plate was clean: and when Mr Langtoft mildly inquired if he would take a little more pork, the preacher stood up and intoned: 'Be not tempted to gluttony, that meks us like the beasts of the field. Thank you, Lord, for the meat we have et, the pudden likewise, what you give to us, and look wi' mercy on

37

them among us as mocks and blasphemes, and dances among the wash-pots, and save 'em from the wrath to come.'

'Won't you stay for a drop o' tea?' Mrs Langtoft said.

'I'm got a long walk ahead of me, on the Lord's business,' the preacher said; and picking up his hat, and getting it on by making a sort of dive into it head first, he marched to the door.

'You're got a nerve, answering the preacher back,' Chad said, while Hester cleared away, and Mr and Mrs Langtoft saw the visitor out.

'Me? I reckon it's him as has got a nerve,' she said indignantly. 'He never said a word of thanks – giving it all to God – it were me and your mother as cooked it. Wash-pots and scorpions, I never heard such stuff.'

Mrs Langtoft was full of praise for the preacher, and shook her head at Hester's obduracy. 'Do you better to tek some of his words to heart, my gel,' she said, 'stead o' fleering. You'll know – it'll come home to you!' But Mr Langtoft sat himself down by the fire, and lit his short 'nose-warmer' pipe, and looked relieved to be contemplating flames of an earthly nature.

Sunday or no Sunday, there were still chores to be done; and after washing up in the scullery, Hester went out to feed and water the hens. Crossing the yard back to the house, she found Chad standing there, holding up his hands and looking at the sky.

'It's raining,' he said.

'Oh! so it is,' she said. Murky, mud-coloured cloud stretched from horizon to horizon. Chad's eyes were baleful. 'What's the matter?' she said.

'Can't you feel it?' he said. 'Temperature's gone right up.'

She noticed it for the first time. 'Well, old Sunny Daintree was right then – it is a thaw. About time too.'

'Don't you see?' Chad said. 'The ice on the washes'll be melting. There won't be no more skating.'

'Oh! of course,' she said. 'What a shame. I was just getting on, as well.'

Chad's face was almost tragic as he stared at the lowering sky. 'I can't believe it. I were so looking forward to it.'

'Still,' she said, wishing to cheer him up, 'shows it's spring.

There's Stokeley Fair at Easter – there's something to look forward to.'

'Will you go to Stokeley Fair with me, then?' he said, quickly.

He looked so miserable over the loss of the skating, that she said promptly, 'All right, Chad. Thank you for asking me.'

'You sure? It don't matter. You needn't, if you don't want.'

The gloaming light showed her his face now withdrawn in the old indifference. It was the face of a man who doubts himself, even as he mistrusts others. For a moment she wondered if she were doing the right thing; but then after all, she thought, it was a pity about the skating.

'Stokeley Fair,' she said.

# Chapter Three

1

The thaw that set in marked the end of that winter, and the flood-waters where skaters had laughed and shrieked rang again with the honking voices of wild geese. The cessation of frost meant the beginning of the turf-digging season; and Chad Langtoft, like other young men wishing to do a little work on his own account, hired a half-acre of peat land, and began to stake it out and prepare it. Turf-digging – the digging out of rectangular blocks of peat to sell as fuel for cottage fires – was an occupation that many old men in the fen had pursued seasonally all their lives, with the result that some of them were permanently bent double, and never saw the sun unless they lay on their ruined backs like beetles. Chad, as a beginner, consulted old Andrew Surfleet as to the best methods; and he was full of his plans, which he confided to Hester.

'I reckon to get a hundred thousand turf out of that plot,' he said. 'Thass what I reckon. Prob'ly I shall only manage five hundred a day to start with – while I git my hand in, like.'

He went over these computations endlessly. Rambling down these paths of arithmetic, he lost his inarticulacy with her. 'Git up to a thousand a day, mebbe, when I git used to it. Reckon to git about seven bob a thousand nowadays. Course, there's the cost of boating them away. Thass about two-and-six a thousand.' He became entangled in his calculations, until it was just as if he were talking to himself. But he was not: he was talking to her, and it seemed that it was only in terms of such abstractions that he could do so freely. The exception was the subject of Stokeley Fair, which he brought up regularly yet always with a great show of nonchalance.

'We still going to Stokeley Fair, are we?' he would say, in the middle of some task about the farm, as if it had just happened to occur to him.

'Oh! yes. Well, unless you're thinking of tekking somebody else.'

But it was impossible to rally him like that. He was too serious; and when she spoke there was something dog-like in the way he hung on her words, though the suggestion was of a dog more cowed than docile.

It was not easy for Hester to comprehend him, though she tried. Always there was about him an uneasy coolness: a dull turmoil. His was one of those natures which are slow to commit themselves, but once committed, fasten like a badger's jaws.

And so while his attentiveness to her was obvious it was also, as it were, not obvious at all: it expressed itself merely in an intensification of his guarded manner. Anyone else might have noticed nothing – which provided her with an excuse (which she was very willing to take) for not thinking about it. They were only going to Stokeley Fair together; and she easily succeeded in convincing herself that he contemplated this as casually as she did.

In truth Hester did not know what she felt. Her father, the higgler, had been notorious for his tendency to take his cart round ten miles in pursuit of some chimerical job involving cut-glass rather than go a mile down the road and pick up some beer-barrels: and she was so far her father's daughter in that, for all her dislike of effort, she would often make the most laborious mental detour to arrive at what she wanted to think, rather than take two steps to the unlovely truth. When the day of Stokeley Fair came, and they set out across the fields, she was aware that plenty of girls on the fen would have been well pleased to consider themselves as in a position to make a catch of Chad Langtoft, even as she felt a little weariness at his beginning to talk again of his plans for the turf-digging; but she kept these two thoughts separate.

It was windy as they walked. The wind here was part of the landscape, as physical as earth: it was possible, turning out of it, to lean on it for a moment like a shooting-stick. The sails of the Hinching Fen mill, black on the skyline, were whirling round as if to outrace the coasting clouds. They passed a group of men dyke-digging, in long stout boots and 'slops', the old-fashioned smocks still to be seen in the world of the railway and the telephone as they had been in that of the stagecoach; and Hester felt that special pleasure of going on a jaunt when others are working. (Mr and Mrs Langtoft were to follow with the boys later: when Will had demanded why they couldn't all go together, his mother had shushed him.) Without need for words they gave a wide berth to the ruins of a farmhouse that had burned down: one of the 'haunts' with which the fens abounded had been seen there, a ghostly horse running in circles. Hester, if you had asked her whether she believed in ghosts, would have said no, but there was no point in looking for trouble.

The chief business of the fair, the buying and selling of stock and seed and tools, and the hiring of labour, had been disposed of earlier in the day; and when Hester and Chad arrived in Stokeley a mass of side-shows, stalls and entertainments had taken possession of the High Street. The great width of this thoroughfare, sufficient for a Parisian boulevard and given an even more expansive aspect by the river running alongside it, bore testimony as eloquent as that of the pure picked bones of the Abbey to the fact that Stokeley was a decayed place. From the days when it had stood as a wealthy island above the drowned fens, and been reckoned with in the counsels of kings, it had undergone a kind of reverse historical process, settling down at last as a pottering market town of a few thousand souls, and consoling itself, perhaps, with the reflection that its name was writ large on maps of the realm when Birmingham and Manchester were blank spaces on the parchment.

'Hey-up there, Chaddy bor! Halloo, Hetty gel!'

A bright check suit, with Uncle Bevis inside it, emerged from the crowd. Laughing like a fusillade of blanks, he slapped a meaty hand on Chad's neck and shook him from side to side, and then butted Hester like a shunting-engine. 'So, they let you come off that ole fen for a change, eh? Well, what do you think of it?' – this with a smirking modesty, as if the fair were all his own work. 'Not a bad show this year, though it's all a bit prettified for my taste. Now in my young days, we used to git a lot of real Romany folk, and they were Rousers. Why, you couldn't call it a proper do till the stallholders had had a free-for-all on the last night. Broken heads ten a penny – you thought nothing of it. There were one Terror name o' Mealy Jack who could pick up a cart on his own and chuck it in the river – I'm seen him do it. I tell you what though –' he took hold of Chad by the waistcoat – 'you want to come over the boxing-booth, bor – there's a lad there from Pondersbridge tekking 'em all on. Very smart little fighter – sharp, very sharp.' He danced about on his toes, like a frisky carthorse. 'Course, it's nowt to the boxing we used to get up to in my day – a fight were a fight then, and I'm had blood pouring out my nose an hour at a time and thought nothing of it. Still, it's worth a look.'

'No, ta, Uncle,' Chad said with discomfort. 'We're got other things to see.'

'Ah, goo on! You'll mebbe see him git beat.'

'Why don't you tek the lad on yourself, Uncle Bevis?' Hester said.

'Wehrr, I wouldn't mind, gel,' Uncle Bevis said. 'Matter of fact there's nothing I'd like better. Only there's my wife's nerves to consider, see, and I don't reckon they'd bear it if she knew I'd been boxing and up to me old tricks.'

'Well, we wouldn't tell her, would we, Chad?' Hester said.

'Aah, ha ha ha!' Uncle Bevis went on laughing for an unnecessary time. 'Wehrr, it'd git back to her though, in a town like this, you know – where everybody knows me. Ah well, I'll leave you to it, then.'

'Phew, I'm glad you got rid of him,' Chad said.

'Wehrr,' Hester said in Uncle Bevis's accents, 'we didn't want to go and watch some silly beggars knocking each other about, did we, Chaddy bor? Let's git some whelks.'

They made the tour of the stalls, and Hester followed up the whelks with peppermint twist and then hot peas – 'she's got cast-iron guts, that gel!' was a frequent exclamation of Mrs Langtoft's. Chad hovered at her side with his peculiar, soft, cat-footed gait, continually solicitous, in his brusque, uneasy way, about what she wanted to do. It was nice, after all, to be made a fuss of, Hester thought: even though Chad's attention seemed more possessive than considerate. They had a go at the Aunt Sally, and the coconut shy, and went into booths to see a waxwork of the beheading of Anne Boleyn watched by a cheerfully smiling Henry VIII, and a peepshow rather ambitiously representing the Charge of the Light Brigade, with the horses running like greyhounds, and seeming to have too many legs. The greatest attraction was a tent where a phonograph was to be heard, and outside this they met Henry Wake and Andrew Surfleet.

'Quite a remarkable invention, that,' Henry Wake said urbanely, tipping his hat to Hester. 'Simple enough once you understand its principles, mind you – but our friend here was quite shook up by it.'

Old Andrew Surfleet, dressed in his best outfit of half-high hat, red neckercher, and shiny trousers with the gusset somewhere around his knees, shook his head and chewed a few snowy strands of beard. 'Well, I thought it were some sort o' trick at first, like when I went to see the hoss with its head where its tail should be, and all it was was an ordinary hoss standing with its arse to the manger,' he said. 'Then when I found it weren't a trick, and that voice were really coming out of summat like a sewing-machine, I felt a bit peculiar. I wun't deny my hand went to my fairy-stone, sort of without thinking.' Some old fen people still carried holed stones called fairy-stones, as a protection against witchcraft. 'Still, I don't feel so bad now Enry's explained it to me.'

Henry Wake fairly beamed condescension. It was a great satisfaction to him, Hester thought, to know someone like Andrew Surfleet, who some said was so daft he'd stick his head out of the window to see if it was daylight, and who believed whatever Henry told him. 'Yes, I'm got a certain grasp of these things,' Henry said, 'don't know why, just one of them matters I happen to understand pretty well. It's the 'lectric that accounts for it, you see – thass the elementary principle you have to bear in mind – the 'lectric. I think you'll find I'm correct.'

'The 'lectric, you see,' Andrew Surfleet repeated. 'I wouldn't ha' thought of that.'

'Why, where's the electric come from, then?' Chad said doubtfully.

'Oh! it's conducted, you know,' Henry Wake said. 'Conducted. I can't really go into more detail than that just now.'

They went into the tent, and heard from the machine an excruciating soprano voice intoning 'Twinkle Twinkle Little Star'.

'There weren't no electric there!' Hester said; but when they came out Henry and Andrew had moved on.

'He'll say anything, that Henry Wake,' Chad said. 'Down the Labour In Vain one night some chaps got a dead sparrer and painted it all wi' blue paint and then showed it to Henry and asks him if he's ever seen one of them before. "Ah," he says, "I'm seen them flying about Holme Woods, and they're called sky-blue warblers."'

Then Hester saw a fortune-telling booth, and wanted to go in.

'I dunno,' Chad said. 'Mother reckons it's heathen.'

'Only if you believe in it. Come on.'

An old man with a shock of white hair and silver earrings read her palm, his jaws working and munching. Suddenly he made a noise like a pot boiling over. 'Tssss! You're going to cross some water.'

It was impossible to go more than a couple of miles across the fens without crossing water, but she let that pass.

'There's fortune coming.'

'Good fortune?'

'Tssss!' He ran his finger round the heel of her hand. 'There's a journey – quite soon. There's money, plenty of it. There's gold, and long life. But you'll wear an eelskin wedden ring, gel.'

'Oh, I want to do better'n that!' she laughed. There were still older women on the fen who wore wedding rings made of a coil of dried eelskin, their husbands having been too poor to afford a real one.

'Eelskin wedden ring,' the old man repeated. 'You'll wait for gold.'

'Oh! well. Chad, you have a go.'

'No, not me,' Chad said, in his most cumbrous way, flushing. 'I don't want to know.'

'It's only for fun,' she said as they left the tent: though the circumstance of the eelskin wedding ring had made a deeper impression on her mind than she pretended. Hester was as little acquisitive as it was possible for a person to be: her imagination was kindled not by the prospect of gold or otherwise, but by the sheer tantalising mystery of her future, and the shapes, fair and foul, that might be waiting there. 'Don't you wonder how your life'll go, Chad?'

'I don't want to know. Leave it dark,' Chad said.

'So there you are, you two!' Lizzie Gosling appeared, and gave them both one of her long, searching, I-could-say-something-but-I-won't looks. 'Where you been hiding yourselves?'

'Well away from you, you ole fishwife,' Hester said. 'Couldn't you git nobody to bring you, then?'

'I'm here with my brother,' Lizzie said. 'He's in the dancing-booth. Ain't you been in there? You want to come and see – there's Sunny Daintree having a dance.'

The dancing-booth was a long tent of striped orange canvas, which filtered the light of late afternoon, so that the interior swam in a warm haze resembling the dim congealed atmosphere of dreams, thickened further by clouds of sawdust rising from the boards that formed the dancing-floor. A fiddle and concertina provided the music which was just audible over the stamping of the dancers and the clapping of the spectators, gathered in narrow aisles on either side of the floor; and standing atop an upturned barrel an old man called out the steps in the nasal carrying voice of a cattle auctioneer. The dancers were a very mixed set: here was a flash of beauty in eye or lip, there a glimpse of grace transforming plainness, and on all sides an enthusiasm and pleasure atoning for the absence of either; youth danced beside age, and girth and leanness trod the same measure. But even in such a harmonising of incongruities the figure of Sunny Daintree was conspicuous. It was often observed, apropos of his bow legs, that he would not stop a pig in a passage; but more remarkable than that was his utterly doleful expression even as he turned, skipped, and pranced to the Cross-Hand Polka, his round face a lugubrious moon in the laughing half-light.

The concertina shimmered a last chord: the dancers dispersed. 'Step up,' cried the old man on the barrel. 'Step up and tek your partners for Speed the Plough.'

Hester turned to find Chad edging away: some of his friends were calling to him from the other side of the tent.

'I just got to say hello to them ole boys,' he said.

'Don't you want to dance?'

'Oh! I can't dance. You do it – you go on.'

It was twopence to go on the floor. Hester did not lack for partners, and she even had a turn with Sunny Daintree, to 'Toast to King Gustav'.

'I never knew you liked dancing, Sunny,' she said as they bowed to each other.

Sunny sighed deeply.

'I can't abide it,' he said, whirling her round.

Out of breath at last, she rejoined the spectators. Chad was still with his friends; but she noticed how he seemed to just inhabit the edge of their circle, and whenever they broke out in laughter he was always the last to join in, as if he first sought to reassure himself that the laugh was not against him.

Lizzie Gosling was at her side. 'Fell out already?' she said.

'Don't be daft.'

Lizzie's face teemed with irony. 'It's not anything serious, then?'

'How do you mean?'

'Well, you coming to the fair with Chad. I mean, there's nothing in it, is there?' And before Hester could answer she added, 'I didn't think so. Not you and Chad. Mary-Ann Cole was saying the other day how she's fishing for Chad – reckoned she wouldn't need more'n a twitch to land him.'

'Mary-Ann Cole!' Hester said. 'Her! She's got a face like a hoss looking over a gate.'

Lizzie was all dark glinting amusement at this. 'True; but if there ain't nothing in it, why should that bother you?'

'I didn't say there weren't nothing in it – I never said that,' Hester said, finding herself thus in a position she had not intended, and, typically, deciding she might as well stay in it.

47

At that moment Chad came over. As he left his friends, one said, 'Going to dance, then, Chad?' and another, with a whoop of laughter: 'Chad, he can't dance to save his life!' It was an ordinary enough piece of banter, but Chad's whole face and neck flamed in a moment.

'Come on Chad – got twopence?' Hester said, taking his arm. 'We're not had a dance yet. You taught me skating – I'm sure I can teach you dancing – thass much easier.' She was not given to analysing her impulses, and a generous wish to save Chad's face was so much the chief constituent of this one, that the minor ingredient of putting the absent Mary-Ann in her place was scarcely detectable, at least by herself.

'Choose yer partners!' called the old man on the barrel.

His eyes fixed on her with a sort of morose struggle, Chad said: 'I'm no good at this'; but he went unresisting on to the floor with her.

'Just do what I do,' she said, and all through the dance, which he managed no worse than anyone else there, his eyes remained riveted on her, just as if they were balancing on some terrible height, and he would be lost if he looked down.

For her part Hester liked to dance, enjoyed the music, and was lifted – by the holiday and by the tent's orange glow that made of the figures of the dancers something strange and visionary – into a mood of inclusive warmth: if she had ever been drunk she would have recognised the sensation.

One dance was enough for Chad; and she was hot and thirsty. They left the dancing-booth, and she refreshed herself at a lemonade stall. The westering sun was firing the roofs of the little town, but the fair was still crowded with people, some having just arrived after long walks from remote places on the fen: the smell of paraffin from oil-lamps joined the medley of fish, gingerbread, calliope-steam, liquorice and manure. They saw Henry Wake and Andrew Surfleet again, at a thimble-rigger's stall; and Henry Wake turned to them and shrugged.

'I wish you'd help me persuade him,' Henry said. 'He's lost near two shilling already.'

The thimble-rigger's equipment consisted of three tiny cups and a dried pea: after switching the cups around with an apparent negligent slowness he invited Andrew Surfleet again to select which of the cups the pea lurked under. 'You're been watching pretty close, granfer,' he said, 'I reckon you're got it this time.'

Old Andrew gazed long at each cup, tasting his beard. 'Why,' he said, putting his money down, 'thass got to be the one.'

The thimble-rigger whipped off the cups. 'Ah, hard luck, granfer – I thought you'd got me.'

Henry Wake clucked his tongue. 'Andrew, Andrew – now will you be satisfied?'

'Well, beggar me,' Andrew said smiling. 'Would you credit it? There's that bloody ole pea up tother end. Beggar me. Beggar my ole boots.' It was of course a trick: the thimble-rigger secreted the pea each time under his long horny thumbnail.

'Come away, my friend,' said Henry Wake, who did not approve of gambling.

'Well, I'll just have another goo,' Andrew said.

'You're being done, Andrew – it's not under any of 'em,' Hester said, while the thimble-rigger attempted to look injured.

'Ah, I suppose so,' said Andrew, unperturbed, and turned his innocent smile on them. 'I'll have another goo, though. Why, thass quite a treat just to watch him dew it.'

Chad had left her side during this: she found him calling to her from a fenced enclosure. 'Hester. Come and see.'

There was a small, scraggy, elderly bear in a cage. There were bald patches on its fur from rubbing against the bars.

'Watch,' Chad said. He picked up a handful of gravel and tossed it into the bottom of the cage: the bear pounced at once on it, leathery nose snuffling, then looked up at them with small, weak, baffled eyes.

'He thinks it's summat to eat,' Chad said. He repeated the action. 'See? He does it every time – he don't learn.'

Hester, in spite of the years on the farm, was uncomfortably humane towards animals: she always had to absent herself when the pig-killer came round, and could not abide to see anything in a cage. Cruelty affected her so much that it caused a horrible tightness, worse than tears, in her chest; and the onset of this, when she had been feeling so happy, undid her completely.

Chad was still laughing and tossing the gravel as she turned and stalked away from him.

'Wait – wait, what's the matter?' Chad came after her.

'Look here; I shan't stop wi' you, if you're going to do things like that,' she cried.

Chad looked startled, then alarmed. 'I didn't hurt it – there weren't no harm in it.'

'Teasing it like that!' She could not look at him: she brushed a tear away.

'Here – wait – I'm sorry. I never meant – I just thought it'd mek you laugh. Thass all. I just wanted to mek you laugh.'

His expression was really stricken. 'Oh, it don't matter,' she said.

'I'm sorry . . . I could git some cakes or summat and feed it if you like.'

He was so remorseful that her feeling of pity partly transferred itself to him. 'No – it's all right,' she said. It was something of a relief, all the same, to have the attention diverted from her by a little boy who in plain desperation began to pluck at her skirts, and declare himself lost.

'Who was you with, then?' she asked, bending down. 'Your mam?'

'Me sister,' the child said, making herculean efforts not to cry. 'I can't find her. Mammy says we weren't to stop out long. I went on a swingboat and I were sick.'

A few more inquiries established that the boy lived in the town, though he didn't know where, except that it was 'near the 'Orse'.

'There's a pub over the river called the Nag's Head,' Chad said. 'I should think thass what he means.' So they escorted the child over the bridge and down to the south end of the High Street, where his excited pointing at the signboard of the Nag's Head confirmed Chad's conjecture, and he was able presently to recognise his front door. The woman who answered thanked them and confided in an aggrieved voice: 'I told her to tie a bit o' string to him!'

The water-meadows at the edge of the town were close by here, and a path led behind the houses to the ruins of the

Abbey, spectral in the dusk. Chad said, 'Shall we go and have a walk round the ole Abbey?'

'All right,' Hester said. She didn't mind; and she was a little ashamed of herself for having the vapours just now. Like one of those drippy girls who piped their eyes at the slightest thing, she thought – like Mary-Ann Cole or somebody. Still, the plight of the bear grieved her.

The noise of the fair faded behind them as they took the path to the Abbey Green, and was lost in the ever-present boom of the fen wind. A slight sensation of going uphill – which a native of a less level country would not even have noticed – indicated that this had once been an island of firm ground standing above a virtual swamp, in the days when the monks had first raised here their great stone standard of faith. Standing sentinel to the remnants of the Abbey itself was a ruined gatehouse, where pilgrims had once waited to be admitted to the presence of the Abbey's relics: it was reduced now to the barest portal, yet so strong was the imprinted sense of those parts of the structure that were gone, like the itch of feeling in an amputated limb, that to pass under it was still to have an impression of entering a place. The Abbey proper reared up in spare profile against a steep chasm of clouded sunset: the large, asymmetrical fragment of west front was joined by the arch of a vanished window to a single shattered column so that it appeared like an old man leaning on a stick. Moss-grown gravestones were planted in the grass at its foot, so old that the carving on them had been weathered away completely, and they seemed to be melting back into the living earth from which their mother-stone had been hewn. Hester and Chad walked down the nave, open to the sky, and haunted by no voices now but those of the rooks that quarrelled in the bare galleries above.

'I want to ask you summat,' Chad said, in his flat way, as they emerged at the open end, where trees were raving in the wind.

'Yes?'

Chad paused in his stealthy tread. 'Well,' he said, 'I want to ask you if you'll git engaged.'

She nearly, very nearly, said 'Who to?' Perhaps it might

51

have been better if she had. But her habitual flippancy was constrained, heathen though she was, by the solemnity of the setting; and just for that moment the romantic in her was seized, really in the abstract, by the sheer idea of a proposal amongst Gothic stones and creeping shadows.

'How do you mean?' she said instead.

'I want you to git engaged to me.'

'Me? But – Chad—'

'I want you to. I been meaning to ask you. You got to – you got to.'

She looked at him, his taut slight figure and his face half-sullen, half-seething. Dusk lay like a thick net over the gaunt spaces of the Abbey; but enough light remained, if he had had eyes to see, for him to read her answer in her face. Though Hester's mouth, pretty and mobile, moved so naturally in mature curves of irony, she had singularly truthful eyes: they were still a child's, with a child's helpless candour; and they probably expressed her more than she knew herself.

'Chad – you can't really . . . You don't really know me, it don't make sense. You got to git to know people first . . .'

He looked uncomprehending. 'I don't care about that. I made me mind up. Look. You got to. I'm gitting a ring – I'm gitting one off Rob Risby – proper, not eelskin like that ole gippo said—'

'A ring?' She was astonished, but also dangerously flattered. 'Oh, Chad, you shouldn't do that—'

'Well, you said you'd like to be bought things – you said it yourself, you can't deny that.' He spoke with harsh challenge.

'But you can't just buy a ring like that, without saying anything—'

'I'm just said, ain't I?' A rook took off with a dry flapping of dusty wings at the sound of his raised voice. He paced back a little way down the path, plucking at his collar as if it irked him. 'You got to. I'm serious – I ain't mucking about. I don't want nobody else. You can't just say no – think about it. Say you'll think about it.'

'I don't know . . .'

He was standing facing her, perfectly framed by a dog's-tooth

52

arch, a solitary soaring bow of stone miraculously preserved on the thinnest of decayed columns. The afterglow in the sky behind it deepened to red as she looked at him, turning the toothed mouldings inside the arch fiercely black and sharp; and suddenly, irrationally, the image terrified her. He seemed to be standing unaware in a sinister mouth, a great fanged maw about to close on him. 'Chad – come away from that arch,' she said.

He did not heed this, and remained where he was. 'Say you'll think about it.'

The jagged mouth gaped, red-rimmed.

'Just say you'll think about it.'

'Oh! all right – yes, I will – just come away from that arch.' She covered her strange panic with a forced laugh, saying as he came forward: 'It looks so broken down, I thought it might fall on you or summat.'

'How long?'

'Eh?'

'How long you going to think?' And before she could answer he went on: 'Two days. Till Monday. How about that?' Again there was something dog-like in his gruff insistence. 'Two days.'

Did she really need two days to think about an answer she already knew deep down? Well, she had said she would think about it – it was done now. And it would postpone it, after all . . . Hester both benefited and suffered from a moral nature that was decidedly not strenuous. As she was generous in her judgement of others, she was correspondingly lenient to herself: she was inclined to give herself the benefit of the doubt, and rely on the universal alibi of meaning no harm. No one had ever asked her to get engaged, moreover: it seemed mere courtesy to give it consideration, rather than a flat no . . . 'All right,' she said, and he looked so relieved that she felt she had done the right thing.

They said no more about it. Chad only repeated once: 'Two days, then.' The business seemed to have exhausted him. They left the Abbey to the rooks and the wind; and on returning to the fair they found Mr and Mrs Langtoft and the boys newly arrived, and went round the fair with them all over

53

again. She acted, she supposed, quite normally, though her mind kept fetching up with a bump against the thoughts: A proposal! Fancy that! And so much for Mary-Ann Horseface! And, occasionally: But I don't love him.


2


The two days passed: Chad was the same as ever, that is, subdued, with a sort of muffled edge about him; and on the Monday morning he returned to the turf-fen to continue preparing his digging. Hester's mind oscillated between wishing she had never got into this, and thinking: 'Ah – well – it won't hurt.' This was a mental habit she had picked up from Mr Langtoft, who was a great bodger: he would perform a perilously makeshift repair on a cart-axle or a coulter, and when asked whether it was safe he would contemplate it with his head on one side and say, 'Ah – well – it won't hurt.' She was equally reluctant to give Chad the pain of a refusal, and to give herself the pain of making it.

At mid-morning Mrs Langtoft told Hester to go and take Chad his dockey.

'Oh – can't Jacob go, or Will?'

'Wha' for? Git on, git on, gel. You mek my blood boil.' Mrs Langtoft was sharp on Mondays, suffering from the pious equivalent of a hangover from the intoxicating devotions of the day before. 'Stand slummocking there. You'd end up on turnip-tops, the whole issue of yer, if it weren't for me.'

Hester placed Chad's dockey – a hunk of bread and cheese, a sliver of pickled pork, and a 'hungin' or onion – in the basket and went out. It was a goodish walk to the turf-fen, requiring a roundabout route to find the sleeper-bridges across the dykes, or places where they were narrow enough to jump; and after a while she was singing under her breath, for it was a spring day of magnificent pearly sky, and along the green dykesides there were wild violets and marsh-marigolds. She was healthy, she was young, she was fed, and for the moment there did not seem very much in the world that could threaten her. As she crossed the brimming main drain she could see the figure of

54

Chad in the turf-fen beyond, with the sun on his pale hair: he straightened up, saw her, and remained stock still, watching her, as she approached.

'I'm brought your dockey, Chad,' she said – rather unnecessarily: but he was staring so. 'I say, you're gitting on well now – have you started the digging yet?'

'No. I'm just finished paring. It just wants a bit o' cleaning and levelling yet.'

The half acre of land was marked out with pegs, and the top layer of earth had been removed by the sharp hodding-spade on which Chad was leaning. At the edge of the pit he had already prepared a flat surface, the staddle, where the blocks of peat would be stacked. She examined all this for some time, while Chad did not touch his dockey, but watched her. They were alone in a vast arena of black earth and blue sky, with only the muttering wind, the old gossip of the fen, beside them.

'Two days is up,' Chad said.

'I know. Thing is, Chad—'

'I give you the two days. I didn't pester you – you can't say that,' he said, with his smothered belligerence.

'I know.'

'Say yes then. Say you will. You know how I feel.'

'But thass it, you see,' she said, snatching at this. 'I don't. I mean, you just up and say let's git engaged all of a sudden, and—'

'You think I don't mean it, then? Is that what you think? You think I'm mucking about?'

'I dunno. You ain't thought about it, Chad. I mean, you only imagine it's me you want.' She hesitated: her honesty censured this as a weak argument. 'You know, there's loads of girls who—'

'I don't want them. I ain't bothered about them. It is you I want. I'll prove it yer. I'll show yer I mean it. I'll prove it – you got to—' He slammed the hodding-spade down: its sharp blade slid into the peat like a knife into flesh. 'If you don't believe me – if you're just mekking fun—'

'I'm not mekking fun,' said she, with truth.

'I'll show yer. What can I do? – I'll prove it—' Then in the midst of his grim flounderings he seemed to strike on the very

55

thing that had released him into articulacy before. 'See this peat? I reckon to cut seven hundred turf when I git started tomorrer. Seven hundred, thass a fair number for a start-off, they reckon. Here's betting I can do two thousand. I'll dig two thousand turf tomorrer – I'll do it – I will. Then will you believe me?'

'Whatever do you mean?'

'Just what I say. That'll be my proof. Will you believe me then? Two thousand turf in one day. For you.'

She stood in amazement and confusion. 'Oh, but, Chad—'

'Three thousand then!'

There is no malice in spring violets and blue skies, and they are seldom the instruments of unlucky fate: but just then it might have been better if Hester's walk to the turf-pit had been a trudge through grey November, for the flowers and the brilliance had got into her head, which at the soberest of times was inclined to lightness and rashness. And as Chad stood there making his wild bet and stabbing the spade into the peat, Hester's first thought was of fairy-stories her mother had told her as a girl: stories where the hero won the girl's hand by the performance of some tremendous and bizarre task. Imagine her being in a fairy-story! There was an irresistible novelty in that, to a girl inured by austerity to the grindingly prosaic. Her second thought was of what a thing it would be to tell Lizzie . . . Between these two, a third thought – of what would happen if she agreed – was quite squeezed out; and her instinctive conviction that Chad would never manage the task obliterated it completely.

'Three thousand! Say the word and I'll do it!' cried Chad.

'Oh! all right then – I'll believe you if you can do that.'

'And you'll git engaged to me then?'

He had not forgotten that part of it, even if she had in the astonishment of the moment: she faltered; but then, after all, it was so ridiculous . . . 'Go on, then.'

Chad clapped his hands once: then sat down and began eating his dockey as if she were not there.

He was still out in the turf-fen that evening when she walked over to Lizzie Gosling's.

56

'Three thousand turf, eh?' Lizzie's black button eyes glittered. 'Let's see – my brother Jack's been turf-digging for a couple o' years now. He reckons to do two thousand on a good day.'

'Oh, I know he won't be able to do it. But ain't it the queerest thing? I nearly went through the floor when he said it. 'Cept I weren't standing on a floor.'

'Three thousand . . . Well, he might manage it.'

'Goo on!'

Lizzie's wry bud of a mouth expressed a world of cynical possibilities. 'He might. Depends how serious he is about gitting you.'

'Oh, but thass what's so daft! He's got hold of this silly idea he wants to marry me . . . But he can hardly find a word to say to me. He stares and stares and gits mardy if I mek so much as a joke.'

'Oh, yes, I know what you mean. But still. What if he does do it?'

Hester actually felt the muscles of her face relax as the smile faded from her face. 'But it's a joke – it's just so ridiculous . . . Ain't it?'

'*I* think it's a good 'un. Best I ever heard,' Lizzie said, and gave one of her most satisfying laughs.

'Well, there you are then.'

'But,' Lizzie said, her eyebrows mounting right up her head, 'I wouldn't say a sense of humour was Chad Langtoft's strong point – would you?'

Hester made her way back to the farm. Giving Lizzie the news had not been as much fun as she had expected. Clouds like ragged witches were sweeping the dimming sky, and a wish came to her that it might rain tomorrow – then Chad might not be able to do the digging. Not that it mattered really – he couldn't do three thousand, surely? That was the trouble with Lizzie Gosling – you could never tell whether she was serious or not.

The little star-like eyes of the flowers on the dykesides were closed now; and the gaiety of the joke seemed to have worn off a little too.

'Well-a-well, who'd ha' thought it!' Mrs Langtoft was

57

beaming when Hester came in. 'You pair certainly kept things quiet, I'll say that.'

Hester glanced over at Chad, eating his supper by the light of the oil-lamp. He did not look up.

'Seems we'll be hearing some news tomorrer then,' Mr Langtoft said, smiling over his pipe.

'Mind! We'll say no more now,' Mrs Langtoft said. 'Not while it's time tomorrer. I declare though, it's quite a romantic sort o' fancy, ain't it – reminds me of when we were courting, Wag, d'you remember? – and you climbed on the sail of the mill and went all the way over, hanging on, just to show off to me, and I begged you not to, though I were tickled in a way.' She gave her husband an affectionate pummel, smiling on Hester all the while. 'Just fancy – still – we'll say no more now. Not while it's time.'

Hester made her excuses straight after supper and went up to bed. She could not believe it. Chad had marched in and told everyone that she was going to marry him. He had announced it flat: with the turf-digging task as a sort of flourish on the contract.

She did not undress: she wasn't ready for sleep – she had some thinking to do. Oh, but she hated thinking . . . She had taken one boot off, when she heard Chad's familiar creeping tread on the stair, and she went hopping out to the landing.

He was dressed to go out, and was just descending the stairs. He looked spruce, and almost cocky.

'Where you going?'

'Just down the Labour In Vain for a spell.'

'Look here – what'd you have to go and tell all about it for?'

His face flushed up in an instant, making his eyes pale. 'Tell what?'

'Me marrying you – all that.'

'Well, you are, ain't you? You said. You can't back out now. You said. You said.'

'I know – but I didn't mean—'

'You said. You said.' He repeated the words like a private charm: he suddenly gripped her arms in a convulsive movement, his fingernails digging into her skin. It was the first time he had touched her like that, and it was not a pleasant touch. 'You can't back out. You said. You said.'

'All right, I said – no call to go blabbing it—'

He let go of her. 'You reckon I won't be able to do it, don't you? Well, I'll prove it to yer. You'll see.' He turned and padded down the stairs.


3


It did not rain: the next day dawned bright and fine. Chad had gone to the turf-fen at first light. He had not stayed long at the Labour In Vain, the pub in the hamlet of Milney St Mary, for he had gone there not to drink but to tell everyone that he was promised to Hester Verney: the Labour In Vain performing for Hinching Fen a function analogous to that of the main drain, and serving as the channel through which all the news of that scattered parish flowed.

Hester remembered not only her mother's fairy-tales but the stories she retold from little yellowback novels which her father, full of pride at her scholarly accomplishment, got for her from the market whenever there was spare money. In these stories men with long aristocratic names and varying styles of whisker competed for the favours of a heroine who was always, throughout her trials, implacably single-minded. *Single-minded* hung round those heroines' necks like the fabulous necklaces with which the whiskered lords were continually presenting them. That Hester was unconvinced by these stories had much to do with the fact that she was not at all single-minded herself. Those single-minded heroines, she reflected, would never have got themselves in this position.

She woke feeling optimistic – the whole thing was after all so absurd and fantastical there could be no harm in it whatever happened: began to feel uncomfortable under Mrs Langtoft's significant nods and smiles; and set out at mid-morning to take Chad his dockey feeling dreadfully uneasy.

She began to see, now, that it would have been fairer to Chad to have turned him down flat straight away, at the Abbey. But at the time that had seemed the very opposite of fair to him.

Anxiously examining her motives, she was unable to acquit herself of frivolity in taking up his challenge, but her wish to be fair was quite genuine; and so was her desire to avoid hurting him. She still did not want to hurt him, but an easy middle way seemed to be petering out before her eyes, and dark extremes closed in on either side of her.

On drawing near to the turf-fen she was relieved, at first, to see some other folk there: and then dismayed when she realised that the gaggle of children, Henry Wake, and Jass Phelps must have gathered about Chad's pit for the sole purpose of witnessing something that had been bruited all over the fen; an idea that was confirmed by the universal gaze of speculative interest that greeted her arrival.

Chad however hardly glanced up, but continued with his digging. He was dressed in shirt sleeves and sweating-cap, and there was already a great stain under his arms. The peat was dug in blocks, called cesses, of about six by four by eight inches, marked out in rows of three by a wooden gauge pressed into the surface: and the cesses were turned off the spade on to the staddle in neat rows, three at first to make a firm foundation, and two above. Veteran turf-diggers took pride in the precision of their stacks; but though Chad's were not as tidy as they might have been, they were already large, and the cut surface of the pit seemed to be growing at disturbing speed.

'I'd advise you to eat summat, Chad,' Henry Wake said, observing the dockey-basket. 'I think you'll find you git on better. It replaces the animal salts, you see. You mustn't lose your animal salts.'

'In a minute,' Chad said.

'Is there any cheese in that basket, Hester?' Henry said. 'Cheese is a very feeding food.'

'People reckon as sugar gives you strength,' Jass Phelps said. 'So they reckon. *I* don't know.'

Jass Phelps was the landlord of the Labour In Vain: he had come over in his little donkey-cart. He was a sleek man of fifty with a dropsical belly, dainty hands and feet, and a crown of oiled hair looking as if it were painted on; with a snub nose and, as it were, a snub mouth and snub eyes too, as if his face were permanently pressed up against a window-pane – and indeed, being of voraciously inquisitive character, he could be said to be habitually pressing himself up against his neighbours' business, and trying to see in. 'I suppose some people might reckon three thousand in a day's too much to ask of anybody,' he said, glancing sidelong at Hester: he seemed to feel that his curiosity was somehow mitigated by inserting it crabwise, in arch generalities. 'Or perhaps I'm got it wrong. *I* don't know.'

'We-ell, turf-digging's not a thing I'm ever turned me hand to, meself,' Henry Wake said, 'but I'm known quite a few turf-diggers in me time, and I'm observed the process pretty closely, so I reckon I understand it as well as anybody, no point in mekking out I don't: and I think you'll find three thousand's well within the bounds of possibility. I think it is, you know.'

'You'll mek yourself ill if you don't eat summat,' Hester said quietly to Chad. He turned off a last row of turf, spat out his sucking-pebble, and picked up the dockey-basket. He ate standing up, quickly, looking at his stacks.

'I suppose you could ask,' Jass Phelps said, 'who's going to count 'em? And I suppose some people might wonder what's going to happen if they're just a few short or something o' that kind. I don't know, perhaps that don't matter. It's nothing to do with me.'

'Oh! if there's a disinterested witness required, I'll be quite happy to step in,' Henry Wake said. 'A 'judicator you call that, you know, but we'll say witness. Not,' he said, smiling pleasantly at Hester, 'that I think it'll come to anything as strict as that.'

Hester found she could not smile back. Chad had finished his dockey, bolting it down, and picked up his spade again.

'Well! I'm got things to see to,' Henry Wake said. 'Better git back. I shall drop by later if I may. It's not the sort of thing you see every day, this.'

'People might say this is what you call a labour of love, ain't it?' Jass Phelps said, staring sideways at Hester. 'Or summat like that. I suppose some people might think it's all a bit peculiar. *I* don't know.'

As it was early in the season, with the spring floods not long past, there was water slopping about in the bottom of the pit, icy with all the stored coldness of winter; and Chad's lower hand, grasping the base of the haft, was raw scarlet. Birds, attracted by the prospect of wriggling eatables turned up by the spade, were continually alighting round the edges of the pit. Hester was sure she saw irony directed at her from their small gemstone eyes.

As she watched Chad digging, mechanically, with morose intensity, Hester seemed to feel the chill touch of the water herself — a cold invasion of misgivings. Not once did he look her way, and that unnerved her. She went away, and was glad to be given the job that afternoon of taking the cow round the droves and dykesides to get a little early grazing, a task of which the solitude usually irked her. She lingered, and found herself reluctant to return to the farm at dinner-time.

'I'm been out to see Chad,' Mrs Langtoft said. 'He ain't half gitting on. You can't top the Langtofts for wukk when they put their minds to it.' For all the irritable impatience and the turnip-tops, Mrs Langtoft nourished a fierce family pride. She enjoyed the privilege of calling her menfolk useless articles, but woe betide anyone else who should slight them: there was something of the mother cat about her, and sometimes it seemed that only her lack of stature hindered her from picking them up in her mouth by the scruff, and taking charge of them that way. Hester did not find these thoughts encouraging. 'Now you get your dinner ate, gel, and when it's settled you can tek Chad's out to him — he ain't coming back here for it.'

Hester watched her wrapping the pork dumpling in a cloth. 'Oh, but he can come home for his dinner, surely. He'll just mek himself ill. It's silly!' She spoke lightly: but a heaviness of foreboding was on her. The day was beginning to seem like one of those dreams in which familiar faces turn alien, and the world becomes a series of jagged distortions.

Mrs Langtoft looked at her in surprise. 'Why, you're an odd one, you are. I'd ha' thought you'd be flattered. I declare it's made you go all shy, and I'm never seen *that* afore. Chad knows what he's about, don't you fret.'

The walk to the turf-fen was becoming a *via dolorosa* for her. This time when she was within sight of it she heard a voice haling her, and Peggy Chettle caught up with her.

'Wait for me, gel. I could tell it were you from other side of the drain. Tell your walk. I can always tell folk by their walk. You walk straight and stick your chest out. Why not – stick 'em out, if you're got 'em. I wish I had a bit more on the sideboard meself, still they did their job, I'm raised four boys and one of 'em drives a hoss-omnibus.'

All of Hinching Fen and many surrounding parishes knew Mrs Chettle, or would know her eventually; for she was of that indispensable race of matrons piquantly known as first-and-lasters, who acted as midwives to the newly arrived and layers-out to the newly departed, and sometimes ministered to minor illnesses in between, in the absence of doctors repelled by the poverty and remoteness of the region. She was a stout and hardy woman, very cheerful about her trade in all its aspects, with a permanently strenuous stride, suggestive of ploughing through droves in all weathers and not minding a bit. Two wings of grizzled hair framed a flat face more honest than comely, split by a great healthy horsey smile like one almighty tooth, and adorned by wiry black eyebrows of almost manly thickness. She did pretty well out of her work, and was always smartly turned out – a straw sailor hat, and tailor-made walking dress with leg-of-mutton sleeves: but there was nothing of vanity or frippery about her. Rubbing shoulders daily with mortality as she did, Mrs Chettle's social manners were inevitably marked by the frankest intimacy – made manifest by her habit of standing very close to you and constantly touching you, in a familiar manner not entirely pleasing, with pink brisk hands that always seemed to have just been washed after doing something.

'I heard the news the smorning,' Peggy Chettle said, thrusting her smile in Hester's face, and kneading her arm in her fingers. 'So I thought I'd come and tek a look for meself, thinking this'll perhaps be summat to remember in after years, and say I was there. Who knows, I might even be recalling it in my professional capacity with you, at the proper time, that would be quaint, wouldn't it? And I'm got to git over and see Coggy Onyett who got kicked in the stones by a cow, though he wants it kept quiet, daft beggar, as if it were some sort of shame to be kicked by anything less than a hoss, and he's such a shy morsel, he won't show the damage, though anybody can see it, and Mrs Onyett's had to cut an extra gusset in his britches to mek room – so it was in me way, like, so I thought I'd tek Chad a dab o' neat's-foot-oil, knowing how the diggers suffer terrible with their hands at the start o' the season, gret blisters and cracks you can put your finger in, still, what's a drop o' pus here or there, when you're soaring on the wings of love!'

There were more people gathered round the turf-pit, Hester saw as they approached: the stacks of cesses had mounted, and from the top of one a tassel fluttered in the breeze – signifying a thousand. At the sight of it Hester swallowed, and tried to hide her dismay from the midwife's benevolently devouring gaze.

'You're looking a bit peaky yourself, gel.' Mrs Chettle squeezed her hand, and confidentially laid her chin on her shoulder a moment. 'I'd say it was green-sickness, if I didn't know you better; you was never the lent-lily sort. Now if it's summat as you think you can't speak of, you know, then you come to me and we'll see you through it, bless you. I'm birthed dozens of 'em what were in the belly before the banns, and they drop out just the same way.'

'Oh, I'm all right, Mrs Chettle, thanks all the same,' Hester said: but this last had hit home direct as an arrow, and had the effect of clearing much that was confused. That she – that she and Chad . . . Impossible! She had got to know him better, and understand him a little, and had enjoyed the skating and the fair, and been flattered by his attentions, all very light-hearted . . . but as for feeling anything like that for him . . . The shock of it went through her like a physical jolt, right down to the soles of her feet. She seemed to behold for the first time the chill, dour aspect of Chad's passion, and something within her recoiled, with uncharacteristic violence.

She remembered an outing to the hills-and-hollows at Barnack – ancient quarries whence had come the stone of Peterborough Cathedral – when she had begun to run, laughing and exhilarated, down a steep slope, and then had found her own momentum carrying her on, frighteningly, against her will, faster and faster. The same helpless sensation came upon her now. If only she could just speak to Chad alone, sensibly, without all these people around, watching and making things worse!

She handed him his dinner, and saw that his hands were indeed cracked and blistered. Peggy Chettle moved in. 'I'm brought you a spot o' salve for them hands, Chad, no, you put them coppers back, I wouldn't think of mekking a charge, not for such a special occasion as this, any road you'll most likely be needing all your money afore long. Now it wants rubbing in deep and then you'll find it eases you, mind, wait while you're et your dinner fust, you don't want none of it gooing down with your dumpling, else you'll find it coming out tother end afore you can shift your braces.'

Lizzie Gosling was among the watchers. Hester took her aside.

'I can't believe it, Lizzie. I never thought he'd tek it this serious.'

'Gitting near his two thousand, I reckon.'

'He'll mek himself ill,' Hester said, watching Chad, having swallowed his dinner like a gannet, set in again. 'I don't want that!'

'What's his mam and dad think about it all?'

'Oh! I don't know, really.' She was afraid she knew too well: they had taken Chad's cause to heart.

The day waned; and as they knocked off work more people came across the fields to watch Chad's labours in the turf-pit. Such a thing was worth seeing, not simply in itself but because there might be a tale in it, and this was important. The existence of the folk of Hinching Fen was bare and plain in the extreme: they lived out lives of narrow poverty in clay-lump cottages, and in the featureless landscape there was little to beguile the eye but the giant kaleidoscope of sky; and remote from modern communications as they were, the oral transmission (and embroidery) of stories, forming an ongoing local epic, was a vital sweetener in a meagre diet of experience.

'There weren't nothing like this in my day,' old Andrew Surfleet remarked to Sunny Daintree. 'You just poddled up to the gel you wanted and ast her to be promised to you there and then. That were usually on the way home from church

– afore the chapel were built, like – I don't know why then 'specially, I suppose it were because you'd had a good wash, and she could see what you looked like without your muck. And if she didn't tek to yer, she said no.'

'If you were lucky,' Sunny said, darkly.

'I had to give up the turf-digging, meself,' Andrew said. 'It were gitting so as me fingers had been gripping the spade so long, they wouldn't uncurl when I got home, so I couldn't eat me dinner: 'less me missis helped me, and she weren't very patient at it, she used to keep poking the next bit o' pudden in me mouth afore I'd swallowed the last beggar. Ah! not that it'll hurt a young feller like Chad, in the prime o' life.'

'Ooh! dear.' Sunny Daintree sucked in breath. 'I wouldn't goo so far as to say that. I knew a young chap once as were lifting taters, and it were past supper-time, but he'd took it in his head that he wanted to git 'em all up that day: so he carried on, and overshot his strength – and his ole mother come out with a lamp and found him there laying dead amongst the taters like he'd been pole-axed.'

'No! What killed him, then?'

'Why, it were the wukk: summat just bust inside him. Ooh! dear. He were about Chad's age. I tell you, if Chad was to fall down dead at my feet now I wouldn't be a bit surprised. I wouldn't bat an eyelid.'

At dusk the Langtofts themselves went out to the turf-fen; but Hester was not with them. She had made an excuse some time earlier of taking Chad a can of tea, and had hidden herself in the barn.

'Oh – it's not my fault if he goes and gits the wrong idea!' she said aloud, making a mouse scuffle in the straw: then paced up and down, and admitted to herself, silently, that it probably was her fault. A moment of light-mindedness had induced her to accept the outlandish challenge; and still she could scarcely believe that such a momentous weight of consequence should be poised on that tiny apex.

It was her misfortune to come into collision with a nature like Chad's: a nature singular and colourless, embracing no diversity, which the belated presence of a passion stained a uniform dull hue; and disabled by a crucial dislocation between feeling and expression. Hester could no longer deceive herself as to the reality of his feeling: but that grim, blank way in which he was labouring in the pit gave her an idea of its quality too, and it did not suggest warmth.

She sat down in the straw. It occurred to her that there was simply no one to whom she could turn: and if she had been prone to self-pity, she would have bewailed her loneliness. As it was, she admonished herself for hiding. 'Well – you did it – you're got to face it,' she said to herself; but still she lingered in the barn, until she could scarcely see her hand in front of her face; when she was roused by a voice in the yard, calling 'Hallo there!'

It was Henry Wake. She left the barn.

'Ah, there you are, Hester – I'm come to fetch you to the turf-fen – Mrs Langtoft were going to send young Will, but I volunteered to nip over meself – I'm always been a tidy runner, I don't know why it is, I think I'm right in saying stamina's the word for it. Well! He's done it, gel – he's done it: three thousand. I did a quick count-up meself, not one by one, you understand, but I think I've a pretty fair eye for these things.'

'I'd better come then,' Hester said faintly.

Henry, in his urbane way, gave her his arm. 'Whole issue of folk stood there watching as he cut the last one – seems to have quite captured the imagination. Might make a nice little item for the *Hunts Post*, if it were written out properly – I'm a fair hand with a pen meself as it happens, it's one of them things you're born with—'

'No, Mr Wake – don't do that.'

He stopped in surprise, and peered at her in the gathering darkness. 'Why, Hester, what is the matter?'

'Oh, this is going to sound awful – but the thing is, I never meant all this to happen – he would keep insisting so, and then he made this silly bet, and I thought it was funny so I said go on then – but he's so terrible serious and he went round saying I were going to marry him – and now I wish I'd never got into it.'

Her choice of Henry Wake as confidant was dictated simply by the pressure of feelings that had been building up all day

67

and now could no longer be restrained: in fact she might have done worse. It was known all over Hinching Fen that Henry Wake, for all his big talk, was as tender as a chicken; he could not bear the sight of distress, and someone else's troubles would afflict him as if they were his own. People put up with a lot of his bumptiousness, on account of this quality which he believed he kept hidden. And so he peered anxiously into Hester's face, and his hand went to his handkerchief.

'Oh! dear,' he said. 'Dear me, I – this rather puts a different complexion on things. I'm sorry, Hester, I had no idea . . .' He gave her the handkerchief, and studied the distance while she made use of it, looking as if he might need it himself.

'I'm been thinking about it all day,' she said. 'I'm got to tell him. I know folk'll think badly of me.'

'I'm rather afraid they might,' Henry said.

'But think how much wuss it'd be if I went and got engaged to him for such a daft reason,' cried she. 'That wouldn't be no kindness to him, would it? Not when I – well, I don't love him. Thass the thing. And he'd find it out.'

'Ah,' Henry said; and stroked his little moustache.

'It'd be a mockery. I know I shouldn't have took him up on it – but wouldn't it be a disgrace to go through with it, and mek two people miserable for the sake of a pile o' turf?' As she spoke she was afraid this would seem a mere cobbling-together of an excuse – yet at the same time she knew she was absolutely right. All the while in the barn she had been fending off this harsh conclusion: it had pain on its side, but truth too, and she must embrace it.

'It'll mean going back on your word,' Henry said reflectively. 'But like you say – the alternative's a lot wuss. Oh! dear.' Timidly he patted Hester's hand. 'Well, you must do what's right, Hester. Better to settle it now than later. I shan't judge you – though I'm afraid some people will; but then it's been a bit of an excitement for them, like, and they'll be sorry at being disappointed.' He expressed these views with a gentle tentativeness, far more convincing than his usual assertive parade of learning. 'Never mind. It'll be all right. Truth's always best, I reckon, in the long run.'

She believed him – for her habit of lying to herself was

really the superficial evasion of a rather frighteningly honest nature: but the trouble was she had always lived her life in the short run. And suddenly that had become a dark thicket of difficulty.

'Do you want to come now?' Henry said. 'I could go back and mek an excuse for you if you like – I could say you're got headache. I could say you're indisposed,' he added, with a flash of genteel inspiration.

'No,' she said, laughing in spite of herself at that ladylike phrase while the odours of the farmyard wafted around them. 'No, thank you, Mr Wake, I'm got to come.' She had hidden enough.

It was almost full dark when they reached the turf-fen; but Mr Langtoft had brought a storm-lantern, the light of which revealed a dozen or more people standing around the pit, and the long walls of stacked cesses with the three tassels waving – at her – in the night breeze. There was a cheer as she approached, and a few ribald comments.

'There now,' Mrs Langtoft said, coming forward and taking her hand in a motherly, or mother-in-lawly, way, 'didn't I say nobody could wukk like a Langtoft when he sets his mind to it?'

Peggy Chettle had returned, and having made Chad sit on the edge of the pit had her hands up the back of his shirt and was rubbing ointment into the muscles. 'Never mind your modesty, dear boy,' she said, 'I'm past fretting about such things meself, why, I have me hands in funnier places than this every day and it don't mean no more to me than kneading a bit o' dough. Now I'm putting plenty on, so you'd best sleep on your front tonight else you'll be sliding about in bed like an eel on a wet oilcloth.' Her great teeth shone at Hester in the lamplight. 'Not that you'll feel much like sleeping, I shouldn't think.'

'See?' Chad said to Hester.

'Well, I'm sure we're all had a very interesting time,' Henry Wake said, 'but Mrs Wake'll be putting a lamp in the winder for me by now, so I reckon I'll be going, and I'd suggest we all do likewise.'

'Ah! you're right, Henry,' Mrs Langtoft said, 'there's a couple of people here wants leaving alone, so let's all say goodnight. Come on, Wag,' and she collected her husband from the edge of the pit with both hands like a wheelbarrow, and having rearranged the load a little, turned him round and trundled him home.

The spectators left: their voices dwindled, very slowly, into the wind-rippled silence of the fen night. The lantern was left behind. Chad picked it up and held it close to Hester's face.

'You never saw me cut my three thousand,' he said.

'No.'

He brought the lamp a little closer. 'So now you believe me,' he said.

'Yes, I believe you,' she said. Her heart began to pound horribly: suddenly she felt like an animal caught in a snare. Part of her longed to equivocate, to sidle out of it, even to give in – an engagement, that was nothing, engagements had been broken before . . . But it would not do. 'You're done wonders, Chad. I ought to be right proud, I know—'

'What d'you mean, ought to be?' Suddenly the lamp was right in her face, hurting her eyes: he had caught something in her tone.

'Well, I am – I mean it's very flattering you doing this – but it still don't mek any difference to what I feel. Or what I don't feel. Thass why I can't get engaged to you, Chad. I'm sorry I took you up on it, I know I shouldn't have. I'm sorry.'

'But I'm done it,' he said, as if not understanding. 'Look – I'm done the three thousand. Dad counted – Henry Wake counted. I'm done it.'

'Oh, but you don't marry someone just because they pile up a load of turf!' she cried, unable to suppress a note of exasperation.

'You said you would.' The lamp was unsteady in his hand: its light fell in ghostly smears on the black walls of turf, so that they seemed to face each other in some sunken prison-vault. 'You said – you said you would.'

'Only because you were daft enough to suggest it! What sort of a person would really marry someone because of a thing like that?'

'You got to! You said! You said!' Chad's face, so cautious of expression, betrayed his fury obscurely: the rising flush

70

of blood merged with the shadows of fatigue until it looked horribly bruised.

'No, Chad. I can't. It's no good. I don't—' It seemed too hard to say *I don't love you* – those cruel words, so stark and deathly; but even as she hesitated to give him this pain, he grasped the unsaid. He stared at her for two more seconds, and then hit her in the face.

Such essentially passionless natures as Chad's, once infected, know no moderation. He might have reflected that his was the moral advantage, having kept his side of the bargain while she had broken hers; but because of that emotional equivalent of tunnel vision from which he suffered, he hit out and forfeited the advantage with a single stroke of the fist. Hester staggered back, more in shock than pain, and nearly fell.

'You said,' Chad repeated, dully, then dropped the lantern on the ground and walked away.

Afterwards she wished she had hit him back; but at that moment she was immobilised not only by shock but by a feeling curiously akin to relief: relief that it was all with utmost cleanness finished, settled, done with – at least where she and Chad were concerned. She knew, however, that those few violent moments in the dark turf-fen had irrevocably changed her relations with the Langtofts: she was their dependant, and utterly vulnerable; and she was afraid to go back to the farm.

At last she wiped her eyes, and made her way, carrying the lantern, over to Lizzie Gosling's, where she explained the mark on her face by saying she had walked into a low tree branch in the darkness. Lizzie bathed it in an eloquent silence.

'What's going to happen now?' Lizzie said, as Hester finally prepared to go home.

She shook her head. 'I don't know.'

Mrs Langtoft met her at the door of the farm; and at once she knew that Chad had told his tale.

'Now git in here, gel, and tell me the truth! You gone and broke your promise to Chad, is that it? You gone and led him on and then broke your promise? Well, come on, out wi' it!'

'Where is he?' Hester said.

'Gone down the Labour In Vain. Terrible state he was in – *that* shows it – he's never been a drinker before. He never

71

learnt that in this house. Well, what's it all about? Lord give me strength, you mek my blood boil!'

The boys had been packed off to bed. Mr Langtoft, looking more than usually perplexed, and also sad, sat in the armchair and patted old Dan.

'I never meant that promise,' Hester said. 'It started as a joke . . . He took it too seriously.'

'Joke? What joke?' Mrs Langtoft snapped. 'Mekking a joke of Chad? What on earth are you playing at?'

'I never really thought of gitting engaged to Chad – you can't do that unless it's the right person—'

'Right person? What's wrong with our Chad?'

'Nothing, nothing. But I don't feel . . .' She went on to repeat the things she had said to herself, to Henry Wake, to Chad . . . but at some point she became aware that Mrs Langtoft, exclaiming, snorting, and pacing around the kitchen as if she felt its walls pressing in on her, was not listening.

'Never heard anything like it in my life – just git the winter over and now this – I thought he'd gone spare when he come in tonight – mekking a promise like that . . .' Her stalwart bosom heaved, and her magnified shadow revolved endlessly. All her loyal protectiveness of family burned in her, and for the moment she did not see the girl of whom she was fond and who had replaced her Meery, but an intruder and betrayer.

In the midst of this Mr Langtoft, speaking for the first time, said quietly: 'What you done to your face, gel?'

'Knocked into a tree in the dark,' Hester said, turning away from the light.

'Is this what we took you in for? Playing tricks like this?' Mrs Langtoft fumed on; and Hester grew weary as she realised there was nothing she could say that would penetrate the shell of Mrs Langtoft's possessive indignation. She was the villain and that was that.

An end was put to this hopeless wrangling at last, when Chad came in, drunk.

'Oh! Chad, you'll do yourself no good this way,' Mrs Langtoft said, fussing him into a chair. 'Git the kettle on, gel, mek yourself some use. And look at them blisters! They want threading – pass me my sewing-box, Wag.'

The huge blisters caused by turf-digging were treated by passing through them a needle threaded with wool, then leaving the wool inside to soak them dry. Chad, slumped in a chair, submitted to this operation silently, his eyes lowered.

'Drink's no answer, my boy,' Mrs Langtoft said, as she tutted and shook her head over the blisters. 'You won't git it sorted that way.'

'Folk were having a rare old laugh at me down the Labour In Vain,' Chad muttered. 'A rare old laugh.'

Suddenly Mrs Langtoft shot at Hester a glance that hurt her – for instead of being reproachful it was hateful. 'Look what you're done!' she said.

'We can git it sorted,' Mr Langtoft said. 'Surely we can git it sorted.'

'I tell you what,' Chad said, lifting his eyes to Hester at last, 'I wouldn't have you if you paid me! Thass what! Not if you paid me, you ole slut!'

'Now then,' Mr Langtoft said, 'no call for that. We can git it sorted.'

But even as he spoke Hester knew that it could not be sorted: that here, among the lamplight and the needles and the hot water, the possibility of reconciliation was receding moment by moment. And in a white glare of instantaneous truth she saw what those few moments of trivial foolishness had led to – the end of her days at Langtoft's farm.

'Just hold your hosses a bit,' Mr Langtoft was saying. 'Remember we're all got to git along together here.'

'We what?' Mrs Langtoft was crushing. 'What peace are we ever going to git with her around? Playing tricks – leading people on—'

'Well, then, I shan't stay,' Hester said, with deliberate dignity. The sight of Chad's blisters had renewed her sense of guilt – but one can only bear so much reproach without sinking into self-contempt, and Hester did not think so badly of herself as that. 'I shall go as soon as you like.'

'Thass the best idea I'm heard yet,' said Mrs Langtoft, with stabbing bitterness.

Hester took a candle and went up to bed. She had not yet begun to undress when there was a tap at the door. It

73

was opened slightly, and Mr Langtoft stood in the gap, not looking in.

'You all right, are you, gel?' he said softly.

She said yes.

'All a bit of a to-do, ain't it? I don't know what to say. You shouldn't have done it, gel. Well, I s'pose you know that. I shan't say no more. Trouble is –' he dropped his voice to a whisper – 'I'm afraid I don't reckon Bess is going to come round, you know. If it were just up to me, like . . .' He left a pregnant pause.

'I know,' Hester said. 'I don't see how I can stop here, any road. Not now.'

'Ah. It ain't that we're not fond of you, gel. You're been a good worker, and all, and I wouldn't ha' wanted you to go. I like a quiet life meself, and if I thought there were a chance of gitting it sorted . . .' His voice trailed off.

'Thank you, Mr Langtoft,' Hester said. 'I'll go. I'll go tomorrow.'

The morning brought no alteration in the facts of the situation: no alteration in Hester's mind, and most importantly none in Mrs Langtoft's.

The truth was, Mrs Langtoft's liking for Hester had been deep and genuine; and for some time there had been at the least an unconscious willingness on her part to look on the girl as a future daughter-in-law. The sudden realisation of this prospect, and its more sudden demolition, had produced in her a combustion of feeling – and its most fiery element was that jealous family pride, taking the form of an indignant rhetorical question: 'So she thinks Chad Langtoft's not good enough for her?' Her husband was forced to listen to several animadversions on Hester's family, who she said were as poor shabby an ole lot as anybody on the fen and nothing to be proud of, but he knew as well as she did there was nothing in them – they were just smoke from the flame of her disappointment and resentment. The flame was too strong and fierce to be dampened down by reflection: and the sight of the baleful, hung-over Chad scarcely able to eat his breakfast for the blisters on his hands, was oxygen to it. 'You still sticking to what you said last night, gel?' was Mrs Langtoft's abrupt greeting of Hester, spoken as it were out of the back of her head; and the girl scarcely needed to reply. It was plain that she and Chad could not remain in that house together – and there was no question of who should go.

Mr Langtoft drooped untidily about the farm all morning, could settle to nothing, and at last went up to Hester's room where she was packing her few clothes and possessions.

'This all seems a bit hasty to me, gel,' he said, plucking miscellaneous straws and seeds from his moustache. ''Twouldn't be so bad if you was just going home to your folks – but you ain't got no folks near, have you?'

'I don't know where Father is now,' she said. 'It don't matter, though. The Goslings'll put me up for a time, while I look for work.'

'Ah. Well, I'll give you a good word, gel, wherever you go – just tell 'em to refer to me.' With great difficulty he took a handful of shillings from his pocket and placed them on the wash-stand.

'Oh! Mr Langtoft – really, I ain't got money owing to me, you know, and I'm got a few bob—'

'I know, gel, but still, you tek it, you'll want a bit by you – you got to look after yourself – we ain't struggling quite so bad wi' winter done now, and there'll be extra coming in when Chad sells his turf – oh! well, we won't talk about that – any road . . .' and beaten about with various sorts of discomfort as he was, Mr Langtoft made a sort of hurried sidle out of the room, colliding with the door-jamb as he went.

'Give her how much?' Mrs Langtoft said when her husband at last told her. 'Hm! One thing's for sure – we s'll end up on turnip-tops yet.' But, more significantly, she did not object.

The packing did not take long. A walk over to the Goslings' secured her a temporary berth there – Lizzie, being the capable only daughter of a not very capable widower, having a good deal of say in the household. Hester had no wish to linger out her farewell to the farm. Life with her father had been a continual round of flitting, but this was different: she had come to regard this as home; and to tear herself quickly and sharply from it, she felt, was the only way of limiting the pain, and making

75

the severance bearable. It still seemed scarcely possible that, virtually overnight, the earth should have shifted beneath her feet like this. The material aspect of her predicament would have daunted a temper less buoyant than Hester's – for she had lost a good job, and was now thrown on the world without means: as it was, her chief sorrow was at the loss of friends. She did not love Mrs Langtoft the less for what had happened, and she might almost have run to her and begged to be allowed to stay, but for one thing: wrong as she had been to agree to Chad's wager, she was sure she had done right in the end.

She went out to the fields to say her goodbyes to Jacob and Will – their respective ages manifest in their reactions to this drama, in that Jacob understood it too well and could hardly look at her, and Will did not understand it at all. Returning, she met Chad in the yard.

She was not much of a hater: the sight of him now produced little more than a weary aversion, insignificant beside her sadness. Perhaps therein lay the essential misfortune of their association – that it was curiously difficult to feel anything much towards him.

'You going then?' he said.

'I reckon it's best,' she said. 'Don't you?'

Still he gave her his dogged, watchful look. He said: 'I meant what I said, you know. Last night.'

Meant what he had said? Ah – that. She allowed herself a grain of bitterness. 'Oh! well, don't worry about it, Chad. I'm never going to pay you. You can be sure of that.'


4


The news of Hester Verney's broken promise and of her leaving the Langtofts' farm under a cloud did not take long to permeate Hinching Fen, and it formed the chief topic of conversation at the Labour In Vain that night.

This public house was the most prominent feature of Milney St Mary, a hamlet which was really only a sort of brief inhabited interlude along the course of a fen causeway – as if the road, tiring of its ruler-straight transit across the flat miles, had momentarily broken out in houses. The peat which formed the soil of this district was notoriously liable to shrinkage, with the result that not only was the road elevated several feet above the fields, but the foundations of buildings were unstable: and so the few dwellings of Milney St Mary had settled at various angles to the perpendicular, with an effect of leaning towards each other in promiscuous and raffish attitudes. The Labour In Vain, a long double-fronted building with a stout chimney-breast at each end, had suffered a variation on the common fate by subsiding in the middle. This not only gave its exterior a broken-backed appearance, but meant that to walk across the bar-parlour was to be aware of a listing sensation, suggestive of a heeling ship – an experience alarming to strangers, and giving rise to wild speculations on their part as to the strength of the beer. For the same reason chairs and tables had had to be tailored to the declivity of the floor, by the sawing off of odd inches from legs to make them level: and it was not an uncommon occurrence for jugs and tankards to make a slow sliding progress to the edge of the shelves along the walls, and be seen teetering there, as if in two minds whether to throw themselves off. To these basic appointments the Labour In Vain superadded an extravagant piece of décor, hanging above the great open hearth fire and running the whole length of it: a painting in oils, representing sheep, stags, and cows all in unlikely proximity to a thunderous waterfall, with a storm and a sunset going on for good measure; the whole blackened monstrosity covering a great deal of wall, and seeming to have been chosen on that dependable old principle, If You're Going to Have One, Have a Big One.

The coming of spring meant more work, and hence more money around, and so the bar-parlour was well-filled. It was expressive of the rough democracy of the fen that labourers like old Andrew Surfleet rubbed shoulders with farmers: including Henry Wake, who overcame his Methodist disapproval of liquor to the extent of supping a half-pint or two, simply for the sake of the gossip.

'There's some as reckons there's more to it,' said Jass Phelps, the landlord. 'Reckons as she was in a certain condition. So they say. *I'm* not saying that, mind you.'

'Why, what condition's that, then?' Andrew Surfleet said.

'Expectin', you daft ole beggar,' grunted an old turf-digger named Artie Gill, a cross-grained fellow whose eyebrows met in the middle, mirroring his moustache and giving his face a sinister symmetry.

'Oh! that.' Andrew Surfleet – who took his beer warm – watched as Jass Phelps plunged the hot poker into the mug, and thought deeply. 'No! Surely not. She'd never have turned him down, in that case. That'd be tother way around.'

'I'm sure there's no suggestion of that,' Henry Wake said. 'No call to bring that into it.'

'Funny sort of business, all the same,' Jass Phelps said, scratching the arched back of one of his cats. He was a man who loved cats, hated children, and believed the worst of people with an almost religious faith. 'She were always a flighty sort, so they say. Always giving the glad-eye one way or tother. Thass what I'm heard. *I* don't know.'

'Oh! she's young, you know,' Henry Wake said. 'Young and a bit giddy. No more than that.'

'Thass Chad I feel sorry for,' said Andrew Surfleet, with the steam from his beer all over his beard. 'I'll never forgit his face when he come in here last night.'

'You weren't here last night,' growled Artie Gill, 'so how could you know?'

'Ah – no, but – I'll never forgit it, from how Jass there, and Sunny here described it – you saw him, didn't you, Sunny?'

'Ooh! dear. Did I?' Sunny Daintree felt in his moleskin waistcoat for his tin watch – a frequent consultation which invariably seemed to indicate that it was later than he thought. 'I thought he'd gone spare, for definite. I wouldn't have been a bit surprised to be fishing him out of the dyke the smorning.' He sighed. 'With a pole.'

'Terrible pity,' Andrew said. 'Not that Chad's such an easy chap to feel sorry for, somehow: he seems to have got there before you, if you see what I mean.'

'It's the gel I feel sorry for – losing a good place like that,' Henry Wake said. 'And no family to fall back on. I'll tek half a pint of Barceloneys, Jass, if you'll be so good.'

'Ah – the family. You might say it's only what you'd expect

from a daughter of Ben Verney – we all knew what *he* was like – not that I'm saying anything against him.' Jass Phelps served Henry with a half-pint of Barcelona nuts, by the direct expedient of emptying them on to the table.

'I shouldn't wonder if he's come to grief by now,' Sunny Daintree said. 'If he were laying in Lincoln gaol I wouldn't be a bit surprised.'

'Come now,' said Henry, 'he were a bit unsteady – no more than that.'

'Ah! but thass just what's coming out in the gel,' Sunny said. 'You tek a gel on to wukk at your house, you want her steady. Ooh! dear. A gel gits that sort of reputation and she's done for. She might as well just tip herself in the dyke and have done with it.'

'They reckon Bess Langtoft took a strap to her,' Jass Phelps said. 'Buckle-end.'

'I don't feel we should judge when we don't know all the facts of the case,' Henry Wake said uneasily. 'And if she weren't quite sure, it would have been a shame to marry him – and then the pair of 'em be unhappy.'

There was a delicate sort of silence, punctuated by a few coughs: for it was known that Mrs Wake was a little on the harsh side, and would make Henry's life seven kinds of hell if he so much as got mud on the boot-scrapers.

'Well, Hester's made her bed now – she must hope it's a soft one, though I'm afraid she'll find it hard,' Andrew Surfleet said.

'Your missus is in bed with a quinsy, you were saying, Andrew?' Henry Wake said quickly – for Chad had just come in.

'No!' said Andrew, slow to catch on. 'I never said that. The ole gel were right as rain the smorning. Well, she were!' he protested, as Sunny Daintree trod on his toes.

'Evening to you, Chad,' Henry Wake said. 'Turning a bit misty out there, I reckon, or perhaps it's clearing.'

'Well, now you mention it she were looking a bit poorly,' Andrew said belatedly.

Chad ordered a pint of beer, drank half of it in one go, and then sat down at the table with Henry, Andrew and Sunny, causing them to shift in their chairs, nod, hum, look at their beer, and all start talking at once: 'Mole-catching season's nearly done, Chad, tell your father—' 'Preacher from Chatteris at the chapel this week—' 'My ole gel's got the quinsy, Chad, did you know—' until Chad silenced them with a belligerent sort of smile, drawing from his waistcoat pocket a small packet of gauze.

'See what I'm got here?' he said, and unwrapped a plain silver, or silver-coloured, ring. 'Got that off Rob Risby.'

Jass Phelps craned over the bar to see like someone at the scene of an accident, and there was silence, broken only by Andrew Surfleet piping: 'Thass nice!'

Chad held the ring aloft, with a general stare at everyone. 'And I'm here to tell you I'm not bought this for nothing. There's half a dozen gels hereabouts who'll be glad to put that on – mebbe Mary-Ann Cole, mebbe Kate Dyer, mebbe somebody else – I'm not made me mind up.'

'Course, you know, it might not fit all on 'em,' Andrew said helpfully, 'fingers being what they are,' and had his foot trodden on again.

'So, if you're all been chuntering over what I'm going to do, now you know,' Chad said, his cheeks very pink, 'and you needn't trouble yourselves any more.'

'Very wise, Chad, very wise,' Henry Wake said. Privately he did not think it wise at all . . . but, for once, Henry held his peace.

# Chapter Four

1

Hester's stay at the Goslings' could not be of long duration.
The tiny cottage was already overcrowded, with Lizzie's father
and three brothers all as sturdily well-built as Lizzie herself:
the money Mr Langtoft had given her would not pay her keep
for long; and moreover Mr Gosling tended to take Chad's part,
giving her the frostiest of welcomes, and when she overheard
some disapproving remarks about her being Ben Verney's
daughter all right, she knew she would have to go as soon
as possible.

Unable to find work in the immediate vicinity, she sought it
further afield by means of Rob Risby the tallyman, who asked
around for her on his travels. At last he brought her the address
of a farm the other side of March where a female servant was
wanted.

'Five pound a year!' Hester said in dismay. 'Why, I'd be
nothing but a slavey!'

'Ah, thass the way of it,' Rob Risby said, feeling his whisker.
'There's precious little wukk about. I should know. My table
don't see meat from one week to the next. I caught my missis
a-kissing the pig tother day. "Robert," says she, "I'm trying
to remember what pork tastes like".'

Hester had deep misgivings about a place offered on such
parsimonious terms: but she did not need Mr Gosling's surly
reminders that beggars could not be choosers. The urgent
necessity of securing a living, which only her own hands and
wit could supply, pressed upon her; and her native optimism,
reasserting itself, did the rest – the place surely couldn't be
*that* bad. She wrote, and received a pencilled reply engaging

her, and telling her to '*Come next Mundy, bring cloths & boots, caps providid*'.

So a new life awaited her. It was not a great distance from Hinching Fen – a matter of twelve miles – but that was far enough to entail a complete separation from the place she thought of as home, and the people that made it so. It was a barren prospect for Hester, who by nature would trade riches for a friendly face. And yet her feelings about leaving were not unambiguous – because of the very thing that had overturned her fortunes. She knew that on Hinching Fen a certain opprobrium attached to her as a result of what had happened with Chad. There were as many varying views on that, of course, as there were people; but she frequently intercepted glances of wary disapproval, and conversations faltered and stopped as she walked by. Pride she normally had little use for, but she certainly had no intention of donning sackcloth and ashes for what she had done. She still maintained it would have been a far greater disgrace to have bound herself to a man she did not love for the sake of a wild bet; and it seemed to her that folk were rather too automatically ready to blame the Woman in the case. Hester was no self-tormentor. If she was irresponsible, it did not extend to refusing to accept the consequences of her own acts: indeed she was far more willing to do that than to think badly of herself. Her heart was sore at leaving, but her self-respect provided an opiate. If she were to be burdened here with the unmerited reputation of a cruel flirt, then perhaps it was all for the best.

To travel to her new place of employ required a roundabout railway journey, from the little halt at Stokeley to the main-line station at Peterborough, and thence to March, a small fenland town which had been hoisted into prominence by the siting there of a great concourse of railway marshalling yards. Lizzie Gosling saw her off at Stokeley. Elastic as Hester's nature was, at the last moment she tasted a rare despondency. 'Oh, Liz,' said she, half laughing and half crying, 'am I going to end up like my ole father – flitting about like a flea in a colander for the rest of my life?'

'Well,' Lizzie said, biting on tears, 'you ain't got a moustache quite like his, any road. Git on, gel. You'll be all right.'

A whistle shrieked, and steam enveloped the two girls. Lizzie said goodbye, giving Hester a hug and one of her most speaking looks – this one saying I-really-don't-know-what's-going-to-become-of-you-but-you-know-you've-always-got-a-friend-in-me.

A train ride was a novelty for Hester: the price of the ticket had absorbed almost all her money, and the two shillings left plus the contents of her two carpet-bags constituted all her worldly possessions as she watched the edge of the upland country, clothed in unfamiliar woods and sheep-pasture, slip by on the way to Peterborough. 'Here I go again,' she said to herself, recalling the day she had stepped down from her father's cart at the end of the Langtofts' drove. Having changed at Peterborough she arrived at March, deep in black fen country again, in the early afternoon. Her enquiries after Gore's Hole Drove met with uncomprehending stares until she found an old man sitting in the spring sunshine in the market-place.

'Noo-oo, you won't git a carrier going out there,' he told her. 'You'll have to try and walk it, I reckon. Whass your legs like, gel?' he said with a meaningful look over her.

'They start at me behind and go down to the floor,' she said.

'Ah! well, they'll dew. You tek the Rings End road and keep going. You'll git there, eventually. I'd offer to carry them bags for yer, but I should want one hand free, at least.'

'Dream your dreams, granfer.'

She was inured to walking long distances, and scarcely noticed the first few miles: she was still fresh when she came to the drove turning. But the drove went on, and on. This was remoteness: and the place seemed to have a micro-climate, for while the rest of the country was dry, the drove was a morass of puddles and ooze. Huge black fields surrounded her, tinted with the merest shade of green growth. When at last the farmhouse did come in sight it seemed for something like an hour to squat on the horizon, and never get any nearer.

At last she found herself knocking on the door, and looking up without enthusiasm at a patched tiled roof, and tottering gutters, and windows grimily opaque that gave the place a blind look. She knocked for some time before the door was finally, cautiously opened by a little old woman, with moist rheumy eyes, a snuffly nose, and a dribbling lip, all swathed up to the chin with a tight winding of shawls and scarves, as if she were inclined to be leaky, and had to be lagged.

'We don't want nothing,' the old woman said; and waved a rusty poker in Hester's face.

'I'm Hester Verney. I've come about the job.'

'We don't want nothing, I tell you!'

'I wrote to you,' Hester said. 'About being the farm-servant. You said to come Monday.'

'Oh! that. No, we got a gel. We already got a gel – she come asking on Sat'dy so we took her on.'

Hester was astonished. The old woman was starting to close the door. 'Wait a minute – you offered me that job. You told me to come today—'

'Oh, I can't help that,' the old woman said, wetly. 'We wanted a gel quick, and this one were handy. Any road, now I look at you, you wouldn't have done at all. A gret thing like you. We wanted a proper young gel, fresh, what we could train up. I should think you're probably got set in all sorts of ways of your own.'

There was a grim resonance in those words *fresh* and *train up*, taken in conjunction with the ramshackle state of the farm. A skivvy – just out of school, and too frightened to protest at being treated like a slave – Hester knew the pattern. An awful prospect – yet she had no other . . . 'But I'm come all the way from Hinching Fen,' she said. 'I'm spent all my money on gitting here. Don't you see – I counted on this job – you offered it me!'

'I can't help that,' the old woman said. 'Folk should stop where they are. Thass none of my business if folk choose to go gallivanting. No, you wouldn't have done for us at all. We don't want no gadabouts!'

The door was closed. For some moments yet Hester did not apprehend the gravity of her predicament, occupied as she was with thinking of those stinging retorts that always come to mind too late, contemplating arson, criminal damage and assault and battery, and furiously pulling faces at the spot where the old woman had been standing. It was only when she turned round at last, and looked at that drove stretching away to infinity, that her spirits really sank.

'Oh! piss-emmets,' she said, and began the long trudge back.

She would have to find something: she had not sufficient money to get back to Hinching Fen – and what was there for her there? She couldn't stay at the Goslings' any longer. Family – well, she had lost sight of her father, who had disappeared north in search of new windmills to tilt at: there remained Aunt Netty, in charge of her younger siblings a long way off in Leicester. No: there was to be no question of turning to Aunt Netty, even if she were in a position to get there. She could just imagine that lady's sour triumph in being sought out for help by the girl she had always characterised as Heading For a Fall.

A couple of hours of daylight remained. There must, she reasoned, be more farms in this fertile area, and there was at least a chance that one of them might be in need of female labour. She tramped down more droves, each seeming longer than the last, as if the farms had been deliberately sited to be as far from human contact as possible; and indeed, one or two of the people here were so accustomed to isolation that company simply frightened them, and they could barely find a voice to answer Hester's inquiries. She had no luck: no girls wanted; labour had been taken on at Easter. One woman advised her to go down to the nearby village – 'it's only a step,' she said, ominously. 'You're more likely to find work there than out here.'

She went, moving like an automaton now: and found the village a straggle of cottages hugging the banks of the Old Nene. The same negatives met her. Exhausted and hungry, with darkness coming down, she turned to a waterside inn called the Ferryman, the chief building of the place, with several barges tied up at the landing-stage: seeking now only rest and food, and undeterred by the palpably seamy character of the inn. This was discernible even at the outer door, through which was exhaled a great breath that was curiously smoky, steamy, fishy, beery, earthy, and oath-y, all at once.

The parlour of the inn was a long, low-raftered room with windows at the end overlooking the river. The windows were open but it seemed none of the smoke was going out: it simply filled the room as water fills a tank, and to Hester's stinging eyes it seemed that the stuffed fish in cases on the walls were swimming in it. Her first thought, as the babble of talk reached her ears, was that some sort of violent quarrel was going on, for every second word seemed to be a curse: but a few moments' observation revealed that the watermen, standing in groups or hunkered round tables, were on the best of terms, and that it was merely a convention that conversation should be conducted in a stream of cheerful obscenities, some of them physiologically impossible. She was not, as she had first thought, the only woman there: several women of her own age (or at any rate wishing to appear so) were joining in the colourful exchanges, seeming by the unbuttoned state of their blouses to feel the heat excessively; and by the window one was seated on a waterman's knee, or in that region, and was responding to the confidences he whispered into her ear by a reiterated squeal of: 'Y'mucky bugger! Y'mucky bugger!'

Squeezing through a sort of corridor of waistcoats, caps and laughing mouths, she found an empty table and ordered a mug of beer and a meal of bread and cheese. She sat with her feet on her carpet-bags and ate voraciously. A few watermen turned to look round at her: she was dressed pretty much in any working-girl's best, a straw boater-style hat, short jacket with high-necked blouse and plain skirt, buttoned boots; but perhaps even that was a little smart for this place, and one brick-red face with a covering of whiskers like a luxuriant growth of mould loomed down and asked if he could buy her a drop of wet.

'No, ta,' she said, keeping her left hand out of sight, 'I'm waiting for me husband,' and the whiskers vanished.

She finished the bread and cheese. It was very short commons compared to what she had become used to at Mrs Langtoft's table, and the landlady passing her just then with a tray, she caught a seductive scent of eel stew. No, she told herself, you can't have none of that – your money's nearly gone, and you'll need a place to sleep tonight – do you hear . . . ? She heard, but did not obey, and was soon digging into a plate of stew, steaming with thyme and sage.

Replete, she sat back, sipping the remainder of her beer, and addressed herself to the problem of what was to become of her. Her money would now only extend to the barest night's accommodation – some cheap lodging-house, which she would probably have to trudge back to March to find. 'I should have throttled that ole ratbag at the farm,' she thought: and as she thought pleasantly of this, and about asking the landlady if she had any skivvy work, washing-up, anything, she found her attention being caught by a conversation going on at a table behind her.

'. . . Farm over Whittlesey way – load of phosphate of lime. Promised to git it over there tomorrow. Now how am I going to manage?'

She turned to look at the speaker, who was seated in the chimney-corner. Oil-lamps had just been lit, and the curling smoke diffused their radiance, so that the interior of the inn was now clothed in a rich chiaroscuro: the man speaking was hidden in one of the pockets of shadow thus created, but he suddenly leaned forward into the light towards his companion as Hester turned to look.

'Not the first time I'm been left in the lurch like this,' he said. 'I wish they'd stick to it, when they tek the job.'

'Whass a matter, bor?' another voice said from the bar.

'I'm got to git my lighters over Whittlesey, and my mate's done a bunk,' the man in the chimney-corner answered. 'Five lighters, heavy load to barrow, I can't manage it on my own. I were just asking Fred here whether he'll tek the job on.'

'Not me!' said his companion. 'I'm a landsman, and I'll stick to it. I went on me cousin's lighters once, just for a lark, and it were such terrible wukk I swore I'd never mourn about digging ditches again.'

'Whass happened to your mate, then, bor?' the voice at the bar asked.

'Oh! he went mortaring after a gel, Outwell way,' the man in the chimney-corner said, in tones of great disgust. 'That were his excuse, any road.'

Several ribald comments followed this, terribly old and stale, but of the sort which men of all ages have taken to be a conclusive demonstration of virility. The man in the

87

chimney-corner paid no heed, but sat staring into the smoke with a deep frown which was doubly expressive: evincing his present vexation, but also appearing plainly as a habitual mien, into which the contours of his face settled naturally. A peculiar immobility was also noticeable about him – he sat there amongst the crowd and movement and noise just as if, Hester thought, he was completely alone; and there was a short-sighted look about his heavy-lidded, dark brown eyes which might have been either physical or a further manifestation of that quality of seeming to inhabit his own circle of space, and to positively not perceive his surroundings. His colouring, naturally dark, was made more so by the typical tan of the waterman, accustomed to a life in the open air, and the large brown hands which tapped restlessly on the table-top were almost of a colour with the chestnut hair, roughly parted in the middle and slightly curling about the ears. His figure, dressed in corduroy trousers, waistcoat, striped shirt and neckerchief, was distinguished by its breadth and bigness of limb, with just a lingering suggestion of the gangling youth – enough to cause Hester to revise her estimate of his age down to twenty-four or -five. That first impressions should have suggested an older man was owing not only to the depth and sonority of his voice but to a certain rigidity about his strongly marked and clean-shaven features, as if he would deny them expression, and impression too, by conscious will.

'Ain't there anyone,' he said, coming out of abstraction again, 'some lad in the village, mebbe, who'd tek the job? I'm the master, mind: but he'd get a share of the profits, fair and square, and a berth and his meals.'

'None that I know on,' his companion said. 'They're all wukking on the land. They're too daft, some on 'em, to blow their noses – but they ain't daft enough to come off the farm and go breaking their backs on the lighters.' And with a dismissive laugh he got up and went to the bar.

The man in the chimney-corner drained his beer, then ran his finger round the rim of his empty tankard, and toyed with it, as if debating whether to have another. In these few moments Hester made up her mind. She gathered up her bags and went and took the recently vacated seat opposite the waterman.

'Not interested,' he said, barely glancing up.

'Nor am I,' Hester said, 'if it comes to that. But I'm interested in the job.'

The waterman frowned at her, then made an impatient gesture. 'You got it wrong, gel. I'm got a gang of lighters, I need a mate to work on 'em. Thass the job.'

'Well, thass the job I'm asking for.'

'Oh! git along. I'm not in the mood for joking.'

'I'm not joking. You need someone to work for you and I need work.'

'A man, I meant, a man,' the waterman said, frowning harder.

'All right – but you can't git one – and I can work just as hard as any man. I'm done three years on a fen farm – I'm used to it. What do you say?'

'You?' The waterman glanced up and down her figure, then shook his head, his lips compressed, as if he could barely even bring himself to laugh. He got up. 'Don't waste my time, gel.'

She watched him go, threading his way through the crowd. Unlike the heroines of her mother's yellowback novels, Hester was not particularly proud: she had never, as far as she could recall, flung her hair out of her eyes in Fiery Resentment, or felt her cheeks Mantle (whatever that was) at an Insult. But she was unaccustomed to being found so unworthy of a second glance, which piqued her . . . and besides, what she had said was perfectly true. Her desperate need for any job had made her speak out: being dismissed as unequal to this one made her more determined to get it.

She picked up her bags and went out after the waterman. It was full dark now, but fine and starlit, and she presently descried him walking down the towpath behind the inn, and then stopping to look at the river where several lighters were tied up. He pulled out a tobacco-pouch and began filling a pipe, visibly falling into that rapt absorption of solitude that she had already noticed in him; so that he started when she spoke.

'These your lighters, are they?' she said.

'Oh! it's you.' He continued to pack the pipe. The starlight, and the soft margin of illumination from the windows of the inn, showed her his uncommunicative profile, and the shapes of the fen lighters, low open barges of a peculiarly native type, moored by the landing-stage.

'I weren't joking,' she said. 'I'm looking for work and I don't mind if it's heavy. I'm young and fit and I got no ties. I don't know much about lighters but I'm willing to learn. You said you need someone bad, and you can't git anybody here. So why not?'

The waterman put the tobacco-pouch away, and faced her at last, turning his whole body in an aggressive presenting of himself. 'Now why on earth,' he said, 'should you want to do this job?'

'Like I said – I need the work. Down on my luck. Nothing strange about that, is there?'

The waterman grunted, studied her for a few moments, then said: 'Wait here,' and turning away from her descended a boarding-plank on to the first lighter, locating the plank in the dark with a conspicuous negligence. With the same casualness he traversed the narrow strip of deck running the lighter's length and from the stern drew out a wheelbarrow and shovel. In a very few seconds he had loaded the barrow with lime from the hold, and was wheeling it down the deck and then up the boarding-plank to the landing-stage, his clay pipe fixed in his mouth. He set the barrow down in front of Hester.

'Now let's see you tek it back,' he said.

Just in time Hester stopped herself from saying she might get her clothes dirty. She grasped the handles of the wheelbarrow and carefully, refraining from tugging, took the weight. It didn't seem too bad. The waterman stepped out of her way as she steered it along the towpath and on to the boarding-plank. The river being low and the landing-stage high, the plank descended at quite a steep angle: gravity suddenly took hold of the barrow and nearly pulled it out of her hands, and only by setting her arms as taut as cables was she able to control it. The water twinkled underneath her as she crossed the sagging plank, trying not to look down. The barrow seemed somehow to have got heavier by the time she reached the deck: her arms juddered as she slewed it round, but she kept her balance, and with a conscious briskness she trundled it down to the stern. Upending the barrow to tip the load into the hold caused her to go rather red in the face, but she felt she presented a tolerably composed appearance by the time she rejoined the waterman on the landing-stage.

'Well,' he said, smoking, 'thass the easier part, of course – barrowing downhill. You'd be barrowing up high banks mostly.'

'Fair enough.'

He continued to contemplate her, his hands on his hips. She returned his gaze steadily.

'You harness a hoss?' he said abruptly.

'Do that in me sleep,' she said – with perhaps a little unconscious mimicking of his manner. It was a job she had done, just occasionally, at the Langtofts'.

'Powerful lot of walking you have to do – leading the hoss.'

'Well, I'm never kept a carriage, you know.'

The waterman sighed and frowned down at his lighters. Reading his thoughts, Hester said: 'You can't manage on your own – I heard you say. And there's nobody else offering, is there?'

From the inn a blowsy, boozy gust of laughter came floating on a smoke-scented breeze, dying away in the purer air. The river made quiet lappings to itself round the struts of the landing-stage.

'All right,' he said. 'Look here. I need someone for the job, so you'll have to do, though I never heard of a woman doing it. You got to be serious, mind – no skipping out if you find you don't tek to it: I'm got loads to deliver, and I'm late as it is. Still game?'

'Oh, yes!' said she: elated by having won her point, and for the moment beguiled by the sheer novelty of the position she found herself in. She had a strong regard for the capabilities of her sex, and it pleased her that she was doing what women had never done before.

'Rules,' said the lighterman. He pointed to the first lighter, where there was a cabin amidships. 'Thass my cabin – there's a little stove there for cooking on – you'll git plenty to eat. My mate used to have one of the bunks, but thass no good for you.

91

There's a cabin on number four – full o' taters at the moment, it ain't been used much – you'll have to sleep on that. I ain't carrying no passengers, mind. You do the work proper, and you'll git your share of the profits, same as anybody else: but like I say, it's a man's work, and you'll have to live as a man. No frocks. It ain't practical, and besides that I don't want folk thinking I'm got a gel faffing about on my boats. I'm got some ole trousers and a moleskin jacket somewhere, and a cap – I s'pose you can put your hair right up?'

'Oh! yes,' she said – she didn't fancy cutting it off.

'Well, we'll have to sort all that in the morning – we'll not be sleeping yet – I do a lot of travelling at night. Not changed your mind?'

'No,' she said: and really she did not see why she should. It could hardly be worse, after all, than life at that old crone's farm would have been. Her decision had been made with characteristic celerity – but part of the reason for that promptness was that little daunted her. Hester's conception of the world, and of her relations to it, was still imaged forth as a slate on which she might write broadly what she chose, and as yet she did not envisage this principle acting the other way round. 'I reckon I can do it. If *you* ain't changed your mind.'

He shook his head, and looked hard at her. 'I dunno. I must be mad. I want my head seeing to. Still, have to mek the best of it.'

'Well, at least you can be sure of one thing – I ain't going to do like your last mate and go mortaring after some gel.'

He did not respond. 'Come on. We'll go and fetch the hoss.'

The inn, like most of its kind, had stabling for the lightermen's horses. Theirs was a strong and thickset beast, and submitted with the utmost placidity to the collar and bridle under the waterman's hands: but when he suggested that Hester lead him out, and she began to do so, the horse kicked and bucked like the very devil.

'Here, here – you ain't up the stick, are you?' the waterman said.

'No, I ain't!'

'Only it sends him funny, that – he knows it somehow. Whoa, steady Boss.'

'It's just he ain't used to me, thass all,' Hester said; and she kept a tight hold of the bridle and crooned some nonsense words that Mr Langtoft had always used to his team. The horse ceased kicking, but shied at passing through the amber shafts of light coming from the inn windows, and she had to lead him round.

'He'll git used to me,' she said as they went down to the towpath. 'I'll bring him round – I'll git him to like me – you'll see.'

The waterman watched her with an expression of profound scepticism. 'Think pretty well of yourself, don't you?' he said.

She was not accustomed to being assailed so frontally. She seemed to come up against a large hard arrogance, like some bulky obstacle in the darkness, and it irked her. 'Well,' she said, 'I don't see why I should be ashamed of myself, instead. Do you?'

'We'll see,' he said dryly.

'Any road – my name's Hester Verney, and I'll let you call me Hester, and I come from Hinching Fen.'

'Mine's Jonathan Eastholm; and I don't come from anywhere in particular; and you'll call me captain, or skipper – 'cos thass what I am.'

2

The waterways of the fens, along which the gangs of lighters carried their goods, comprised a mixed network of the Rivers Ouse and Nene and their tributaries, and artificial drainage channels, of varying age, and testifying to the long and still continuing struggle to free the land of its burden of water. The route that Hester and her new employer took that night led from the Old Nene into the straight cut known, from its width, as the Twenty Foot. Leading the horse, she found that he soon lost his nervousness of her, seeming glad of any company in the lonely darkness. She soon found, too, the impracticality of her normal clothes. Though the weather had been dry, the towpath along the high banks, with their soft soil, was in that permanent condition of mud known locally as slub, which coated the hem of her skirt in no time, and then seemed to creep on upwards as if possessing a life of its own. In places the fences of the surrounding fields came right up to the bank – and coming across one without a gate, but only a stile, she stopped: only to hear Jonathan Eastholm bellowing at her from the lighters: 'Don't let the rope go slack, damn you, I lose steering-way! Jump him over it – he's used to it!' And indeed the horse, though not appearing to relish the effort, cleared the stile quite easily. Then there was a bridge – which necessitated untying the horse, and trotting him over the top, while the lighters drifted through below, and then retying again on the other side, with the rope all wet and slippery, the horse skittish from his few moments of liberty, and Eastholm cursing at her to git on. Everything seemed slimy, damp, difficult, and frustratingly laborious; and add to this the wind which came howling down the straight funnel of the Twenty Foot, always full in her face of course – the fens being the only place in the country where two people can be observed walking in opposite directions into a head wind – and altogether Hester saw the sun rise on her first day on the lighters in a state of the severest dejection and exhaustion.

By that time they had passed into Whittlesey Dyke, and it was necessary to untie again while the lighters passed through a lock. Waiting on the towpath with the horse, she leaned her head against his neck, and could almost have fallen asleep there and then.

'Hoy, look alive there!' Eastholm called. 'Tain't a pleasure cruise!'

'Aye, aye, captain,' she said under her breath, except that captain was not the word she used.

Soon after that, however, to her intense relief, they moored just below another bridge, and the waterman proposed some breakfast. There was grazing for the horse on the bank, and Hester was glad just to place her aching bones on a canvas stool in the doorway of the cabin on the house-lighter, and smell the bacon frying in a blackened trivet on the little oil-stove.

'Out of eggs just now,' Eastholm said, producing bread and a parcel of butter from a foot-locker, and knives and plates from another. 'We'll mebbe git some from the farm where this lime's going. Git that ate, and I'll brew some tea in a minute.'

Hester was not particular, and was too weary just now to take much notice of her surroundings; but she did notice that everything was surprisingly clean and neat in a spartan sort of way, and that the tiny cabin seemed to contain most domestic necessities; though getting at them entailed on Eastholm's part a complicated set of manoeuvres, dictated by the impossibility in the confined space of opening more than one drawer at a time, and requiring him to squeeze his long limbs into unlikely postures. Extracting a box of cutlery from underneath the bunk compelled him to lie on his side, and swing his great legs round so that his boots touched the wall, as if he were going to walk up it like a fly. That he was plainly unaware of the incongruous appearance of this, demonstrated further what Hester had observed from her first sight of him – that he was a creature of solitude, who carried that quality with him into company, as a fish in a glass bowl inhabits its own miniature element amidst the alien one that surrounds it.

A great wedge of lean bacon, and a slab of bread and butter which the waterman cut as if he were sawing wood, with tea in a mug like a pint-pot, did much to revive Hester's spirits – as did the thought of that dingy farm, and the sort of victuals that moist old woman was likely to serve up. Eastholm, having disposed of his meal very much as he stowed away the utensils in his cabin, occupied himself with sorting appropriate clothes for Hester.

'You git these on,' he said. 'We'll be delivering to the farmer upstream in a bit, and I don't want it looking like I'm carryen some fancy-piece with my cargo.'

'Well, you could always pretend I was your wife,' Hester said.

Eastholm gave a grunt, something like 'Pah!' and, collecting the plates, rinsed them by the simple expedient of lowering them over the side in a net.

The cabin on the fourth lighter was the barest hatch, with an earthy smell of the vegetables stored under the bunk. Here she stored her bags, and changed into the clothes he had given her. The coarse calico shirt and the moleskin jacket fitted well enough, their roomy folds being filled out by Hester's figure, for as Peggy Chettle had remarked, she had plenty on the sideboard: but long-legged as she was, she could not compete with the waterman in that respect, and she had to roll the bottoms of the trousers up into great cuffs that flapped as she walked. Her hair she gathered up into the flat cap, and finished off the ensemble with a silk square scarf of her own, tied as a neckerchief.

She went down the towpath, trying to walk like a man (however did they manage it?), to where Jonathan Eastholm was harnessing the horse, and drew his attention to the trousers.

'Ah! well, they'll have to do for now,' he said. He clucked his tongue. 'You still don't look like a chap really.'

'Well, I ain't going to wear a beard, if thass what you're thinking.'

Eastholm shook his head and turned back to the horse. 'I dunno. I want my head seeing to.'

So Hester Verney, having left Hinching Fen to be a farm-servant, found herself a waterman instead.

The men who plied the gangs of lighters around the fens were the survivors of a much more numerous breed, having their origin in the days when the waterways were the easiest, and in some cases the only, means of transport in that remote part of the kingdom. The antiquity of their trade was sufficiently exhibited in the very design of the lighters, which was traceable to the shallow-drawing boats of the Vikings, who had penetrated the channels a thousand years ago to lay waste to the fenland abbeys. The lighters were flat-bottomed and rounded at bow and stern, forty feet in length and ten feet wide, sturdily built in oak with deck planking of elm, and coated with pitch: they were not equipped with rudders, the leading lighter in the gang being steered by a pole, and the following lighters linked by seizing-chains and a system of ropes which kept them aligned. These craft, though reduced in number, were still a familiar sight despite the coming of the railways to the fens; the lightermen surviving by working at cheap rates, and carrying heavy local loads – sand, bricks, clay for stabilising the peat soil, and in particular the ubiquitous turves for domestic fuel. A spirit of comradeship accordingly existed among them, as Hester soon found when they passed a gang coming in the other direction. 'What you carryen?' was the standard greeting shouted across the water – accompanied, as was the reply, by a volley of curses casting vivid aspersions on the other's parentage, eating habits, and sexual endowment: the whole, however, as mechanically harmless as the passing of remarks on the weather.

Having delivered the load of lime at Whittlesey on time, they were at last permitted a rest, and Hester lay down in her clothes in the musty bunk and slept a drugged sleep. In the afternoon Jonathan Eastholm outlined their itinerary.

'Load o' tiles to pick up at Yaxley, and mebbe some turf; then back down the Twenty Foot, through Outwell, through Denver Sluice, down the Ouse, down Brandon Creek and back, down to the clay-pits at Ely; round Pope's Corner, up the Old Bedford, and down the Forty Foot to Stokeley.'

They proceeded via the King's Dyke; and it was suggestive of the persistence of the past in this land that the King in question was Canute. The banks were tree-lined here, the interlacing branches bristling with new green buds: spring growth quickened in the fields below. Everywhere was transfixed with the light of the limitless sky, to a bright glassy stillness. In such conditions, rather than at night, the possibility of those ghostly apparitions common in the fens seemed tinglingly present; and time appeared a porous membrane, through which at any moment the past might leak, and the carved prows of the Norse longboats be seen nosing round the bend in the stream, or the tramp of the legions be heard on the ancient wind. The horse pricked up his ears at the brilliance of the day; and Hester felt that life on the lighters had, after all, strong charms, and that she had rather fallen on her feet.

She continued to feel this over the next few days. Unfortunately, this optimism alternated with times when it seemed hell on earth.

It was him that was the trouble – him with his great stern frown of scepticism, always watching her for a mistake. She was soon on good terms with the horse, who was pretty well accustomed to the places where he had to jump a stile – and there were places too, where if he could not negotiate the obstacle and the banks were not high, the lighters would be brought in to the side and the horse would jump on to the first one, sailing on for a few yards as if it were the most natural thing in the world before leaping back on to the towpath. But still there were occasions when Hester would start woolgathering, and the horse would very willingly dawdle too – and soon the shouts of the captain would alert her, in withering terms, to the fact that the tow-rope was slack.

'Wake your bloody ideas up there! I'm damn near into the bank! Bugger my ole boots, I never see the like of it. Whoever told you you could be a waterman?'

'You did!' she cried back.

Then there was her first experience of barrowing goods up the high flood-banks which carried many of the fen waterways above the level of the land. The trick, of course, was to take the barrow up the plank at speed, the momentum carrying you through without that horrible wobbling, sagging moment in the middle: but this was a lesson more easily apprehended than put into practice. She was afraid of dropping the load into the water, she was afraid of dropping herself into the water, she was afraid that her arms would come out of their sockets, and she was afraid that Jonathan Eastholm, impatiently waiting behind her with the next barrowload, would see all these things; and the resulting paralysis of caution made her more clumsy than she was. At Yaxley she lost control of a barrowload of tiles just as she reached the bank: it overbalanced, and a few of the tiles smashed as they hit the towpath.

'Cack-handed sort of ole boy you're got there, ain't it?' said the man collecting the tiles.

'Oh! you have to tek what you can git,' Eastholm said. He unloaded his barrow, then told her to follow him to the cabin. A piece of slate was nailed to the cabin wall, on which he noted details of loads and payments: and here he chalked the letters H.V. and a minus sign. 'Them tiles are coming off your pay,' he said. 'Probably a bob's worth. We'll call it ninepence,' and he chalked the figure up.

Then there was the long heavy shower of rain – which was

snug to hear drumming on the roof of the boathouse, but less fun to slop through leading the horse. Eventually, with the rain coursing off her hat and her trousers clinging round her legs – how did men bear to wear them? – she pulled the horse up and trudged back to the first lighter.

'Whass up?'

'I'm gitting soaked! Can't we moor for a while?'

'Just for a drop of rain?' Eastholm was standing on the deck with all his perpendicular sturdiness, gripping the steering-pole, bare-headed and with his shirt plastered down to his square torso by the wet so that its contours showed through like a Roman breastplate. 'Git along.'

'Well, ain't there a bit o' tarpaulin or summat I can put over my shoulders?'

'Coh! give me strength,' he muttered, and presently an old oilcloth was flung in her direction. 'Goo on, we're losing headway.'

The clearing of the rain, thankfully, threw everything into a different aspect. The long straight channel of Bevill's Leam stretched ahead like a spear aimed at the horizon: the sun glittered on the water; a pair of swans drifted by, pure white and unruffled. It was impossible not to wonder at the ingenuity and aspiration of man, wrenching this inimical landscape to his own purposes, and to feel a sort of proud solidarity with those whose past labour, so often heartbreaking, bore renewed fruit in each crop that was lifted from the jealous fields. But for all her exhilaration, there he was still behind her, watching out for a slip, and getting out his tobacco in that slow thoughtful way that infuriated her.

But when they moored things were better. He caught a fine bream in his bow-net, and they cooked it on the oil-stove, and there was a wonderful quiet between the high banks roofed over with red-ribbed sky. He had told her that she would have to live as a man on this job; and that certainly extended to the meals, which were huge and satisfying, and which he dispensed with a rough liberality.

'Here – git that down you. Goo on – tek some more. Plenty where that come from.'

At these times all the brusque urgency of work subsided in

him, and he sat on the canvas stool in a kind of massive repose
that had in it something suggestive of the large elements of
water and earth with which he was so plainly at home. He
looked about him at the changing colours of the sky with a
dwelling eye, as if he were conning the pages of a book, and
his voice sank to a deeper register as he placed his hands on his
knees and remarked on their progress or the weather. 'Wind's
shifted. Reckon it'll be fair tomorrow. Git through Outwell
afore sun-up.'

'Well, I'll say this –' she wiped her plate with bread – 'you
git fed as well here as on the ole farm.'

'How'd you lose your work then?' he said. 'Farm go bust?
– I know a lot do, on the fen.'

'No . . . it weren't that.' She watched a cluster of wild duck
fly overhead, briefly traversing their roof of sky as sparrows
will pass through an open warehouse; and her mind suffered
the mental equivalent of a sigh. It was a pity, after all, that a
part of your life should be finished, cut off as if it had never
been: was it always to be like that? Sadness touched Hester's
shoulder, and for a moment she could not brush it off. 'It were
one of them personal things – a disagreement. It's a shame,
because I liked the work, but you can't go on once that sort
of thing happens.'

The waterman nodded, slowly, and seemed to look down a
deep well of thought. He took the pipe from his mouth and
said with deliberation: 'It's gitting all involved and tangled up
wi' feelings that causes half the trouble in the world.'

'I suppose so,' she said. 'But then you can't just live life all
on your own, can you? Thass no way to live.'

The look he gave her was more of surprise than anything else.
'It's the *only* way,' he said. He knocked out his pipe, stood up
and stretched. 'Well, I reckon I'll gi' meself a bath.'

'Oh! Where do you do that?'

'Why, where d'you think?' And he gestured over the side.

'Oh! I see.'

For some moments she did not understand the uneasy frown
he gave her. At last he said: 'Well – you git up tother end, if
you want to do the same.'

'Ah – sorry.'

100

She went down the towpath to the other house-lighter, smiling to herself: he was as modest as a girl! A splash, and some satisfied baritone gasps, indicated that he had gone in. She considered going back and saying she had forgotten something – but she more than suspected he was not amenable to that kind of teasing.

Her amusement at his unexpected pudency, however, gave way at the first touch of the water on her bare legs to amazement at his hardiness: it was freezing! She contrived to bathe herself with piecemeal splashings, and with the help of a bucket to wash her hair. She was combing it, and despairing of ever getting it dry, when he came down the towpath to fetch a bait for the horse. He was all in a glow, and not shivering in the least.

'Ain't you got a mirror anywhere?' she said.

'What would I want a mirror for?'

'Well! not to look at your beauty, thass for sure,' she said. But again, these sallies simply rolled off him, leaving him as unmoved as the icy water had done.

'We'll git going in a minute,' he said, digging in the tub of oats and bran.

'All right,' she said. She looped her hair into a great bunch, combing it over her shoulder. She wished there was a mirror: when she had it down you could really see the sheen on the black, almost indigo in the sunlight. Suddenly she noticed he was staring at the long sweep of hair. Well, she thought, consciously spreading it out, he wasn't completely made of stone after all.

'I hope all that stuff's going to go back in your cap when it's dry,' he grunted, going away.

He took his cold plunge whenever the opportunity was furnished by a quiet stretch of water. It was part of that same stoical impassivity that made him stand out on the deck in the east wind in no more than shirt and waistcoat; that enabled him to barrow the heaviest load of turves without so much as an extra puff of smoke coming from the clay-pipe jammed in his mouth; and that manifested itself in a complete indifference to her own shivering dips into the water from the other end of the gang. Of course, she would soon have told him where to go if he had tried to sneak a look – but still it was a little provoking to feel that for all he cared she might just as well have been the man into which the borrowed clothes imperfectly transformed her.

She hated the sight of those turves – and not simply because of the memory of the awful débâcle of Chad's wager. Delivering them a few at a time, to cottages close to the waterside, was not without its novelty: Eastholm would throw them up to her from the lighters, and she was deft at catching them; and occasionally housewives would come down to the towpath, and hold out their hessian aprons to catch them as he tossed them up. But mostly, alas, they were dealing in hundreds. Back on the Old Nene towards Outwell they were sailing between high flood banks; and pushing a barrow of a hundred turves up these was like pushing a boulder up a hill. And the fact that whenever she thought she had taken the last load, there always seemed to be one more waiting for her, added to the sisyphean quality of this nightmarish labour.

And him, of course – always watching her with his arrogant eye and his sceptical scoffings.

'Stop watching me – you put me off!' she exclaimed once.

'Watching you? I have to watch you – Lord knows what you'd do if I didn't.'

It was at Outwell that it happened, at last. There was a big load to deliver, and half-way through the muscles of her arms felt as if they were drawn out like soldering-wire. 'Just let me have a rest a minute,' she pleaded.

'A rest? What for?' Eastholm said. 'I don't want a rest.'

'But my arms ache – I'm afraid I shall drop 'em if I carry on.'

'Pah! Do as I tell you, and git on.'

Muttering some words she had learned from the watermen under her breath, Hester manoeuvred the barrow on to the plank and gritted her teeth to go at it at a run. Half-way across she realised she had lost her momentum – it was just as she feared – the barrow wobbled wildly – she could not hold it – her wrists gave way, and the load of turves toppled into the water, Hester just managing to save the barrow from following them.

'Coh! bloody hell fire me,' Eastholm said. 'I reckon you did that on purpose!'

Hester opened her mouth to protest: could not speak for sheer indignation.

Eastholm put down his barrow and walked slowly to the cabin. 'Better chalk that up, hadn't I? Shilling a hundred.'

She had always thought 'seeing red' was just an expression: in that moment she knew better. She was even-tempered by nature, but something about this man made her hackles rise; and somehow all her strength came back. She waited till Eastholm had emerged again from the cabin. Then she trundled the empty barrow back to the lighter, loaded it with another hundred turves, wheeled it half-way across the plank, and calmly and deliberately tipped the whole load into the water.

Eastholm's mouth was open: she saw she had got to him, and she swelled with black, devilish satisfaction. She walked past him into the cabin, picked up the chalk, and wrote another shilling on the slate.

'*That* was on purpose,' she said, dusting her hands.

They finished the delivery in silence: sailed on a little way in silence, then moored, in silence, for supper. Hester gave the horse his feed, and came back to the house-lighter to find bacon on the stove, and Eastholm standing looking down at it, his tobacco-pouch in his hands.

She turned the rashers over, whistling, and aware of a pair of glowering chocolate-brown eyes fixed on her.

'That were a bloody daft trick you played,' he said.

'Well – next time you'll know what to expect,' she replied – her anger by no means over.

'Next time? Any more o' that and I'll dump you on the bank and leave you there – where I should have left you in the first place!'

'Try it! You wouldn't git anybody else to put up with you!' The sight of him aloofly filling his pipe was too much: he even conducted a quarrel from a lofty height! Wildly she snatched the tobacco from his fingers and tossed it over the side. 'And I'll chuck that in the river an' all if I feel like it!'

'Why, you little beggar—' He seized a broom-handle. 'I'll tek this to you—'

'Don't you hit me wi' that! I'll hit you wi' this!' she exclaimed, grabbing a wooden shovel and brandishing it.

He hit her with that, and she hit him with this. She came off best: for while he only paddled her behind with the broomstick, she brought the shovel down on the back of his neck much harder than she intended. 'Oh no!' she said, dropping the shovel, and convinced for a moment that she had killed him; but he straightened up, rubbing the back of his neck, and swearing in surprise.

'Did I hurt you?' she said.

'Well, that was the idea, weren't it?' he said, throwing the broomstick down. They stared at each other a moment: then Eastholm picked up the pan of bacon and began slopping it out on to plates.

'Here,' he said gruffly.

'Thank you,' she said, with equal shortness: and they ate their meal in silence, each selecting one of the high featureless banks to gaze at throughout, as if it were a view teeming with absorbing detail. This restful repast over, she returned to the towpath, and he to the steering-pole, to move on for an hour or so before finishing for the day.

Along the towpath, besides flag irises and purple loosestrife as high as the horse's withers, there was a thick spring growth of reeds and thistles. Hester was in that sullenly smarting state in which we tend to barge about with a sort of masochistic defiance, and if we get hurt, well, that just shows how cruel the world is: and so she ploughed through the foliage as if she had the strength of the horse, with the result that one tangled clump of knife-edged reeds fairly lacerated her bare leg just above the boot. When they tied up for the night, it was bleeding heavily; and as Eastholm was putting the kettle on the stove for a last brew of tea, he noticed the blood.

'What you done to your leg?'

'Nothing.'

Unceremoniously he pushed her on to a stool and yanked up her trouser leg. 'I'm got summat for that,' he said. 'You don't want it turning nasty.'

'It ain't anything much,' she said.

He ignored that, and went into the cabin, where he underwent his familiar contortions to extract a tin from under the bunk. She watched him crushing some leaves in a bowl, adding a little hot water, and mixing. There was a piquant contrast between the big-hewn character of the man and the nimble nicety with which he performed these actions: in spite of herself she smiled.

'Right, come here.' He knelt and pulled off her boot, and applied the poultice with more gentleness than the size and work-roughened texture of his hands suggested.

'What is it?' she said.

'Water-bitney,' he said. 'Grows all down the river.'

Hester was particularly susceptible to small pleasant sensations, one tincture of them being sufficient to colour her whole mood: and so the soothing of the poultice, taken with the unfamiliar sight of the russet crown of Eastholm's head – a part of the body that communicates a peculiar vulnerability – was sufficient to relax, mellow and generally transform her straight from ill-humour to content with no gradations in between.

'Feels nice,' she said.

'It's good stuff. That'll all be healed up tomorrer.'

'I'm sorry I hit you with the shovel,' she said.

Eastholm sat back on his haunches. 'Well . . .' he said, and then seemed to make a mental swerve. 'I ain't sorry I hit you with the broom – you deserved it.'

The peacefully unvarying panorama of level horizons, dykes, and cloudscapes scumbled here and there by the smoke of pumping-stations, was interrupted after Outwell by a stop-and-start passage of locks and sluices, culminating in the great engineering feat that acted as the heart to the fenland's arteries, Denver Sluice. It was as they lay up in the late evening waiting for a passage through Salter's Lode that Hester, just about to catnap on her bunk, heard the sound of music, small and faint above the lapping of the water. Having been accustomed all her life to the home-made music of poor fen chapel-goers, she immediately recognised the timbre as that of a concertina.

She got up and went down the towpath; and saw Jonathan

Eastholm sitting in the doorway of his cabin, his back against the jamb, with a concertina of ancient appearance, with a turkey-necked look about its leather bellows, on his knee. He was working his way, with terrific concentration, through the melody of 'Tom Bowling': his performance being of that pluckily amateur kind which the ear follows with a sympathetic suspense in apprehension of a wrong note. Hester, liking a tune, and no more able to play an instrument than fly, heard its halting progress through with pleasure: struck too by the altered appearance of Eastholm, who bent over the concertina with something of the perplexed, encumbered look of large men when engaged on small tasks of tenderness with babies or animals.

'That was nice,' Hester said.

Eastholm nearly jumped out of his seat. 'What you doing there?'

'Listening. I didn't know you could play that.'

'I can't – I can't play it, really.' He shoved the concertina out of sight, as if to deny the very fact of its existence. 'It's just an ole thing I'm got – it ain't anything.' He had gone red in the face, and seemed thoroughly and disproportionately embarrassed by the whole thing. 'Ain't you going to git some sleep? Don't want you dragging your feet in the morning.'

She went back to her cabin, framing to herself a sketch of his character headed by the word Impossible.

With the passage of Denver they left behind the locks and sluices, and entered the River Ouse, wending its way south through a sea of rich earth on which Ely Cathedral, in the limpid dawn, could be glimpsed like a distant galleon. Here the waterway was busier, and Hester more conspicuous: other lightermen called greetings to Eastholm, and asked who he'd got working for him; watermen outside riverside taverns and at ferries watched her leading the horse with the frank curious stare of the isolated country district; and once a fisherman on the towpath asked her the time.

'Whass a'clock, bor?'

'Bout half arter,' she muttered, pulling her cap down.

They were to make a diversion down the tributary known

as Brandon Creek to deliver turf. The venerable Ship Inn commanded the turning into the Creek, and they moored here to eat some dinner – fish again, cooked on the stove.

'Can't we go up to the Ship to eat?' Hester said.

'No we can't,' Eastholm said. 'Likely to be a whole issue o' chaps I know there, and they'll soon want to know all about you.'

Even as he spoke, a man sitting underneath the trees on the grassy plot before the inn stood up and hailed him: 'Jonathan! Is that you, you ole bugger?'

Hester found herself being abruptly bundled into the cabin. 'Here, what's to do?' she cried.

'Git in there and lay low. Thass Shush Hubbard coming over – I'll never hear the last of it if he cottons on you're a gel.'

'Well, I am! It's nothing to be ashamed of.'

'Just git in and stay out of sight.'

'Why's he called Shush?'

'Because he don't, thass why – he's got the biggest mouth between here and Boston Stump. Every tale you ever hear started with Shush Hubbard. I'll try and git rid of him.'

He shut the cabin door on her, and presently she heard the usual cuss-strewn exchange of greetings, with a great yelping laugh that could only be Shush Hubbard. She sat down on Eastholm's bunk and peered round in the semi-darkness. There was a narrow shelf above her, stocked with a handful of books: *Old Moore's Almanac*, for the tides, *Pilgrim's Progress*, the Bible, *Robinson Crusoe* and *Paradise Lost*. The further shaft of light thrown on Eastholm's character by this mini-library was not without interest: she was tantalised by a glimpse into a bafflingly inaccessible personality; but there was insufficient physical light for her to read in the books, and she grew bored. Outside the conversation went on, dominated by the deafening counter-tenor of Shush Hubbard: 'What you carryen then? – *Are* you? – Down Brandon, then? Ah, *I'm* been up Burwell – few bricks, poor ole load, *poor* ole load' – all interspersed with the shrieking laugh, which seemed not to derive from anything funny, but to be a kind of reflex like the rattling of a jester's bells. Boredom, instinctive dislike of self-proclaimed wits of Shush Hubbard's sort, and hunger for her dinner got the better of her: she pulled her cap low over her face, opened the cabin door and went out.

Shush Hubbard and Jonathan Eastholm were standing on the towpath close to the lighter; and the latter, turning, threw Hester a wild glance, with more than a dash of murder in it. Shush Hubbard – a plump ginger specimen with a mouth which bisected his face like a split in an apple – raised his eyebrows and said, 'Who's that then? That your new mate?'

'Ah,' Eastholm said, through clenched teeth. 'Thass it – Jack – thass his name.'

'How do,' grunted Hester, stumping over to the stove with hunched shoulders. She slapped some of the cooked fish on to a plate and squatted down on a stool with her back to them. 'Scuse me – got to git some bloody grub down me – I'm that hungry I could eat a dish o' pigshit wi'out a spoon.' And she began gobbling the fish down with appreciative smacks and slurps.

There was a moment of surprised silence, and then Shush Hubbard said: 'Been on the lighters long?'

'Not long – used to wukk on the wharf up at Lynn,' she growled. 'Chucked it in when I saw a chap git caught by a load o' timber right in the knackers – sod that for a lark, I says.'

Shush Hubbard let out a gurgle of laughter, though a little uncertainly. 'Whass he like to wukk for then, ole Jonathan here?' he said.

Hester risked a glance round, seeing what appeared to be a carved statue of Jonathan Eastholm standing on the towpath, with a most lifelike expression of smothered anguish. 'Ah! he ain't a bad ole bugger,' she said. 'Bit of a tight-arse, you know – put a foot wrong and he gives you a look as black as a coalman's cods – but he ain't bad.' She spat out a fish-bone.

'Ah! Right.' Shush Hubbard's laugh trailed off again. 'Well, I reckon I'll goo and git meself another drop of beer. Yew coming for one, Jonathan?'

'Er – no, ta all the same, Shush.'

'What about you, Jack?' Shush Hubbard said.

'Not that bloody ole beer they serve here,' Hester said. 'You might as well drink a pot o' piss and cut out the middleman.'

'Ah! Right.' Shush's laugh faded completely. 'Cheer-oo

then.' He started down the towpath, and then she heard him say to Eastholm – with a totally ineffectual attempt to lower his voice – 'I say, Jonathan, that ole boy you're got wukking for you – he's a bit foul-mouthed, ain't he?'

Hester carried on eating – aware of Jonathan Eastholm's footsteps coming slowly up the boarding-plank, and ready to seize the shovel again if it came to it.

He sat down on the stool opposite her, picked up a plate and served himself with fish, cut a slice of bread, put both down on the deck, and burst out laughing.

It was a pleasant sight to see. The set, curtailed lineaments of his face broke up: he gave himself up completely to the laughter, which afforded an instructive contrast to the forced hootings of Shush Hubbard – it was a young laugh, the laugh of a boy still inhabiting the deep-chested figure of the man, and gladly breaking out as if he had been suppressed a little too early and a little too strictly. Tears started to his eyes, and he slapped his legs helplessly, and at last choked and half-strangled.

Hester jumped up and slapped his back. 'I made you laugh! Hooray! I did, I made you laugh!' she said, her hands on his shoulders.

He groaned, wiping his eyes. 'Oh, you little beggar. I never thought I'd see somebody shut Shush Hubbard up – I never did.'

'So my name's Jack, then, is it?' she said. 'What made you pick that? – Jack's as good as his master?'

He made to shake a fist at her, but was still too weak. 'I dunno,' he said. 'Whatever happened to my quiet life?'

They moored that evening at Littleport, having returned from Brandon Creek to the Ouse. Littleport had a bad name in the fens: seventy years ago it had been the centre of food riots, as a result of which six men were transported and five publicly hanged for refusing to starve quietly; and perhaps the fact that these sentences were meted out under the merciful authority of the Bishop of Ely was not without influence in the turning of the fen folk to the chapel. If the loved and respected lord and clergyman were ever to be found outside the pages of novels, they were not to be found in the fens – where the deepest pride in lineage still attached to an ancestor who had fought for the good old cause of Oliver Cromwell.

No wronged shades, however, troubled their peace as they tied up at a tree-fringed mooring below the town. It was an April evening of rare beauty, with a sky bearing both the colour and something of the bloom of rose-petals, reflecting in the water with yet softer hue, and casting glancing shadows amongst the trees. Hester had found flour and dried fruit amongst Eastholm's miscellaneous stores, and had contrived to make a nodding-cake, which they ate hot from the pan, sitting on the deck and watching the river banks dissolve into violet shadow. There was scarcely a sound beyond the quiet croppings of the horse on the grass; and it was possible to sense the broad unpeopled distances that lay on either side of them, and to receive the impression of the primeval, paradoxically, in this man-made landscape – to taste that ancient loneliness, of when humankind was few, and the world vast.

'Hark at that quiet,' Hester said. 'We could be on a little island in the middle of the sea – like in that book you're got – *Robinson Crusoe*.'

'How'd you know I'd got that?'

'I saw it in your cabin – when you shut me in.'

'Oh! then,' he said, and gave a retrospective chuckle.

'Thass what it's about, ain't it? I remember being told about it at school.'

'There's more to it than that – but thass the main bit, and the best bit.' With a sudden uncoiling of reserve he said: 'I must have read that a score of times – can't git enough of it.'

She was going to make a remark about him being quite a scholar, but stopped herself. It was by no means unheard of for men in the fens, isolated in mills, farms, boats, to turn despite ill-education to a little store of books; and besides, she did not want to inhibit his newly expansive mood.

'How's he end up on this island then?' she said. She was sitting directly on the deck, her back comfortably against the outer cabin wall – sitting just how you liked, she decided, was one advantage of wearing trousers. 'Tell me what happens.'

'Well . . .' Jonathan scratched his head, the hair quite coppery in the rays of dusk. 'He's shipwrecked on the island, the one survivor. It's all uninhabited, though there's goats what he kills for meat and skins, and he manages to salvage some tools and things from the wreck: and he meks a pet of a parrot, and teaches it to say his name. But he has to do everything hisself, all alone, from scratch – all these things you don't think twice about: growing corn, mekking bread, mekking an oven to mek the bread; he's only got hisself to rely on. And so you watch him struggling with this, and then conquering it – and realising that you can manage all on your own, quite apart from all the world. That everything you need's in yourself. Just in yourself.'

His voice had assumed the tones of a dreamy incantation: his eyes were not seeing her.

'It sounds awful – I'd go stark mad,' said she, with conviction.

'Oh! well, some other people visit the island eventually – cannibals. And he saves one of their victims, and he stops with him. Course he don't speak English or anything. He names him Friday, because thass the day he found him.'

'There – thass what you should call me.'

'I found you on a Monday.'

'Well, Monday then – Jack Monday, how's that?'

'Ah! well, the thing is about poor ole Friday – Robinson Crusoe kept him as a slave.'

'Sounds more and more like me all the time!'

Jonathan smiled as if he could not help himself, and took out his pipe. Hester saw this with unease – remembering she had thrown his tobacco in the river. 'How'd you git started on the lighters then?' she said quickly.

'Started wi' just two – hired 'em, and carried stuff for the brickyards at Whittlesey. I'd been working on the land till then. I saved all my harvest money to put the deposit down – I'd got my heart set on the lighters, see, so I worked every day of an eight-week season.'

'It don't run in the family then? Your dad weren't a waterman?'

'No.' He looked at the pipe, put it away. 'He were a banker over Wisbech way.' This description did not indicate that the Eastholms had fallen from high estate – a banker in the fenland

111

context being not a man in charge of vaults but a worker engaged on the repair of waterway embankments.

'He ain't around now, then?'

'No,' Jonathan said, with that attentive look in another direction which indicates that a subject is closed.

'So you ain't got a home then – apart from the boats?'

'Just the boats,' he said. 'Everything I'm got's in these five ole buckets. Oh, I know folk reckon there's not much future in 'em any more – the railways finished a lot of the trade. But it's the life that suits me. Always summat new to see – but you only look on, and don't have to git mixed up in it, and go on your way when you're seen enough.'

All of a sudden a heron, which must have been standing motionless in the shallows all this time, took off with a great ponderous noise of wings, seeming to make a palpable disturbance in the air, and becoming in a moment an elongated silhouette diminishing against the sky.

'Creaky old hernshaw,' Jonathan said. 'They always look ghostly to me – a ghost of some other bird, mebbe.'

'You ever seen a haunt?' Hester asked.

'I don't know. I'm seen summat odd: I'm often thought about it. I were tied up just this side of Huntingdon one morning. It were a bright day, birds singing, everything plain and ordinary – not when you'd expect to see a haunt, I suppose. I were sitting up on deck, like this, and peeling a few taters, when I saw a little boy running along the bank up above. I'm tried since then to think whether I saw him come from anywhere in particular, but I'm not sure. He were a boy, but he had long curls, and he were wearing skirts – summat like a pinafore, which I thought were strange. He were sort of laughing, and cheerful-like; I couldn't hear any sound, but then he were a little way away from me. He kept looking over his shoulder, as if there were somebody following him. Then he went down to where there was this patch of reeds on the edge of the bank, and he seemed to sort of dip down – whether he'd fallen, or jumped in the water, or what, I couldn't tell. I never heard no splash: but I jumped up and ran down the towpath, to see if he were all right. I looked and looked, but I couldn't find no sign of him.'

112

Hester let out a breath, and found the back of her neck tingling. 'D'you reckon that was a haunt?'

'Like I say – I ain't sure. But I believe in 'em, all right.' He looked at her sharply. 'Whass up?'

'Nothing. Just you're the last person I'd have thought of as believing in 'em.'

Suddenly he looked displeased, and was curt. 'Well, you don't know me, do you?' he said.

'I suppose not. But you don't seem to want anybody to know you, any road,' she said – curious about him, and not meaning to be rude.

'Mebbe I don't.' His face contracted into the old frown, then he gave his dismissive grunt: 'Pah!' and stood up. 'Come on, Jack Monday – git up off there and git the kettle on for tea. I never saw such a lazy article.'


3


They had much business at Ely: unloading of fertiliser and several thousand turf, taking on of gault from the Roswell clay-pits and a load of cinder and gravel to go to Stokeley. Eastholm drew up the profits of the run so far, and gave Hester her share – at the same time wiping off the debits he had chalked up in the cabin.

'Why'd you do that?' she said.

'Why? Because I want me head examining, thass why. Tek it before I change me mind.'

He had provisions to buy in the town, too; and while he was gone Hester slipped up to a little dry-goods shop on the waterside and bought him an ounce of tobacco. It was nice to have money in her pockets. What she was a little tired of was having pockets: she had an urge to wear some decent clothes again.

They moored for the evening near Waterside Quay, beneath a row of massy chestnut trees just breaking into blossom, with a crazy huddle of ancient warehouses on the other side, staggering down into the river on decayed struts like invalids taking the waters.

'Here,' she said, presenting him with the tobacco. 'Present from Jack Monday.'

'Whass this?'

'Fairy dust, whass it look like?' She grinned at him. 'Tek it before I change me mind.' She had been feeling guilty about that tobacco: she had always abhorred pettiness, and had been disturbed to discover it in herself.

They had stabled the horse at the Cutter Inn, whence Hester had caught a tantalising whiff of good food and drink and a lively intimation of company. Jonathan was about to light the oil-stove when she said: 'Oh, can't we go up to the Cutter for summat to eat? It looks good there. I'm fed up with the boats. Let me put my glad rags on and mek a night of it.'

'That money burning a hole in your pockets already, is it? Oh! goo on then. No stopping late, though: we're got to make a start tonight, to git to Earith in the morning – d'you hear?'

'Yes, master,' she said happily, and ran off to change.

She put on her best stiff-boned blouse, with at the neck a little cameo brooch that Mrs Langtoft had passed on to her, and a pair of earrings that she had got from Rob Risby the tallyman, which he said were garnets, meaning they looked a bit like garnets, from a distance, if you half-closed your eyes, and had had a drop to drink – and which Mrs Langtoft said were a bit trollopy . . . but then what did an old married woman know about looking nice? She fastened her hair above her ears, as best she could, with a bowl of water as her only mirror, and decided she ought to turn at least a few heads tonight, if those ratty old haybags she had seen at the Ferryman were anything to go by.

Jonathan was waiting on the towpath for her.

'Bet you'd forgot I could look like this, hadn't you?' she said.

He stared at her.

'Suppose I had,' he said.

He dug his hands in his pockets, and spoke little as they walked up to the Cutter. Every now and then he gave her an abrupt sideways glance, with something like affront in his eyes at her altered state. It seemed to throw him into difficulty. The ease with which he had spoken to her last night of the haunt and of Robinson Crusoe was replaced by his old, short, bristling manner.

The first thing she saw in the Cutter Inn was a large pier-glass on the wall, which sent her spirits higher. It was like meeting an old friend to see a clear reflection of herself, free of that wretched cap and old moleskin jacket. And she did look all right! She scarcely noticed the meal of chicken and ham pie they ate, except that it was rather salty and gave her a thirst. The bar-parlour was noisy, and full of watermen: not just lightermen, but denizens of the quayside quarter of the little city; and she was on her second mug of beer when some acquaintances of Jonathan's hailed him, and they began a familiar conversation bewailing the state of the trade.

Hester considered herself not unused to light liquor: at the Langtofts' she had drunk the home-made wine to which Mrs Langtoft, like others on the fen, somehow considered her Methodist views on temperance inapplicable; she was accustomed to a drop of small beer on fair-days and feast-days, and felt she knew her limit. In short, she was soon thoroughly tipsy. After staring in perplexity for some time at a girl her own age, and having the stare returned, she at last recognised her as someone she had known years ago, when her father in his wanderings had settled briefly at nearby Sutton-in-the-Isle: and they fell on each other with all that superheated warmth of acquaintance renewed in the cups. The girl, whose name Hester never did remember, introduced her to her two female companions, whose names she did not catch, and they were soon all firmly bonded in conviviality. Suddenly Jonathan Eastholm's head appeared over her shoulder, seeming to bend from a great height.

'Don't forgit – no stopping late. We got to git moving. D'you hear?'

'Oh! all right,' she said: she was sure it was not late yet.

'Is that your chap?' whispered one of the girls.

'Him?' said Hester. 'Why, he ain't interested in anything that ain't shaped like a boat and got three layers o' pitch on it.' And as they laughed she went on, more in soliloquy than dialogue: 'It's all self with him. He don't see no farther than his own nose.'

At some point someone began playing the upright piano that stood in the corner, and a man was prevailed upon to sing – not that he seemed very reluctant. This was a man of abbreviated stature, dressed in a suit of startling check that even Uncle Bevis might have baulked at, and brought up to reasonable height by a tall bowler hat. It soon appeared that the hat was an indispensable adjunct to the singer's performance, his repertoire being of the comic-sentimental kind, and the final vibrato cadence of 'Polly Perkins' being given a most affecting pathos, by his raising the hat perpendicularly off his head, and waggling it in the air with his eyes closed. He followed up this triumph with the 'The Death of Nelson', clasping the hat impressively to his heart, and then signalled his transition to the comic mood by setting the hat on his brow at a racy angle, and making motions suggestive of riding a galloping horse. All this Hester saw and enjoyed through a haze of what she took to be tobacco-smoke, until three young men who had been nudging each other for an unconscionable time came over to her and her companions and offered to buy them a drop of wet; and she soon found herself flirting with them. What a relief it was, after all that dour grind of lock-gates and turves and hard boots and hard bunks! None of the three men was up to much – but it was delightful to feel herself admired and appreciated at last.

Her attention had been diverted from the singing for some time, in half listening to an interminable anecdote told by one of the three young men, who was attempting familiarity by proxy, by caressing the back of her chair, when the piano introduction to a song struck her with a peculiar recognition. The singer expressed a nautical mood by placing one hand on his stomach and the other in the small of his back, and crooned: '"Here, a sheer hulk, lies poor Tom Bowling . . ."'

Hester listened raptly: the melody, sweetened perhaps by her own tipsiness, seemed to fairly wrench her heart from her breast; and all at once she recollected that it was that same tune that Jonathan had pieced out on the concertina, alone in the evening. 'Oh! I say, Jonathan – thass your song,' she said, 'there's the song you were playing the other night.' She turned to where she had last seen him. He was not there. How long was it since she *had* seen him? She had rather lost track

116

of time. She evaded the tentative grasp of the young man, who had forgotten the punchline of his story, and made a struggling, squeezing circuit of the packed parlour.

'"His form was of the manliest beauty,
His heart was kind and soft . . ."'

Eastholm was nowhere to be seen: he must have gone back to the lighters. Hester groaned inwardly. She supposed it was getting rather late: but how dreary to have to go back to work, just when she was feeling human again . . .

She left the inn; and the cold night air reproached her, with a dizzying slap in the face, for having that extra drink. She walked down to the moorings, and stood looking at various unfamiliar shapes of boats under the chestnut trees, until her mind numbly registered the fact that Eastholm's lighters were not there.

He had gone on without her. Disbelief was followed by fury, to be succeeded again by disbelief. She began walking down the towpath, exploring in her mind various alternative scenarios – but of these even the least unlikely was that all five lighters had suddenly and noiselessly sunk to the bottom. No: he had gone on. 'I'll murder him,' Hester said to herself, stumbling as she hurried in the dark.

She had passed the railway bridge, and left the environs of Ely behind, by the time she discerned the squat outline of the rear lighter on the dim river ahead; and then, beyond that, the white shirt sleeves of Jonathan Eastholm leading the horse. Confirmation converted her anger into the form of new energy: she ran; the speed of her sudden approach startled the horse, and seemed to startle Eastholm too, who had a job to hold him.

'What's the 'nation idea of that – going off and leaving me behind?' she cried.

'Whoa, steady there – it's all right,' Eastholm said – to the horse, not to Hester. To her he presented a face of which the arrogant neutrality was perceptible even in the dark. 'I told you not to be late,' he said. 'I told you we'd got to be moving tonight. Tain't my fault if you don't listen.'

'You could have said! You didn't have to just go off like that!'

117

'Look here – you work for me, and you work by my rules. You shouldn't need telling – it ain't my business to go chasing you up.'

'Oh, you – you ain't human, I swear you ain't!' His harshness seemed the blankest affront to her melting mood of a few minutes ago. 'You're got no more feelings than your ole boats!'

'I'm got a bloody living to earn, thass what I'm got – small chance wi' you around. Now tek hold of this hoss, and git going – I want to see Pope's Corner by sun-up.'

She glared at him – he glared back; but the darkness intervening, they faced each other as it were insubstantially, like two irate ghosts, and after a moment she reached up to grasp the horse's bridle. What seemed at first a reluctance on the animal's part to take the strain quickly revealed itself, in the tension of the tow-rope, to be something more serious. Turning back, they found that the lighters, having lost steering-way, had drifted into the reedy shallows of the bank – the case being made worse by the jambing-poles getting caught up in the tangled scrub that came to the water's edge.

'Stuck,' Eastholm said. 'Look at 'em – stuck fast. You satisfied now?'

'Me? Thass your doing – tekking off on your own with nobody to steer.'

'I wouldn't have had to, if you'd done as you were told.'

Abruptly he put an end to these recriminations, flinging off his boots and stockings and clambering down into the shallow water, where he began clearing away the weedy obstructions from poles and ropes with his bare hands. Pausing, he stared up at her.

'Well, don't just stand there.'

'You don't think I'm gitting down there in these clothes?'

'Change 'em then! Coh – I swear to God I'll never crew up with a woman again. I must have been mad.'

In a sort of savage compression of mutinous feeling Hester changed in her cabin into the hated men's clothes and then joined Eastholm in the water. It came up to her waist: it was bitterly cold, silty, weedy, reedy, and scummy; the river that was so sparklingly innocent in the sunlight became in darkness a sink of clammy unpleasantnesses, nameless sticky and slimy things that clung to her skin and were the more repulsive because they could not be seen. Her foot slipped on the muddy bottom and gave her a ducking; overhanging branches raked across her face; she skinned her hands on the thick ropes and on the pitchy hulls of the lighters. What am I doing? she asked herself once – what am I doing, working like a slave up to my neck in freezing filthy water in the middle of the night? – when there's people down at the inn living a normal life?

'Shove harder!' Eastholm commanded, as they put their shoulders to the hull of the first lighter, and strained to heave it out of the silt. 'Goo on, push!'

'I am pushing!' she wailed: the lighter shifted: she lost her footing again, and went under. The water sang in her ears, and then Eastholm dragged her out with one strong arm, and deposited her on the bank.

Convulsed with shivers, Hester pulled a clump of stinking weed out of her hair, then sat back aching and exhausted, aware that something alive was wriggling on her upper leg. Eastholm, having freed the waterlogged tow-rope, heaved himself up by his arms, like a muscular Triton, on to the bank. She regarded him standing there, and his great robust dripping figure seemed an emblem of imperviousness to her misery. 'I shall never git dry – and when I do I shall go down with rheumatics,' she lamented, with more feeling than logic. 'What a way to live!'

'You shouldn't have took the job on if you can't manage it,' he said. 'I told you it was a man's job.'

'Man's?' All the toil and discomfort of the lighters seemed to boil up within her and condense in a single protest, a cry in the chill comfortless dark. 'Man's? This life? This is no life for a human being at all – it's no life for a dog!'

'It's my life, and it's always suited me,' Eastholm said, after a moment – his words simply a flinty articulation, without emphasis.

'Well, you're welcome to it,' Hester said, hauling herself to her feet. She hugged herself, and tried to stop the wild chattering of her teeth. 'I'm had enough.'

'So you're backing out then, are you? Just what you said

you wouldn't do – leave me in the lurch half-way through the run—'

'Oh, no,' she said. 'I'll carry on to the end of the run – as far as Stokeley, weren't it? Yes, I'll do that. I'll keep my side of the bargain – I shan't let you reproach me with that. But then thass it. I'm finished. I'll try my hand at road-mending or summat. It'll be a holiday after this.'

'All right.' He turned away, and his expression, if any, was lost to her. 'Goo and lead the hoss, then. Quicker we git to Stokeley, quicker you can pack in.'

'I don't suppose you'll be sorry to see the back of me, any road,' she said. 'Will you?' This little coquettish fishing was no adulteration of her resolve to go, which was as genuine as her wretchedness: it was rather the tic of a still irrepressible vitality.

'Well, you said it,' Eastholm said.

He presented to her his broad back, shoulder-blades outlined where the wet shirt clung. Hester looked around for something to throw at it, but something more than her weariness prevented her. To her own surprise she plumbed a momentary desolation: the surprise being not so much that she had not Jonathan's good opinion, but that she really cared, pig as he was, to have it.


4


Hester, like many pliable personalities, could adhere to an idea with dogged persistence once she had set her mind to it. The compensations of life on the lighters made themselves felt during the rest of the journey to Stokeley – interludes of charming peace, with fish popping to the surface of the water and the cry of wildfowl across the sunlit Ouse washes, strewn with marsh-marigold; but these little persuasions could not compare in eloquence with aches, blisters and chills, nor with the voice of Hester's inward resentment. Enough was enough: though one thing might have changed her mind. A soft word of commiseration, apology – anything – from Eastholm, and her hard resolve might yet have been flipped over on its back like a turtle; but nothing of the sort was forthcoming from the waterman, who accepted – indeed seemed to welcome – her decision with finality. He conducted himself for those two days pretty much as if she were already gone – that self-containment which she had first noticed about him merely deepening a shade into finished introspection.

So a bright morning found them leaving the Forty Foot and approaching the familiar environs of Stokeley: the Abbey's ruined beauties rising above the low roofs, and painfully reminding Hester of those rash moments with Chad which had been the unwitting beginning of this odyssey of hers. The last load to be delivered was of cinder and gravel to a horse-dealing establishment in the town, of which the exercise paddock came down to the towpath; and the banks were sufficiently high and the barrows heavy enough to dispel any traces of regret in Hester's mind, leaving only a grim thankfulness that this was the last time.

A little crushed-looking groom, with bow legs and sorrel hair all flat on his head as if he had been curry-combed, superintended their unloading of the cinder and gravel in a corner of the paddock; but as Hester tipped out the last load, an elderly woman came from the direction of the house, beyond the row of stables, to inspect the goods: her proprietorial manner, and loud insistence that they'd better not be diddling her, proclaiming her as the owner of the establishment. Hester, considering her obligations finally discharged, sat herself wearily down on the edge of her barrow whilst the old woman haggled with Eastholm, and pondered her next move. She was without work again. There might be something in Stokeley; but if not, she would go and throw herself on Lizzie Gosling's mercy once more – the journey having brought her back to the old district of Hinching Fen – and from there she would have to swallow her pride and write to Aunt Netty. Horrible thought! – and redolent of defeat: but the compass of her options was so contracted. There must be something wrong with her, she thought: here she was with no home, nobody, nothing – no eye to pity, and no arm to save, as they said on the fen; and quite downcast, she buried her head in her hands.

'We're laying an exercise track for the horses, for all

weathers,' the old woman was saying to Eastholm. 'Paddock's a mess in winter. Could do with someone to help lay the gravel. You interested?'

'Can't help you, I'm afraid,' Eastholm said. 'I'm moving on.'

'What about you, boy?' the old woman said. She carried a long walking-stick, less it seemed to support her figure, which was noticeably upright, than as a brandishing instrument; and as she spoke she gave Hester a hard poke in the ribs. 'You afraid of a bit of hard work?'

Hester did not greatly like being poked in the ribs, and the imputation just then touched an equally tender spot. 'No, I ain't,' she said, 'but I'm had enough of loading and barrowing, and I'm finished with it. And I ain't a boy – I'm a girl,' and she snatched off her cap and pulled down her hair with a feeling of liberation.

The woman stared, thumped her stick on the ground as a horse will stamp its hoof, and let out a shout of hard laughter. 'Well, damn me, so you are! Damn me – I never saw the like of it! What's a gel doing working on the lighters?'

'I took it on because I had to – temporary-like,' said Hester, rising with an assumption of dignity, and picking up the empty barrow.

'Well, damn me!' the old woman said again; and she continued to laugh, and exclaim, and stare after her, as Hester and Jonathan wheeled the empty barrows down to the paddock gate and out to the riverside.

Hester went into her cabin for the last time, threw off the waterman's clothes, changed into her walking-dress, packed up her two carpet-bags, pinned on her hat, and emerged again to find Jonathan Eastholm waiting for her on the towpath.

'Not changed your mind then?' he said.

'No,' she said. She looked up at him in surprise – his hair was white. 'Whatever's that?'

'Eh? Oh, that—' He brushed a hand over his hair: it was blossom which had fallen from an apple tree at the end of the paddock.

'Thought for a minute I'd made you go grey,' she said.

'Here – here's your share of the money.' He dropped the

coins into her hand, and bent his frown upon her. 'How you going to manage now?'

'Don't suppose that bothers you much, does it?' she said; and then, relenting: 'I'll git work in Stokeley. How you going to manage?'

'There's a berth up past the bridge – I'm tying up there for a while. I'll find somebody proper to do the job at Stokeley market, mebbe.'

Somebody proper indeed! Till then she had been ready to say farewell to him on friendly terms: they had been through some experiences together, after all; but now she glared at him, and her glare was about to translate itself into scathing speech, when they were interrupted by a loud 'Hem!' from the paddock gate above the towpath. A maid, in the form of one great starched frilled affronted stare, was standing there, and addressing Hester said in frosty accents: 'Missis says WOULD you be so good as to step up to the house as she'd like a word with you IF you wouldn't mind.'

'Me? If it's about laying that gravel, I – oh, well, beggars can't be choosers. All right.'

She turned back to say goodbye to Eastholm; but he was already walking away from her, down the towpath to the horse, brushing the blossoms from his bowed head.

'Well – and ta-ta to you too,' she said tartly under her breath: though it gave her a queer pang to see him go like that. At last she picked up her bags, and followed the ramrod back of the maid through the paddock gate and up to the house.

'What's it about, then?' she asked, as they crossed a stable yard, watched by the elegantly protruding heads of horses in loose-boxes.

'Oh dear don't ask ME I'm sure I don't know I'm only the MAID,' said the maid, in terrible capitals.

'Who's the missis, then?'

'Oh dear me Mrs SAUNDERS is the name of the mistress of the household as such,' the maid said, leading her in through a back kitchen, and pausing on the threshold to wipe her feet on the mat with such pointed emphasis that she looked like an exceptionally unsubtle mime artist doing the same.

Hester was conducted into a parlour, furnished with an eye

123

more to massiveness and durability than refinement, where the elderly woman was seated in a wing chair before the fire, grasping her stick before her.

'Ah, there you are, gel! And you *are* a gel – I can see that for sure now. Well, well, that's the funniest thing I ever saw – when you whipped that cap off and gave me a mouthful out there. You could have knocked me down with a feather. Come a bit closer – let's have a look at you. Pretty gel, too! Don't mind me asking you in here – but it's tickled me so, I had to get to the bottom of it.' All this was delivered in a powerful, indeed booming voice, which not only betokened strength of character, but suggested that the lady was somewhat deaf, and so assumed that everyone else was. 'There must be a story behind this, I said to myself – gel like you doing work like that. Go on – sit yourself down, you look worn to a shade – go on, and tell me.'

Hester complied: it was very welcome to find herself the subject of kindly interest at last, and moreover she glimpsed a chance, given the size of the establishment, that she might beg a little work here. She gave an outline of her career which glossed over the reasons for her leaving Langtoft's farm, and which at several points caused Mrs Saunders to break again into sharp-edged laughter.

'And you've been swanning about in men's britches, with a lot of hard-swearing watermen! Oh! I shall have to tell Gideon this one – I shall have to write and tell Lyle. It'll tickle him to death.'

'Well, I needed the work, you see,' Hester said, blushing a little but laughing too. 'And I thought if men could do it, I'm sure I could just as well. If not better.'

'Ah! you're right, there, gel,' Mrs Saunders said, thumping her stick on the floor, and disturbing an indiscriminate basketful of fur by the fire, which resolved itself into two drowsy tortoiseshell cats. 'Don't ever let them tell you otherwise, though of course they will. A woman can get through a day's work while a man's still wondering which side of his mouth to put his 'bacca in. Look at me – finest horse-yard in the country. Gentlemen and ladies of the aristocracy come to Saunders' for their carriage-horses and hunters – and that's

*Mrs* Saunders and they know it. Optional extras, men,' she declared. 'I've buried two husbands, I have—' the dismissive tone in which she added this, suggesting that in thus disposing of them she had not regarded their decease as a necessary preliminary.

'I had to pack it in, though,' Hester said with honesty. 'I'm not afraid of work – but I just couldn't tek that life any more.'

'Oh! they're a rough set of men on the river, right enough,' Mrs Saunders said. 'That's no place for you. Still, I like your spirit – I like that. I can't abide these mincing chits of gels you get nowadays, frit to step in a bit of muck. I hope he dealt fair with you – that waterman – eh? No funny business.'

'Oh! no – nothing like that,' Hester said. 'I might just as well have been a man.'

'Eh! you in those trousers,' Mrs Saunders said, with a reminiscent chuckle: then fixed Hester with an acute look. 'You got any work to go to now?'

'No,' Hester said. 'I was going to look for something in Stokeley – service, or anything.'

Mrs Saunders' eyes, glinting amidst shrewd wrinkles, dwelt on Hester for some moments. Hester decided the best thing was to gaze straight back.

'You know what a companion-help is?' Mrs Saunders said abruptly.

Hester said yes: and tried not to betray her jolt of astonishment at what seemed to be coming. Amongst girls of her class, going as companion-help was the very best sort of service: lady's-maid was nothing to it. Many were the tales of girls on the fen who had gone as companion-helps to rich widows or genteel spinsters, and been left fortunes – though of course there were tales of the opposite sort, in which the employers turned out to be old dragons, and made the girls' lives a misery. Hester held her breath.

'Well, I've been looking out for a companion-help for a while,' Mrs Saunders said. 'I've buried two husbands like I said, and there's just my two sons now, and one of them's away. I'm a busy woman still, with the yard to see to, and there's a few things I can't manage. Folk say I'm going deaf, though I reckon it's just that they mutter; and I'm getting arthritis in my hands, which is a nuisance when you want to be well turned out, though I've never been one for titivating. Anyway, I've worked hard for nigh on forty years, and I reckon I've earned the right to be waited on. I didn't know whether I'd find a gel as would suit me: I had one call about the position the other week, but she was such a mousy thing she got on my nerves after five minutes. I make my mind up quick when I meet folk, and I either take to them or not; and I reckon you might do. I like a gel with a bit of pluck, and not afraid of rolling her sleeves up. Perhaps I've got you wrong – or perhaps you don't fancy the job – what do you say?'

'Oh! Mrs Saunders – I dunno what to say. Thank you!'

'Should be a step up from the lighters. Won't be soft, mind you: I'm particular, and what I say goes: we'd best have a month's trial. You'll have your own bedroom – you won't be expected to share with a maid or anything like that. You'll get your keep, and an allowance for clothes, and a bit of pocket money: I don't believe in throwing money at gels of your age, it only turns their heads. Well then! Tell me your name.'

'Hester Verney, ma'am.'

'You needn't ma'am me – Mrs Saunders will do. Well, Hester Verney: it's a good position – do you want it?'

Did she want it! Even the mention of a bedroom, after the musty bunk on the lighters, fell on Hester's ear like a promise of oriental luxury. There were lines round Mrs Saunders' mouth that suggested she could be a Tartar . . . but all in all, it was a piece of the greatest good fortune. Jobs like this were not going begging: Hester's head began to swim as she took it in, and she could not help smiling as she said: 'Oh! yes, please, ma'am – I mean Mrs Saunders.'

'Good. You've got sense in your head. No more cap and trousers, eh?' She checked herself in another chuckle, and said with a thump of her stick: 'Mind, there's one thing I won't put up with, and that's canoodling. I won't have canoodling and spooning under my roof – you hear?'

'Oh, yes, Mrs Saunders,' Hester said. She wasn't too concerned about that just at present – and that could surely be got round, anyhow.

# Chapter Five

1

Hester was allowed one day off per fortnight. She used the first of these to go by carrier's van out to Hinching Fen to visit Lizzie Gosling, and give her the news of her alteration in fortune. Wearing a new velvet-edged cream frock bestowed on her by Mrs Saunders, she surveyed the familiar landmarks, which she had last beheld under the shade of obscure disgrace; and she would have been less than human if she had not felt a little pulse of triumph, and vindication, though she was amply conscious that she owed her new vantage to nothing more than luck.

'Mrs Saunders of Stokeley – I'm heard of her. What a turn-up!' exclaimed Lizzie. 'There's gels on the fen'd give their eye teeth for a job like that. Course it depends – what's she like?'

'Well, she's nice to me, mostly. She's a masterful sort of woman, though, and got a terrible temper when she's roused. You have to tread careful. But I'm got my own bedroom – and I git clothes, and I eat at table with her, and everything!' Hester concluded with uncontainable elation.

'Well – talk about falling on your feet. I don't suppose you miss the farm, do you?'

'Oh! well – I think about it sometimes. I wouldn't mind going over and saying hello to Mr Langtoft, but I suppose I can't do that . . . Folk are still talking about it, I suppose?'

'Not so much now. There's always summat new to gossip about. Fact is, Chad Langtoft's turned to courting Mary-Ann Cole, and they reckon there'll be an announcement any day now.'

'Has he indeed?' Hester spoke grimly. 'Well, good luck to 'em.'

The days at the farm seemed very far off to Hester now. Not only had the mode of her working life wholly changed, but she was living in a town for the first time. Stokeley was small as towns went: to the birds that alighted in its gardens it represented no distinguishable habitat from the fields in which they chiefly lived, and the pollen clouds of early summer blew straight down its wide High Street. But the town's distinct separation from the country consisted not so much in its modest concentration of bricks and mortar as in its function. There was a world of economic specialisation within its small bounds, with at least one tradesman for every trade imaginable, rising to a rarefied upper atmosphere of the professions in the odd solicitor and schoolmaster. On the fen the absence of large manorial landlords and the universal struggle to earn a living placed everyone pretty much on an equality: on walking into Stokeley, one entered the labyrinth of class. And Hester soon found that in this world where everyone was striving for importance, Mrs Rachel Saunders, her new employer, was very important.

She had not always been so. Her father, who had barely been able to write his own name, had kept a decayed inn on the Great North Road, a dozen miles to the west on the edge of that foreign country known as the upland. But for the stable, with a few ponies and carts for hire, it was practically an ale-house. Rachel, on her father's death, had taken on the stable side (in both senses) of the business; had united her knowledge and instinctive understanding of horses with the capital of her first husband, and found herself at his early death the proprietor of a small horse-dealing yard. The move to Stokeley followed her meeting and marrying her second husband, Saunders, a native of that town, who also possessed a store of capital which it took his wife's acuity to put to good use. Two children and seven years later, he followed his predecessor to the churchyard, leaving Mrs Saunders a well-set-up widow holding in her capable hands the reins of a large and profitable horse-dealing business, located in a sturdy three-storey brick house by the river, with two rows of stables, yard and paddock, and an auxiliary cottage for grooms, as well as an outlying farm property. The whole formed a realm of which she was absolute monarch – her wealth and force of character giving her a sort of suzerainty over much of the town as well.

Hester learnt most of this history from the servants rather than from Mrs Saunders herself. She was a proud woman, and in spite of her frank and down-to-earth manner she did not encourage familiarity – as Hester quickly learned, when some initial democratic casualness in her own demeanour was sternly reprimanded. One piece of equine argot which Hester quickly picked up was 'Plenty of Bone': this seemed to be a good thing in a horse, and if Mrs Saunders' opinion of herself was anything to go by, a good thing in a person too – for she was a big woman, tall and bulky, with the cast of figure called statuesque, though the sort of statues she brought to mind had more of Mars than Venus about them. Her long, strong, dark-complexioned face had no curves in it, and was graven with firm lines: two especially deep ones ran from the sides of her straight nose to the corners of her mouth – and, as Hester soon learned, if the science of palmistry had extended to the face, these might have been aptly christened the Lines of Awkwardness. Her hair, scarcely greying though she was getting on for sixty, was severely parted and bound up in plaits at the back of her head; and Hester, who had seen many prints and peep-shows representing the terrible Red Indian chiefs, could well picture Mrs Saunders in fringed buckskin at the head of a company of braves, and felt that if she had been, the settlers of America would never have stood a chance.

The binding up of these plaits every morning was one of Hester's tasks, as was assisting at Mrs Saunders' dressing, and the care of her wardrobe, which consisted chiefly of a hulking platoon of black bombazine frocks, with several black fur-trimmed capes, heavy as pieces of armour, for outdoors, rigid high-button boots which were tortured every night on a boot-tree but refused to yield, and for evening wear some ropes of pearls, so weighty to manipulate that it was like handling anchor-chains. A portable writing-case was also in Hester's charge, in which to Mrs Saunders' dictation she made various memoranda, and fired off endless notes to tradesmen, very seldom of the complimentary sort. She likewise officiated at the making of tea, which Mrs Saunders drank strong and black throughout the day; accompanied her on shopping trips, dealing with the terrified clerks and cashiers who were beneath that lady's notice, and plucking her out of the path of advancing waggons – Mrs Saunders serenely assuming that what she could not hear did not exist; dispensed her medicines, which she took in large quantities and did not believe in; interpreted for her the 'mutterings' of people who did not shout loudly enough to penetrate her deafness; acted as a partner for her nightly, and highly competitive, games of rummy; fetched and carried, and generally performed any little task for which the fluctuating arthritis in Mrs Saunders' hands incapacitated her; and received, when no one else was available, her blasts of bad temper.

These were frightening. They rose, like bubbles to a calm surface, without warning.

'I want my spectacles,' she would say. 'Look in my ridicule.' (Meaning her reticule – which was the size of a small flour-sack.)

Hester looked. 'I can't find 'em.'

'What do you mean, you can't find them?' Suddenly Mrs Saunders was snarling, fierce, terrible. 'Look, gel, look!'

'Oh! I remember – I put 'em down on the night table upstairs.'

'Well, don't just stand there! Go and fetch them! What in the name of all the saints do you think you're doing?' Mrs Saunders' mighty voice shivered the ornaments on the mantelpiece. 'Look alive!'

The heroines of her mother's yellowback novels would not have stood for this: they would have gone all spirited and lifted their chins and tossed their hair and so on. Hester soon knew better, and simply rode out these brief storms. There was nothing personal in them: Mrs Saunders breathed occasional fire, and if you happened to be in the way, you got scorched. The most concentrated salvoes were reserved for tradesmen, who were all, every one, out to diddle her. They were criminals of monstrous artfulness. To hear her talk, you might suppose that the tradesmen of Stokeley were in the habit of meeting by night, in ceremonial conclave, to plot the sole ruin of Mrs Saunders.

One of these was Uncle Bevis, the butcher. It was significant of Mrs Saunders' prestige that Uncle Bevis himself, not the manager who looked after the shop, came to the house at her summons. Hester met him in the hall.

'Wehrr, beggar me – what are you doing here, gel?'

Hester explained her position. Uncle Bevis stood there holding his bowler hat, and looking doubtfully into it, and seeming to shrink inside his check suit.

'Not a bad place, eh –'cepting the mistress is a bit of a fire-eater, eh? Ah, there's no harm in her, you know – I'm known her for years – we understand each other.' But he did not say this very loudly.

'She's waiting to see you,' Hester said.

'Is she?' Uncle Bevis essayed a ghastly sort of smile at this prospect, and scratched his fat shaven neck. 'Good sort of mood, would you say, gel?'

Hester sharply sucked in breath, and looked noncommittal.

Uncle Bevis was not invited to sit down. He endeavoured to make light of this, as if standing in the middle of the room suited him best of all things in the world; but his hands seemed to incommode him, as if he longed to put them in his pockets, and jingle.

'I suppose you meant it as a joke, did you?' Mrs Saunders said, with an alarming lack of preamble.

Uncle Bevis smiled at the word joke, saw that wouldn't do, and turned solemn. 'Why, what's that, then, Mrs Saunders?'

'Sending us horsemeat instead of beef – us dealing in horses as we do.'

'Horsemeat?' Uncle Bevis tried bluster. 'Now, now, steady on – I can assure you there's never been any of that in *my* establishment.'

'Well, it certainly wasn't beef,' boomed Mrs Saunders: it was futile even for Uncle Bevis to attempt to compete with her in volume. 'Some folk might say sending a side of horsemeat instead of beef's bad enough; but then some folk are strict; I'm the forgiving sort myself. I've buried two husbands, and both of them were always telling me I'm too soft – I suppose it's my nature. But when the meat's off as well, I think I've got a right to complain – what do you think?'

'Off, Mrs Saunders? Meat supplied by my establishment? Oh, now, I say—'

'High as old game!' Mrs Saunders cried, with a thump of her stick. 'When they brought it in even the flies walked out! I suppose you think because I'm a poor old widow-woman you can fob me off with that sort of muck. Take advantage of me – poison me into the bargain – why not! I dare say you'd like to see me dead – I dare say it'd please you – I dare say you'd Laugh!'

Uncle Bevis denied these aspersions in a very humble, shuffling, sweating, and small-boyish manner.

'Well, I've put up with a lot. I've put up with burying two husbands, and arthritis in my hands so I can't hardly take the top off an egg, and having my good nature traded on, and having tradesmen diddling me every which way. But I shan't put up with this any more. I shall have to take my custom to Mason's. I dare say they'll rob me like the rest, but perhaps I won't be poisoned.'

A few minutes later Hester was showing Uncle Bevis to the door. He looked a broken man, and scarcely had the energy to give her one of his genial punches. He had just managed to hold on to Mrs Saunders' custom by means of an abject apology, a promise to do better and an offer, grudgingly accepted, of a joint of beef gratis with a couple of chickens thrown in. He mopped his brow with a handkerchief and looked at Hester in wistful appeal.

'That beef weren't so bad really – was it, gel?' he said in a whisper.

'Not really,' she said.

There had been nothing wrong with the beef: a little gristly, merely, by the high standards of Uncle Bevis's meat – a man can be a fool and good at his trade. The remarkable thing was that Mrs Saunders really seemed to believe that there had been something wrong with it: she grumbled afterwards to Hester that that fat fellow had better not diddle her again. Every egotism is sustained by its delusions, and those of this highly realistic woman were that everyone was trying

132

either to do her down, or affront her by canoodling under her roof.

She hated canoodling – or spooning, or poodle-faking, or making sheep's eyes, or carrying on: all her words for loving dalliance were mocking and a little contemptuous. Hester had to accompany her on periodic forays into the servants' quarters of an evening, when she would burst in on the grooms and maids in the hope of catching them up to something; and it was a by-blow of her deafness that she was convinced people were always murmuring endearments behind her back. 'What are they saying?' she demanded of Hester, if she saw a maid pass a word with the stable-boy; and Hester would have to repeat the most innocuous commonplaces about tea being ready. Mrs Saunders' detestation of this most natural of human predilections seemed to originate in plain incomprehension.

'What do they want to do it for?' she protested to Hester. 'Making up and carrying on. Billing and cooing. I don't see the point of it all. I just don't understand why they want to do it—' an assertion which the rather glum faces of her buried husbands, staring sadly out from framed photographs above the mantelpiece, seemed to corroborate.

Hester never saw any canoodling amongst the servants – with whom, as a glorified servant herself, she had much to do. Judy, the parlour-maid who had taken against her so emphatically on her first meeting, did not relent: she had a habit of stiffly placing herself in Hester's way, and then noticing, and exclaiming: 'Oh do pardon ME I'm SURE': and she was no more encouraging to men. The kitchen-maid was more of an age to be interested in dolls than chaps. The two grooms and the stable-boy, who slept above the tackle-room across the yard in a leathery ambience of saddles and bridles, spoke a strange language which sounded saucy, until you realised that they were referring to horses when they rhapsodised about sloping shoulders, good withers, sweet-itch, snaffles, wisping her over, and Damp Legs. The domestic arrangements were presided over by the cook-housekeeper, a sallow matron named Mrs Dawsmere.

Mrs Dawsmere did much to make Hester feel at home in the first difficult weeks, when she was in sore need of a friend. She was a kindly soul whose view of the world was obscured by a fog of superstition. Hester, living on the fen, had unconsciously picked up a few of these – never put shoes on the table, turn your money over when you see a full moon. For Mrs Dawsmere, the whole of life was a terrible maze of omen and augury.

'Don't put that down there!' she cried, as Hester brought Mrs Saunders' tea-tray down to the kitchen.

'What's the matter?'

'The spoons are crossed – cross your spoons, and you'll come to want. Oh! no – don't turn 'em that way – see your face in the back of a spoon, and you'll never marry.'

Hester laughed. 'How would it be if I just chucked 'em out the window?'

'You laugh, gel. You want to be careful – specially wearing that brown.'

'I thought it was green that was unlucky?'

'Ooh! Brown as well. Wear brown above your waist, and you'll never suckle your children. There's truth in these things.' In fact there seemed to be so many unlucky colours that Mrs Dawsmere was forced to wear nothing but a shadowy grey.

'Don't put your feet on there!'

'Why not?'

'Rest your feet on another's chair, and they'll never again be sitting there.'

'Is it all right to put 'em on the fender?'

'Ooh! Spit on your shoe if you do – spit the devil away,' Mrs Dawsmere said – the devil in her cosmology seeming to be a feebly persistent little nuisance, who had nothing better to do than pop up in tea-cups and fireplaces, and be endlessly repulsed with salt and spit. She cleared the tea-things away, disposing of them in various auspicious attitudes, and suppressing a yawn – it was doubtless unlucky to yawn when your hands were wet, or something. She always looked tired: probably, Hester suspected, because going to bed involved so much treading on the right stairs, and taking off the right pieces of clothing first, and touching wood, that before she was finished it was time to get up again.

Domestic life at Mrs Saunders' was subordinate to the horse.

The furnishings of the big high-ceilinged rooms were, like the mistress, burly and solid – great chairs and tables of oak and mahogany with shin-catching legs, thick cretonne drapes sagging under their own weight, thumping brass lamps with swollen heads – but the only adornments were of an equestrian character. There were glass cases full of cups won by Mrs Saunders' horses at shows, statuettes of horses, paintings of horses, books about horses – the very leather of their bindings seeming to whiff of the saddle. When Mrs Saunders occasionally took a horse out to ride – arthritis permitting – she became a centauress in riding-habit and hard hat. For Hester horses and ponies had always been convenient four-legged machines for pulling ploughs and carts – and now lighters; when she walked down the stable-yard past the protruding heads she could not tell which were new arrivals and which had been sold: it was one undifferentiated stream of horseflesh. For Mrs Saunders, it was poetry.

Her son Gideon, and the head groom, did the day-to-day work – travelling to shows and fairs to buy; breaking in; training for riding or draught or carriage-work; negotiating sales – but Mrs Saunders' was the guiding hand. She inspected each new arrival, and could tell its height at a glance, for she knew how many hands high her chin was. Every morning she went out to the stables to cast her eye over the daily operations, the mucking out and feeding, the grooming, and then the saddling up for exercise; and she was always snatching the broom or the bowl of oats from the stable-lad's hands, and doing the job herself. She grabbed muzzles, to peer into that most unlovable orifice, a horse's mouth, and ensure that the teeth had not been filed down to make the animal seem younger: she put hoofs over her knee like a blacksmith, and barged fearlessly into loose-boxes with notorious kickers. Periodically she went out in the trap to look at the stock at grass in a meadow on the upland near Holme, driving the trap herself, with Hester accompanying her. Mrs Saunders was at her most queenly on these outings, her hat tied on with a veil, her gauntleted hands waving condescending greetings to trembling tradesmen. This was an occasion when her deafness sustained her dignity, for though the little fat pony broke wind stertorously all the way, Mrs Saunders remained heedless and serene – only once remarking, above the trumpetings, that the country smelt very rich today.

It was all a strange world to Hester, but an interesting one; and once or twice it afforded her a glimpse into a much higher sphere. Whilst the yard dealt chiefly in stock for farm work and tradesmen's carts, they handled carriage-horses and hunters too for the shires to the west; and rich gentry who would not so much as tie their own bootlaces came in person to Mrs Saunders. Hester, rather to her surprise, was specifically told to be present when Mrs Saunders received these influential customers: afterwards she thought that lady was seeking to impress by thus displaying her own waiting-woman. One of these customers was actually a Sir Something; another was a lady whose name was prefixed with The Honourable, though Hester couldn't see what was honourable about her, except that she had gloves that buttoned right up her arms, and a whole dead bird on her hat. There was, after all, some sort of fairness in the world, Hester thought: for though these people had all the money, they talked like congenital idiots.

Someone who was always present at these occasions was Mrs Saunders' eldest son Gideon.

Gideon was something of a dandy – something, but not much. His lilac suede gloves and double-breasted waistcoats had an air of belonging to someone else: he seemed rather to lurk within his chimney-pot collars than to wear them. His hair had a habit of sticking up at the back, which no amount of macassar oil would remedy, and when he paused, as he often did, before mirrors, he seemed to hover in a brooding region between vanity and doubt. A new mother-of-pearl tie-pin, patted at frequent intervals, cried out for comment: Hester obliged, saying, 'Oh! I do like that tie-pin'; Gideon said, 'Oh! that,' appeared to have forgotten it, patted it again, then glowered suspiciously at her as if fearing mockery; and further convinced Hester that she and Gideon were never going to hit it off.

He was a thin sandy man of thirty, with small eyes and an undernourished moustache marooned on a long expanse of upper lip. His prominent Adam's-apple was offset by an absence of chin – just as if he had swallowed it at some point in his nervous chewings and munchings, and it was now only to be seen forever bobbing up and down his hairless throat. His mother called him Giddy (which he was far from) except when they were receiving that top-drawer company, when she addressed him as Gideon in awful tones. Leaning with uneasy negligence on the mantelpiece, Gideon hung on every constipated word that fell from the lips of Sir Something or the Honourable Dead-Bird, his face frozen in a half-smile of ingratiation; and sometimes he would fling himself rashly into conversation:

'Shall we see you at the Norfolk Show, I wonder, Sir Leonard?'

'Gideon,' Mrs Saunders would say, her voice coming down like a guillotine, 'go and bring the mare in out of the paddock.' And off, crushed, he would go.

His subservience to his mother was complete. It had given him a sort of habitual furtiveness, so that he even ate his breakfast eggs as if they were so much humble pie, and drank his tea as if quite prepared to be told to stop doing it. He was busy all day, training and riding, clipping new stock, and travelling often to horse fairs and auctions; but Mrs Saunders poured him only a half measure of responsibility, and none of that strong liquor authority at all. One morning he brought home from the station a horse he had bought that was no bargain: it turned out to be lame in the left front foot, which the dealer had concealed by the old trick of bruising the right front foot too, thus disguising the favouring. Mrs Saunders was scathing. 'You ever throw money away on such a pig in a poke as that again,' she said, 'and you can do the stable-lad's job, and I'll promote him to yours. He couldn't do worse.' Gideon's ears went crimson – but it was Hester he glared at. He was used to his mother's browbeatings, but not to having them witnessed by this newcomer; and as he plainly dared not resent his mother, he seemed to transfer the resentment to Hester – and it was no good her trying to look away, and appear not to have noticed his humiliation at all.

'Ooh! she can be terrible sharp with Mr Gideon,' Mrs Dawsmere said in the kitchen that night. 'With Mr Lyle, too, though it's not so bad for him, because he don't seem to mind it, and just laughs it off. Mr Gideon teks it more to heart.'

'I wonder he don't just up and start on his own,' Hester said.

'Well, it wouldn't be easy for him. He's hardly got a penny to bless himself with.' Mrs Dawsmere lowered her voice. 'Oh! I know he's got all them fancy clothes – and that smart hunter what he goes to hounds with, though thass mainly to git business – but what I mean is, she gives him an allowance for things like that – very strict – he has to go cap in hand and ask for every last sixpence. Why, there ain't a nail in this whole place what ain't in her name alone, and Mr Gideon and Mr Lyle won't git a morsel of it till her time's up – and mebbe not then if they don't behave theirselves. Such a masterful woman as she is – she'd burn the whole place down to spite 'em, if it meant getting her way. Oh! God forgive me for saying it—' And Mrs Dawsmere incapacitated herself for some moments crossing her fingers, touching wood, and performing some complicated charm involving a lump of coal, the sugar-bowl, and seven human hairs.

'I know how close she is with money,' Hester said. 'She bought me a frock to wear when she's got company, but when I asked her for some pocket-money she nearly bit my head off.'

'Ah! She gives me my wages like they're a favour,' Mrs Dawsmere said, having warded off the evil eye for a few moments. 'But thass just it – there's no wage at all for her sons. I'm heard her say to 'em: what d'you want money for? – you git everything you need here. So they're cheap labour for her, you see. And there's poor Mr Gideon been walking out with Miss Phoebe Purefoy for five years – her father's the corn merchant up Infirmarer's Street.'

'Five years! Why, don't they want to git married before it's too late?'

'Thass just it – there'd be such a to-do if Mr Gideon was to git his courage up and try and git married – Coh dear! I daren't think of it!'

'What about Lyle?' Hester said.

'Oh, Mr Lyle's never give no trouble that way, not yet.

I don't reckon she'll ever let either of them go, though. Not her.'

Well, Hester thought, they must be a poor pair if they'll let one self-willed old woman stand in the way of their happiness. She felt she could perhaps believe it of Gideon: any temptation to sympathise with Gideon Saunders was obviated by the unpleasantness of his character. Privately Hester thought he resembled a weasel. He never laughed but with a cackle of spite; he jealously guarded a dignity he did not possess. To her he adopted a sneering condescension when Mrs Saunders was not around, though she could put up with that: what repelled her was the way he sucked up to those brainless blue-bloods and bullied the stable-boy, whom he addressed with seigneurial disdain; and he made a very sanctimonious fuss when one of the grooms got drunk one night, though Hester often detected on his own breath the smell of surreptitiously supped whisky. But the younger son, Lyle, was an unknown quantity to her – except through his letters to his mother, which it was Hester's job to read out to her.

Lyle Saunders was in Belgium, living with an eminent horse-dealer in Brussels, and establishing a Continental trade link for the Saunders' yard: he had already sent over several pairs of magnificent Percherons which had made the other horses in the yard look like pygmies. His letters were frequent, informative and affectionate; and after Hester became Mrs Saunders' amanuensis for her replies, there was always a friendly mention for her. *'I hope you are not ill-treating that companion of yours, Mother. If she is half as nice as her handwriting I look forward to meeting her. I dare say you let her sleep on the cinders, and feed her on potato peelings: I don't suppose there are many princes round Stokeley way, but you never know – there might be the odd prince out on Chatteris Fen, down on his luck, and lifting carrots with his crown on – so you'd better watch out.'*

'Daft beggar,' Mrs Saunders said, laughing and tutting at herself for doing so. 'He always was as daft as a brush.'

It was an odd sensation for Hester to be writing and reading letters to and from a person she had never met. She found herself looking forward to the arrival of those envelopes with the funny foreign stamp and violet ink: and wondering greatly what Lyle looked like. She could of course have asked Mrs Dawsmere, but she did not do so, perhaps from fear of being disappointed – he might look like Gideon.

She had entered her fourth week of employment at Saunders' horse-yard when Gideon's paramour, Phoebe Purefoy, was invited to Sunday tea – or at least, Gideon tentatively announced that she was coming, and Mrs Saunders acquiesced with an ominous silence. Sundays there were not characterised by the strong devotions of the Langtofts' farm. Mrs Saunders was Anglican – on taking Hester on, she had sharply demanded of her whether she were church or chapel, which was like asking a cat whether it preferred turnips or parsnips – and apart from the mandatory visit to Stokeley's old abbey church, where she gorgonised various tradesmen as they tried to hide behind their hymn-books, she chiefly marked the Sabbath with vast meals, so that the big house was all a-swelter with roasting and baking from dawn to dusk. Tea was a gargantuan affair of ham and potted meat and pork-pies and fruit tarts; and contemplating the laden table on the day Phoebe Purefoy was expected, Hester thought there was something specially daunting about it all. Everything was weighty in Mrs Saunders' house: the great cut-glass salad-bowl could only be moved by putting both arms around it, and the cake-stand was like an altar; and all the clumsiest, most stiff-necked china and cutlery seemed to have been got out for this occasion – as if with the intention of confounding Phoebe Purefoy with sheer weight of crockery. That her welcome was not to be a genial one Hester had already gathered, when helping Mrs Saunders to dress: 'I'd better put on my best, I suppose,' she had said, 'seeing as we've got Miss coming to quiz us.'

At four o'clock Gideon came in attended by a sort of supernumerary shadow, which gradually detached itself and became a young lady dressed, with Gideon's gingerly elegance, in a tight-waisted dress and a zouave jacket over puffed silk sleeves. She was introduced to Hester, and gave her a little cold apologetic hand, as if she were purchasing with a ten-shilling note from someone who had no change; and in the same shrinking manner greeted Mrs Saunders, who intoned in a voice like a gong: 'I hope I find you well, Miss'

– giving this title a terrible bitterness – and led them straight in to tea.

Phoebe Purefoy, by the equine standards prevalent at Saunders', must have been judged deficient in Bone. If Mrs Saunders was a good strong hack, Phoebe Purefoy was a soft-mouthed pony, sufficient only to pull an old lady's dog-cart. She was a very well-washed young woman, apparently in some peril of being washed away completely, with neat coils of buttery hair and a pretty heart-shaped face that continually blushed, not in becoming touches of pink, but with a brick-red glow: Hester sitting opposite her could almost fèel the heat. It was clear that her attitude to the world was deferential, not only from the way she seemed to wind herself placatingly round the table leg, but from a habit she had of murmuring 'Thank you' at arbitrary moments, in a sort of universal propitiation. Hester already knew Mrs Saunders well enough to see that, quite apart from her general disapproval of canoodling and all its works, Miss Purefoy was not the sort of girl to please her: what converted worse to worst was the fact that Gideon's sweetheart had a very soft and low voice. And what Mrs Saunders could not hear, did not exist.

'Mother,' Gideon said, 'Phoebe's father was telling me his carriage-horse was sickly, and he had a farrier in from Chatteris, instead of old Reeves. Found him much more reliable.' Mr Reeves, the Stokeley veterinary surgeon, was not found very satisfactory: rather to the disadvantage of his professional authority, he was frightened of animals. 'What was the man's name again, Phoebe?'

'Ashley, I believe,' Phoebe said. 'Which is rather odd because that's my mother's maiden name, though there's no relation, but it shows what a small world it is, as they say. Of course she came from—'

'Reeves ought to retire and let a younger man in – that's what he ought to do,' declared Mrs Saunders, cutting across Phoebe's cooings like an axe through cobwebs. 'The man's got a few bob – he's diddled enough out of me.' She munched loudly: Mrs Saunders had all her own teeth, and seemingly a few more.

'Father thought at first that what the poor horsey had was

141

something called glanders,' Phoebe said – making, Hester surmised, a valiant attempt to tailor her conversation to Mrs Saunders' interests. 'I always thought that was a place but apparently not. They do say you learn something every day. It turned out that the horsey only had—'

'Hester,' Mrs Saunders said, 'did I tell you I've run out of my liver pills? Anyway, I have. You'll have to run over to Robson's after tea and get me some more.'

Phoebe being placed on her right, behind a monstrous glass vase of irises, Mrs Saunders was able to stare chewingly straight ahead, and not see her. Perhaps in an attempt to counteract this, Phoebe leaned forward across the table in a wriggling manner, and said, 'Oh, do you suffer from the liver, Mrs Saunders? So does my father – sometimes he's hardly able to stir out of the house – though Mother says that's a good thing in a way as it stops him overworking which he's rather inclined to do – so as they say it's an ill wind that blows nobody any good—' seeming thus to habitually fall back on the proverbial, for sheer fear of committing herself to a personal opinion.

'Pass me the cress, Hester,' Mrs Saunders said – for, of course, she could not hear.

'Do you ride, Miss Purefoy?' Hester said, feeling sorry for her.

'Oh! I've been learning to – thank you – Giddy has been teaching me for a year or more but I'm afraid I don't get on very well. At least, I can get on all right, but somehow I can't make the horsey go where I want it to – I keep clicking my tongue and saying giddy up – which is quite a funny thing when Giddy's standing by because he says "Up where?" – pretending he thinks I'm talking to him, you see – and we do laugh – thank you.'

'You're improving all the time,' Gideon said. 'Just takes a bit of confidence.'

'Oh! well, I'm sure Giddy – thank you – I feel very confident with you helping me.'

'That hackney you bought's a sticky trotter,' Mrs Saunders thundered at Gideon, visibly shaking him out of canoodling mood. 'You still hoping to drive that at Peterborough Show?

I doubt it'll be trained in time. Got a bit of a wooden mouth too, if you want my opinion.'

'What does that mean – a wooden mouth?' Phoebe said.

A large black-clad patch of silence met her.

'It means the horse doesn't respond very well,' Gideon said.

Mrs Saunders' resolute deafness persisted to the end of the meal. By that time Phoebe Purefoy seemed herself to doubt whether she actually existed, and appeared to catch sight of her reflection in the hall mirror with a start of surprise. A short interval in the parlour followed, during which Phoebe was obliterated again, by being buried in the most massive of the wing chairs, and towered over by a giant potted fern. She very soon took her leave, quite beaten down by overpowering furnishings, and utterly defeated by Mrs Saunders' determination not to know she was there at all.

Gideon went too, to see Phoebe home. Hester saw a glitter of triumph in Mrs Saunders' deep-set eyes, but all the old lady said was, 'Bah, it wears me out, entertaining all this company. Well, go on, gel – step over to Robson's and get me my pills.'

'Mr Robson perhaps won't like being disturbed on a Sunday.'

'Won't he indeed! I don't know who Pop Robson thinks he is to put on airs. The day he got married they had to have a midwife as a bridesmaid just in case. Go on, don't dawdle.'

Robson was a pharmacist, whose shop was at the other end of the High Street. The town was quiet at the glimmering candle-end of the spring day: nothing moved on the river, and there were only a few strollers, wearing Sunday hats and faces. Hester lingered on the narrow stone bridge, looking down at the green water steeped in sky. Suddenly another head appeared beside the rippling image of her own.

'Oh! it's you,' she said, finding herself face to face with Jonathan Eastholm.

'Hullo,' he said awkwardly. He seemed unchanged since their last meeting: shirt-sleeved, brown, hard-lipped, frowning as he looked at her as if she were a bright light: though she had forgotten just how much height and breadth there was to him.

'You back in Stokeley, then?' she said. 'Well – I can see you are.'

'Moored down by the Abbey. Moving on soon,' he said. 'Fact is – I'm glad I saw you.'

'Are you? Well, that's a first, any road.'

'Ah – I just wondered – whether you were all right. Whether you'd got work.'

'Oh! yes. I had a bit of luck.' She told him of her job with Mrs Saunders: though the meditative gaze he threw down at the water below made her wonder if he was listening.

'So you're all right then?' he said at last.

'Yes,' she said. 'Thank you.' Now I'm sounding like Phoebe, she thought. 'Are you?'

'Eh? Oh! yes.' He continued to stand there, like some muscular excrescence grown out of the bridge. 'I just wondered. As long as you're all right.' And then, abruptly, he walked past her.

'Goodbye,' she said; and went on to Robson's, thinking to herself that her absence from the lighters had done nothing to improve Eastholm's command of the social graces. All very well to go asking her now if she was all right, she reflected as she returned home with Mrs Saunders' pills (huge pink bullets that she swallowed in horse-like quantities): it might have been better if he'd been a bit more solicitous when she was wearing herself to a frazzle on those wretched lighters. But perhaps that was what was behind the odd little scene – a belated guilt on his part at the way he had treated her.

Gideon had just arrived back before her, and was closeted with his mother in the parlour. Hester went up to her room to change out of her walking-dress, and was half-way down the staircase when she was arrested by a great wail issuing from the parlour.

She ran in, and found Gideon standing on the hearth-rug, plucking his lip, his face as white as flour: and Mrs Saunders in her chair, emitting another moan of lamentation. It seemed she had had one of the cats on her lap when stricken with this loud grief, and in the absence of an apron had buried her face in the animal, and was sobbing into it – the cat reacting to this unexpected turn of events by peering over its shoulder and looking exquisitely displeased.

'Whatever's the matter?' Hester said.

Gideon shot her a bitter glance, as if her being privy to this was another mark against her. 'Nothing,' he said unconvincingly.

'No! it's nothing,' Mrs Saunders groaned, muffled with cat. 'Just my own son turning against me – that's all.'

'I'm not turning against you, Mother,' Gideon said. 'I'm only saying what we want to do – I didn't mean—'

'Oh! you do what you like,' Mrs Saunders said. 'You just carry on. I've had my time – just leave me here to die, seeing as that's what you want.'

'That's not what I want, Mother—'

'If I was a horse you'd shoot me – you would!'

'Mother, I wouldn't—'

'And it'd be kinder. It'd be kinder if you'd just shoot me here and now. Your father's old gun's in the tackle-room – you might as well go and get it. Hester, fetch me my smelling-salts.'

'You haven't got any smelling-salts,' Hester said in surprise.

'Even my help's against me!' wailed Mrs Saunders. The cat had had enough and bolted from her arms. 'And Tipsy as well. I wish I were dead.'

'Mother,' Gideon said, 'please don't take on like this. I only suggested . . . I never meant—'

'I know what you meant! Help me to bed, gel.' Mrs Saunders struggled out of her chair and leant on Hester's arm, though her touch did not feel noticeably weak. 'My son doesn't want me around any more – I may as well get out of his sight.'

Hester accompanied her upstairs. 'Mrs Saunders, what is the matter?' she said – though she had a fair idea.

'Draw the curtains, gel. Shut out the light. I can't bear it. I'm fit to fly. What's the matter? Me – that's what. I've done my best for my boys, but they don't want me.' She went down on the bed like a dropped sack of oats. 'Giddy came back from seeing Miss home and marched straight up to me and stabbed me in the heart. Or that's what it felt like. He says he wants to get engaged – him and Miss. Engaged. You know what that means. Oh! I don't know why he had to come and tell me –

seeing as he's made his mind up. Just to crow over me I suppose – just to rub salt in the wound – just to see me weep.' All this in a loud voice, conspicuously audible to Gideon tapping at the door outside. 'I thought I'd a bit of life left to me – I thought my boys would allow me that, after all I've done for them. But no. He wants to just chuck me away like an old shoe. Don't let him in, gel! He doesn't want to see me anyway. The only way he wants to see me is in my shroud – and he will soon – it'll not be long.'

Mrs Saunders took to her bed. This, Hester learned from Mrs Dawsmere, was not a new strategy where a conflict of will with her sons was concerned; but she pursued it with grim application. For three days the curtains remained closed and Mrs Saunders lay in stately despair: the face of a stony martyr, above a black crocheted bed-jacket, scrutinised the ceiling. Meals were sent away untouched, and only Hester was allowed in the shaded room. Gideon came periodically to knock on the door and plead with his mother.

'Let me in, Mother – please. Just let me explain. I only wanted – that is, we only wanted – to ask your permission—'

'We, he says!' cried Mrs Saunders. 'Oh! it's We now. Well, that says it all. I suppose Miss wants this bedroom, does she? Well, I'm dying in it as fast as I can. I'll be leaving it soon. That should be some satisfaction to you.'

He came back again. 'Mother, listen. All I meant was that we – I – was thinking about an engagement. Nothing more than that for the time being—'

'For the time being! Ah! I know. Just give it a little while, you said to Her, and then we can get rid of the old nuisance. I know. Well, I'm trying to save you the trouble, son. You'll be shut of your burden soon.'

'What's she doing in there?' Gideon said to Hester, when she came down for dinner.

'Just lying there,' Hester said.

'I wish she'd just listen for half a minute,' said Gideon in his whining way, gnawing at his lips.

But she is listening, Hester thought: she's listening to every word you say. And none of it's any good. She's not going to

146

meet you half-way, or one-tenth of the way: that's the point. She won't be satisfied till you and poor old Phoebe have surrendered completely. And then you'll be walking out for another five years . . . Hester would have counselled him to stand up to her, but she knew Gideon would be uppity if he thought he was being given advice by a paid servant; and besides, it was not easy to feel for someone who had so little that was likeable about him.

On the third day Gideon came supplicating to the closed door on another matter – business. A wealthy customer had taken a fancy to that grey hunter, and was prepared to pay any price – but they had half promised the animal to that lady from St Ives . . . what was he to do? Such knotty decisions had always been taken by Mrs Saunders, and Gideon was helpless. His mother had ensured this helplessness, of course, by exactly that tactic of never allowing him responsibility. Hester had to admire her shrewdness.

'But what shall I tell him, Mother?'

'Oh! don't ask me, son,' Mrs Saunders said mournfully from the bed. 'You don't need me now – you said so yourself. You're the one who knows it all. I'm just a makeweight about the place. Ask your Miss – she's the important one, apparently.'

Gideon gave a wretched little groan, and his footsteps died away down the stairs.

'I hope he's not such a fool as to turn that offer down,' Mrs Saunders said to the ceiling.

There was discussion in the kitchen that night. Judy the maid, vengefully sewing, said it was only to be expected when folk would get involved with Attachments: the head groom recalled a time when they had a stallion that was so savage nobody would go near it, except Mrs Saunders herself, and she just slipped a halter over its head like a ribbon on a kitten, and said he wouldn't put it past her to starve herself to death up there; Mrs Dawsmere said this was the longest she had ever gone. Hester was about to say that if Gideon had any sense he would call her bluff, when Gideon himself appeared at the top of the kitchen steps.

'Hester – will you come please – Mrs Saunders is getting up –

and Mrs Dawsmere, boil a couple of eggs and make some toast and tea . . .'

Hester found Mrs Saunders sitting up in bed and dabbing her eyes with a handkerchief. 'Ah, there you are, gel,' she said in a weak voice. 'Pass me a clean handkerchief out of that drawer, will you?'

Hester did so: though neither the first handkerchief, nor Mrs Saunders' eyes, seemed at all wet.

'You will eat something now, won't you, Mother?' Gideon said, sitting down in the chair by the bed.

'I'll try and swallow a morsel,' Mrs Saunders said. She turned a marmoreally tragic face to her son. 'I did hear you right, didn't I, Giddy? – because you know I'm a bit troubled in the ears. I couldn't bear to think I'd heard you wrong.' She glanced briefly at Hester – who realised she was being used as a witness. 'Just – just tell me again.'

'Yes, you did hear me right, Mother,' Gideon said, with a glance of his own at Hester, not at all friendly.

'Tell me again.'

'I shan't say any more about – I promise I shan't say any more about getting engaged.'

'Or think it?' Mrs Saunders said, her voice noticeably less weak.

'Or think it. I shan't get engaged. You're to forget it ever happened.' In Gideon's demeanour as he said this there was more than a little of the reprimanded schoolboy, which formed a droll contrast with his man-of-the-world collar and two-tone shoes. Hester was amused: but with a twang of distaste. Poor Phoebe! So he had unconditionally surrendered. She knew one thing – she wouldn't put up with that sort of pusillanimity in a man.

Mrs Saunders exhaled a sigh. 'I suppose you think I'm a silly old woman.'

*Silly*'s not the word I'd use, thought Hester, as she went down to fetch the eggs and toast.

'Oh! I shall never manage all this,' Mrs Saunders said, on being presented with the tray. But she did, pausing only to complain that the eggs were overcooked. Within an hour she was up and dressed, and ramping about the house and stables, setting to rights everything that had been neglected during her absence from its affairs. 'Can't take my eye off things for two minutes,' she declared: while Hester followed in her wake, dispatched hither and yon to fetch and carry and to tell Judy this and Mrs Dawsmere that, and barely able to keep up with this elderly woman who a short while ago had been ready to turn her face to the wall. By the time Hester retired to bed, she was more weary than she had been since she had worked on the lighters.

Sinking into bed, she was reminded of the strange meeting with Jonathan Eastholm on Stokeley bridge. There were still times, if she woke in the night, when she thought for a moment she was still on the lighters, and seemed to hear the lapping of the water round the bows. Now an idea occurred to her – perhaps he had found no one else to do the job, and had been about to ask her to come back! Now that *was* funny.


2


The elderly man who was Hester's replacement on Eastholm's gang of lighters was an experienced waterman who could do the work in his sleep, and sometimes seemed to. Not only was he capable but he was extremely taciturn: he could go a whole stoical day without uttering more than a couple of monosyllables. All in all Eli, as he was called, was an eminently suitable companion for Jonathan Eastholm. And Jonathan Eastholm found that he hated him.

At first, Jonathan thought he knew how to account for this. He must be suffering from an attack of the Old Goblin. This was a term that he had privately framed for himself to express the fits of fierce melancholy that seized him from time to time. Such a mood assailed him without warning, and had done so ever since he had reached manhood: the mood seemed to both darken and intensify his vision, so that the simplest external events rasped against his consciousness like sandpaper, and the disregarding flux of the world suddenly bristled with menacing import. At such a time the not uncommon sight of a stray dog drowned in the river, for example, filled him with black thoughts: cruel aimless presences stalked his dreams, and the hand of an injudicial dispenser of suffering seemed discernible behind all the processes of the universe; he found himself both tending to a cosmic pessimism, and deprived of the sense of proportion that would have allowed him to laugh at himself for it. The way in which this mood overcame him, as if it were some extrinsic visitation rather than an inner state of feeling, caused him to give it the name of the Old Goblin: and he believed it must be the Goblin's unwelcome presence that was making him sharply dissatisfied with Eli, with the lighters, with himself, with everything.

And yet it did not have the familiar malicious features of the Old Goblin. It looked somehow different.

Jonathan Eastholm was not born complete, fully formed and alone out of the waters of the fens, though such was the impression he often gave, and perhaps chose to give. Scarcely anyone knew his history: he did not care to tell it. Its leading event was the death of his father when he was a boy, and his mother's subsequent remarriage. His father being a man kind only in his cups, and seldom then, and given to augmenting the miseries of poverty by a liberal use of the strap on both wife and son, there could only be the prospect of better times in the acquisition of a stepfather who seemed demonstrably fond of his mother, did not drink, and was a market-gardener in a small way, in the orchard country around Wisbech. Such was the supposition of the boy Jonathan – who, it turned out, was the one unwanted factor in this comfortable equation. The market-gardener wanted a wife: he did not want a ready-made son, already growing tall, and with a deplorable habit of eating. The memory of the methods by which his stepfather had signalled to his young and vulnerable self that he was to get out and not come back remained fresh to Jonathan yet, in his twenty-fifth year, but he would never let that memory out. A similar pain attached to the memory of his mother, too crushed and ineffectual to protest at her son's treatment – a treatment which did not last long, for Jonathan put an end to it by leaving: he would not plead or cling. While other boys, even on the ill-educated fens, were still at school, he went to work on the land, at a good distance from the home he could no longer claim. The crucial junction of feeling at which he found himself at this time of his life might have been expressed in three words: 'All right: alone.' But he did not say them to anyone; for the resolution embodied in those words precluded trust, confidences, or communication.

His years of labour on fen farms, where his strength and endurance became a byword, were terminated as he had related to Hester, by his scraping up enough money at last to hire his first lighters. This was a life that had long attracted him by virtue of its complete independence. By this time all his ties were gone. His mother had died in giving birth to his stepfather's child, which had outlived her but a few days. His stepfather, perhaps finding the management of his business a strain, perhaps remorseful, had soon afterwards invited Jonathan back. Jonathan was having none of it. The self-reliance which had been forced upon him, he had now come to embrace: the solitariness that had been grafted on to his personality was now an ingrained part of it, as a living tree will grow round a nail. He loved his life on the waterways of the fens, and wanted nothing better.

He prospered modestly on the lighters, having few wants and no dependants. He earned a name for driving a hard but scrupulously fair bargain. That he never at any time engaged in the mildly shady dealing that most watermen did, was attributable to a fastidious and rather severe sense of what could only be called honour – an abstraction he valued the more, because he had been treated with the opposite. Probably the same causes lay at the root of his somewhat sternly judgemental attitude to others. He had grown to a young man with only a limited tolerance of human frailty, who was more surprised than gratified when people behaved well.

The books which Hester had observed in his cabin had for some time been his closest companions, and with his formal education having been early terminated, he schooled himself to learn their ways with much labour and struggle. *Pilgrim's Progress* and *Robinson Crusoe* he knew virtually by heart: *Paradise Lost* he had begun several times, always retiring defeated by its difficulty, though never without a sort of swimming wonder and a sense of having glimpsed something as elusively glorious as the vaporous galleries that opened up momentarily in the vaulted clouds of the fen sunset. He dearly loved a song, too, but was disabled by a conviction that this was somehow unmanly of him, and a sort of shame clung about the old concertina he had bought and taught himself to play. It was an uncompromising version of maleness that Jonathan Eastholm had constructed for himself: it combined with that rigorous code of honesty which made him intolerant of those who did not come up to similar standards, and with the sheer habit of being alone, to make him cold and short in company. Added to this was an aggressive species of egalitarianism natural to horizontal landscapes, which historically has made flat lowland countries the most anti-aristocratic; and it was no wonder that he was known as an unapproachable customer. If his great generosity, a warm lining to a rough topcoat, was less well known, it was partly because he was always afraid of its being abused.

There was more than a touch of the ascetic about him, as Hester had discerned in his addiction to cold plunges – and in deference to her he had moderated a habit of semi-nudity, which had once led him forgetfully to enter a neat little waterside shop clad in only his trousers, to the screams of the maiden lady behind the counter. In his moral scheme simplicity assumed the value of the highest good: he was uncomfortable in towns, and of the sophisticated appurtenances of technical civilisation he made use of little more than the printed book and the oil-stove. To see Jonathan Eastholm standing on the deck of his house-lighter whilst in the background a steam-train beetled across the fen, was to see the juxtaposition of two different worlds, and to feel that this oaklike figure had more in common with his Saxon ancestors than with his coevals speeding on their coal-driven, steel-thewed way. That he was impervious to cold and wet and discomfort did not generally mean that he was insensible, but that he was occupied with his own thoughts, which in his solitude came to represent a much nearer reality. In another age and clime Jonathan might have submitted himself to the disciplines of the Spartan mess, the monastic cell, or the bare feet and begging-bowl of the mountain mystic; but these would have lacked the elemental pleasures that constituted the charm of the life he had made for himself. Such were the sight of cornfields waving under moonlight; the orange-tipped flight of swans against the fiery cold of a winter sunset; the fatly buoyant shapes of ducks on the water, scarcely troubling themselves to hustle out of the path of the lighters, as if he and his boats appeared to them as no more than gently gliding aspects of the natural landscape. Lying flat on deck and looking up at the stars, which on a summer night could seem as near to the terrestrial observer as cottage lights, he felt there was nothing more to be asked of life. What was most disturbing about his new mood, was that he no longer felt that. Somehow, relish had departed, and Jonathan's palate began to taste the jaded dregs of discontent.

Having been ground in the mill of some pretty hard experience, Jonathan Eastholm considered his development complete, and did not believe he had anything more to learn about life. Womanhood belonged only to the irrelevant margins of his actuality, and the taking on of Hester Verney as a temporary workmate had not seemed to threaten this. He had been heartily glad to get rid of her – and once she was gone he could not stop thinking about her.

He thought, repetitively, maddeningly, of everything that had happened while she had been on the lighters, until that short time seemed to stretch and fill half his past life. What an infuriating little beggar she could be! – the way she had chucked those turves in the river, just to get back at him! He should have known she was that sort from the moment she came and took the empty chair opposite him that night at the Ferryman – there was something about her mouth – even when it was not smiling it seemed just about to. The devilish sort. He hated that sort. But then the way she had outfaced old Shush Hubbard – that was a good one. And then that wonderful clear still evening at Littleport, when she had got him talking about *Robinson Crusoe* . . . How had she done that? His pleasures were personal and private – a part of himself: it alarmed him, the way she had drawn him out, and tempted him to share them.

Still, she was a giddy beggar – and fancied herself something rotten – always after a compliment. Well, she *was* pretty, no doubt about it, but he wasn't going to play that game. Nosy too.

'Git used to anything, I suppose,' he said to the horse – it was no use speaking to Eli, that was like talking to the wall. 'Miss an ulcer when it's gone.'

He had got used to her, in a way – which was why it had been such a shock for him that last night at the Cutter when she had suddenly appeared in her woman's clothes again. There had been something baffling and dismaying about her beauty, and the realisation that he had been so close to it all this time: that these distracting eyes, lips, and other things had been smuggled into the jealously guarded confines of his independence. He could not have described the way he had felt that night as he walked up the towpath to the inn beside her, looking the way she did, except that there was something in it of pain, of being probed and invaded. His silence that night had belied a great internal noise of tocsins and alarums, manning of battlements and raising of drawbridges.

She represented something quite new in his view of the world. As a native of the fens, and travelling constantly about their high-banked waterways, Jonathan was accustomed to contemplating far horizons: his eyes dwelt often too on the detailed foreground, in the pages of a book; but towards the middle distance of life he had developed a certain blindness, which found a correlative in the short-sighted look of his eyes. Now, occupying this former blankness was the figure of the girl, even more vivid to him since she had gone, so that he found himself staring at the canvas stool on the deck and thinking, 'That's where she sat – just there – I can see her now.'

'Whass up?' said Eli – who was sitting on the stool. This was a long speech for him.

'Oh! nothing,' Jonathan said: but he knew something was, very gravely, up. These feelings were strange to him: he was adrift and without bearings. The books he had read gave him no guidance, being of the stern kind, puritan not cavalier. In this benightedness, he at first mistook the specific for the general, and sought a solvent for his unrest in making a night of it with some fellow-watermen at a riverside inn where the girls were known for their friendliness – thinking that what ailed him was a late manifestation of a trivial urge which he had hitherto dismissed as a fool's game. But the laborious flirting in the smoky parlour bored him within a few minutes: he supposed, in the abstract, that the girls were pretty, but their dull talk and sheepish faces repelled him; and he very soon sloped off.

The experience was useful, however. It threw into stronger relief the figure of the one girl, the unique girl, and compelled him to confront the implications of the way this figure haunted him. She was the first thing he thought of when he woke: at intervals during the day he suffered something like mental palpitations when the image came to him unbidden of some element of her, such as the way her pink tongue showed against her teeth when she laughed. (He thought of this, of which Hester was unaware, rather than her hair, of which she was so vain: the things people love about us and the things we expect to be loved for seldom coincide.) And he came out of his reveries to see the plodding horse, and the river banks, and another lock ahead, and the familiar crabbed face of the lock-keeper leaning on his gate, and it all seemed dismayingly aimless and tasteless.

She had broken up his carefully constructed life, and he half hated her for it. He seemed to lose his identity. The precincts of self in which he had loved to dwell were no longer an ample habitation containing all he needed, but an airless prison, from the walls of which his sole voice resounded in dullest echoes.

'Well, this can't go on,' he said to himself. 'I shall have to do something.' For Jonathan the accession of these disturbing feelings was not an occasion of joy in itself: the springs of his nature were still too tightly wound for that; he sought the restoration of the lost equilibrium. 'I shall have to marry the girl,' said he. 'Thass all there is to it!'

It was all an infernal disruption, not what he had intended for himself at all, but he was lost without her, and there was no help for it. His mind leaped forward from perplexity to decision with characteristic directness, and with never a glance to right or left, wherein he might have seen the more dubious aspects of his case – those shadowy regions of contingency in which most lovers dwell, touched by subtle winds of fear and hope.

The recognition of his longing, and the possession of its object, appeared to him as successive stages linked by a straight smooth path. The fact that he and Hester Verney had fought like cat and dog virtually throughout their short association seemed an insignificant eddy against the tide of his will.

It would be unfair to Jonathan to state that he scarcely thought of Hester's possible feelings at all: even the most altruistic love, looked at in a certain light, is mere indulgence of self; and besides, the moment of his decision was immediately succeeded by his asking himself the question: would she have him? In this he was deeply influenced by her final verdict on life as a waterman: 'This is no life for a human being at all – it's no life for a dog!' These words had burned into Jonathan like a cattle-brand: they stayed with him through all the restless, empty days following her departure, until the awakening of his feelings for her, and their prospective resolution, became inextricably linked with them. She had left because she found the hardships of the lighters intolerable. She would never marry him whilst that was the only life he could offer her. The lighters would have to go. She would want a house.

Habituated as he was to living at the pace of a dawdling barge-horse, Jonathan could also be extraordinarily swift both in the making of his decisions and their execution – a speed facilitated by his austere circumstances, untrammelled by ties. When Hester met him on Stokeley bridge, his choice was already made – he had been asking after her in the town that day – and only the fact that his plans were not quite complete had prevented him speaking out there and then. He had already concluded a deal to sell his gang of lighters to a small Whittlesey brickyard, who were seeking to do their own transporting: and he had a house in view.

That the house was not finished did not daunt him. It stood at the end of a long drove on Hinching Fen, a tiny cottage built of clunch and thatch – with only half a roof, and windows yet unglazed, and a bare earth floor. It belonged to an acquaintance of his, a former waterman, who had found himself in possession of five lighter-loads of building materials when the dealer for whom he was carrying them defaulted, and so had decided to realise a long-cherished dream of settling down as a one-hoss farmer. At the depressed prices typical of these remote spots he had bought a building-plot and hired a few acres, begun his house and his new life, and found the whole business intolerable within a few months, so that he had not even the heart to finish the building, and was rained on through the gaping roof while his heart hankered for the freedom of his old brawny, boozing, rootless ways. He was desperate to sell up, and could hardly wait to get Jonathan to the solicitor's in Stokeley, and be rid of the place, stock and all.

'I'll be honest with you, Jonathan bor,' he said. 'It's the loneliness I can't abide. Thass a different sort of being-on-your-ownsome from the lighters, somehow: I hope you can tek to it.'

Jonathan was not listening. He was looking round at the four walls, and picturing bringing here the girl whose image gave him no rest. A house: a house was the one thing needful; she would want a house. It did not occur to him that he might be starting from the wrong end. The sheer idea of a house had become so firmly linked in his mind with the success of his suit, that he considered them as good as married by the acquisition of it.

He would purchase it. The sale of his lighters would only just meet the cost: he negotiated a further advance of money from the proprietor of the brickyard, who knew him well, and trusted him. Such a wrenching and uprooting of the massive solidity of his nature had these new emotions caused that he was able thus, in the space of a few weeks, to completely transform the conditions of his existence with equanimity, and even with impatience that the processes of law did not allow it to go through more quickly. But there was nothing else for it: the life of the waterways had formerly defined his personality, but it did so no longer – he was like a scripturalist scuttled by Darwin – he would have been living a lie.

There was ten days' hiatus between the brickyard's entering into possession of his lighters, and Jonathan's entering into possession of the half-finished cottage. For that time he lodged there with his friend, and threw himself into the working of the few acres – only half of them planted – as the latter had never

157

found the energy to do. One fine May morning, however, he left the seed-drill and the hoe, put on his best neckerchief, and set out to walk across the fen to Stokeley.


3


Gideon Saunders' wild gesture of rebellion had ended in defeat and capitulation. He knew better than to dispute the terms of the peace. But if his subjugation to his mother was complete and unprotesting, his resentment of Hester, the witness of his humiliation, became more sharply defined. A needling slyness entered his manner to her. He would seek the newspaper when she was looking at it, and then on her offering it, say airily, 'Oh! no, don't mind me, I wouldn't dream of troubling you.' He delighted to bring her messages from Mrs Saunders: 'Mother says would you go down to Robson's for her embrocation. Sorry to put you to such trouble. It's a hard life, isn't it?' Hester met all this with a brilliant glassy smile which seemed to satisfactorily unnerve him, and indulged herself with private fantasies of sneaking into his room when he was asleep and snipping off his ridiculous moustache.

From the absent son, Lyle, there had been no communication for a while, so when a letter with the familiar Belgian stamp arrived one morning, Hester took it straight out to the yard, where Mrs Saunders and Gideon were watching the clipping of a young bay that had just been fetched from the station. This was the first stage in a process at which the Saunders establishment was adept – the transformation of unpromising horseflesh. After the clipping, which left just a saddle of longer hair on the back, came the trimming and thinning of the tail, the plaiting of the mane, the burning off of whiskery hairs round muzzle and ears, and then a long course of brushing and currying. The plainest animal came out of the Saunders stables sleek and shapely – and, of course, fetching a higher price.

'There's a letter from Mr Lyle, Mrs Saunders,' Hester said, handing it to her. She turned away so as not to see the application of the twitch to the bay's nose. This was a cord tightened round the flesh between the nostrils with a pole:

its effect was to numb the horse, so that it would not feel the painful pulling out of hairs, but it always made Hester's eyes water to see it.

'Ah! I thought as much – he's coming home. Lyle's coming home – d'you hear, Giddy?' Mrs Saunders said.

'Oh, is he?' Gideon said without enthusiasm.

'He's coming – when's that say, gel? I'm hopeless without my spectacles – read it.'

'He says the end of next week,' Hester said. Lyle had made an arrangement with an English-speaking agent in Brussels, the letter disclosed, who would maintain their contact with the Percheron dealer: the latter was closing up his house for the summer. '"The Dielmans have been very kind to me",' Hester read, '"but oh how I long for English cooking. I keep dreaming about hills of Yorkshire pudding and mountains of Cheddar and lakes of onion-sauce."'

'Ha-ha!' Mrs Saunders' big hard laugh made the horse jump. 'I knew that would happen. They're not as bad as the Frenchies, but still, they're not English, and they do funny things with food. Mix it up together, so I've heard, instead of cooking it separate like civilised folk. Oh! we'd better get ready for him. His room's been shut up all this time. Hester, go and tell Judy to have Mr Lyle's room swept and aired – clean laundry and a fire to take the mustiness off – I want everything homey for him when he comes.'

In the kitchen Mrs Dawsmere was delighted with the news. 'Thass always nicer when Mr Lyle's here. There's more of a smile about the place somehow. That'll be a treat to see him. Oh! now I'm done it – I'm counted me chickens – and him having to cross the water as well – I shall have to sleep with me stockings on tonight, else he'll never git here.'

'Hem!' said Judy, who had just answered a knock at the back kitchen door. 'Pardon ME I'm sure, but it appears there's a Person who wants to see you.'

'Me?' said Hester. 'What sort of person?'

'OH I'm sure I don't know I'm only the MAID after all it's none of MY business,' Judy said on one long plain-song note, gliding past Hester as if she were on wheels, and adding out of the back of her head, 'It's always been MY understanding

159

that the staff weren't allowed FOLLOWERS but there I dare say it's nothing to do with ME.'

Hester went to the door. She was astonished to see Jonathan Eastholm standing there.

'Oh!' she said.

'Hullo,' he said. 'I wanted to speak to you.'

Hester pulled the door to behind her. 'What about? I'm not supposed to have people calling here, you know. Mrs Saunders'll have my head.'

'It's urgent.' He frowned on her. 'Don't they ever let you out?'

'Well – I'm got my day off on Saturday—'

'Right then.'

'But I'm going to see Lizzie – my friend – on Hinching Fen. I go on the morning carrier.'

'Where's the carrier leave from? Spread Eagle yard, ain't it? Right. I'll meet you there. Day to you.'


On Saturday morning Hester walked down Stokeley High Street to the Spread Eagle inn in a condition of perplexity which two days of wondering had done nothing to elucidate. Could it really be that Eastholm wanted her to come back? She knew little enough of him, but she did know he was far from stupid. Did he really believe that she would give up this comfortable job for the purgatory of the lighters? It was baffling.

The Spread Eagle was a large inn which had formerly served as the centre for such coaching trade as the little town had enjoyed. Now its capacious yard, entered by an ivied arch, was the depot for carriers' vans and the gigs of marketing farmers; but the inn still wore a mellow and sleepy look, as if it had scarcely awakened from a dream of former days, and high up on the forehead of its gable-end there was a sundial marked in vague gradations from seven to five, and seeming to say that if there were any more precise ways of measuring time, it didn't want to know about them. The latticed windows were open to the spring day: from the upper storey there was a flapping of sheets and dusters, and from the lower a murmur of talk from farmers smokily taking refreshment in the parlours, which the sunlight never seemed to penetrate, and left as cool, congenial dungeons. Along the outer gable wall there was a high stone bench, and here sat a row of women waiting for the carrier, some who had come in early from the fen to sell a few eggs or a little butter, others setting out on visits to relatives: hopping down from the bench now and again to rearrange something in their baskets, or to shake out their black shawls or re-pin their black bonnets, hopping up again and chatting all at once, like so many inky-plumed and cheerful crows. At the other side of the yard was a solitary cherry tree, leaning at a slouching angle, as if it had imbibed the beeriness of the spot through its roots, and was permanently foxed: an old wooden seat was fixed around its base, with below it a smooth circular groove in the earth, worn down through long years by the shuffling feet of sitters there; and here in the bright sunshine Hester sat and composed herself to wait for the carrier to Whittlesey which passed through Hinching Fen on its circumambient way.

The carriers were more reliable than prompt, and you would have to be pretty late to miss one. A couple of the vans were standing in the yard, their horses stabled in the inn's stalls. They were broad four-wheeled carts, open-ended, with plank seats along each side for passengers and a wooden top. Parts of the fenland were served by the railway, and within the environs of such places as Cambridge and Peterborough the horse-omnibus had lately appeared; but the mass of ordinary folk depended for local transport on these sturdy waggons, which would have been recognisable in their essentials to their ancestors of the Tudor age. The carrier himself did more than just drive the van: for isolated cottagers he was a link with the wider world, fetching miscellaneous shopping from the towns, and carrying in his roomy pockets an item of ironmongery to be mended, a pair of boots to be hobnailed, a couple of plucked chickens to be sold. As a consequence his journeys were slow and roundabout in the extreme: a typical carrier's detour would take him a mile down a drove to deliver a broom-handle to a cottage – the presentation of the broom-handle itself being performed with all the deliberation and ceremony of Black Rod. But no one seemed to mind the slowness; and Hester had once heard an old woman declare, as they rumbled to a halt outside her cottage after three hours had brought them as many miles: 'Well – here we are already! All this flying about meks your head spin!'

Hester had been sitting only a few minutes when she saw the tall form of Jonathan Eastholm appear in the archway, and walk purposefully in her direction. It was the first time she had seen him wearing a hat – a peaked cap, which he swept off as he approached, less it seemed from gallantry than because it irked him. He ran a large brown hand through his hair, and stood looking down at her from his great height, for all the world as if it were she who had asked him for this meeting, and he was wondering why.

'I wish you'd sit down,' Hester said uneasily. 'It meks my neck ache looking up there.' And indeed the upright size of him, interposed between her and the morning sun, created a patch of shade in which she was entirely enclosed.

'No,' he said. 'I don't think I'll sit down.'

'Oh! well – shall I stand up then?'

Jonathan shook his head. 'I wanted desperate to speak to you—'

'Well, I don't know – one minute you can't wait to get rid of me, and the next you're seeking me out again.'

'—And now that it's come, I don't know how to do it,' he concluded, paying no heed to her interruption.

All sorts of vague surmises had begun to crowd in on Hester: but persisting in her first idea she said, 'If it's about going back to the lighters, then you needn't ask. I'm got a very good job at Mrs Saunders' – I know you give me a job when I was down on my luck, but that don't mean—'

'I'm sold the lighters.'

'You never have!'

'I'm sold 'em, and bought a house. A cottage on Hinching Fen – with a bit of working land. It wants the odd finishing touch, but it's a house, fit to mek a fair life in. I worked on farms for years – you know that – I can manage it.'

'I'm sure you can,' she breathed – quite taken aback. She could scarcely picture him separated from the waterways. 'But I thought you loved the lighters.'

'You hated them. That was no life for a dog, you said. I knew

162

you'd never go back to them, so I bought a house.' Jonathan pronounced this as straightforwardly as if he were talking of buying a loaf of bread. 'It ain't a bad little place – come and see it before you decide, if you like.'

'Decide what?'

'Why,' he said with difficulty, 'I wanted to ask you to marry me, you see.'

Part of her mind knew he was quite serious; but another part reacted with disbelieving flippancy. 'So,' she said, 'you have a woman for a week or two on your ole boats, and then you suddenly fancy you want a wife, eh?'

'I'm never wanted a wife,' Jonathan said reflectively. 'Not till now. I don't know as I want one now, come to that. It's all come on me so sudden and I'm not sure I like it. But that don't matter.' For a weird moment she thought he was going to kneel, but he only dropped down on his haunches – the sun's rays streaming in again where his figure had blocked them – so his head was level with hers. 'I can't get on without you, you see,' he said with grim earnestness. 'I don't know how it's happened, but I'm all of a mess. I'm tried to put it out of my mind but I can't – it's made me fit for nothing. So that's why I bought the house, see. For you to live in. The lighters were no good. I knew you'd want a house.'

A suffocating sensation overcame Hester: utterly unprepared as she was, she panted like an animal tensed to flee. 'I don't want a house,' she found herself saying, with some inconsequence.

'Well, thass a story!' Jonathan declared. 'You couldn't abide the way we lived on the lighters – thass why you packed it in. And I suppose it ain't much of a life for a gel. But the house now – thass different.'

'I don't understand you,' cried Hester. 'Do you mean to say you're gone and sold up, and got a house on the fen, just because you took it into your head that – well, that I might marry you?'

'I didn't tek it into my head. You put it there.'

'I never did no such thing!' said she, sharply, for there was accusation in his tone.

'Well, I don't know what else to call it. I never wanted this

163

to happen. I never thought I'd git caught like this – but it's happened, and there's no help for it. I'm got to have you.'

For the moment any incipient feeling of flattery or gratification at this avowal was eclipsed in Hester's mind by indignation. The disaster of Chad and the turf-digging rose vividly before her: here it was repeated! A pile of turf, a pile of bricks – these men seemed to think she was a piece of property, and they had only to put down a material deposit to secure her.

'But you shouldn't have done this thing,' she faintly said. 'Thass not the right way – you should have asked me before.'

'Should I?' It seemed quite a new idea to him, and he bent his eyes thoughtfully on the ground at her feet. 'Well – I never thought you'd have me the way I was, see – with the boats, and no home. Still!' Jonathan stirred, and fixed her with a penetrating look. 'I'm asked you now – never mind which way about. It's done now. Come and see the house – I know you'll like it.'

'No – I mean, I dare say it's very nice – but there's no point in me going to see it.' There was something overwhelming in his rugged ardour – alarming too: her palate shrank from such a concentrated essence of decision.

'Why, you want to see what sort of a place you'll be living in, don't you?'

His choice of tenses pricked her – releasing her confused feelings into the safer channel of vexation at his arrogance. 'Oh! what a fellow you are! Who said I'm going to be living in it?'

'You did – just now – you said I should have asked you to marry me before.'

'Oh, but what I meant was, you should ask a person such a question before you go and get a house for 'em – I didn't mean I'd say yes,' exclaimed Hester, conscious that this statement, though perfectly true, had a coquettish sound. Her fear on this point was confirmed by Eastholm, whose frown deepened. 'Well,' he said, 'after all that, what *do* you say?'

Hester looked distractedly around the innyard as if for guidance, but the carts, the heaped baskets and beer-barrels wore only the smug, stupid look typical of the external world at such critical moments. She groped for the lightness and clarity in which she trusted, but his presence cast her into doubtful unease: he made her feel terribly unsure of herself, and she did not like that. 'I don't know what I can say,' she said. 'You're the last person in the world I'd have expected to ask me.'

'Why, I'm not an old codger, you know,' Jonathan said, with a little pique.

'Oh, but you never even said a single nice thing to me!'

He shrugged, as at a supreme irrelevance. 'I suppose so – but then I'm no good for that sort of canoodling.'

There was that word again! It infuriated her. What was so wrong with the small change of love, that it had to be dismissed so?

'But whass that got to do with anything, any road?' he went on, with honest scepticism. 'I dare say it's true – I dare say I'm not like other chaps in that—' this with rather more pride than humility. 'Perhaps I'm more serious about things. Thass why I bought the house.'

'Oh! you and your house! Really, you must think pretty well of yourself if you went and bought that, never even thinking I might say no.' Her indignation, which had begun as the froth from a troubled swirl of emotions, took solid form. 'And you reckoned it was me who fancied meself! Why, I think it's men who are the vain ones.'

'But I did it for you, damn it.'

'To get me, you mean – to possess me. Well, I won't be bought like that.'

'Beggar me! you are a skittish one.' Jonathan had subsided to his knees now, though more for ease than in the posture of a suppliant. 'I don't understand you. What more can a man offer you than what I have?'

'Well,' said she, hesitating, and trying to look elsewhere than the large expanse of striped shirt and braced thighs that still filled her view, 'well – there's love, you know.'

For the first time his eyes left her, and a little of the air seemed to seep out of his tight resolution of manner. Then he rose to his feet and, placing his hands on his hips, spoke with such deep-toned emphasis that Hester seemed to feel his voice as a perceptible reverberation through the ground. 'Now look here,' he said, 'I'm gone to a deal of trouble for you – I'm give up my occupation, and everything that mattered to me, and staked it all on one chance.'

'But I never asked you to!' cried Hester, both distressed and angry.

'Never mind that – I won't be put off. I'm dealing fair with you, and I expect you to deal fair with me. It's a good offer – tek it or no.'

'Oh, dealing – you talk like you're trying to sell me a hoss! I declare you're the most pig-headed man!'

'Well: mebbe – I won't be made a game of,' Jonathan said sharply. 'I s'll only ask you once, you know.'

'Oh, I'm honoured!'

Jonathan snapped his fingers. 'A man must be a fool to put hisself through this, and set hisself up as an Aunt Sally for a gel,' said he, as if giving rein to a compelling bitterness. 'I'm always thought so, and it goes hard with me to do it: I never thought I would, till you come along.'

Hester might have been disarmed by this tribute to her power – had it not been couched in such unflattering terms, which seemed to transfer all the virtue to his part. And she was being represented as a mere destroyer: it was so unjust! 'Well, if it's such a pain to you, why do it?'

'Because I can't help it,' he gruffly replied, and his glare was so baleful she could not meet it. 'You're made a proper mess of me. You going to give me your answer?'

'I already have, haven't I?' she said, with some asperity, for she felt herself more accused than appealed to. 'You must be more pig-headed than I thought if you can't see that.' She was the least pitiless of girls, but at that moment it hardly seemed to her that she could hurt such a flinty surface as he presented to her.

'Very well then.' Jonathan, instead of putting on his cap, screwed it up in a ball and crammed it into his pocket as if he had no more use for it. 'I'm asked you – I shan't ask again.'

With no word of goodbye he walked away, with a certain slow deliberation, as if he were carefully carrying something – perhaps a large vessel of pride, from which he did not choose to spill a single drop.

\* \* \*

A further twenty minutes' wait for the carrier ensued, but this and the journey itself were fused for Hester into one long brooding abstraction of thought, such that she stared for a couple of hours at the wedge of moving scenery between the two passengers opposite, and saw not a leaf of it. She was profoundly upset, but could hardly tell why. Some vulnerable part of herself seemed to have been laid bare and scarified. Her dominant sensation was one of regret: but it was regret not so much for what had happened as for the pattern of which it seemed a specimen – a pattern which had her as its protesting centre. It was not entirely the twist of perversity in Hester's nature that enabled her to feel, directly after a proposal of marriage, that nobody valued her. She considered that she had good grounds for feeling slighted. Practical as she was, she had a certain contempt for the material – perhaps inherited from her father – and she could only see the matter of the house as a proposition of barter, with herself as the complementary item.

Canoodling – what was wrong with canoodling? Jonathan had made it sound like a diminution of love – or whatever hard, immutable version of love he countenanced – instead of its expression. Hester was as susceptible as most mortals to the pleasure of making conquests – but in this case the conquest seemed a highly ambiguous one: it was as if he had made a grudging concession to the overmastering elements, like lighting a fire against the cold. Perhaps it was this elemental aspect about him that nonplussed her. She could understand a man wanting to kiss her, but not a man wanting to build a house for her: she could frame no conception of sincerity that would include them both.

'And even then, I don't reckon he said a single nice thing to me,' she mentally grumbled. 'No – he didn't – it was all as if I'd done him a wrong. Arrogant – that's it – I wish I'd used that word to him.' The idea of what it would be like to have Jonathan saying nice things to her was quite swallowed up in her resentment that nobody did.

She tried then to dismiss the whole thing – he had said that was the end of it, and besides it meant nothing to her anyhow: but that this was not true was illustrated by her decision, as she alighted from the van at last, to say nothing to Lizzie about it. Lizzie would mock. Somehow she found the experience, far from being superfluous, had alerted her to a consciousness of lack within her – a lack which Eastholm's brusque proposal had highlighted by its very failure to fill it in the right way. Hester wanted to enjoy the sensation of being loved, not be violently presented with love as an achieved fact. If there was a certain sophistry and self-justification in this reasoning, it was perhaps because Hester felt an uneasy need to go all round the houses in order to avoid the thought of that one house, bought for her; and to avoid a suspicion, subversive to her view of life, that even bricks and mortar might be an emblem of passion.

# Chapter Six

1

The day before Lyle Saunders' return was expected, Mrs Saunders and Gideon made a visit to a wealthy gentleman at Warboys who was offering for sale a desirable thoroughbred that had been a racehorse. This was clearly a deal, and a social contact, that could not be trusted to Gideon alone. Before she left Mrs Saunders gave Hester a shopping-list of various small items requisite for her younger son's return: this occupied her morning. Hester enjoyed going into Stokeley's shops nowadays – the authority of Mrs Saunders clung about her, and when she walked in the shopmen flapped like hens before a vixen. Back at the house, she applied herself to the laborious task of pressing Mrs Saunders' lace jabots, tippets and bands, all of intensest black. Coming downstairs from putting them away, she stopped. It occurred to her that she was all but alone in the house: it was Judy's half-day, and Mrs Dawsmere inhabited the kitchen like a cuckoo in a cuckoo-clock, emerging only at rare and prescribed intervals. The staircase on which she paused set the tone of massiveness that characterised Mrs Saunders' house: it comprised enough wood for a small plantation, in colour like petrified chocolate, with newels crowned by great brown footballs. Hester never ran her hand along the broad, highly polished banister without a sort of tactile speculation about what it would be like to slide down it: and here at last was an opportunity to find out.

She went down the first time side-saddle: it was disappointing – she had to hang on so awkwardly. As there was no one to see, she hitched her skirts up between her legs, and slid exhilaratingly down astride the banister.

'Whee!' she said – *sotto voce*, as a gesture to decorum. She came to rest by a collision of her behind with the newel-post – that was less pleasant; but she scrambled down, and ran up the stairs again to repeat the exercise. This time she essayed to twist her body at the end of her descent to avoid the posterior impact: lost her balance; and would have landed in a heap on the hall rug had not a pair of hands come from nowhere and stopped her fall by seizing her round the waist.

Hester let out a shriek of surprise – also of surprising volume – the hands of her supporter left her waist, and went to his own ears. 'By the left!' he exclaimed. 'You must be Hester – now I know why she picked you – I'll bet she can hear you *quite* plain!'

With the echo of her scream still springing about the hall, Hester turned to the speaker. She found herself looking into the amused blue eyes of a loose-knit young man, somewhat above medium height, dressed in a light suit and turn-down collar with a straw hat, which he removed to reveal a crown of short fair hair, slightly curly. Though there was nothing in his features reminiscent of Mrs Saunders or Gideon except for the pronounced curve of his mouth, she knew him at once to be Lyle: something about his looks immediately recalled the tone of his letters. His was a notably open face, with something gently mocking about the upward configuration of the eyebrows; and an odd little smile, mostly cheer, with a moiety of melancholy, like a spring sky brushed with cloud. There was an assurance in it which curiously communicated to Hester as reassurance, as if she had long known him.

'Well, even if you're not Hester,' he said, after she had stood mute for some moments in embarrassed confusion at the way he had found her, 'I'm Lyle Saunders, and how do you do.' He proffered his hand.

'Yes – I'm Hester – I mean, how d'you do.' She shook his hand, and said: 'But you're not supposed to be here till tomorrow!'

'That accounts for my welcome. Are you the only one here?'

'Just me. Mrs Saunders and Mr Gideon have gone to Warboys to look at a horse.'

170

'Oh! well, it don't signify. Fact is, I was able to get a night packet across, and then I got a train straight from London, rather than hang about there. My luggage is still at the station – I just walked up from there – funny, I don't feel a bit tired.' He turned to close the front door, which was still standing open from his sudden entrance, and came back to Hester. 'Well, I feel like we've met already, through those letters, and d'you know your face is very much as I pictured it. Not that your *face* was my first introduction to you . . .'

Hester, most unusually for her, blushed. 'I don't know what come over me,' said she. 'I didn't think anyone would see.'

'Oh! your secret's safe with me. *I've* been pulling faces at myself in the glass, on the train journey – it whiles away the time – I think this was the best one,' and he grotesquely sucked in his cheeks and screwed up his eyes, looking not unlike a caricature of Gideon. 'What d'you reckon?'

'Why, you don't look any different,' Hester said.

'I see. One of these sharp women. Come on, let's go to the kitchen, I'm starving. Everybody well? Mother still fit?'

'Yes – excepting the arthritis, of course – I'm afraid she can't hardly fasten a button some mornings.'

'Sad,' Lyle said. 'Why an active woman like Mother, eh? Still, she's got you now – I'm glad about that – I wanted her to take on a help before I left. What about Giddy? Still walking out with Phoebe Purefoy?'

'Yes – well, at least, I presume so . . . I think perhaps Mr Gideon or your mother had better tell you about that.'

'Oh! dear, like that is it?'

They descended to the kitchen, where Mrs Dawsmere was so delighted to see him that she spilt salt with impunity, and could not find a bad omen anywhere. 'You're looking thinner, though, Mr Lyle,' she said. 'I was afraid they wouldn't feed you proper over there.'

'Not feed me! You should see the way the Belgians eat. Thumping great sausages and sticky pastries every hour of the day. Huge tankards of beer you can hardly lift. And that's just the ladies. I'm starving now, though – what can I eat?'

'Oh, I'm afraid dinner won't be ready for a couple of hours

yet,' Mrs Dawsmere said. 'I know there's a couple of kippers, if you want something hot—'

'Can't wait for that – let me forage in here,' Lyle said, with his head in the larder. 'Can I chew on this mutton-bone?'

'Oh, yes, sir – I was going to give it to the cats.'

Lyle made his meal standing up at the kitchen table, gnawing on the mutton-bone, with a plate of radishes and bread and butter, and spoke of his life in Belgium. 'Quite a rich sort of place. Crops growing on every inch of ground, and some of the farmers make our fen-folk look like paupers. You see 'em driving about in these enormous wagons, with horses like elephants.'

'Did you manage to speak the language, sir?' Mrs Dawsmere said.

'I got by with a bit of French. Of course, some of them speak Flemish instead, and I couldn't follow a word of that.'

'Fancy. You'd think one foreign lingo would be enough for 'em,' said Mrs Dawsmere, as if they had two out of mere perversity.

'What were the people you were staying with like?' Hester said.

'Mr Dielman is about five foot nothing, with a little pointy beard. Mrs Dielman is about six foot tall and six foot round. But somehow they've got two daughters – they always seem to be either at Mass or confession, and one of them wants to be a nun.'

'Oh! Papists!' cried Mrs Dawsmere, with a native disgust unmodified since the days of Cromwell. 'I hope they didn't try any tricks with you, Mr Lyle – trying to mek you one of 'em. I've heard things about them Nuns.'

'No, I was too much of a benighted heathen for that,' said Lyle, amused. 'Mind you, I would have followed the eldest girl practically anywhere, if not quite to the convent. She was a dazzler.'

'Why, what's she want to go and hide herself away in one of them places for, if she's so pretty?' Hester said, feeling somehow piqued.

'Well, her eyes weren't fixed on worldly things,' Lyle said, with a glance of some interest at Hester. 'Certainly not on me.

Ah! I'll go—' There was knocking at the front door. 'That'll be my luggage.'

The driver of the station brake brought Lyle's bags into the hall, one of which Lyle seized and carried into the parlour, saying, 'Hester, come and see what you think of these. Presents for Mother and Giddy.'

In the parlour Lyle sat himself down on the rug and began to rummage eagerly in the bag. 'Now then. This for Giddy. You should see the Brussels shops – all gilt and velvet and cherubs with fat behinds. D'you think he'll like that?' It was a boot-jack inlaid with silver. 'I suppose he still wears those crippling tight boots? Sorry – shouldn't ask you that really.' But he gave her a droll look, which established the matter of Gideon's vanity between them, without either of them mentioning it.

'I'm sure it's just the thing,' Hester said.

'And this for Mother.'

It was a dressing-case, again inlaid with silver, and it was the most luxurious thing Hester had ever seen. 'Coh,' she said. 'Coh.'

'I'm glad you like it. I dare say it'll be mostly in your hands, what with Mother's arthritis. I've got some fancy Belgian chocolates for Mrs Dawsmere and Judy somewhere – where are they – hope they're not squashed. Anyway – this is for you, Hester. Now you see my problem. I didn't know what you looked like. For all I knew you might have been a right old gargoyle, instead of – well, the way you are. Anyway, I thought I couldn't fail with Brussels lace. I hope it's all right.'

From a wad of foreign-looking wrapping paper came forth a lace fichu, of unendurable delicacy.

'Oh dear,' Hester said.

'What's wrong?'

'I can't take this.'

'Eh?'

'Well – what I mean is – I don't know you.'

Lyle burst out laughing. 'True. But I shouldn't let that stop you, if you like it. Anyway, you *are* going to know me, aren't you? I mean, now I'm back.'

'Shall you be stopping here permanently, then?'

173

'I should think so. We've got the contact on the Continent now, and it's a lot of work for Giddy to manage on his own here. Give me England, anyhow. I got fed up with rolling my Rs. Letter Rs, that is. Ha! I've been waiting to use that joke. You do like it, though, don't you – the lace?'

'It's lovely,' Hester said. 'Thank you very much.'

'That's all right then.' Lyle suddenly yawned like a cat. 'Phew, I think I am tired after all. Hope you don't mind if I go to sleep. Can't be bothered to shift all that luggage yet. Would you wake me in an hour, if Mother and Giddy aren't back by then?'

He took off his jacket, climbed up on the sofa, curled on his side, and fell asleep in a few moments. Hester had thought she was the only person who could do that. She lingered in the parlour to have another look at him, with that slight uneasy feeling of guilt attached to observing a sleeping person. It was not enough to say that the face, fair-complexioned with a pleasant straight nose, was a boy's face – Gideon's could often be that: rather it was, unlike Gideon's, the face of a boy when he thinks no one is looking at him. What strange differences there were in families! There seemed nothing of Mrs Saunders in him at all, and he appeared the temperamental opposite of Gideon.

'But then, after all, you don't know him,' Hester told herself – feeling, however, that she did. She went upstairs to admire herself in the lace fichu, in Mrs Saunders' dressing-table mirror, and presently heard the sound of the trap entering the yard.

'Mr Lyle,' she said, going into the parlour. 'Wake up.' She shook him by one warm, shirt-sleeved arm. 'Wake up – your mother's here.'

Lyle sprang up with his hair in a mess. 'Ow! My leg's gone to sleep,' he exclaimed, and ran with a hopping, hobbling, pins-and-needles stride out to the hall.

'Lyle!' Mrs Saunders' voice must have been audible at the other end of Stokeley. 'You beggar! We didn't expect you till tomorrow!'

'Hullo Mother – hullo Giddy.' Lyle kissed his mother and shook hands with Gideon: there were greetings, laughter, inquiries. Out of the blue, Hester was assailed by sadness. Though she had seen the unedifying spectacle of Mrs Saunders' possessiveness, still there was real warmth and affection here: and she felt a little forlorn. No one ever kissed her affectionately. She was momentarily brushed, in fact, by the claw of the Old Goblin, though she did not know it.

'Well, my son,' Mrs Saunders said, 'I suppose you've met my help, then?'

'She was just coming down the stairs when I walked in,' Lyle said, and Hester caught the faintest wink.

'Ah, she's not a bad gel,' Mrs Saunders said, all the lines of her face deepened in a big harsh smile. 'You have to watch her, though.'

'Oh! I'll watch her,' Lyle said.

Life at the Saunders yard was different following Lyle's return. Formerly there had been an odd sort of balance between Mrs Saunders, who was a vivid physical expression of the idea of will, and Gideon, who was a colourless distillation of submission. Beside these two elements, Lyle was an ambiguous alloy. It was very soon clear to Hester that Mrs Saunders tyrannised her sons indiscriminately: she was quite as severely dictatorial to Lyle as to Gideon, and he had barely settled in when he was set to work; but there was something pliable about him, something india-rubbery rather like the smile of comic irony often to be seen on his mobile lips, that meant he was not ground down as his brother was. He was adept at the soft answer, even when his mother berated him at length for his bad habits.

'You've got settled into your bad habits, you have,' she stormed at him. 'That's what happens when you don't have my eye on you. You go all to pot. D'you hear?'

'You look just like the Queen of Belgium,' Lyle said dreamily, and kissed her hand.

'Get away with you! I'll give you kings and queens—' But he had already gone off, chuckling.

Lyle's bad habits were not far to seek, though they were of a sort which Hester, for one, found forgivable. He could work hard enough – once you had got him out of bed, which, Mrs

Saunders said, was like trying to prise a brick out of a wall. While he could be gently ironical about Gideon's attempts to be a masher, he had a weakness for clothes himself, and was always appearing in new neckties. He had a frank liking for a drink, and on one of his first evenings back home, took Gideon down to the Nag's Head to make a night of it: they returned very late and convivial, and Hester was woken by a strange muffled yodelling which she afterwards learnt was the sound of Gideon being rather ill into the water-closet. Mrs Saunders was very sharp with a somewhat grey and chastened Lyle in the morning; but it was better, Hester thought, than those secret tipplings of Gideon's. Lyle's general friendliness towards Gideon, which met with a decidedly mixed return, somewhat surprised Hester. That this proceeded too from a certain indolence, and that Lyle preferred amiability because it was simply less strenuous, she dimly discerned; but she was far from thinking any the worse of him for that, and her prejudice in his favour had material grounds, in that her position in the household improved in comfort following his return. He was always taking thought for little things that would never have occurred to Mrs Saunders – that the fire should not be allowed to go out simply because there was only Hester in the room, that she might want some paper to write a letter, that she might be introduced when folk called rather than left sitting there like a piece of furniture.

'Huh! you'll spoil the gel, you will,' Mrs Saunders said. 'She fancies herself as it is.'

'Better to spoil her than lose her,' Lyle said. 'Anyway why shouldn't she fancy herself? Blow your own trumpet, I say.'

'Ah, I know you say that!' Mrs Saunders said. 'You kept me waiting five-and-twenty minutes this morning – you with your titivating.'

'Well, after all, it was Colonel Napier we were going to see. You need to be turned out like a gentleman for the Master of the Fitzjohn Hunt.'

'You need to arrive on time, not five-and-twenty minutes late!'

Lyle laughed at himself for this, but it did not stop him doing the same again. This was a characteristic, Hester thought, that was more Verney than Saunders – Lyle, though candidly averse to effort, would nevertheless go to enormous trouble dressing himself to the nines, if the fancy took him, just to go down the street. Similarly, he took a liking to a chest of drawers that was standing in the spare room, and decided he wanted it in the bay window of his bedroom. One of the grooms came up to help shift it: they measured the bay window, measured the chest of drawers, measured again.

'No – I'm afraid it won't fit,' the groom said.

'No,' Lyle said, 'I suppose it won't.' He looked again at the bay. 'But then – perhaps if it stood out a bit – I think it might, you know.'

'I reckon it's too narrow, sir.'

'Too narrow – it is, you're right. Silly idea.' He measured again. 'Still – you know – I think it might squeeze in.' And in the end nothing less than the laborious shifting of the chest of drawers from one room to the other, and the demonstrated physical impossibility of its going into a space six inches narrower than its width, would satisfy him.

He called it optimism: Mrs Saunders, pig-headedness. Hester inclined to his side. She was prepared to make a good deal of allowances for a person who made her laugh. The seed of flippancy in her own nature had borne bitter fruit in the dark turf-pit that disastrous night, but that did not mean she wished to uproot it: hers was no parable mentality, eager for a large dividend of precept from the small investments of experience. Lyle's capricious attitude to life was one she understood. She recognised the way that boredom came upon him, not by degrees, but instantaneously, in the manner of young animals: he would abandon a whole project in momentary lassitude. Mimicry diverted him in the same way. Walking down the stairs quite normally, he would suddenly become Gaffer, a creaking tottering character he had invented who spoke with a whistle through his teeth. 'Ah! beggar theshe old shtairsh. Play merry hell wi' me jointsh. Hark at 'em popping. Like a load of ole sheed-podsh. You shtand there laughing, gel. You'll be old yourshelf one day.' His sudden humours were always catching her unawares. One evening she was sewing, and Lyle was reading the newspaper. All at once she became aware that

177

he had gravitated to a seat near her, and was regarding her solemnly with his chin on his hand.

'Whatcha doing?' he said, hushed.

'What's it look like I'm doing?' she cried, beginning to laugh.

'Sshh!' he admonished, finger to his lips, though there was no one around. 'I won't tell anyone,' and he tiptoed back to his chair, and read the newspaper with ferocious concentration.

When rich and influential customers came to the yard, Lyle was usually on his best behaviour: he did not lack that most salient feature of the Saunders' physiognomy, a nose for business, and he was a ready flatterer. But then one morning came Mr Maurice Pimlott, who while not a Sir was the son of a Sir – six feet two of genial vacancy wrapped in a dove-grey frock-coat, with a painted-on smile like that of a marionette, and no back to his head; who was, he said, after a soft-mouthed Anglo-Arab with well let down hocks. Though this flower of the nation's élite was a valuable customer, it was difficult for Hester at least to keep a straight face when he was talking; and when young Mr Pimlott took tea with the Saunders in the parlour, Lyle began to catch Hester's eye, and a little devil entered him.

'So you've been in Belgium, I understand, Saunders,' Mr Pimlott said, manipulating with difficulty the complexities of cup, saucer and spoon. 'That must be a devilish queer sort of place.'

'Very queer indeed,' Lyle said, gravely. 'One gets used to some things, you know: but it was the sun I couldn't get used to – rising in a different place. The sun rises in the west there, as I'm sure you know, Mr Pimlott, because of the latitude; and I just couldn't take to that.'

'By Jove, does it really?' Mr Pimlott sucked tea from his moustache. 'Where *is* Belgium, exactly?'

'Quite near Africa,' Lyle said, deadpan.

'Yes – of course – near Africa. I suppose they don't wear clothes like ours, do they?'

'Well – pretty much the same as ours,' Lyle said. Hester risked a glance at him: his eyes met hers for the merest instant, but his face remained utterly sober as he went on,

178

'Except for the unmarried women over forty, that is – they don't wear anything at all. Except a sort of apron, for modesty. It's some curious old custom left over from the Dark Ages, and the Belgians aren't too keen on its being known – but it's sanctioned by tradition, you know.'

'Oh, quite.' Mr Pimlott pondered: giving him the appearance of a man who begins to suspect he is sitting on something nasty. 'Don't they get awfully cold?' he at last said.

'Well, it's a very hot climate, you see – tropical – being near Africa,' Lyle said.

'Shall you be going to the Huntingdon Show, Mr Pimlott?' boomed Mrs Saunders, who had caught enough of this through her deafness to find she did not like it.

'Yes, I believe so, Mrs Saunders.' The young man turned back to Lyle in fascination. 'I say – people are *white* over there, aren't they?'

He's going to say they're green, thought Hester, with her hand over her mouth: he's going to say they're green, and I'm going to scream.

'Oh, yes, they're white,' Lyle said. He paused. 'That's the Russian in them, you see. The country used to belong to Russia – and some of the older men still wear fur hats and boots, in spite of the heat. Tradition, you see.'

'Oh, quite. I've a great respect for tradition.' Mr Pimlott pondered again. 'Still, they're queer, these places. Aprons, eh? Damn me.'

Gideon cut in then, and diverted the visitor's fragile mind to the safer subject of hunting till his departure. But as they stood in the yard to see him off, Mr Pimlott turned to Lyle before climbing into his gig, and said, 'Those aprons, now – what are they made of?'

Lyle, almost thrown for a moment, seemed to cast wildly about in his mind.

'Seaweed,' he said.

Hester had a fit of coughing, whilst Mr Pimlott nodded reflectively. 'By Jove,' he said. 'Jolly interesting – but awfully queer. No: you've convinced me, Saunders – the diplomatic service would never have done for me.'

'You'll see,' Mrs Saunders reproached Lyle, after Mr Pimlott had left, 'one of these days you'll be so sharp you'll cut yourself.'

'By Jove,' Lyle said, giving Hester a smile of Pimlottesque foolishness. 'Will I really?'

One morning Mrs Saunders sent Hester out to the paddock to fetch Lyle: he was to accompany them on a charity visit to some of Stokeley's poorer townsfolk, to whom she was a staunch if rather browbeating benefactress. 'Tell him not to keep me waiting,' she said. 'Now means now.'

Outside the spring sunlight had all but attained to the high brightness of summer, and the callow green of the new leaves on the apple trees around the paddock seemed to deepen visibly in the warm air. From the paddock there was a strong and rank smell of bruised grass and earth, being trampled into a yet juicier compound by the thudding hoofs of a young cob, which had shown the most prolonged resistance to bit and bridle, and had yet to be broken in to a rider. Lyle and one of the grooms were standing at the paddock gate, watching the skittish trottings of the animal, and conferring.

'I'm going to give him another go,' said Lyle, who was in riding-breeches and boots. 'I think he's quietened down a bit. Hullo, Hester.'

Hester gave him her message.

'Oh! I'll be along directly,' he said. 'I just want to try this chap again – I think he's getting used to me. Don't come into the paddock, will you, Hester – his hoofs fly a bit.'

Hester needed no persuading. The cob, though it had been given the typical Saunders gloss, yet had something wild and swarthy about it: the innocence of its long eyelashes did not disguise the dark glitter in its eyes, even as it submitted to be caught and held by the groom. Lyle patted its neck and spoke cheerily to it, measuring it with his eye, and looking very slight beside its thick black quarters: then all at once he swarmed up on to the cob's back like a man besieging a rampart. The horse gave a great galvanised twist in the air, describing almost a full circle, and landed only to spring up again, and career at zig-zagging angles across the paddock in a series of buck-jumps, each fiercer and more frenetic than the last. Lyle, braced backwards in the saddle, hung on, and even seemed, with his clenched rictus of effort, to smile grimly. The muscles of his thighs were so taut that they seemed quite as anatomically delineated, through the riding-breeches, as the rippling sinews of the horse, so that rider and mount might have been one infinitely steeled and compelling creature. The strenuous snorting of the horse's mouth and nostrils produced a cloud of moisture in the sun's rays that enveloped the two like a film as they bounded and plunged about the paddock; and this added to Hester's impression, derived from the balletic arch of the cob's back and the way it kept its feet almost daintily together, together with Lyle's stylised posture, of a weird dance – something at once graceful and violent. She watched in a suspense of troubled fascination.

Suddenly horse and rider, unpredictable as a jumping-jack, were right over by the fence where Hester stood: automatically she recoiled at the frantic rolling eye and staring neck-veins of the horse, and the spray of froth that rained on her; then the cob twirled again, the pounding of its hoofs perceptible as a vibration through Hester's feet, and Lyle twisting in the saddle was unseated at last. He grasped at the pommel for a moment, could not hold it, swore, and slid off, landing heavily on the grass, and straightaway rolling out of reach of the prancing hoofs. His roll took him a little too far, and he struck the side of his face against the lowest bar of the fence.

'Oh! you've gone and broke your head – I knew you would,' cried Hester, falling on her knees beside him, 'it ain't safe!'

Lyle sat up and tenderly touched his upper cheekbone. 'Ow! Silly bloody thing to do. Go through all that and then go and knock my own silly bloody head against the fence. Sorry – pardon my Belgian – ladies present.'

'Don't worry. I should think I can swear as well as you.'

'I'll bet you can as well.' He smiled at her, then winced.

'Oh, does it hurt?' She touched his shoulder. 'You ain't cracked a bone, have you?'

'Just bruised, I think. But you can kiss it better if you like.'

'Indeed I won't!' She let go of him.

'Well, I thought you might like a treat.'

181

'Huh!' She had caught this emphatic exclamation from Mrs Saunders. 'I can git them ten a penny.'

Lyle got to his feet. 'Ow – I think I'm bruised somewhere else as well—'

'Don't you say it!'

They went into the house, where Mrs Saunders rounded on him. 'There you are – hurry up! Go and get changed. Keeping me waiting till bull's noon. And you, gel, go and get your hat on.'

They raced up the stairs. Hester was ready in a few moments: there was no sign of Lyle when she came out on the landing.

'Hester!' Mrs Saunders bellowed from below. 'Tell that son of mine to hurry up – he needn't titivate himself for where we're going.'

She went to Lyle's bedroom door, which was ajar: he was scrutinising his face in the mirror on the wall.

'I hope it won't mark,' he said, touching his cheek. 'There'll be girls on both sides of the Channel mourning if my looks are spoilt.'

'Well, here's one who won't be,' Hester said.

There is a peculiarly enhanced intimacy in the meeting of eyes in a mirror. The solitude of self is startlingly broken, and the two reflected seem bound in a common consciousness, seeing themselves and each other in one closed circuit of vision. Lyle held Hester's eyes in the glass for some moments, then smiled: then ceased to smile, and turned to the bureau by the bed.

'Hester – look here – I want you to have these. I brought 'em back from Brussels. Look. I had to have them.' He held out on the palm of his hand a pair of jet earrings, like black pendant raindrops.

'I – I can't tek them,' she said.

'You're a rum one. Why not?'

'I just can't . . . You already give me one present.'

'Oh! that was because I brought everybody a present. That was just formal – I didn't even know you then. These are different. Look – I'll be honest. When I saw them I had no idea of a girl to wear them – I just bought them sort of on the off-chance. Now I know what you look like – and you're just the one to wear them.' He held them for a moment by her hair. 'You've got the colouring – everything. I want them to go where they'll suit.'

'But I can't,' she said. 'It wouldn't be right—'

'Oh! right, wrong – who cares about that? I want you to have them. Go on – else I'll give them to Phoebe Purefoy.'

'I don't know when I'd be able to wear them – your mother likes me turned out plain.'

'That doesn't matter. The best gifts are useless ones. Now then – mind your blushes – I've got to get changed.'

'Oh yes – sorry.' She left the room: and on the landing found, without quite knowing how, that she had taken the earrings on to her palm.


Early summer saw the beginning of the show season, an important time for the Saunders' establishment, which entered horses and ponies at all the various agricultural shows around the fenland. Gideon and Lyle were continually busy schooling animals to be ridden and driven in the ring. Lyle had particular hopes of a smart dappled pony he had named General Blucher, and spent hours with it in the paddock, preparing for the Huntingdon Show. Hester frequently watched him: sometimes sent out to take a message from Mrs Saunders, more often drawn of her own accord.

'I believe you'll be sorry to see that pony go,' she said to him.

'Oh! well – you mustn't get too attached to them,' he said, stroking the General's nose. 'But we're going to win a cup together first – aren't we, old fellow?'

'All that effort for a cup!' said Hester – who, despite a couple of months in the Saunders' ambience, still viewed things equestrian in the most prosaic light.

'Ah, but it's not just the cup – it's the acclaim. When I'm riding in the ring, I like to pretend I'm taking part in a tournament – knights of old and all that. Where the victor receives a kiss from a lady fair. You know. Some filly in a pointed hat.'

'A lady fair at Huntingdon Show – you daft beggar.'

'I know. Lady Fitzjohn usually presents the cups – pointed

head, more like. Moustache like Giddy's. Tell you what – I'll claim a kiss off you if I win the cup.'

'I'd sooner kiss General Blucher!' she said.

'No, you wouldn't. He's not your type. Anyway he can never have children. Oh! go on, Hester – promise – it'll spur me on.'

'I just don't know what to mek of you. Go on then, Sir Lancelot. First prize only, mind. If you git second prize, there's no kiss from me.'

'What then?'

'Kiss from Judy.'

'Ech, now I've got to win!'

Both Gideon and Lyle, with several horses to display each, were at the showground early on the day: Hester drove over later with Mrs Saunders in the trap. Mrs Saunders' arthritis making it sometimes difficult for her to handle the reins, she had lately been teaching Hester who, having taken charge of Mr Langtoft's farm cart occasionally, was a ready pupil; and this was the first occasion on which Hester was the driver for the entire journey.

'I don't know,' Mrs Saunders sighed. 'Only just sixty, and I can't even drive a little dumpling of a pony.'

'Oh, but Mrs Saunders,' said Hester, who knew how to butter her up, 'thass only right you should have things done for you – having got to your position. Specially at the show – you don't want folk thinking you're a farmer's wife or some such.'

'True, gel: true – I reckon I've got a bit of respect due to me. Well! I hope we shall win a fair few prizes today. That pony of Lyle's looks a certainty.'

This was a subject on which Hester did not know what to think: she attempted to solve that problem by not thinking about it at all. She and Mrs Saunders took their seats in a small stand at the edge of the main show ring, beside the presentation dais. A feeble white-gloved waving at the edge of Hester's vision resolved itself into Phoebe Purefoy, sitting with her father a few seats along.

'Hello there – how d'you do – thank you – lovely day – they do say flaming June, don't they?'

184

Hester greeted her, and said to Mrs Saunders, who was fixedly staring at a spot of sky, 'There's Miss Purefoy, Mrs Saunders, saying hello.'

'I see her!' Mrs Saunders said out of the corner of her mouth, and added with vicious indignation, 'Hello, is it! I know what she means by *that*!' And she continued her resolute study of the sky whilst poor Phoebe helplessly pantomimed civilities across the intervening row of hats and knees.

Lyle's fantasy of the show as a medieval tournament did not quite accord with the large hoardings advertising cow-cake and fertiliser, or the bowler hats and furled umbrellas; but the colour of the marquees, the flags rippling against the blue sky, the rich grass that surely merited the word greensward, and the mixture of voices – the broad ones at the rails speaking in Anglo-Saxon terms, of Hosses and Kine, whilst the clipped accents on the dais talked of Stables and Cattle, recalling Norman French – established the show as a recognisable descendant of those occasions. And Hester, sitting through the displays of pony-and-trap and sulky-driving with amiable disinterest, felt her blood quicken at the sight of Lyle riding into the ring, quite as much as if he had been clad in mail, with a scarlet cross on his chest.

She had seen him practising on General Blucher a score of times, but never had the two seemed more elegantly, gracefully fused than now: and she seemed to feel herself moving with them, through every step of their routine, and holding her breath against a slip. She wished to catch Lyle's eye, but it was impossible here: the situation was the reverse of when they had looked at each other in the mirror, and she felt herself receding from him into the mass of the encircling crowd, as alien and separate as if they had never met. Her suspense was sharpened when the time for the judging came, and she barely noticed Mrs Saunders tugging at her sleeve.

'What are they saying? I can't hear a word. What are they saying, gel?'

'They're judging the riders – Yes, it's Lyle! First prize!'

'Oh! the riders,' Mrs Saunders said. 'I knew he'd get that. That don't matter.' It was the value of a prize pony that mattered to her; and soon enough, the chairman of the judges announced first prize in the pony class to General Blucher. 'There! I knew he would!' Mrs Saunders cried. 'Good old boy, Lyle! – I knew he was schooling a champion. That pony'll fetch a blinder of a price. Hester – go and tell Lyle congratulations – he'll be in the enclosure – and say he's not to take any offers. They'll be at him like flies round jam. Tell him to say we've had an offer – two fifty – that'll push 'em up. Quick now.'

She found Gideon in the Saunders' partition of the enclosure, with their horses. He had won a blue rosette for carriage-driving, and was in high spirits – or some sort of spirits: his whisky-flask protruded from the pocket of his hacking-jacket. 'Lyle?' he said. 'Yes, he's over there,' and he gave her an unpleasant smile. 'If you can get near him.'

Lyle was receiving the congratulations of two young women whom Hester did not know. She stood around for a minute, like a fool, before she could attract his attention.

'Hester – hullo – this is my mother's companion – Miss Bowen, Miss Blythe.'

'How d'you do. Mrs Saunders says congratulations, and – er—'

'Oh! I see. Excuse me a moment, ladies.'

He took Hester to one side, and she gave him Mrs Saunders' message. 'Two fifty, eh?' he said. 'Well, if she says so. See him go, Hester? I hardly had to guide him.'

He was happily smiling, and gazing directly at her as he said this, but there was nothing whatsoever to suggest that he remembered the promise attached to the winning of first prize. 'Tell Mother I'll be along to see her soon,' he said, and went back to the two young women, one of whom was examining the silver cup and getting fingermarks all over it. No – he had forgotten! She noted the two women – turning on all the charm – oh Mr Saunders this and la Mr Saunders that – she knew the type. The giggly sort, who made fizzing noises through their teeth when they laughed. She thought he'd have better taste.

The vehemence of her own reaction to this disconcerted Hester and made her a stranger to herself all the rest of that day. She was a stranger to herself because she was for the first time feeling something like jealousy – a large emotion springing from small and trivial causes, in direct contrast to the usual straightforward progression of her feelings. 'You all right, gel? You're quiet. Not got the curse coming on, have you?' Mrs Saunders said, in her plain way, when they drove home. She had not; but it felt not unlike that.

The Saunders' establishment had made several good deals that day: Lyle and Gideon went out in the evening to celebrate. 'Landlord of the Nag's Head getting all our profits,' Mrs Saunders grunted, but without malice: she was in a good mood. Everybody was, it seemed, except Hester. They had the nightly game of rummy. Sometimes of late Lyle would join them for this. He had several flashy ways of shuffling the cards, which never quite came off, so that they ended up fluttering all over the floor. 'Oh, it does work, though,' he would say, scrambling for them, 'let me have another go—'

'Get on, you great fool-jabey!' Mrs Saunders would say, clipping his ear.

Hester went up to bed and, inhibited from sleep by some vague shape of discontent, pillow-punched for an hour or so. She scarcely seemed to have been asleep a few minutes when she was woken by a thunderous banging noise. She thought for a moment it was Gideon and Lyle, coming back soused again; but country living had given her the ability to tell the hour of the night quite precisely by the shade of the sky, and a glance at the window told her it was well past three – too late for that. She put on her dressing-gown and went out to the landing. Someone was lighting an oil-lamp in the hall: the illumination revealed Lyle, dressed in shirt and trousers.

'What is it?' Hester said.

'Just a horse got cast in the stable. Giddy's up. Tell Mother, will you? – and tell her we'll deal with it – don't let her get up, it's a bit nippy.'

Hester did as she was bid, and then went down to see if there was anything she could do to help. In the stable-yard light was streaming from one of the stalls, whence came the banging: the two grooms, coats thrown over their nightshirts, hurried towards it. The unsettled occupants of the other stalls were shuffling and whinnying in the darkness. For a horse to get cast was a not uncommon occurrence: the animal, enjoying a roll on its back in the stall, found itself unable to turn on its side and get to its feet again because it had edged too close to the wall, and the noise it made in its struggles was enough to wake the household. Looking in at the open stall, Hester found that it was a young mare that had got cast. Lyle and Gideon had already fetched ropes from the tackle-room and were tying them on to the flailing legs.

'Take hold of this lamp, will you, Hester?' Lyle said. 'She'll have it over in a minute. Hold it high – that's it. All right, Tom – let's pull her over.'

Lyle, Gideon, and the two grooms wrapped the ropes round their arms, braced themselves against the opposite wall, and with much heaving and straining, pulled the mare over to the centre of the stall so that the animal was able to get to its feet. The grooms quietened the mare with their peculiar crooning stable-talk whilst Lyle and Gideon untied the ropes and ran their hands along its flanks to check for damage.

'She's all right,' Lyle said. 'There, you silly old devil. Don't do that again.'

They returned to the house, yawning, Hester carrying the lamp, and Lyle and Gideon drooped back to bed. On the landing Hester heard Mrs Saunders call to her, and opened her bedroom door a little.

'No damage done, is there, gel?'

'No, everything's all right, Mrs Saunders.'

She closed the door, and crossed the landing to set the lamp on a small table there. Lyle emerged from the shadows. His hair was the colour of dull gilt in the lamplight.

'It wasn't old General Blucher, anyway,' he said softly. 'He wouldn't do anything so daft.'

'I suppose not,' Hester said. Her limbs still had the kittenish weakness consequent on awakening from sleep, and the lamp wobbled as she set it down.

'Now then,' Lyle said, standing quite still, 'I think you owe me something, don't you?'

'Eh? Oh! that. I thought you'd forgotten about that.'

'No, I hadn't forgotten.'

'You didn't seem in much of a hurry to claim it,' said she, hearing in her own voice a pettish resentment she could not control.

Lyle's expression was unperturbed. 'Ah, at the show, you mean? That was no good. Not in front of those two old cats. No pleasure in that.'

Hester felt herself outfaced: and had a sensation too of being suspended between intense wakefulness and drowsiness.

'Oh! well,' she said, trying to sound careless. 'If you still want it.'

'Only if you do.'

She did not answer; and a moment later the white shirt had advanced towards her out of the darkness, like a moving patch of moonlight, and Lyle's lips touched her own.

'First prize,' said he. 'Good night,' and light and quick as a panther, he disappeared back into his own room.

The following Saturday was Hester's day off: mentioning this at breakfast, Lyle said, 'I suppose you go and see your family?'

'I'm got no family local,' Hester said. 'I go and visit my friends on Hinching Fen.'

'Someone fetches you?'

'Oh! no. I go by the carrier.'

'Mother!' Lyle said. 'You mean to say you make the poor girl travel on those lumbering old carriers? I should think half her day's gone by the time she gets there.'

'Why, what else should she go by – magic carpet?' said Mrs Saunders. 'I wasn't ashamed to use the carriers when I was a girl – I don't see why she should be. She's only a paid help.'

'Well, you're not going by carrier today, Hester,' Lyle said. 'I'm taking you in the trap. I was going to take it out today anyway – that grey we bought wants more schooling.'

'Huh!' Mrs Saunders said. 'I wonder you don't take her in a coach-and-four – with a footman to boot! She'll start to expect it, I'm sure, the way you're going.'

'Oh, I'll hit her with a stick every now and then, so she doesn't get proud,' Lyle said.

'I took a stick to you when you were a lad,' Mrs Saunders said grimly, 'but look how you turned out.'

'I was an angelic child, you know, Hester,' Lyle said confidentially. 'Mother had to cover me up when I went out to stop rich ladies stealing me and making me their own.

Crusty old men used to burst into tears at the sight of my curls
– and thieves turned reformed characters with one look at me,
and devoted their lives to the church.'

'Bah! He could wriggle his way out of anything – that's what
he was like,' snorted Mrs Saunders. 'And he's no different now.
If he fell in the river he'd come up with a fish in his mouth.'

The trap was soon waiting in the yard, in all its compact
smartness, with polished brass side-lamps and whip-socket
and black-and-white check seats. The grey pony, which Lyle
was schooling as a carriage-horse, was a much leaner and more
wiry animal than their own steady dumpling, and was restless
to be off.

'Up we go,' Lyle said, handing Hester up, and then stowing
a wicker basket on the backboard.

'What's in that?' she said.

'Cow's eggs,' said Lyle, taking the reins. 'Now then, old
girl!'

The pony sprang forward, and they were borne briskly out
of the yard and down the High Street, pedestrians stopping to
admire the whirl of the red wheels as the trap whisked by, and a
draught-horse stationary in the shafts of a dray turning its heavy
head slowly at their passing, like age contemplating youth. In
a few moments they had left the arches of the Abbey behind;
and Hester suddenly marking the road they were taking, said,
'You're going the wrong way – you want the other road for
Hinching Fen.'

Lyle slackened the reins, and said: 'Oh! you want to go there,
do you?'

'Why – what else?'

'I thought you were coming for a day out with me. I've got
a picnic lunch in the basket – I asked Mrs Dawsmere to make
it up for me.'

'Well! you *are* a story.'

'Not really. I'll take you to your friends' if you like; or you
can stay with me. Which is it to be?'

He turned his face to her, haloed by his straw hat, and all at
once she laughed, reaching up and pinching his nose between
her finger and thumb.

'Ow! what's that for?'

'Thass to be going on with. Come on then – the picnic it is.'

'I shall cry if you're going to knock me about.'

'Oh! git on and drive.'

He did so, clamping his hat down on his head and with a grin setting the pony off at speed, so that Hester was thrown backwards in her seat. It was a clear summer day, warm and windless, and the pony was full of vigour, scarcely noticing her light burden. The merest dab of Lyle's whip sent them bowling along, the wheels below seeming rather to skim the ground than actually revolve on their axes, and a vortex of onrushing air funnelling between Hester and Lyle, so that a third person seemed to be sitting there, rubbing against their shoulders.

'Can't you slow down a bit?' Hester cried.

'Can't hear you.'

'Slow down!'

'Why? It's the pony – not me,' he said – at the same time giving the reins a flick. 'Anyway, it's grand, isn't it?'

The straight road ran directly parallel with the high banks of the Forty Foot, which traversed the open fen like a backbone in the earth. Fields of pale olive-green wheat rippled away to the encircling horizon, on which in the bright air landmarks could be seen at such distances that a couple of miles' progress along the road could be made with no apparent change relative to the position of a far-off steeple or barn: so that they seemed at the same time to be plunging along at furious speed, and standing still. Starlings fluttered up from the roadside in fright, just as their ancestors had done at the spiked wheels of Boadicea's war-chariots; and butterflies were caught up in the momentary turbulence of their passing, spinning helplessly for an instant in dusty whirlpools of air before being deposited again on the flowered verges. At some point Hester – unable now even to protest, as the whipping air snatched the breath from her open mouth – passed from fear to exhilaration, though this feeling was not without its coppery tang of alarm: at some point too she had put her arm about Lyle's shoulders, as the most convenient means of holding on, and when he suddenly pulled on the reins, tugging them to a slewing halt on the grass of the verge, she

191

was compelled to cling to his neck to keep her balance, and was thrown full against him.

'Hester – I declare you've got designs on me,' he said, looking down at her gloved hand clasped close to his face. Her recent indoor occupation, and the regenerative power of youthful flesh, had rendered the former farm-servant's skin as white and smooth as a lady's, so that the two inches of wrist between sleeve and glove appeared like a splash of milk against Lyle's navy jacket. Before she could move he had bent his head and kissed the exposed skin; and her heart still beating fast as it was from the excitement of the ride, she seemed to feel the pulse of her own blue veins against Lyle's mouth, like the ticking of a watch.

'Here,' she said, drawing back from him, 'you're already had your prize.'

'Oh, that was *your* prize.'

'You conceited davil!'

'Not enough, eh? Have another one?' said he, and kissed her lips.

Hester felt the kiss as something warm, sweet and bright – like some detached aspect of the deep blue summer air in which a lark was singing. Her happiness came to her with a curious unsurprise: it was not at all the proverbial happiness too deep for expression – it made her smile. She looked at him through eyelids half-closed against the sunlight, so that his face was fringed like a cameo by the glowing nimbus of her own lashes. 'You are a davil,' she murmured.

'Ah, you like me, though, don't you?'

'Sometimes.'

'Only sometimes?'

'Well – I was mad as fire with you the other day – flirting with them two old cats at the show.'

'Aha! Hester, that's a confession!'

'No – I only meant—'

'Too late,' he said, kissing her again. 'Secret's out. Jealous, eh? Why, they didn't mean anything at all.'

'Thass what you say.'

'Well, I wouldn't take *them* out for a picnic. Strait-laced little misses they are – Phoebe twice over. No fun at all.'

'Oh! I see – not the sort you can tek liberties with – not like me – thass what you mean. Well you're wrong there.' But almost before she had finished speaking she suffered a sort of mental flex of impatience at herself, for there was something perfunctory about this coquetry now that she had been brought to acknowledge what had been inexorably stealing on her ever since Lyle had come home – and so she effectively contradicted her words with an eager embrace which took him by surprise and sent his hat rolling on to the grass.

'By the left,' he said, when he had recovered his breath. 'I don't feel safe with you!'

'Oh! I won't hurt you. Now where you going?'

'To get my hat.'

'I'll git it,' she said, springing down from the trap. She got to the hat first, and put it behind her back.

'You Pampered Jade – Unhand My Boater,' Lyle said in his theatrical voice.

'Say please.'

'Please.'

'No.'

She ran up the bank. Lyle came after her as Gaffer, knees wobbling. 'Ooh! I shan't get down from here. Not with my anklesh. I shall go arshey-vershy. You young beggar! Thish were all fieldsh when I were a lad. And you never had to lock your door in them daysh.'

Hester made as if to skim the hat into the water.

'No! please – Hester – no, not my best hat!'

She put it behind her back again. 'Give us a kiss then.'

'Another one? She's insatiable.'

At last they returned laughing to the trap: drove on till they found a dry place shaded with a few rare trees by the waterside, and got out their picnic, sitting on carriage-rugs spread on the ground, whilst the pony cropped the grass and was teased by flies. The precipitancy of the drive and the chase with the hat was now replaced by a brilliant stillness; and when Hester lay back on the grass, after eating with her usual appetite, the only movement to be seen was directly above her, where a few white clouds travelled in a slow arc from horizon to horizon; the fens at such times offering a perceptible intimation of the spherical

193

nature of the earth, which their very flatness seems curiously to reinforce.

Propped on his elbow, Lyle leaned over her and tickled her face with a blade of grass.

'What a bit of luck, meeting you!' he said.

'True.' She felt utterly, blissfully relaxed with him: not a cell of self-consciousness in her whole body. 'Lucky boy.'

He stretched out his legs in his feline way. 'Folk are so serious, aren't they?'

'Terrible serious.' She snatched the blade of grass from his fingers, and poked it down his collar. 'Wouldn't it be funny if Gideon came along now, and saw us?'

'Mr Gideon to you, serving-wench.'

'Yes, Mr Lyle.'

'Oh! just My Lord will do.'

She put one hand to his face, and held it there. 'It's an odd sort of situation, ain't it?'

'How odd?'

'Well. Funny. Tricky.'

'Oh! it would be, I suppose – to serious people. Which we're not. I knew you were my type when I saw you sliding down that banister.'

'I don't know what I'll say to your mother if she asks me whether I'm had a nice day.'

'Well, you are having a nice day, aren't you?'

'Oh! fair – fair to middling. But you know what I mean.'

He subsided beside her, placing his hands behind his head and tipping his hat over his eyes. 'Just fib. It's easy. I've been fibbing all my life, and it's never hurt me yet.'

'You'd better not fib to me!'

For answer he merely curled his lips in a smile, his eyes invisible beneath the brim of his tilted hat.

'Oh! Lyle,' she said, 'just think – it's a whole fortnight till my next day off.'

'Trust a woman to think of that, when this one isn't even over! Anyway – a fortnight – that's years away – that's practically infinity. I can't think that far ahead. Besides, there's always a way round things, my dear. Always.'

'Is there?' Scarcely listening, she laid her head on his gently

194

rising and falling chest, gazed at the sky, and felt herself to be closer to that blue ether than to the earth below.


2


Jonathan Eastholm tended not to measure time in weeks. Though he had read much in the Bible, so that its accents often coloured his speech, he had little time for church or chapel, which divided time by Sundays; and the solitude of his life on the lighters having estranged him from the workaday world, and made the moon his chronometer, he habitually thought in fortnights – thus unconsciously evading fifteen hundred years of Christian history, and perpetuating the mental forms of the ancient Druids. When that June fine weather came, he had been precariously established as a one-hoss farmer in the little half-finished house on Hinching Fen for nearly four fortnights.

Even the poorest cottager from the upland shires might have been aghast at the bareness of his situation; and there were moments when even Jonathan's mind, schooled to hardship, staggered a little at the consequence of his reckless action. When he had first seen the house, he had viewed it in the light of a bower to bring a bride to; and so that vision had transformed it, and cloaked with romance the rough edges of reality. The failure of his suit – worse, its revelation as the purblind fantasy of a beleaguered egotism – had lifted the spell, and forced him to contemplate what he had done. Three things kept him from despair in the first days: the resilience of his own nature, the kind weather which eased a prospect that in winter would have been grim indeed, and the fact that, the lighters being untenable now by their sheer force of tormenting association, he would have had to change his mode of life anyhow.

The floor-space of the entire cottage was about the size of a prosperous tradesman's drawing-room. The single downstairs room, the house-place as it was called locally, had a brick floor and an open hearth for a turf fire, along with a few sticks of furniture which the former owner, Jonathan's friend, had left

195

behind him, having no use for them on the boats to which he had returned with hungry eagerness. A ladder-stair led to the room in the roof, which when Jonathan moved in still gaped with unfinished thatching, so that sparrows popped in and out, as if the house were no more than a negligible interruption to the sky: the windows too, at first, were only shuttered. Jonathan slept on a straw palliasse on the floor. The cottage was damp, of course – most fen cottages were; but this was particularly so, owing to its very recent and flimsy construction, and the thinness of its foundations on the peat. In consequence, the walls were inhabited by crickets, which after dusk made the whole place ring with their stridulations, and disturbed Jonathan's rest by making wild Cossack leaps over his body, and sometimes landing on him, with a disagreeable scratchiness. He countered this in an old fen way, by obtaining a young hedgehog scarcely out of the nest, and inducing it with libations of milk to become a house-pet. The hedgehog found the cottage a very comfortable berth, and its nightly trundlings around the walls soon reduced the cricket infestation; though if nature roused him in the night Jonathan was always careful, for both their sakes, lest he set his naked foot on the creature in the darkness.

As he lay on his straw bed, his large limbs disdaining clothes in the warm nights, Jonathan bore something of the appearance of a warrior of antiquity, taking his statuesque repose within arm's reach of sword and shield. Bone-weary from the day's work as he was, he always thought long, staring at the ill-laid rafters above, before going to sleep: thinking being something he had always enjoyed, as an active process. The silence of the fen pleased him, as did the sense of being his own master, and he felt that this new life promised some satisfaction. Still, troubled currents moved in him, swirling about the thought of Hester Verney, and the strange effect she had had on him. At times he could scarcely believe that he had been such a fool as to propose marriage, and all it entailed: that he had actually contemplated exchanging the purity of independence for the tainted pleasures of a cloying proximity. At such times the chance meeting with the girl at the Ferryman assumed the dimensions of a vast mistake in his life, engineered by a capricious fate which owned no higher aims than the vexation of mortals, and the confounding of their attempts to order their existence. But at other times, the image of the girl continued to haunt him in a peculiarly remote way, as if those eyes, that mouth, that laugh had only existed in one of those dreams which linger long after waking, and during which one seems to have been living in a parallel universe. He was not a good liar to himself, and could not deny that these latter times were the more frequent.

In fact his disappointment had changed Jonathan, more perhaps than he yet knew, and the change was not without benefits. There was something of liberation. The soul of the boy had been purposefully smothered on the day he left his stepfather's house, and the premature manhood on which he had entered had the slightly showy and unnatural quality of all forced growths. Now he had received a severe knock, and its effect was to release some of that buried youth, which was not without poetry. He had elevated self-sufficiency to a religion, of a stern and jealous kind: now the revelation that he was vulnerable after all left him a freer if more bewildered man, doubt replacing dogma. Most importantly, the disappointment he had suffered was notable for its sheer commonness: he had loved and known rejection, and so at a stroke found himself involved in the universal experience of humanity – which hitherto he had tended to regard, if not to despise, as an alien and irrelevant abstraction. The dammed springs of sympathy and generosity began to play again on his too long arid nature. He was carrying in his heart an image of beauty glimpsed and lost, which worked its age-old alchemy upon him; and the true man was beginning to emerge from the hard chrysalis of the persona.

Strangely enough, Jonathan seldom wondered what she might be doing now, or thought of seeking her out again. Her rejection had been absolute, so it seemed, and he was used to thinking in absolute terms. That he had gone about it all wrong he now knew, but that did not mean he knew of a right way to go about it, nor that he cared for a second time to expose the tender tissue of his pride to the lacerating scalpel of feminine scorn; and that element of the Spartan in him told him the only thing to do was to abjure the sight of her, and give himself up to work.

Work was, in any case, a pressing necessity, for the loan from the brickyard owner could only be repaid from the harvest of his first crop, and his friend the previous owner had only half-heartedly cultivated his few acres. He had sown some potatoes, which came as stock with the property, but Jonathan had done most of the planting, rather late, on land that had not been well ploughed. Of course, only the completest beginner could fail to get a crop from the rich peat: it was the very fertility that was the problem. Weeds were rampant: Jonathan, labouring with mattock and hoe, often thought he could see them growing out of the corner of his eye: even tall, thick-bladed reeds sprang up. However, he was no beginner, having done farm-work since boyhood. What he chiefly lacked was materials. He began as a farmer with one horse, stabled in a lean-to, a rusty plough and harrow, and a few other dilapidated implements which his friend had left behind him. That ingrained and rather rigid independence of his baulked at seeking help from neighbours; but he soon found it generously offered. This perplexed him at first, for he had yet to recognise that nobility did not only reside in an aloof self-reliance.

There was great interest in him, he knew, as a newcomer to Hinching Fen; but fen folk not being of the sort to impose themselves, and Jonathan keeping himself very much to himself, there was virtually no contact. The little world of the fen, its only landmark the windmill which Jonathan's front window framed exactly like a Dutch landscape painting, was spacious enough for him to avoid company if he chose. He seldom went to Milney St Mary, the village; a long drove separated his house from the high road; the nearest cottage was half a mile away. All this allowed him to embrace solitude as devoutly as he had on the lighters. One morning, however, he was returning from a walk far afield in search of mushrooms, his favourite food, when he caught sight of a youth standing by the boat-dyke, throwing his cap forcibly on to the ground, and bursting into noisy tears; and Jonathan could not pass by on the other side.

'Now then, boy,' he said, more gruff than he intended, from sheer lack of use of his voice, 'whass up?'

The youth, a tall stripling in that raw state of adolescence where the elbows and knees seem to belong to some maturer individual, beheld Jonathan through a mask of tears, and cried, 'Oh, mister! Look what I'm gone and done! Oh, 'ell! I let Molly git in and now she can't git out!'

Below, Jonathan looked into the large helpless eyes of a cow which, led round the dykesides for grazing, had obviously climbed down into the dyke to drink, and now found it could not climb out again. The animal had its hindquarters in the water, and looked like a person demurely testing a bath.

'Thass my fault!' the youth bellowed. 'I were dreaming again – mairster tells me off for dreaming – but I done it again – mairster'll have me guts for garters – I wish I were dead!' And seizing his cap, he threw it down on the ground once more, then picked it up and crammed it on to his head, as if he were a candle, and he were trying to extinguish himself.

'Who's your master, then?' Jonathan said.

'Mr Wake, mister. Oh, 'ell!'

'And where's his farm?'

'Oh – way uvver yonder,' the boy said, without any accompanying gesture, as if 'yonder' were a sufficient direction in itself.

'Well, now, stop roaring, do,' Jonathan said. 'You stay here, while I go back to my place, and fetch a spade and a bit o' rope. We'll soon have Molly out, and she won't come to no more harm than a wet behind amounts to.'

The boy gazed up at Jonathan as if he were some superhuman being sent to his aid, and he was still rooted in the same awed posture when Jonathan returned, bearing over his shoulder a hodding-spade and shovel and a coil of rope.

'Now then,' Jonathan said, clambering down the dykeside using the spade and shovel like crampons, 'I'll see if I can dig out a bit of a slope for her.' He cast one end of the rope around the cow's neck. 'Catch hold of tother end – whass your name?'

'Charlie Smeeth, sir.'

'You needn't sir me. They ain't knighted me yet. You give her a pull when I say.'

The dyke walls were in a soft condition, and it did not take long for Jonathan to dig out a rough ramp, shallow enough for the cow to manage; but the animal merely looked round at him with bovine obtuseness, giving an apologetic moo, and had to be encouraged to scramble up by the youth's tugging on the rope, and Jonathan giving her rump a hearty slapping.

Once this crisis was over, and Molly was safe, Charlie Smeeth gave a great display of emotional volatility, by bursting into a great high-pitched laugh of relief, with the tears still wet on his cheeks, and throwing his cap repeatedly into the air, as if headgear was a sort of auxiliary channel for the expression of his feelings. 'Hooray! I thought Molly was drownded. Hooray for you, sir!'

'Well,' Jonathan said, not without amusement, 'don't go dreaming again, will you?'

'Oh! no. Oh, 'ell!' said Charlie. 'I'm got to git back to mairster – and I'm ages late now, and he'll want to know why, and what I'm been up to – and I dursn't tell him! Sir, will you come wi' me, and tell mairster? Please, sir!'

'Well, you are a dippy beggar,' Jonathan said frowning, but as the round eyes of the boy seemed to presage further tempests, he said, 'Oh! come on then. I don't know. I never see such a panicky article.'

'Yes, sir. Thass what mairster says. He told me to try tekking deep breaths – but all it did was mek me heart go pitter-pat even wuss – and once I even keeled uvver and went head-fust into the pig-bin, because I'd sucked all this breath in and not let it out – so I don't do that no more, sir.'

'Don't sir me,' Jonathan said, between laughter and annoyance. 'Well, next time you feel yourself going panicky, try repeating a bit of poetry to yourself, just in your head.'

'Don't know any, sir. We used to have a bit at school, but I never got none, because I used to sit at the back, on account of the stink coming off Daddy Lucas – that were the schoolmaster, sir – he was as old as the hills, and I don't reckon he ever got a wash any more, because he used to bottle summat chronic – and he hadn't got much of a voice either, just a sort of wheezing, so I never heard nothing.'

'Hmm. D'you know any psalms?'

'I know The-Lord-Is-My-Shepherd-I-Shall-Not-Want.'

'Well, try that. Let's hear you say it.'

In this way, driving the cow before them, they came to the drove which led to Charlie's master's farm, and found Henry Wake coming down the drove to meet them.

'There you are, Charlie Smeeth!' he said: 'And me thinking you'd run away to sea! What's it all about?'

'Please, Mr Wake – I had a bit o' trouble – and I axed this mister to come and explain, because he got Molly out of the dyke.'

Charlie told his tale, wrenching his cap into various illustrative attitudes.

'Now, Charlie Smeeth!' Henry Wake said. 'Do you mean you're fetched this neighbour here, who I don't know the name of, but I shall be glad to, out of his way for this, besides putting him to so much trouble?'

'No trouble,' Jonathan said.

'Well, you're good enough to say so, neighbour,' Henry Wake said. 'Only if I know Charlie Smeeth here, you're had a teasing enough time on it. Charlie, what am I told you about dreaming, and gitting in a panic, and how one follows another? And look! here's our neighbour all drenched up to the thighs, on account on it.'

'Oh! that,' said Jonathan who, between the lighters and the damp cottage, was as seldom dry as a frog, and had not even noticed it. 'Tisn't anything.'

'Well, here's my thanks, any road,' Henry Wake said, holding out his hand, which was as slight as a cat's paw in Jonathan's. 'I think I'm right in saying you're our neighbour at the new cottage. I'm Henry Wake – everybody calls me Henry – I think you'll find I'm pretty well known around these parts—' this with an air of modestly refraining from saying why.

Jonathan introduced himself, and on Henry Wake's inviting him to step up to the house for a pinch of tea, declined, saying he had to get back to his work.

'Of course you have,' Henry Wake said. 'And here's this boy been keeping you from it. Charlie, when will you learn? Well, I'll walk as far as the high road with you, if I may, neighbour.'

So Henry Wake, taking three brisk steps to his one, accompanied Jonathan on the way back, talking volubly. The conversation turning naturally on farming, Jonathan was soon perforce confessing his deficiencies in tools and other necessaries, and Henry Wake offered him help with alacrity.

'I know I'm got a coulter in my shed – you must have that. I'm got onion-seed too – plenty to spare. As for a long-handled rake, I'm pretty sure Wag Langtoft's got one he could lend you.'

Jonathan was embarrassed, wishing he had not said anything, and afraid of seeming to cadge. But it appeared that this was only in his own mind, not Henry's: the latter came right to the cottage with him, and took great pleasure in assessing what he needed. 'Don't lay out capital on tools – not while you're just starting,' he said. 'I can help you to them. I say, that roof's a bit of a nuisance, ain't it?'

Jonathan had covered the unthatched gaps with rick-cloths. 'Thass another thing that'll have to wait, I'm afraid,' he said.

'I think I'll ask Sunny Daintree about that. He's our molecatcher – he turns his hand to all sorts of things out of the mole season. I reckon he's done a spot of thacking in his time.'

'Well – I'm really not able to lay out money at all just at the moment.'

'Don't worry about that. Sunny's not the sort to dun you for money if you ain't got it. I'll see how busy he is.'

From this moment, Jonathan's relations with the people of Hinching Fen changed, willy-nilly: he became a known quantity, and an object of practical interest. Sunny Daintree came ambling over one evening, with ladder and reed-sheaves, and laconically began patching up the roof.

'I shall pay you, soon as I'm able,' Jonathan said.

'Oh! no,' Sunny answered from the roof, in a voice like the sigh of wind through grass. 'Thass a poor ole world if you can't do a neighbour a service. We're only here the once, you know; and we never know when we'll be took. It always comes when you're not expecting it. We might be took tomorrer – both on us. I wouldn't be a bit surprised.'

202

'You're right there, Sunny,' said a little white-bearded old man, who had been approaching down the drove for an enormous length of time, like a clock-hand reaching the hour. 'How do, bor,' he said to Jonathan. 'I'm your next-door neighbour –' meaning he was the inhabitant of that nearest cottage, a mile down the road '– I'm come to watch ole Sunny thacking your roof.' For in the fens any such operation assumed the character of a public spectacle, and it was accounted natural to go along and watch it.

'This won't be a proper job, mind,' Sunny Daintree said. 'I'm only a bodger at thacking, and I dare say a real thacker would turn up his nose at it. But there ain't been a real thacker on Hinching Fen since Mucky Strode died. And he was an example, the way he was took. Right in the middle of a big swear he was, when an apple-plexy hit him, and he were took straight up to answer for hisself before you-know-who, with that on his lips. Ooh! dear. Terrible swearer he was. He could swear for ten minutes without repeating a word – couldn't he, Andrew?'

'I'm heard him meself,' said Andrew Surfleet (for it was he). 'It were quite a thing to hear him, in a shocking sort of way. Not that I understood half of the words he used. And when 'Enry Wake explained 'em to me, I still didn't. I'm always got by with a few damns and beggars, meself, and never felt the need of owt stronger. Thass like when Farmer Mather give us a drop of brandy one day, on account of his wife had give birth to two twins: I couldn't tek to that sort of drink at all, for it gits you drunk straight away, and you don't git the pleasure of feeling it creep up on you; and then you're got to the headache before you know where you are. Well, bor, I reckon you're doing a fair ole job wi' that thacking – I wonder you don't tek it up proper.'

'No,' Sunny said, 'I git by wi' the molecatching, and the gravedigging when I'm wanted. Matter of fact, I were up at the churchyard yis'dy, mekking hole for that chap over Milney Bank passed away Friday. He'd worn the same weskit for twenty-five year, you know: and then on the Thursday he bought hisself a new one off the tallyman, and the very next day he were took. Ooh! dear. Thass what you git for vanity, you see. Any road, the vicar was wittling at me to dig the hole a bit deeper. Now you know, you dig too deep in that peat and the hole just fills up wi' watter: but there were no telling him. So I did as he said, and they lowered the coffin in, and down it went wi' a gret splash like a bucket in a well. Ooh! dear. I could have told 'em that would happen. Git one big shower of rain, and I wouldn't be a bit surprised to walk in that churchyard and see all the coffins floating about like a load of ole boats. I wouldn't bat an eyelid.'

Presently another visitor came down the drove, with much greater speed than Andrew Surfleet. Peggy Chettle, bearing her great toothy smile before her like a torch, gripped Jonathan's hand quite crushingly. 'How do, dear boy. Thought I'd come and see how Sunny's doing, and mek meself known at the same time – not that you'll be wanting me yet, me being the midwife and you being a single man I'm heard, though how long that'll last I'm not sure –' genially fingering the open throat of Jonathan's shirt, and peeping down it – 'not long I reckon – no spare fat there, just like a washboard, what would you give to have a figure like that, eh, Andrew Surfleet?'

'Aye – a tidy figure of a man,' quavered old Andrew – he and Jonathan together looking like an illustration of the extremest variations possible to the human body. 'Not that I reckon I could tek to being quite so tall, meself: things must look so different from up there.'

'Now then, dear boy,' Mrs Chettle said, 'you may be big as a Grenadier Guard, and such a pair of calves as, dear me, quite a pleasure to look at 'em, but you git an ague on that chest, even though it looks like two pillows on a bed, and before you know it you'll be weak as a seven-month delivery, and there's nothing worse for the ague than a damp floor – so I says to Chettle the smorning, I shall tek that chap at the new cottage some of my horehound tonic, and here it is.' Peggy Chettle seized Jonathan's hand, and pressed a small bottle into it. 'You tek that regular, and you'll stay as strong as, well, as strong as you are, dear boy, carryen sacks of taters on your back like they were a couple of young 'uns not yet breeched, and looking at you I dare say we'll see that before long, dear me, such a breadth of back, quite like one of them ancient chaps you see in pictures, driving chariots with nothing on.'

'Thass very kind of you,' Jonathan said awkwardly, pocketing the bottle. 'Thank you.'

'Don't speak of it, dear boy. Now you feel badly any time, you come to me, the nearest doctor's in Stokeley and he charges a guinea just for tekking his gloves off, and though birthing babies is my business, and laying out of course, I know a bit about most ailments, and don't feel shy on account of me being a woman, why, I'm been seeing to Chettle's little trouble for years and it don't mean no more to me than peeling a mushroom. Well. I'm sure you'd keep me talking here all day, but I shall have to git on. I've only stopped on me way to Mrs Binns who's gitting near her time, her first, a bit over-anxious she is, merest gripe of wind and she's laying on the floor with her legs up, goodbye, all!'

'She ain't a bad soul, Peggy Chettle,' Sunny Daintree said when she had gone. 'She do rather talk, though.'

'Ah! she do. You can do wuss than tek her remedies, though, neighbour,' Andrew Surfleet said. 'She cured my rheumatiz years ago. Course, it's come back since then.'

So Jonathan went to bed that night beneath a whole roof; and the timing was fortunate, for there was a shower of rain before dawn. He was grateful, but confused. His independence seemed to be slipping away from him: and he still associated that independence with selfhood. He had read *Robinson Crusoe* not as an allegory of hard-headed Protestant man overcoming his environment, but as a romance of ideal life, the sort of uninvolved and uncompromised life he had fought to attain ever since he had been turned out on the world alone. But now that was being undermined. Perhaps it was the business of Hester Verney that had started it: his conscious mind still sought to stigmatise his falling for her as an infiltration of weakness, rather as the watermen held that hot baths enfeebled you. But his certainties were gone. He had always proudly refused to lay himself under obligation: now he came up against the fact that to proudly refuse Henry Wake's offer of tools was mere churlishness. Andrew Surfleet began to call in to see him every evening on his way home from work; and Jonathan came up against the fact that, in spite of himself, he looked forward to the company.

Sometimes Jonathan would be out in the field when Andrew dropped by, and the old man would take up the hoe or the rake and potter around lending him a hand. 'Ah, it wun't hurt me, bor,' Andrew said when Jonathan protested that he must already have done a hard day's work. 'I'm been digging gault for Farmer Mather all day, which is a stale sort of job when you git a lot on it, and doing this is just like having a skerrick of jam to tek the taste away.' Once he came when Jonathan was eating his tea – a plate of cold potatoes left over from his dinner (which had been a plate of hot potatoes). Andrew Surfleet seemed to grow thoughtful at this: and the next day when he called, he said, 'You swack your hat on your head, bor, and come along of me. My missis has got a pork dumpling waiting, and it'll tek three on us to eat it.'

Jonathan's first instinct was to refuse with thanks, but the thought of the lump of dry bread and cheese on his larder shelf got the better of him, and he found himself going along to Andrew's cottage, deploring his own laxity.

'Ah, course, you don't wear hat, do you?' Andrew said. 'Well, we're all made different, and I dare say your head don't git so cold up there. They reckon it gits colder, higher you go, but I can't see that meself, seeing as it's nearer the sun.'

Mrs Surfleet was a dainty old woman even more diminutive than her husband, with white hair as fine as cobweb combed in two wings over her head. Seated at their little table, Jonathan felt himself rather too prominent in point of knees and shoulders, and afraid to move his feet for fear of treading on someone. How many years this venerable couple had between them he could only guess, but neither was at all impaired in hearing, and their conversation was all in gentle cooing undertones, so that Jonathan had a strange sensation of having squeezed himself into a dovecote: Mrs Surfleet in particular did everything with the utmost quietness, and once or twice he was startled when a disembodied voice like a gnome's whisper spoke in his ear – 'Ha' bit more. Goo on. Tek bit more' – and he found that she had crept unseen to his side and was shyly offering him the rest of the dumpling. The meal was very good, and was lent extra savour by Jonathan's perception, as he looked round at the bare scrubbed house-place, unadorned but for a piece or two of pewter and some pots of musk and geraniums, that his hosts had never had a penny to spare all their lives. It was natural, perhaps, that one so full of years as Mrs Surfleet should refer to him several times as a 'growing boy', though if he had grown any more he would have broken his chair in two: and when he left, thanking them for their hospitality, she tugged his sleeve and softly entreated him, 'Mind the road,' though between their two houses the incidence of traffic was about one slow farm-cart per week.

Such marks of generosity strengthened Jonathan's resolve to work every moment of the day, so as to be in a position eventually to reciprocate. But even his diligence was circumscribed by the hours of daylight. One night in June, when the descent of darkness found him still not ready for sleep, he took a walk down to Milney St Mary, and outside the Labour In Vain he paused. The pub was a temptation he had so far successfully resisted, but tonight he was transfixed by something more insidious than the odours of smoke and ale. There was music playing within. Jonathan had sold up his old concertina, along with practically everything else, when he left the lighters; and had been starved of music ever since. There had, typically, been a touch of the anchorite's renunciation about this – but now, standing in the dusty road outside the glowing window, on which shapes moved as in a shadow-play, Jonathan gave himself up to sensual indulgence, and listened with a throbbing heart. It may have been that his encounter with Hester Verney had deepened this susceptibility which he had always been a little ashamed of, and given it a more tender resonance: certainly he hearkened to what was in truth an indifferent performance, on a kit-fiddle in need of tuning, as if the melody were wafted to him from Arcadia. A gusty wind, which had been getting up since sunset, boomed about his ears and impeded the music: so, thrusting his hand in his pocket to make sure he had twopence for a glass of ale, Jonathan went in.

He was greeted at once by Henry Wake, who was standing on the hearth before the enormous painting. 'Evening, Jonathan. I thought I saw you outside the window just now – just in silhouette, as it were, but thass not a build as one can mistake,' he said civilly.

Jonathan, a little embarrassed that his lingering outside had been observed, ordered his beer and joined Henry at the fireplace. The music was being played by Artie Gill, the old turf-digger, though attention to it among the drinkers seemed to have passed its zenith: Artie Gill having this in common with amateur musicians throughout the ages, in that he seldom cared to play when he was asked, and when he did play he would not leave off.

'You've an ear for a tune, neighbour, I can tell,' Henry Wake said. 'I've a tolerable ear meself, no point in pretending I haven't: when we lack an instrument at chapel I'm often called upon to give the note for the hymns, and I'm seldom far out. Hark at that wind rising!' he added, as a gust moaned down the chimney, and scattered some unswept ashes in the grate.

'Hope we're not in for a blow,' remarked Sunny Daintree, who was sitting on a bench by the wall, the slope of the floor causing him to lean at a compensating angle, like a man taking a corner in a fast buggy. 'Not with the new crops just up. It wouldn't surprise me. It were black over Will's mother's the smorning' – this expression not signifying a particular locality, but being a variant of yonder.

'Jonathan, I don't believe you're met Chad Langtoft, are you?' Henry Wake said, gesturing to a thin fair young man at the bar. 'Chad's got something to celebrate today – he's got hisself engaged to Mary-Ann Cole, and they're gitting married as soon as ever is. Chad, this is Jonathan Eastholm.'

Jonathan gave his congratulations. Chad Langtoft, with a slightly glassy stare of beer and elation, said, 'Come to the wedding, neighbour. It'll be a good do, I tell you. And tek a drink on me now.'

'Much obliged to you,' Jonathan said. 'I'm got one here barely started, thanks kindly.'

'Oh! well, if you say so,' Chad said, with a covert look at Jonathan, as though he suspected a snub.

'When's it to be then, Chad?' asked Sunny.

'Right after harvest, I reckon. No point in waiting, is there?'

'Unless there's summat up as won't wait,' grunted Artie Gill, pausing in his fiddling to dunk his mouth in beer.

'Why, whoever said anything of that?' Chad said, turning round taut as a whipcord, and flushing a terrible red.

'No one, no one, Chad,' soothed Henry Wake. 'Just Artie's joke, and not a good one. I'm sure we're all looking forward to the wedding, aren't we?'

'Ah!' said the company in unison. 'If we're spared,' added Sunny Daintree.

'Well, I'd better git off hum,' Chad said. 'Don't want to start wedded life set in bad habits,' and, rather unsteadily, he took his leave.

'So it's a forced job, then?' said Jass Phelps, the landlord, when Chad had gone.

'No-oo!' said Sunny. 'That were just Artie, stirring trouble.'

'It's nice for the lad, I reckon,' Henry Wake said. 'He's soon got over Hester Verney, as it's turned out, so thass a blessing.'

'What's that about Hester Verney?' Jonathan said, abruptly roused from listening to Artie Gill's mournful rendering of 'Spanish Ladies' and presenting a face of such fierce interrogation that Henry Wake jumped.

'Why, nothing, neighbour,' Henry said timidly. 'You know her, then? Chad Langtoft had a taking for her, thass all; but now he's found hisself another gel.'

'Oh,' Jonathan said, relapsing into meditation. 'Yes, I know of her.'

'Hester's left the fen now, of course, and gone Stokeley way. Lizzie Gosling sees her odd times,' Henry said. 'A very nice gel, I always said. But I reckon Mary-Ann Cole's more suited for Chad.'

Presently Henry announced he was off home, and Jonathan, regretting the way he had alarmed him, elected to walk with him. He could find little to say. The simple mention of Hester Verney – the reminder that she really existed in the world, when in some odd way she had become for Jonathan an entity in a private mythology, with significance for him alone – had unnerved him, and thrown the world momentarily out of joint. In this agitation of mind, he noted as merely complementary the commotion in the sky, where the wind, veering to westerly, was driving before it a multitude of mangled clouds, which streamed headlong across the face of the moon as if in flight from some direful catastrophe.

'Gitting up,' Henry Wake said, gripping his bowler hat to his head. 'It'll 'bate by morning, I reckon.' Their ways parting, they said goodnight, and Jonathan proceeded deep in thought to his cottage, where he laid himself down in his shirt, and passed at length into an uneasy sleep, threaded through with fragmentary dreams. One of these jolting him awake, he looked round to see the sickly pallor of the fore-dawn steeping the room, and realised at last, from the sound being repeated, that it was not a dream but an actual crashing noise that had roused him.

He lit the oil-lamp, which in the dim greyness glowed like rotting matter, and dressed himself. A snuffling alerted him to the presence of the hedgehog, which instead of going on its prowl, was curled in the farthest corner of the fire-grate, and winked its weak eyes at him. Jonathan opened the door, only to find it snatched from his hand, and flung with violence against the outer wall. Stepping outside, he thought for a moment he had blundered into some large yielding object: it was the wind, hurling itself against him with a solidity that seemed scarcely possible to mere air. He stumbled out, forced to turn his face so as to catch his breath, and found the source of the noise he had heard in two slates which had been lifted from the roof of the lean-to and dashed on the ground: inside his horse was unsettled, quivering all along its flanks, and rolling a wild eye at him as he spoke to it. A squawking chorus of alarm came from the chicken-coop: it seemed quite secure, but for safety Jonathan weighted the roof down with a couple of bricks. In the sky a fragile light was beginning to appear, dissipated by a confusion of scurrying clouds, so that it scarcely amounted to a dawn at all, but it was sufficient to limn the thatched roof of the cottage, and to reveal that Sunny Daintree's workmanship was standing firm against a westerly gale that seemed to shake the very chimney-stack.

Jonathan returned inside, and made himself a hasty and absent breakfast of bread and cheese with a pennorth of milk, his ear cocked all the while to the wind, which seemed to stretch all around in a multiform clamour, like the passage of some vast and ragged army across the country. A long interval of muttering quietness was succeeded all at once by a fortissimo shriek, which burst open the shutters at the window as if the gale had suddenly turned all its potent attention to Jonathan's cottage alone, and funnelling inside, set the pans that hung above the hearth clanging like so much percussion, and riffled in an instant through every page of the *Old Moore's Almanac* that stood open on the table.

Jonathan sprang up and heaved the shutters to, and then bound the latches together with twine. A tremendous diapason sounded down the chimney, as if a giant had blown across the mouth of a titanic stone jar. Throwing on his jacket and buttoning it to the chin, Jonathan went out to his fields.

A lemon-yellow morning was beaming fitfully through the wrack of cloud. Jonathan, trudging along with bent head, saw little rills of fine black dust dancing along at his feet, and in these trivial signs read the terrible magnitude of what was happening. The wind was not, as Henry Wake had said, going to blow itself out. What might be no more, within the confines of a town, than a slightly perturbing gale, became in the open spaces of the fens the unchaining of an element. Across this flat land, scarcely broken by so much as a hedgerow, the wind walked at will, and in spring and early summer a westerly traversing the great plain could whip itself into a sheer frenzy of force. The danger in the phenomenon called a fen-blow lay not so much in the damage to human habitation as to the soil. Heavy clay land was resistant to the scourging of the gale, but here there was only light and vulnerable peat, which before Jonathan's eyes was being sifted in the wind's fingers and whirled into the air.

The soil-dust was beginning to choke him: he took off his neckerchief and tied it around his nose and mouth, screwing up his eyes at the gritty particles that were swirling and eddying about in miniature tornadoes. Drifts of lifted peat like rapidly forming dunes were beginning to obscure the field-path. The water in the dyke running alongside was blown into a furrowed pattern like the roof of the mouth, whilst a continual rain of pulverised peat dappled its surface. Looking out across his mangold-field, Jonathan saw the tender young plants fluttering and trembling in the blast.

He ploughed on. Uprooted shrubs were bowling across the fields, and he caught one full in the face. For a few moments he thought he was blinded, and when he opened his stinging eyes at last it was to the hallucinatory sight of the sun shining in a black sky. The soil-storm was sweeping across the fen in a silky curtain, and darkening the light of morning to the hue of an unearthly dusk. On the horizon he could just make out the shapes of a row of old pollard willows, bent over like saplings so that their topmost twigs brushed the ground, and the spinning sails of the mill.

Grainier fragments were striking his face now, and peppering the dyke, and he recognised seed – late seed that he had planted, and that the wind was simply planing off with the surface peat. He battled on, thinking of the potatoes, the turnips, the peas; but he knew there was nothing practical to be done. If rain threatened ricked crops, you covered them; if fire, you put it out: but if a fen-blow assailed the fields, you were helpless. He knelt down and lifted a seedling, and found the young leaves shredded by the flying granules of soil as if grubs had eaten them away. All across the young green of the field, specks of naked white were appearing where roots were being exposed by the clawing of the gale.

He turned back out of the blast in an impotent sort of fury, and saw a little figure tottering towards him up the field-path. It was old Andrew Surfleet, gripping on to his hat with both hands, his white beard turned to pepper-and-salt by the soil-dust.

'I'm been up Farmer Mather's,' Andrew shouted above the howling. 'All his gates are gone down like a pack of cards. You sealed up your house, bor?'

Jonathan shook his head dispiritedly.

'Come on, then. That'll all be a davil of a muck if you don't. You can't do no good out here.'

Jonathan followed him. In spite of the neckerchief, his mouth and nostrils were filled with dust. A few hapless starlings, their feathers clogged, whirred clumsily over their heads for a moment and then were lost in the turbulent murk, which mounted right into the upper air in teeming cataracts, closing out the rays of the sun like a thick gauze. On lifting a hand to push back his hair, Jonathan observed that the black coating on his skin continued up his arm even where it was covered by his sleeve: he pushed his fingers under his shirt, and found that his midriff was the same, and that his body must be as effectually covered with the soil-dust as if he had gone out naked.

They arrived at his cottage at last, and Jonathan found that though he had fastened the shutters and the door, everything within was covered with a fine black bloom, right down to the inner surface of the teapot and the edge of each page of *Robinson Crusoe*. Andrew Surfleet helped him seal the door-jamb and window-sill with rags. 'Might as well stop it gitting any wuss,' the old man said. 'You can't keep it out completely, though. Even the crocks packed away in my missus's cupboard'll want washing after this.'

Jonathan found he had not the heart to start clearing up: he felt ridiculously weary. He slumped in a chair, and listened to the shrill melisma of the wind and the endless scurrying of the peat, whilst Andrew puttered around putting things straight and lighting the turf fire to boil a kettle. 'You got a pinch o' tea, bor? May as well have a drop. Farmer Mather sent me hum, there's no work doing today. Ah! we don't often git a blow this late on, but it happens. There ain't a beggaring thing you can do about it. Still, no cross, no crown, as they say.'

They sat for some time drinking the tea and listening. The fury of the wind raved on, and its declension to a lower note was so gradual that only a brightening of the light in the shuttered room alerted Jonathan at last to the fact that the fen-blow was abating. He got up and opened the door: this time, it was not torn from his fingers. Followed by Andrew, he went out.

Dust still bleared the air, but the wind was tiring of its ghastly dance with the earth, and was relinquishing its partner by degrees, the soil sinking downward in hazy vortices, with brief scutterings as it subsided like the convulsions of death. The drove leading up to the house had disappeared beneath a drift of peat and seedlings – not his own: these must have been blown from the next farm, or further. Mechanically Jonathan walked out to his fields to see the damage to his crops. Except, of course, there was no telling where his crops were. They might have been amongst the mass of dislodged seedlings choking the dyke and strewn about the field-paths: they might have been hurled right over to the other side of Hinching Fen. Some few of the stronger young plants remained, half-buried in black dunes, shredded to tatters: the rest were scattered broadcast, their fertiliser with them. The wind had whisked off the cultivated layer of the fen like a tablecloth, and torn it to shreds.

'Ah! well, bor – never mind,' Andrew Surfleet said, patting Jonathan's back – he had to reach up on tiptoe to do this. 'You'll just have to drill again, like everybody else on the fen I shouldn't wonder.'

Jonathan nodded. He had thought of that: had been thinking, indeed, all the time he was sitting slumped in the cottage. He already owed money, and had none with which to pay for new seed and fertiliser; and to drill all over again, this late in the season, would produce at best a much enfeebled yield, certainly nothing sufficiently profitable to pay off his debts. Moment by moment it was being borne in on Jonathan that, insecure seedling of a farmer as he was, this morning's work by a skittish wind had undone him, and it was doubtful that he would be able to keep the cottage and its holding. Reproachful thoughts of his rashness in buying it were not slow to occur to him, as he contemplated the prospect, perhaps measurable a few fortnights hence, of losing his cherished independence at last: but he thought too, with a certain wistful twist of humour, that it was fortunate that his proposal to Hester had been unsuccessful, and that the trials coming to him would not be rendered sorer by the torment of knowing he had embroiled her in them too.

The gusts were growing fitful now, and carelessly tossing down the last clouds of winnowed peat. Jonathan stooped and picked up a sliver of metal. It was a coin, of some antiquity judging by its abraded condition, turned up by the soil-storm: in the fens nature is her own archaeologist. Normally Jonathan was intensely interested in these finds, but after a glance he let it fall to the ground.

Andrew Surfleet reached up to pat his back again. 'You come along o' me, bor,' he said. 'We'll see if my missus has got summat to eat.'

# Chapter Seven

1

The summer when Hester fell in love drew on, marked by strong, dry and glassy heat, which seemed to burn with full maturity from the very first moment of dawn, and to subsist long after sunset, in the manner of a cooling brick oven.

The horses in the yard thirsted with heaving sides, and grunted with pleasure when the stable-lad came along with buckets of water, the merest splash from which brought sparrows darting down to fill their tiny bills and bathe their dusty plumage. Even the draped and vault-like rooms of the Saunders' house were stifling, and the dropsical vases and jardinières that stood in the windows were as hot to the touch as if they had just come out of the kiln. Hester's feelings were wrought up to intensest pitch in just the same way, and when she restlessly threw back the bedclothes and stared at the first torrid smears of sunrise, she hardly knew whether she laboured under heat or love.

From her earliest childhood Hester's emotional life had tended more to diversity than singularity, and flux rather than fixity. Instead of a home she had had a series of insecure habitations: in place of a mother and father, a vague gentle memory and a vaguer presence whose very insubstantiality eluded the grasp of anything stronger than affection; and her naturally keen and intelligent mind being denied a prolonged education, she had none of that attachment to an idea which makes saints and tyrants. So her feelings were warm, but diffuse: she would far more readily have sympathised with the pagans who saw a deity in every leaf and stone, than with her contemporary worshippers of the one God. And yet inside

Hester, like a grown chick within the egg, there was the most ardent and partisan of romantics waiting to be born. Some people fall in love as dogmatically as others embrace politics or religion; and it was perhaps typical of Hester's streak of perversity that she, who valued lightness above everything, fell in love with Lyle Saunders so heavily that oblivion shrouded every other dimension of her consciousness. The spectrum of her emotions was refracted to the purest and fiercest ray. Lyle became her metropolis, to which everything else in life was an indifferent hinterland.

It was a truism to reflect that she had never felt like this before: more accurately, she had never felt anything this strongly before. She was a coaster who suddenly found herself in deep waters. Not merely the pleasures, but the luxurious pains of the lover were opened newly to her: the latter occurring not through quarrels, doubts or misunderstandings, but as a result of the difficult soil in which their affair took root. She was with Lyle for a great part of each day, and for a great part of each day she was forced to affect towards him the respectful formality appropriate to the son of her employer: to observe with equanimity the smooth hands which fitted her own so well, and never betray her urge to seize them; to watch the cat cross the room and sit on his lap, conscious of the stark impossibility of her doing likewise; to intercept his smile across the dinner-table, and yet stay fixed in her seat, instead of soaring up to the ceiling and careering about the dusty chandelier like a balloon. The strains this placed on Hester, who was not used to dissembling her feelings, were great: the compensations, as is the way with love gratified, both ample and dissatisfying. Her days off she spent entirely with him, but it was never enough. As she said to him, she was not greedy: twenty-five hours a day of him was all she wanted.

The season was favourable to a romance that was of necessity pursued mostly outdoors. Sunlight, blue sky, heat and burgeoning greenness formed the medium in which her love was cultivated, and it grew up as rapidly and sturdily as the wheat which stirred about them in tawny seas as they drove out in the trap. Hester's practical nature was turned on its head: the utilitarian landscape of the fen, which she had always associated

217

with back-breaking labour, all at once became a picturesque setting for the drama of her feelings; she saw meads of asphodel in a field of mustard-seed, the scrubbiest orchard glowed like the garden of the Hesperides, and the enchantment of an idyll transformed the humble banks of the Nene. She was ready for these outings from dawn, and was reluctant to return at dusk: and though she told Mrs Saunders that she was visiting her old friends on Hinching Fen, in fact she neglected them most shamefully. There was no help for it. In her first exhilaration, friendship seemed to stand to love in the same relation as pap to solid food – impossible to savour the one after a taste of the next.

The minutiae of the process by which Hester surrendered a heart that had hitherto been given over to little more than frivolity were commonplace enough – insofar as any of the daily miracles of human life may be accounted commonplace. They went out in the trap, Lyle always driving recklessly fast, they explored the countryside, they talked, laughed, ate picnics. Lyle, who pecked erratically at food, liked to watch her eat. 'What an appetite!' he would say, admiringly, as she finished off the contents of the picnic-basket; and for the first time Hester began to be self-conscious, and tried to eat a little more daintily, without it being obvious that she was doing so. Why she should do this, when her appetite was one of the things he liked about her, she could not have said: perhaps she was touched by insecurity. Hester, who had always had a healthy sense of her own merits, discovered that the experience of being loved did not necessarily reinforce it. As the slightest comment on our physical appearance sends us flying to the mirror, Hester found that the apprehension of Lyle's loving her set off an anxious mental review of all her qualities: she submitted to endless examination a self that she had always taken for granted. The result, of course, was that disturbing feeling that her lover did not really know her at all; that she was two people; that what he saw was not what was within, and that at any moment the mask might fall. This unavoidable disjunction in human intercourse troubled Hester particularly because she was supremely honest. She valued Lyle's love so dearly that she could not bear to think it might be based on a false premise.

Lyle was amused at the pleasing torments she put herself through on this account. 'But you must have known a lot more interesting girls than me,' she would say.

'Interesting!' he laughed. 'What a word! How do you mean – girls who smoke cigars, or do the Indian rope-trick, something like that?'

'No – you know. I'm never done anything, Lyle – nothing but donkey-work on the ole fen. Thass all there is to my life.'

'Why, what do you think the young misses in the smart houses in Huntingdon have done in their lives? Sewed a few samplers and gone out with their mamas to sip tea with a lot of other young misses. I'm sure you've had a lot more worthwhile experience than that.'

'They're got more education than me.'

'Have they? What education do you suppose Phoebe Purefoy has, for example? A couple of chords on the piano, the names of the kings of England, and a few French verbs which you could pick up in a week or two, if you wanted, and if there was any point to it, which there isn't. Besides, Giddy and me never got much schooling. Mother had us working in the stable-yard practically as soon as we could read.'

'Well . . . I wish I knew what you really think about me.'

'What a wittler you are! My dear, I think –' suddenly he became young Mr Pimlott – 'I think you're an absolutely *topping* gel.'

Such questioning was also, of course, a way of hearing nice things about herself – a harmless lovers' subterfuge which Adam and Eve probably adopted: but Hester was quite in earnest. She desperately wanted to be loved, and feared being found unworthy. Having enjoyed a sturdy independence of mind for so long, her loss of it was the more complete – a girl who was forever falling in and out of love would have assumed more, and hungered less. All this did not mean that she spent all her time with Lyle in a gloomy fidget: she was happier than she had ever been in her life – indeed it seemed to her that only now had her large capacity for happiness met with its proper object.

Often she thought how intolerable the two of them would have seemed to a third person. They laughed at each other: they

219

laughed at anything. They put on each other's hats. She plaited his hair like a stallion's mane, then sat back and screamed at the sight of him. He draped the picnic-cloth around him like a toga, and delivered an oration to the waterfowl. Once they called at an isolated farmhouse in hopes of buying some milk, and were greeted by a little mad old woman wearing a bonnet entirely covered with nodding wax cherries, who confided to them in a whisper that she could not sell them any milk because a bear had come along and drunk it all; and after that Lyle only had to say the word 'Cherries' for Hester to be in danger of hysterics. Sometimes, for devilment, he would do so at home, even with Mrs Saunders or Gideon around. 'Cherries, my dear,' he would intone gravely, passing Hester in the hall or the yard, 'cherries'.

'What's the matter with you, gel?' Mrs Saunders cried.

'Got a bit of a cough, Mrs Saunders,' spluttered Hester into a handkerchief.

'Huh! Don't give it to *me*.'

It was typical of Lyle to sail close to the wind in this way. The convention they observed of giving no hint of their relationship at home was always at risk from a wink or chance familiar remark from Lyle. 'Oh! I don't reckon anyone's going to notice,' he said, when they were alone and she mentioned this. He kissed her fingers. 'You worry too much. What do you do?'

'Worry too much. Ooh, you want a shave.'

'So do you.'

'I suppose your mother'll have to know eventually, anyway.'

'Eh? Oh! yes. Don't mind about that.' He subdued her fears with a kiss. When she was alone, however, they returned, with all the painful earnestness that had hitherto been conspicuously absent from her life. All sorts of shadows were newly fretting the clear light of Hester's personality, and not the least of these was guilt at deceiving Mrs Saunders. She tried to tell herself that it was the old lady's fault, after all, for being so unreasonable about canoodling; but she found it would not do, precisely because she was so serious about Lyle. She might have concealed a mere flirtation with an easy conscience – but this was much more than a flirtation. It was certainly conducted in that manner, because of the light-heartedness that was the natural mode of expression for both of them. But Hester was in deep: her heart seemed to throb distractingly from waking to sleeping, and she moved about the Saunders' house and yard in a state of disorientation. Everything there was defined by Lyle's presence. A footstep in the hall, and she was tensely listening lest it was that light and mercurial tread of Lyle's; on Gideon's birthday she scrutinised Lyle's characteristically lavish present to him as if it were for her; when a groom came to the door with a question, it was Lyle she automatically fetched, as if no one else lived there. With this glowing consciousness on her, to dissemble what was going on seemed not only treacherous, but downright fantastical – rather as if she should carry on with blithe normality when the house had turned upside-down and stood on its roof.

And so her proximity to Lyle was both a delight and a torture. He was cunning in manufacturing pretexts for them to be alone – even inventing a nervousness on the part of certain newly-acquired horses, which only Hester's presence would quell; but there were long periods in which no such opportunity presented itself, and she was forced to yoke together the violent antitheses of lover and spectator. When he was not at work Lyle exhibited a sort of restless idleness. He would sleep on the sofa with profound abandon, as if he had just fought a battle, for a couple of hours, then rise abruptly with his face all creased and attempt as if his life depended on it some trifling task, like mending an old clock which Mrs Saunders was going to throw out anyway. He could remain in bed until it seemed he would never surface again, but stayed up the whole of one night with one of the cats while it gave birth to kittens, and then was bright as a bee all next day. Some evenings he went out to the Nag's Head, and came back with a high colour, and a conspicuously careful step; others he read the newspaper from front to back and back again, one slender leg over the arm of his chair, yawning and eating his way through a whole bag of grapes, which was the sort of nibbling food he preferred to orthodox meals. A year ago Hester would have thought herself daft to find in all this such a tantalising fascination. She would have thought herself daft, too, and rather contemptible, for having a sort of weepy tantrum.

It happened on her day off, when for the first time Lyle could not go out with her: Gideon, who was to have gone to an important auction, was ill with toothache and Lyle had to take his place. They were under the trees by the paddock when he gave Hester this news: she stood still for a moment, caught in a green net of glare and shadow created by the sun beaming through the branches, and all at once she felt crushed: an insupportable woe overcame her, and to her own astonished shame she was in tears.

'Oh! it's no good, this,' she stuttered wretchedly. 'We might as well give it up – there's no point to it at all.'

Lyle looked as surprised as she was at this outburst. 'Yes, there is,' he said.

'No, there ain't,' cried she, driven contrary by the pressure of disappointment. 'It's nothing but hiding, and pretending, and sneaking, and it just spoils it.' Such were the doubtful feelings that had been building up in her over the summer – something like a photographic negative of her happiness; but she had not anticipated expressing them like this. 'Oh, Lyle, what I mean is – everything's so sort of underhand between us, and it makes it seem like it don't mean anything real and true – and it does to me.'

'It does to me too, Hes,' Lyle said. 'Did you think it didn't?'

'No,' she said, 'no, no,' scrubbing away her tears, and suddenly conscious of seeming to extort an emotional blackmail – a despicable proceeding. 'I didn't mean that. I know it's not easy. I know you're got to go to the auction. I don't know what's the matter with me – I never git the miseries like this – honest.'

'Poor old girl – you are in a state,' he said tenderly, curling his arm about her waist. 'It is pretty awful for you having to go without me for a day – that's enough to make any girl cry – but there'll be lots more days, you know.'

'I do love you, thass the trouble,' she murmured, 'swell-head.'

'That's no trouble. That's very handy, because I'm pretty

keen on you too. What could be better? Ah, I know. You're afraid you're going to end up like Phoebe Purefoy, with nothing ever coming of it. Confess, now.'

'Well,' she said, a little prideful, 'maybe – except I'd never wait for you for five years – sweet as you are.'

He laughed. 'Oh! yes, you would. But you won't need to. Don't you worry. I'm not going to give you up, Hes. Where am I going to find a girl to suit me like you do? Why, you're the only one I could bear to marry.'

Hester swallowed, and almost choked. 'Lyle Saunders! Is that meant to be a proposal?'

'Why not? We're right for each other, aren't we? Oh! don't shay I've got to get down on me kneesh. Not with my legsh . . . Tell you what. I'll marry you, if you'll marry me. Bargain?'

'You gret fool,' said she, between laughing and crying. 'You gret yawnucks. I'd say yes if I thought you were serious.'

'Serious as I'll ever be. Don't cry any more, Hes. You look like the very devil when you cry.' He touched her chin. 'And I do mean it about getting married. You're the girl for me – don't think I don't know it. By the left, I do believe you're speechless! Now that's a first. Why, you didn't reckon I was a Trifler, did you?'

'Oh! I don't know what you are,' she said, unable to do more than bathe in the moment, with Lyle's arm about her waist, and the sunlight scattering like gold treasure through the canopy of branches.

'Now no more of that stuff about giving it up.'

'Wait a minute – I ain't said yes yet, you know.'

Sternly he said: 'Hester Verney, if you don't take up this offer, I shall go and chuck myself in the river, and you'll never see me again – except when they drag me out all slimy, and nibbled at by fish and other freshwater creatures; and then you'll spend the rest of your life in regret and remorse, and end up a mad old woman tippling gin, and wearing a hat covered with cherries. So, make your choice.'

She was laughing, but her heart was full as though she would cry again: she was a very pincushion of stabbing emotions. 'Oh! give us a kiss,' she said. 'I'd better say yes – no one else'd put up with you.' Still, as he kissed her she heard the faint insistent note of doubt; and the honesty of her nature compelled her to express it. 'It's not me that's the trouble, though, Lyle,' she said, fixing his light blue eyes with her own, 'it's your mother, ain't it?'

'Mother? Don't worry about that. Her bark's worse than her bite, you know.'

She was silent: she thought they were both pretty formidable.

'Now, my love,' he said, pressing her waist, 'you're wittling inside – I can tell you are. You just leave it to me. I know my mother. I've known her all my life, funnily enough. All I've got to do is pick my time, and use my charm, et cetera, and everything will be all right. After all, she likes you, you know. She even likes me, in her way.'

'But she don't like her sons gitting married,' Hester said – clutching thus at a fugitive pessimism, even as Lyle's gaiety blew it away.

'She hasn't tried it yet, has she? I'll soften her up. Trust me.'

Hester wondered whether even Lyle's powers of persuasion might meet their match in Mrs Saunders' obstinacy: but she did trust him; and now she had a fund of delighted anticipation, which she continually drew on and which never diminished. She spent her day off walking by the river, her feet scarcely touching the ground: nervously happy, and exulting that the Promise had come true at last. The Promise was a hazy embodiment of her optimism, which from her earliest youth had fulfilled in Hester's mind something of the function of religious faith. She had never known what form this distant vindication might take, but through every vicissitude, however dispiriting, of her life, the vision of it had hovered before her, a bright patch in the blur of futurity. And here it was – sooner than she had thought – in the quicksilver shape of Lyle. She could not let it slip from her hands. A hole-in-the-corner affair was no good – she felt too much. Nothing could have made her interrupt the pleasure of loving him but the fear – which had burst out in tears among the paddock trees – that it might never come to fruition.

But she did not press him, after that: the visions of what

was to be were so beguiling as to suspend the uncertainty of the present hour, and her discomfort at deceiving Mrs Saunders was assuaged by the assurance that it was a temporary expedient: she could enjoy the sailing all the more, now she knew that land was in sight. Memories of what had happened when Gideon had raised the idea of marrying Phoebe she dismissed: Lyle was not Gideon; she knew Lyle's propensity for getting his own way, and had seen him gain concessions from his mother on other matters by catching her at the right moment. As it happened, she was wrong as could be in dismissing those memories – partly because while she waited for Lyle to make his move it was Gideon, of all people, who forced the issue.

It is simple enough to disguise a liking for someone – countless romances have begun with a long prelude of silence and cool looks; but it is practically impossible to disguise a dislike for someone. The most disingenuous face betrays itself – whereas Hester's might have served as an illustration to the phrase about the eyes being the windows of the soul. That said, she had always rubbed along with Gideon as well as she was able, and never meant him any harm. Hester's was as free from malice as it is possible for a mortal nature to be; but what was in her a mere trace-element was much more substantially present in Gideon – and it was active.

Afterwards, what happened seemed inevitable, as she retraced its stages in memory. She recalled a day when she had been shopping in the town for Mrs Saunders. Lyle was supposed to be taking the trap out that day, and when she saw it standing outside the tobacconist's, she assumed the boatered figure bending over the tail-board to be Lyle: she hurried across the street calling his name, and realised her mistake just as Gideon straightened up, turned, and gave her a tremendous stare, which did not moderate at her feebly and uselessly saying, 'Oh . . . sorry – I thought it was Mr Lyle.' Then there was the morning when, Mrs Saunders having complained to her that the parlour looked like a bear-pit, Hester tidied round: Gideon, coming in, protested that he could not find his papers.

'Did you put them away?'

'Yes – in the bureau.'

225

'They'll be all mixed up now,' Gideon grumbled. 'They're important accounts. It's not your job to mess about with things like that. You should ring for Judy, it's the housemaid's business, not yours. Your job is to attend to Mrs Saunders—'

'Leave her alone, old man, can't you?' said Lyle, who was reading the newspaper. He spoke lightly, but his cheeks had gone pink.

'I didn't suppose it was your business either,' Gideon said.

'Well, I'll make it so, if you don't stop going on at Hester,' Lyle said, his eyes still on his newspaper.

'Oh! pardon me,' Gideon said, looking narrowly at his brother, and then at Hester. 'I seem to be the odd one out here.'

It was curious, as Hester had noticed before, that Lyle was uncomfortable at quarrelling with Gideon, even when the latter provoked it: he seemed to prefer to be affectionate even with no return, and at dinner that day he stood up for his brother. Gideon mentioned that he would not be here on Sunday for tea – he had been invited to the Purefoys'.

'Well, I've got Mrs Fowler coming,' Mrs Saunders said, 'and I want you here.'

'Really, Mother—'

'You'll be here on Sunday. I'm telling you. That's the end of it,' said Mrs Saunders, stonily.

'That wouldn't be fair on the Purefoys, if Giddy's accepted the invitation, Mother,' Lyle said casually. 'You know how you hate it when people cry off. I'm sure Mrs Fowler will understand – and I'll be here, and—'

'You'll both be here, I say so, and that's all there is to it,' declared Mrs Saunders, glaring into the middle distance, and looking like a carving on a totem-pole, perhaps representing the Spirit of Pig-Headedness. 'Judy, clear away.'

But if Lyle radiated affection indiscriminately, Gideon's resentment seemed to work in the same way. Instinct told Hester that Gideon suspected them: instinct told her too that if suspicion became knowledge, they could scarcely rely on him not to convert it into credit. Sooner or later, however, Lyle's rather flagrant nonchalance made it inevitable that Gideon would observe something that could not be mistaken. It came sooner; the very day after the dinner-table row about the Purefoys. Lyle was exercising a mare, and Hester was sent out to give him a message from Mrs Saunders. With an impulsive bravado, Lyle bent lithely right down from the saddle, like a circus-rider, to plant a kiss on her lips. She turned round from the kiss to look straight into the small eyes of Gideon, watching from the back window of the tackle-room.

'Get in here, gel.'

Mrs Saunders was seated in her wing chair by the bare hearth, nursing her stick, her large feet up on the fender. The curtains were drawn against the bright August sun, embrowning the room, and for a moment Hester did not see Gideon's elongated form, standing like a footman behind her. It was the gleam in his eye that alerted her to his presence.

'Come here,' Mrs Saunders said. 'Let's get this sorted. Giddy, you leave us alone.'

'Yes, Mother,' Gideon said, dutifully, and without looking at Hester he softly went out.

'Now then, gel. All I want is the truth. Giddy saw you canoodling with our Lyle this morning: says he's seen such things before. You needn't deny it.'

Gideon had allowed half a day to elapse before telling his tale – relishing it, Hester supposed – and Lyle had gone out in the meantime. She wished Lyle were here; but her first emotion was one of relief, that it had come at last, even so inopportunely. 'No, I don't deny it, Mrs Saunders,' she said.

'Well! What's it all about? He's been pestering you, is that it? I know what he's like. Thinks he's the cat's whiskers. If you've been afraid to tell me, gel, you needn't be: you shan't suffer for it: I'll just tell him straight off to stop bothering you. He'll do as I tell him. You're here to wait on me, not for him to amuse himself with.'

'No, Mrs Saunders, it ain't that,' Hester said. The old lady's eyes, ensconced in harsh wrinkles, drilled into her. Hester had repeatedly told herself that she wasn't frightened of Mrs Saunders: it was dismaying to find after all that she was. In all her life Hester had never had the slightest power, and now in

227

Mrs Saunders she seemed to confront power incarnate. 'The thing is – me and Lyle—'

'EH?' bellowed Mrs Saunders, the monosyllable rising through a whole chromatic scale. 'MISTER Lyle—!'

'But thass it, Mrs Saunders – we ain't on that sort of terms any more, because, well, Lyle was intending to speak to you about it, you see—'

Thump went the stick on the floor. 'He's got you in the family way! God help us, that's what it is! The silly young beggar, I'll skin him—'

'I'm not in the family way,' Hester said hotly. 'It ain't that at all. We want to git married, Mrs Saunders – we're in love and we want to git married, and he was going to speak to you about it, as soon as—'

'Huh! I know – he's *afraid* he's got you in the family way, and so he reckons he ought to marry you – that must be it.'

'No, it's nothing like that,' said Hester, losing her temper, and with it her fear. 'I don't know why you have to make everything sound so cold and nasty – I don't know why you won't believe that people can – well, can really and truly fall in love! It does happen!'

Mrs Saunders pointed her stick at Hester like a sabre. 'You've trapped him. That's what you've done. You're that sort – you hook your claws in like our Tipsy, so they won't come out. Well! I knew you fancied yourself, but if I'd known you were one of that sort I'd never have let you through the door. You needn't think it'll work, gel. I didn't get where I am now just to see my son throw himself away on you. Lyle's got better things in view than that. He's had chits like you throwing themselves at his head before—'

'It ain't like that at all!' protested Hester, both indignant and pained: all that was precious to her was being pelted with muck. 'Mrs Saunders, Lyle and me have been walking out, properly, on my days off: and he asked me to marry him, and I said yes: and he was going to tell you all about it—'

'Properly? What do you mean, properly? My son canoodling with a servant – a waiting-gel off the fen – what's proper about that? Lord give me strength. He must have gone off his head!

Lyle, and you! Why, what can he get off you that he can't get for a shilling against the railings?'

'I'm glad I am just a servant-gel, if being rich gives you such a dirty mind,' Hester said with disdain.

'Now you listen to me, my gel. You've been treated well here, and allowed to sit at table with the family, and given clothes, and I dare say it's gone to your head, and given you ideas. You get rid of them ideas right now, and maybe we can work something out.'

'There's nothing to work out,' Hester cried, despairing of compromise. 'Lyle wants to marry me, and he's a grown man – he can do as he likes.'

'Can he?' All at once Mrs Saunders seemed to shift her ground. Her eyes glittered craftily. 'All right, gel. Say he thinks he wants to marry you – I'll suppose that for the sake of argument. What do you suppose he's got to live on? Hm? You bringing him a dowry, are you – a little fortune you never told me about?'

'I don't care about that,' Hester said, haughtily, and with truth.

'Well, perhaps I believe you there,' Mrs Saunders said, softly for her. 'I'll give you that. But Lyle, now! Is he really one for love in a cottage, do you reckon?' She shook her head. 'I'll tell you what it is. I think this is one of Lyle's jokes. It's not one of his better ones, and I shall tell him so: he shouldn't tease a simple gel like you.'

'Ask Lyle, then!' exclaimed Hester – and then, with a surge of relief and joy, she heard the sound of the front door. 'There he is – you'll see!'

She ran to open the parlour door, surprising Lyle on the threshold. 'Now that's what I call service,' he began: looked into Hester's face, and took in the whole situation in a moment. 'Ah,' he said.

'Get in here, my son, and shut the door,' Mrs Saunders said. 'We're going to get to the bottom of this.'

Lyle came in, very smart and cool – the heat never seemed to affect him – hands in his trouser pockets, reefer jacket unbuttoned. 'Now what's up?' said he in his lightweight way, propping himself against the back of a chair, and smiling slightly on his mother, with his eyebrows tilting into that ironical curve. To Hester, in her rather fevered state, the scene looked like an angel confronting a gargoyle.

'There's nothing up with me, my boy,' Mrs Saunders said. 'There's something up with you, though, if half of what I've heard is true.'

'Heard from who?' Lyle said. 'Or is it whom – I can never work that out. Let me guess, anyway – Giddy. Well, he's saved me the trouble, though I somehow don't think that was his intention.'

'Never mind that – you been turning this gel's head?' barked Mrs Saunders.

'She's been turning mine,' Lyle said, with a cheerful glance at Hester. 'Lord knows why – she could have her pick of chaps—'

'You mean to say it's true? You've been poodle-faking with this gel under my nose?'

'Oh, come on, Mother. You're no fool. What d'you expect? You throw a pretty girl and a rather handsome bloke together – and then you're surprised when they fall for each other. It's the most natural thing in the world,' Lyle laughed, breezily inspecting his patent-leather shoes.

Mrs Saunders stared: gasped. 'But she's a paid help!'

Yes, thought Hester – and your son's an unpaid help, and that's why you don't want to lose him. But she held her peace: she could see Lyle's mind working, and she was confident that for all the big guns his mother carried, he would disarm her.

'You know Hester, Mother. You know all her ways – and you like her, I know that. So isn't that better than if I'd suddenly brought home some miss you'd never heard of, all airs and graces and having a good look at you and making everybody uncomfortable? I know you're not sentimental: what you've got is bags of sense, and I know you'll see the sense in this.'

'So she has trapped you,' breathed Mrs Saunders.

Lyle laughed. 'Why are women so uncharitable to each other? I haven't done anything against my will, you know.'

'Then you're more of a fool than I thought!'

'Well, I dare say I am. I'm not the only one. Look around, Mother – there's fools going two by two through the church door every day of every week – and they don't come to any harm, do they?'

Mrs Saunders curled both her hands, gnarled by arthritis, round her stick: Hester, looking at them, felt a moment of pity – one of those dashes of contrary feeling that season even the purest emotions; for certainly Mrs Saunders looked hateful, stubborn and despotic enough for anything at that moment. 'So you've been carrying on behind my back,' she muttered.

'Well, blame me for that, Mother,' Lyle said. 'That's exactly what Hester wasn't happy about: but as I intended telling you anyway—'

'Telling me what? What daft promises have you been making this gel? She reckons there's talk of marriage. Did you put that in her head?'

'You do make things sound dramatic. Anyway I am daft – you've always said so. You shouldn't be that surprised.'

'Did you say you'd marry her?' thundered Mrs Saunders.

'Of course I did. Didn't I, Hes? Lucky to find anyone who'll have me. And we do want your blessing, Mother – that's why I waited: it's too important to just casually mention it over the rice pudding. I wanted to wait until you could give it a bit of thought and attention – because I know you, you're not half as awkward as you pretend. Hester's a fine girl – I'm mad about her – and I know you're fond of her. So come on – what do you say? Isn't it really a good thing all round?'

Mrs Saunders was silent for some moments. Then she levered herself out of her chair. 'I'm going to my bed,' she said. 'No, not you, gel—!' as Hester moved to help her. 'I don't want you near me. Ring the bell for Judy – Judy can help me.'

'Oh! Mother, lie down here if you're going to, it'll be hot as hell up there,' Lyle said.

'I can't feel any worse than I do,' Mrs Saunders moaned.

Judy came, rigid with triumph, to take Hester's place and assist Mrs Saunders to bed. Mounting the stairs, the old lady exclaimed of a sudden: 'I've nourished a viper in my bosom!'

Lyle gave a shout of laughter. 'Oh! I wish I'd said that.' He came back into the parlour and shut the door. 'If she says never darken my door I'll scream. Oh! poor old Hes.' He kissed her brow. 'I'll bet she gave you a proper grilling, didn't she?'

'Both sides,' she said, smiling with more confidence than she felt. 'I'm done to a turn.'

'That was a mean little trick of Giddy's, wasn't it?'

'I suppose it was bound to happen eventually.'

'Of course it was. And I'm glad it did, in a way,' said Lyle with energy. 'Silly of me to have waited. I should have just spoken out straight – needn't have worried. It's turning out all right.'

'Is it?' said she – uncertain whether or not he was joking.

'Yes, of course! We nearly had her just then, you know – oh, she tried not to show it – but she was weakening. Bless her, she took to her bed because she knew she was losing. Like I said, she's not as stiff-necked as she pretends. And it does make sense, doesn't it – you and me? Anyone can see that.' He took her hand, and twirled her in a dance step. He was at his most blithe and engaging. 'Giddy did us a favour, really. He sort of threw the idea of us at her, and so she didn't have time to think up any arguments against it. See?'

'Yes . . .'

'Doubting Thomas. I'll let her stew a few minutes, and then go up and see her.'

Whilst Lyle was in his mother's room, Hester waited nervously in the parlour, staring into the sphinx-like eyes of the cats, who lay on the floor, boneless with the heat. At length he returned: a little more subdued, and irritably unfastening his collar.

'Phoo, it's like an oven in that bedroom,' he said, flinging himself into a chair.

Hester sat opposite him. It was strange that now they could be alone with impunity, but could not enjoy it. 'What did she say?'

'She says . . .' Lyle rubbed his hair. 'She says if we'll break it off she'll think about not sacking you.'

'Huh!' cried Hester. 'As if I cared about that!'

'It's a good position,' Lyle said, looking wryly at her.

'It's nothing,' she said fiercely. 'It's you I want.'

He reached out and squeezed her hand, then leant back wearily. 'Oh! Mother, Mother, why do you have to be so difficult . . . ? Well, she accepts that we're serious, Hes. She actually brought herself to speak of our marriage as a possible thing. That is, she says if I go ahead and marry you, she'll have nothing to do with me ever again – melodramatic enough: and, more to the point as far as Mother's concerned, I'll get nothing.' He waved a hand round. 'The horse-dealing business – all Mother's, you see. I don't get a penny of it if she chooses. And that's what she says.' Frowningly he nursed his leg and studied the sole of his shoe. 'That's what gets my goat – the way she thinks I'll care more about that than marrying the girl I love. Pretty insulting to both of us, that. She's a mercenary old stick, that's her trouble. Money before everything.'

'She'd do it, wouldn't she?' Hester said. 'If you went against her will. She'd cut you off. I can just see her doing it.'

'She would,' Lyle said, brooding; then he grinned. 'Except that I'm going to win her over.'

'But what if you can't?'

'O ye of little faith! Hes – you don't really think if it came to a choice I'd give you up just to keep a stake in the business?'

'Oh, no,' said she passionately, reaching out for both his hands: there seemed blasphemy in the very idea.

'Well, it won't come to that anyway, my dear – because I'm going to have both.'

At tea-time Mrs Saunders sent for Hester. The bedroom was stifling, and Mrs Saunders had all the blankets on. She lay huge and supine just as she had done when she had taken to her bed over Gideon and Phoebe. On her lip was a sheen of perspiration, which stubbornly she would not wipe off.

'Pull that chair up, gel. Judy, you leave us.'

Judy exited, stiff as a clockwork toy, her chin pointing at the ceiling.

'Well, you've got your claws into him good and proper, haven't you? That boy never gave me any trouble before – and here he's been swearing he's going to stick by you – fleering in my face. I hope you're satisfied with what you've done.'

'No, Mrs Saunders,' Hester said, 'I ain't. I never meant to make any trouble with you and Lyle, and that's God's honest truth. We can't help the way we feel—'

'If you think so much of him, then leave him alone! I suppose he's told you what'll happen if he carries on with it? I mean it. He marries you, and I'm finished with him. He won't get a penny. I know him – he thinks he can wheedle his way out of it. Well, he's wrong, gel: and I think you know it.'

Hester was silent. She did know it: wish otherwise as she might, she could see that the old lady was utterly, fanatically in earnest.

'So you'll be doing him no favours, gel. You'll be the ruin of him, that's all there is to it. Oh, I know you're full of fine ideas now; you think it doesn't matter; you think canoodling's enough. How long do you suppose that fairy-tale's going to last, eh? Well, it'll be on your head when Lyle looks around him and realises what he could have had, and starts complaining about the prospects he lost when he married you.'

'I'll tek my chance,' Hester said. 'Is that all you're got to say?'

Mrs Saunders stirred angrily, plucking at the coverlet: she seemed to perceive that in this, at least, she was facing a will as strong as her own. 'Damn it all, gel, who do you think you are? Can't you see that my son's got better things ahead of him than tying himself to you?'

'Better things? Like what? To be a slavey to you all his life?' cried Hester, determined to prick that monstrous selfishness. 'Thass all you want for Lyle – and Gideon come to that! It don't matter whether I'm a servant-gel or one of them toffee-nosed misses who come here in carriages – you just don't want your boys to have any life of their own – and I reckon you're bloody lucky they don't hate you for it!'

It was out before she could stop it. Mrs Saunders' face went red, a thing she had never seen before.

'Well, you've finished it now, gel. You'd better start looking for a place, because I want you out of here by the end of the week. Giddy'll give you your wage, and then I want you out of my sight. I don't let anybody talk to me like that – least of all a little trollop I picked up out of the muck. I don't know where you're going to go – but I hear there's a street in Cambridge where gels of your sort ply their trade.'

'Where'd you hear that from?' Hester said, getting up. 'Your husbands?'

Somehow she managed to get to the bottom of the stairs

without falling – she was blinded with tears, and in the hall she ran into a warm obstruction, which turned out to be Lyle.

'Here, here, what's going on?' said he, looking closely into her face. 'Hes—?'

She could not speak: gently he guided her into the parlour and sat her down.

'What's she been saying to you?' Lyle said, kneeling beside her.

'Oh – we got into a bit of a row – silly,' said Hester, who despite the openness of her nature was always curiously ashamed of being seen in tears. 'It's nothing.'

'Oh, yes, it certainly looks like nothing,' Lyle said frowning.

'Well – she wants me gone by the end of the week. I don't care about that . . . but I ain't what she said I am!' she burst out, with fresh distress.

Lyle's lips had gone thin. 'I'm not having this,' he said. Absently he patted her hand and stood up. 'I don't care if she is my mother – I'm not having her speak to you like that.'

'Well – I did lose my temper as well,' Hester said, wiping her cheeks.

'It's no wonder!' said Lyle, pacing. 'About time somebody did lose their temper with her. No, no, she's gone too far.'

'Lyle – she said to tell you that she means it – about you gitting no share in the business, and all that.'

'Did she?' He stopped. 'And now she's waiting to see which way I'll jump.' He came back to her, kneeling again. 'Well. What do you think I should do?'

Hester put up a hand to smooth his tousled hair. 'I think,' she said, 'you should stand up to her – and call her bluff – but then I'm biased, because I love you.'

'You're right. Of course you are.' He was on his feet again. 'Damn it, I shall do as I like! We'll get married, and if she doesn't like it she can do the other thing. Pooh! she thinks she can scare me off with all this talk about cutting me off without a shilling. Don't you worry about that, my dear. I've got money of my own. Not as much as her, maybe, but I've got a good bit salted away. I did plenty of trading on my own account in Belgium that Mother never knew about – why, I've been doing deals on my own for years – else I *would* be a fool, like poor old Giddy. Dry your eyes, my girl, because it's all right!'

'They're dry,' she said, jumping up and kissing him. 'Oh, Lyle, do you really mean it?'

'Of course I do. Let her stay in her wretched bed. We're going to have our life together, Hes, and that's a promise.'

'And you're sure you can manage? I don't like to think—'

'Bless you, love, there's money in an account in my name lying there in the bank in Huntingdon just waiting for us.'

'And Lyle –' she held his shoulders for a moment – 'you really don't mind, that you'll be cutting yourself off from your family and everything, just for me?' She spoke very seriously: there was a crucial importance in this. She wanted him, she would have him at any price: but to feel that she had torn him, reluctantly and acrimoniously, from his family; to feel that she had created an estrangement which he would find bitter – it would give a taint to the taste of her love.

'Pah! she asked for it,' Lyle said lightly. 'Anyway . . . it's not as if it'll be for ever, you know – even Mother couldn't keep that up.'

'How do you mean?' said she, touched with misgiving.

'Eh? Why, what I mean is, some day she'll relent – that's all.'

'But if she didn't, Lyle.' She hated herself for pressing this point: she wanted to give in to jubilation. 'Just suppose she didn't – ever – you won't mind? It'll be all right?'

'Of course! Time I broke the apron strings anyway. It's *you* that's more important, Hes.'

She put her arms around him, surrendering to her happiness: too happy even to be troubled when he added, hugging her, 'And besides – we'll surely patch it up, eventually.'

All the next day, and the day after that, and the day after that, Mrs Saunders remained in bed. She did not call for Hester, or mention her at all except, as Judy exultantly informed her, to ask whether That Girl was still around, and to remind her to be gone by the end of the week. Hester was past the stage of being hurt by this: she had had a certain admiration for the old lady's qualities, affection for her indeed, but they were

236

no more. What was more disturbing was Lyle's expression of disappointment and frustration when he emerged from the curtained bedroom; but he always brightened on seeing her. 'She thinks she's wearing me down,' he said, 'but oh no! Not this time.'

Gideon was evasive, and kept out of Hester's way in particular: he had had the courage to make mischief, she thought, but not to face the consequences. But she met him on the stairs once, and she shifted across a little so that he could not hurry past her and had to stop. His Adam's-apple pumped up and down like a piston, and his little winking eyes avoided hers.

'I'm been meaning to say thank you, Giddy,' she said. She had never called him that before! – he gaped in surprise. 'You're done us a service, as it turns out. Now why don't you do the same by poor ole Phoebe, before she finds somebody else?'

He did not answer, and after a moment she let him go by.

Lyle told her, categorically, not to worry about that business of being out by the end of the week: anxious in spite of herself, she pressed him, but he only smiled and tapped the side of his nose. On the fourth day he was out all morning: returning at noon, flushed with heat, elated and mysterious, he beckoned Hester into the parlour and stood there smiling.

'What are you grinning at?' she said.

'Hester, do you still want to marry me?'

'No,' said she, 'I fell in love with somebody else this morning.'

'Well, that's a pity, because –' he tapped his breast pocket – 'I have taken out a marriage licence, and we are expected at All Saints', Stokeley, at eleven o'clock on Saturday.'

Hester caught her breath. Surprise and joy were only the first of a whole flood of feelings: in that moment everything about her took on a sharp-etched, unforgettable look of enhancement; and she had an almost physical sense of leaving behind her old life for her new, as if a mooring-rope had been cut through.

'It is all right, isn't it?' Lyle said. 'I'm sorry – did you want the banns and everything? I thought the way things are—'

'Is it all right?' she said. 'Oh, Lyle, it's more than all right. You gret fool, I – I don't know what to say . . .' Helplessly, she looked down at her clothes. 'D'you mind marrying me in this frock?'

'Well, I'd rather wear a suit. Ha, good one! Come on –' he seized her hand – 'let's go and tell Mother.'

'Now?'

'Of course!' His face was humorously artful. 'And won't *this* fox her.'

Judy opened the bedroom door. Lyle poked his head in. 'Hullo, Mother. It's me and Hester, can we come in?'

'Not that gel!' boomed Mrs Saunders' voice. 'Don't you bring her in here!'

'All right then, I'll stay here. I shan't come in if my fiancée can't,' Lyle said cheerfully. He took hold of Hester's hand. 'How long are you planning on lying there, Mother? Only we're getting married on Saturday, and we'd like you to come to the wedding.'

There was a silence from within the darkened room. Hester, not without a little grim satisfaction, pictured Mrs Saunders' face above the black bed-jacket.

'Is that all you've come for?' came the reply at last. 'To make daft jokes?'

'No joke,' Lyle said. 'I've got the licence here – like to see it? All Saints' Church. Eleven o'clock. It's all fixed. I'm going, Hester's going – why don't you come too? Please.'

There was a creaking of bed-springs. For a brief moment Hester thought that Mrs Saunders was getting up – Lyle smiled, as if he thought so too, and as if he had won; but almost immediately her hope was replaced by sombre suspicion. She remembered the intransigent glitter in the old lady's eyes, the deep intolerant lines that ran to the corners of her mouth; and she wondered whether she perhaps knew Mrs Saunders better than the fondness of a son ever could.

At last Mrs Saunders' voice came again. 'You're a fool.'

'Oh! I suppose I am, but it doesn't matter,' Lyle said. 'Come and see the fool get spliced, anyway.'

'You can do what you like,' Mrs Saunders said. Her tone was level, harsh, and completely controlled. 'It's of no interest to me. I won't see you wed: I won't see you after you're wed:

you'll get nothing from me. I've done with you. That's all. Shut the door, Judy.'

The door swung to. The smile froze on Lyle's face.

'Lyle,' Hester said, 'come away now.' She touched his arm: it had gone rigid. 'Come away.'

Lyle was staring at the door. He suddenly struck it with his fist, and for the first time ever Hester – with disbelief – saw Lyle furious. It was unbelievable because his easy, supple nature had never seemed susceptible to anger, any more than a liquid could have a sharp edge. She knew then how confidently he had counted on this daring stroke to win his mother over: how stunned he was by the repulse. 'All right then, Mother!' he shouted. 'Damn you then! Lie there and rot, you miserable old crow! I'll make my own life!'

There was no sound. He struck the door again, jammed his hands in his pockets and stalked away. Hester followed him downstairs.

'Now what?' she said.

Lyle glared round at her abruptly: he hardly seemed to see her. 'We get married, of course,' he snapped, 'and be damned to her. Let her go to hell.'

It was satisfying to hear a son of Mrs Saunders say that – except that she herself almost seemed to have been forgotten in the revolution of the moment. 'Well, in the meantime, where am I to go?' she said.

Lyle's expression softened: the stare of a resentful youth left his eyes, and he was himself again. 'Sorry, Hes. Don't look so worried. Let's go out this afternoon and buy some wedding clothes – a ring – the lot. Everything'll be all right.'


2


Mrs Saunders declared her intention of remaining in her room until That Girl was out of the house: Lyle, restored to a buoyancy that expressed itself as frantic energy, laughed and said that suited them admirably. He rented a set of furnished rooms in Huntingdon as a temporary base, chastely establishing Hester there the night before the wedding.

'Furniture's pretty ghastly,' he said. 'There'll be no one to help you dress in the morning – damn, what a mess – I bet you never pictured your wedding-day like this, did you?'

'Help me dress?' she laughed. 'Why, no one's helped me to dress since I was two years old. It ain't the wedding,' she said, her eyes shining at him, 'it's who you're marrying that matters.' And she was happy: the informal spontaneity of it all accorded exactly with her temper. Away from the baleful ill-wishing of Mrs Saunders, her misgivings receded, her spirits rose, and her eyes were fixed on the immediate prospect, which was so radiant to the view that the past and the remoter future scarcely merited a glance.

A hired phaeton, tied with white ribbons, conveyed them to All Saints', Stokeley, the next morning: children ran cheering down the streets after it, old women stared with their customary affront at other people's happiness, and Hester was conscious – with a sort of half-measure of vanity – of being half of a handsome couple. Lyle had asked Gideon to come to the service, but he had made an excuse of obedience to his mother's wishes.

'Poor Lyle!' she said. 'No family there. It don't seem right.'

'Oh, pooh, I never like a lot of fuss at weddings. It's just between us, after all, isn't it?'

But waiting outside the church, to her surprise, was Phoebe Purefoy. She had heard the news from Gideon, she said, and she wanted to be there to wish them joy. They had both rather laughed about Phoebe in the past, and Hester greeted her with a guilty compensatory warmth: wondering if the girl perhaps saw a personal omen, hopeful or otherwise, in the marriage of a Saunders son, and thinking not for the first time that she could surely do better for herself than Gideon.

Hester's background was chapel, and though folk on the fen used the church for weddings and christenings, she felt herself to be on foreign ground there. The frowning parson seemed to know that she had no religious faith, and that the lips of a pagan mouthed the responses: the cool stony solemnity dismayed rather than uplifted her, and she inclined her shoulder so as to touch Lyle's arm, and be reassured of the warm presence of

240

the one element in all this that mattered to her. He returned the pressure: clearly churchiness did not oppress his elastic spirit. How wonderful it was to be with him, who took everything in his stride, and gaily side-stepped the craggier obstacles of the world!

They emerged from the gloom of the church into brilliant sunshine, and it seemed to Hester like surfacing from a dream into reality. Phoebe Purefoy apologetically scattered rice: Hester hugged her, and resolved to be more charitable to people in future. Their luggage had already been sent to the station, and they went straight there to begin the long train ride, first to Peterborough, thence to London and then Bournemouth, where Lyle had booked in a hotel for their honeymoon: a novelty in itself for Hester, who though she had covered just about every inland part of Anglia during her father's wanderings, had never seen the sea. Since he had struck his fist against his mother's door, Lyle had thrown himself single-mindedly into these preparations, and now he looked a little weary as he sat opposite her in the railway-carriage.

'Rubbish,' he said. 'Lively as a cricket. This is the best way of doing things, isn't it, Hes? I'm sure we've done right. I reckon it takes the bloom off it, making a long drawn-out song-and-dance about it.'

He had a way thus of reasoning himself into approval of a *fait accompli*, which touched her. 'It suits me best,' she said. 'Only thing is I can hardly believe it – all of a sudden I'm Mrs Hester Saunders, and yet I haven't changed. I just know I shall feel like a hussy when I walk in that hotel with you. It ain't *too* smart, that hotel, is it, Lyle?'

'Don't know – never been there. It was recommended. Why, you're not frightened of that, surely? Just look confident, and you can carry anything off.'

'I suppose so,' she said, smiling, but nursing secret dubieties about some uppity chamber-maid seeing her petticoats and combinations.

They ate on the train: the miles flashed by unheeded, and then there was London: the steam and smell and noise of a vast station, a brake-ride through glaring, horse-crowded streets, and then another vast station, and they were on their way to the south coast. Hester was too absorbed in Lyle, and in trying to comprehend the sheer incredible fact of their being married, even to notice the unfamiliar sight of downs and hills beyond the carriage window: everything passed her in a whirl; and it was with the profoundest disorientation that she found herself all at once in Bournemouth, in a soft-aired dusk, amongst pine-woods and cupola-crowned mansions, with lights winking on along the promenade – just about as far from the atmosphere of the fens as it was possible to be. The hotel was imposing enough, but nobody seemed to stare at her, and she loved the room, which had a view of the sea, rich red damask wallpaper, and a gaselier shaded with ruched silk. The dining-room was rather more intimidating, until Lyle looked over his shoulder to another table and, turning back to Hester, whispered, 'Do you know what they're having for dessert, Hes? Cherries. Cherries, my dear.'

'Lyle – don't you dare start me off!' she gasped, cramming her hand over her mouth. They were aching with laughter when they returned to their room. Lyle lit the gas, and hung his jacket over a purple crewel-worked fire-screen, which he said made him feel bilious.

'Hark at that,' said Hester, standing by the window and running her hand along the sill in sudden nervousness. 'The sea – don't it sound peaceful?'

He joined her. 'That's not the sea,' he said. 'That's the wind in the pines, isn't it?'

'That it ain't.'

'Yes it is – listen.'

'Lyle Saunders,' said she, turning her face to him, 'I ask you, is this the time to be having our first quarrel?'

'Wrong time altogether.'

'Well then . . . Thass more like it . . .'


3


August had burned into September, freshened by breezes but still hot and cloudless, when Hester and Lyle returned from the south coast to the fens to begin their married life.

The rooms in Huntingdon, on the top floor of an old house overlooking the little school that had seen the boyhood of Cromwell, were clean but drab, and Lyle was adamant that they would not stay in them a day longer than was necessary. He visited his mother immediately on their return, and was met with a monumental huffiness, and a refusal even to mention the fact of his marriage. Hester was dejected by this – the honeymoon had been so happy that she had almost forgotten the extent of her mother-in-law's resentment – but Lyle snapped his fingers. 'Pooh, she's got to keep it up, for pride's sake. Let her stew in her own juice – can't be bothered with her just now – we've got plans to make.'

He was enormously sanguine about these plans. 'It's not a bad little sum I've been salting away: now all we've got to do is turn it to good account. All sorts of possibilities.' Each day he returned from visits to auctioneers and estate-agents, and each day it seemed he had a new project in view. 'Now this is the just thing for us – seedsman's business in March. Nice brick-built premises, plenty of accommodation. What do you say?'

'Well . . . I can't really see you as a seedsman, Lyle.'

'No? Well, we'll see. I reckon it would suit me just right.' But on viewing the property, he changed his mind. 'No – that would never have done. Imagine me trying to sell seed to a lot of shrewd old fen farmers! That was an awful idea.'

Then there was a confectioner's shop in Peterborough.

'Does that appeal to you, then?' she said to him.

'Oh! yes – there's scope for a tea-room, you see – you could make it a really smart little place, get the carriage-trade when they're shopping.' But the next day, the confectioner's was a wretched idea: poky little hole, dreary occupation, miserable profits, he didn't know how he could ever have considered it.

'What we really want, you know,' he said finally, one day in October, 'is a house with a bit of land. I'm not cut out to be a shopkeeper or anything like that.'

'Thass exactly what I think,' Hester said smiling.

'Do you? I should have taken your advice in the first place. Sarsby's had a couple of fen properties the other day, but they were small fry – just cottages – we can do better than that.'

'Well, don't go bankrupting yourself, love – I'm not after a mansion. I only wish I brought a few bob to this marriage!'

'Bah, you're worth a fortune in yourself. We'll do pretty well, Hes. And even apart from this money – well, Mother won't hold out for ever, you know.'

He said it lightly; and she replied, trying to be just as light: 'We won't actually count on that, though, will we?'

'No?' He grinned. 'Don't trust my charm to work on Mother in the end, then?'

'Oh! I'd trust your charm for anything,' she said, briefly touching his face. 'But – let's not count on it, eh?'

'Whatever you say, my love.'

The very next day Lyle returned from Walton's, the land-agents, with the details of a farmhouse on Hinching Fen, with seventy acres of land. He strode about in his excitement, rubbing up his hair into unlikely shapes, and painting a vivid picture of the prospect. 'Brick-built house and outbuildings, barn – stock and implements – it's a going concern, not some run-down shell. Can't you just see me as an independent farmer? – answerable to nobody – yes, I should have done this years ago.'

'It does sound nice,' Hester said. 'And I should certainly know my way round a fen farm!'

'Of course! It's made for you. Except you'd be in charge this time, love – not doing the donkey work. But now – this is the best part – "extensive stabling and paddock". You see? I could do what I know best – horse-dealing. Isn't that perfect?'

'It certainly sounds it. What – do you mean do the horse-dealing instead of the farming?'

'Oh! combine the two, you know – it'll work out – one will pay for the other, or the other way around – I don't know,' he said, with his infectious laugh. 'No need to cut off any options. Anyway, Walton's going to take us out there in his gig tomorrow morning.'

Later, when Lyle had gone out to buy a newspaper, she studied again the details of the farm, written out on foolscap with auctioneer's flourishes. It was hard to address her mind to practical considerations: she was still all aglow with the sudden transformation in her life, and every morning when she woke her mind had to leap a mental ditch of disbelief that it had really happened so swiftly; moreover it was difficult to attach the idea of life with Lyle Saunders to the idea of everyday prosaic reality – it was like trying to nail down bubbles. For her part the opening chapter of married life had been so happy – the days and nights by the sea, able at last to enjoy the fun of being with him freely and without fear, seeming simply an intensification of their courtship – that she just wanted to prolong it under any conditions. Their material situation she saw in a neutral light: the only thing that could darken it for her was the shadow of Mrs Saunders. The old woman could burn the horse-yard down or give it to the Salvation Army for all she cared – at least then they would know where they were. What she hated was Mrs Saunders using it as a standing reproach to her son for his folly – a physical reminder of what he had forfeited: and if possession of their own farm would negate that, then all the better.

Mr Walton, the land-agent, was a very fat pink moist man, bald, with the merest suggestion of features, like a great bowler-hatted tweed-smelling baby. It was quite a squeeze for Hester and Lyle to get into his little gig beside him, but he seemed used to taking up a lot of room, and as they drove out to Hinching Fen he talked too in a swaggering oracular voice, as if the broad countryside were his own house, and he were showing them round it.

'You'll observe, sir and madam, that we are traversing some of the finest peat land in the county. The productive capacity of this soil is not to be exaggerated. This may be amusingly illustrated, in the remark of the natives, to the effect that one may plant a walking-stick in the ground and it will sprout.' Mr Walton offered this with a short peremptory laugh, as a limited gesture of condescension to the natives, who might be supposed from his tone to be an aboriginal residue imperfectly acquainted with the use of the wheel. 'On your left, sir and madam, if I may presume to indicate, you will observe the Hinching Fen windmill, furnished also with a pumping-engine, providing a reliable system of drainage, and insuring against Inundations. To your right, various rustic operatives, and a cow being grazed on the stubble subsequent to the harvest: and ahead, the drove leading to the aforesaid deseerable property, which, sir and madam, we will proceed to view.'

The drove, overgrown with grass, led between bare fields to a tiny thatched cottage, which exhibited boarded windows and other marks of desuetude. Mr Walton pulled the pony up short and, taking off his hat, mopped his spherical brow, staring.

'Good Lord,' Lyle said, 'you don't mean this is it?'

Mr Walton snapped his chubby fingers. 'Pardon me, sir and madam – I see it now – I've proceeded down the wrong drove. I was deceived by the absence of landmarks and distinguishing features. No, no: this is quite another property, the merest smallholding – just come on the market. Pardon me – we'll retrace our steps.'

'Thank goodness for that!' Lyle said, as Mr Walton turned the pony about.

'Oh! I don't know,' Hester said, craning round to look at the cottage, which seemed to her forlornly to watch them go. 'It's quite a sweet little place. Shame to see it all abandoned like that.'

'A deseerable property in its way,' Mr Walton said, 'but not appropriate to the requirements of sir and madam. The correct property, to which I shall convey you without further mishap, is a far more considerable establishment, boasting a panoply of conveniences. Ahead of us, observe a bridge constructed I believe of railway-sleepers, traversing the dyke.'

Hester was observing something else – a glimpse of the turf-fen where Chad Langtoft had laboured. She suffered a pang at the memory of what a fool she had been; but it all seemed a very long time ago, and herself a completely different person; and the farm, it turned out, was a good distance further on, almost on the edge of the upland, and was not at all familiar to her.

'Ah, that's more like it,' Lyle said as they approached down the drove. The farmhouse, a solid square Georgian structure, appeared gradually between a screen of mature and tortuously leaning trees, the leaves of which were beginning to turn. It was a building of two storeys, with a shallow hipped roof of tiles, a stout chimney-breast at one end, and angled bays either side of a central front door; but the first impression it gave was somehow of a peculiar tallness, an effect which Hester could not for a moment account for.

'You'll observe, sir and madam,' Mr Walton said as they got down, 'the advantageous situation, facing west, and protected by a fortuitous plantation from the ravages of the elements. Glazing, quite new. Gutters, in good repair. Birds,' he added, waving a hand at the sparrows pecking before the threshold, 'contributing to the rural scene or aspect. The steps up to the door do not indicate the presence of a basement. These are of recent date – the foot of the door having originally been parallel with the ground: but the shrinkage of the peat, common to this region, has lowered the level of the soil over the years, with the effect you observe.'

'Ah, thass what it is,' said Hester. The sinking of the earth had exposed a foot or two of the foundations of the house, which were whiter than the mellow brick above – it reminded her of a countryman's sleeve rolled up beyond the tan of the forearm – and that was why it seemed to stand proud of its surroundings in that curious way.

'Is it safe?' Lyle said.

'Oh! of course,' Mr Walton said. 'Many dwellings in the black fens are subject to such a change. This one, as you may observe, was built with deep foundations, as a precaution against just such an eventuality. Shall we enter?'

The farmhouse had not been long empty: the creaking floorboards seemed still to yield to the feet of the previous occupants, and there was a faint olfactory ghost of homely cooking in the big whitewashed kitchen with its long black range. Hester, brought up in the country, immediately felt more at home than ever she had in Mrs Saunders' varnished and antimacassared house – and how roomy it was after their digs in Huntingdon!

They inspected the yard and farm-buildings – stepping out of the back door with rather a jolt, for the doorstep was about two feet off the ground. All was in good repair. There was a block of brick-built stabling, and Lyle squeezed Hester's hand and gestured expansively. 'See? Ample for dealing in a few draught-horses, maybe even riders. Keep my hand in till I'm back in Mother's good books.'

'Oh! I shouldn't count on that,' she said, retaining his hand and watching his expression: he had proudly burnt his bridges, yet still, laughingly, he believed one was intact. 'The farm's the important thing.'

'Oh! no. I'm not counting on it. Just saying – you know – it'll be something extra.'

Mr Walton led them to the paddock: pausing, with conscious effect, to point out to their surprised eyes an ancient gate, the bottom of which, because of the lowering of the land, was several feet above the ground, so that a small pony might just as easily have passed under it as through it. 'I imagine this is preserved more for novelty than utility,' Mr Walton pronounced, huffing with genteel humour.

'It's a bit like a crooked house out of a fairy-tale, ain't it?' Hester said aside to Lyle.

He chuckled. 'You do like it though – don't you?'

'I do,' she said. She was on home ground: the barn, the rick-staddles, the hen-coops met her eye with an effect like that of seeing a familiar face in a crowd.

'Just think – all ours,' Lyle said. 'Mr and Mrs Lyle Saunders, of the Crooked House, Hinching Fen.'

4

The damage done to Jonathan Eastholm's precarious independence by the fen-blow was not put right by the glorious summer. He had replanted, at great cost – an advance from the seedsman sinking him further in debt: but the tardy harvest his ruined fields yielded was negligible. The loan of money made to him by the brickyard owner had been at a moderate rate of interest, but it was strictly short-term; and that gentleman, somewhat in low water himself, could not or would not postpone repayment, and wait for the doubtful prospect of next year's harvest. Jonathan, denied recourse to mortgage and the other financial devices of more sophisticated milieux, gazed down a winding, darkening tunnel of debt. His sharp sense of honour demanded what expedience suggested: he would have to sell up, satisfy his creditors straightaway, and then see where he stood.

This was a bitter draught, but he took it at a swallow: he did not seek to linger out a struggle that could have only one end, for he was temperamentally averse to half-measures; and even losing his independence was more tolerable than gaining a name as a welsher and bad debtor. In many men this might have been humbug, but it pressed on Jonathan almost as a physical imperative. All the same, it was depressing to contemplate the work he had put into the little holding all coming to naught: to reflect that he had failed in an enterprise which had engaged so much of his energy, confidence and hope. It was with a resolute mind but a heavy heart that he turned the hedgehog loose to get its living, surrendered his title to the property to the land-agents, who had quickly snapped it up at a very fair price, and left the little cottage to the sad state of vacancy in which Hester had glimpsed it from Mr Walton's gig. The sale cleared all his various debts, leaving him solvent and unencumbered – an enormous relief that felt to Jonathan like the removal of a throttling collar – but without sufficient funds to pursue any occupation on his own account, as had long been his custom and desire. The notorious unpredictability of the fen soil had been the agent of an entire reversal of his fortunes, and he found himself in the self-same position as when he had been labouring on the land and striving to save enough for his first lighters.

Youth and strength are not perhaps the palliatives of despair that they ought to be, and Jonathan was hard put to it to fend off a fierce attack of the Old Goblin, who spoke desolate innuendoes about the relentlessly downward course his life seemed to be taking. But to his surprise he found he had allies against his old adversary. There would always be willing hands to help you support a burden of good fortune, but under a burden of ill-fortune you staggered alone – such had been Jonathan's somewhat cynical credo. It was proved wrong. The kindly interest of his neighbours did not disappear with his independence. There was a deep vein of fatalism in fen-folk: they knew that the dyked and embanked fields, so apparently tamed and harnessed, were at the capricious mercy of storm and flood, and so theirs was an instinctive sympathy with mortal frailty – a sympathy Jonathan, in his proud way, had so signally lacked. They commiserated, they condoled, and they encouraged: and it came as a revelation to him to find that this strengthened rather than enfeebled him. Others had suffered from the fen-blow – Henry Wake frankly confessing that he would only just survive this year – and it was a further revelation for Jonathan to find himself commiserating in turn. This simple experience forced on him an entirely new perception – that self-reliance and selfishness melted into one another, and you could cross the border without knowing it.

The surrender of the deeds of his little property left him without a home and without work: but he had already been offered a lodging by old Andrew Surfleet, who engaged too to ask Farmer Mather, his 'mairster', if he had any work for him. 'That'll be hard, I know, having to work for another, once you're been your own mairster,' Andrew said. 'But Farmer Mather's an easy sort of man: and mebbe if you sort of mek-believe, and pretend thass your own ditch you're digging, that wun't sting so.'

'Well, I'm been a labourer before, Andrew,' said Jonathan, 'and it won't hurt me to do it again.'

And so that autumn he found day-work clearing dykes and digging gault – hard and exhausting work for which his large frame, as Farmer Mather's eye discerned, was admirably fitted: and took up his lodging in Andrew Surfleet's cottage. His bedroom beneath the roof-beams had once contained the Surfleets' three sons – now mere striplings in their fifties, living on the other side of the fens – but plainly they must have been built along the economical lines of their parents, and Jonathan had to move about with the utmost circumspection, for fear of putting his elbow through the window, or his head through the thatch. There was a feather bed, an heirloom of great antiquity and softness; but of such modest dimensions, that he had to take the precaution of folding the blankets under the mattress very tightly, and sliding into bed like a letter into an envelope, to prevent himself toppling out in the night. When he came

250

stooping down the stairs in the morning, his stature seemed to strike Mrs Surfleet afresh each time and, recalling the legendary fenland giant, she declared it was like having Tom Hickathrift living with them.

Jonathan scrupulously paid a reasonable rent, and shared at the Surfleets' table the plain diet of the fen labourer: bread, potatoes, onions, home-made lard, and salt pork made to go as far as possible by means of dumplings and puddings: once or twice he walked over to Stokeley market to buy for a few coppers a sheep's head, which made a rich broth called shackles. Whenever he left the house after breakfast Mrs Surfleet would be putting on her hessian apron for her day's work: when he returned at night she was always transformed by a clean white apron and a chignon bag enclosing her wisps of hair. Whilst she laid the table he went to fetch water from the dipping-hole at the dyke and washed himself from a bowl that stood on a stool outside the back door – Mrs Surfleet sidling past the window with her face averted, so as not to glimpse him with his shirt off. (When he had his bath in the tin tub on the kitchen floor, she always took herself off to sweep upstairs – Andrew confiding to Jonathan that she was as shy as a mouse, and she'd always done the same when *he* had a bath, for fifty years.) Often in the evenings, after supper, the Surfleets would set the oil-lamp on the table, and entertain themselves with the neat pile of newspapers that stood in a corner of the house-place. These were all rather old, and some of the yellower ones were rather history than news, but that did not diminish their interest for the old couple. Mrs Surfleet would draw a newspaper out at random, spread it out on the table, and read aloud from it – the ole girl, as Andrew remarked, being a rare reader, whereas he could only struggle his way through a few bits of the Bible that he knew reasonably well already. Mrs Surfleet exercised no editorial discrimination, and read her way through every column: Andrew blinking at the turf fire, listening with devout attention, and taking a personal sort of interest in the intelligence, as if he were hearkening to an intimate letter.

'"Indisposition of Prince Alexander of Teck",' read out Mrs Surfleet. '"His Royal Highness is reported to have been suffering from pharyngitis, which has restricted his public engagements. The royal physicians give a good account of his recovery".'

'Oh! dear. Poor ole boy,' said Andrew with feeling. 'Thass a shame. Thass nasty, that is.'

'"The celebrated actor Mr Henry Irving, whose notable impersonations of the tragic heroes of Shakespeare have formed the chief adornment of the modern stage and earned him the universal respect and admiration of connoisseurs of the dramatic arts, has been awarded a knighthood, and becomes the first of the thespian fraternity to receive such an accolade".'

'Ah! thass nice for him,' Andrew said, nodding approvingly. 'I'm glad about that. Thass nice to git a bit o' credit. I suppose he'll be gooing to see the ole Queen, and she'll be tapping him with a sword – well, well!'

'"Accession of Tsar Nicholas the Second Celebrated with Ancient Formality in St Petersburg".'

'We-ell, I wouldn't swap with him. He wants to be careful. I remember the last one of them Stars – they blew the poor ole boy up. Riding along in his carriage he was – I'll never forgit that. No-oo, I wouldn't want to be a Star – I shouldn't feel safe.'

Occasionally in the evenings Jonathan would walk with Andrew over to the Labour In Vain for a half. Here the topic of conversation, having moved on from the wedding of Chad Langtoft and Mary-Ann Cole, had for some time been Jonathan's own misfortune; but one night, to his secret relief, he found that it had been superseded by a savoury new morsel of information. Jed Gosling, the mill-keeper, had been drunk on duty once too often, and the Drainage Commissioners had given him notice.

'Found him laying flat on the mill-'us floor, dead to the world, with his head in a bucket,' said the landlord, Jass Phelps. 'So they say. Thass what *I'm* heard. *I* don't know.'

'Ah! he'd always pour a pint atop of enough, Jed Gosling would,' said Andrew. 'He were bad enough at Chad Langtoft's wedding-feast – singing them songs wi' wicked rhymes, what made you blush for the chap who thought 'em up.'

'It's a pity for young Lizzie,' said Henry Wake. 'She works

252

hard, that gel, and does her best to keep the family going, and she's had less help than hindrance from Jed, I'm afraid. I don't reckon it's right to put upon your own child like that: I wouldn't do it – at least, in theory, as it were – Mrs Wake and meself not being blessed with issue.'

There were various significant nods at this last, as at a subject better understood than expressed.

'Well, he'll wish that drink back in the barrel before he's done,' said Sunny Daintree. 'Git a reputation for supping on the job, and no mairster'll touch you with a long-handled rake. Ooh! dear. You might as well knock on the work'us door and have done with it.'

'Does this mean the miller's job's going begging, then?' Jonathan said with interest.

'It does, neighbour,' Henry Wake said, 'and they'll want someone as soon as may be – Jed's to be finished by the end of the month. D'you fancy tekking it on, now?'

'I might, at that,' Jonathan said.

'Ah! he's the very man,' Andrew said. 'You should see him digging in the gault-pit, with all the muscles standing out on his shoulders, like a galloping hoss.'

'You're a tidy worker, Jonathan, we all know that,' Henry Wake said. 'I'd put my name to that, if called upon. Mind you, I think you'll find the Commissioners hoping for a man with a bit of knowledge of machinery: do you reckon you're got a bit of that?'

'Lock-gates and threshing-tackle is about as far as I go,' Jonathan said meditatively. 'But I can learn.'

'Thass the spirit,' said Andrew. 'Why, if you could see him washing of hisself in the evening, you'd trust him to any job in Chrisseldom: I know I would.'

'How should I go about applying?' Jonathan asked, addressing himself to Henry Wake – more from a consciousness that he would be flattered to be asked, than a conviction that he would know.

'Well now – if you'll tek my advice,' Henry said with boastful modesty, 'you'll go to the Commissioners when they meet in Stokeley, and put your case to them straight. Farmer Mather's on the board, I believe – that'll stand well for you. They meet on the first Thursday each month – I think you'll find my information's correct.'

'They had a special meeting about Jed Gosling,' Sunny Daintree said. 'Poor ole boy had to stand there afore 'em, and be now-thened and my-manned till he didn't know where to put his head.'

'He were drunk even then, so I'm heard,' Jass Phelps said.

'Course, milling's not a job as everybody'd tek to,' said Henry Wake. 'The pay's not a great deal – but then in fair weather, neither's the work, and you can do other jobs in between whiles.'

'Not that Jed Gosling ever did,' Jass Phelps said.

'And of course there's the solitude – minding the mill all on your ownsome, through the winter nights – that wouldn't suit everybody,' Henry said.

'Suited Jed Gosling, he just used to sup,' Jass Phelps said.

'You do it, bor,' Andrew said. 'We want a reliable man tending the ole mill. Miller Eastholm – I can see that now.'

The solitude of the miller's avocation was scarcely a disadvantage in Jonathan's eyes, and he was anxious for something more secure than day-work: moreover he had always found something pleasing in the sight of the Hinching Fen windmill, which seemed to unite beauty and utility in harmonious proportions; and so on the appropriate day he walked to Stokeley, and presented himself to the Drainage Commissioners as a candidate for the vacant post. The Commissioners were meeting at the Spread Eagle Inn, in the yard of which Jonathan had made his memorable error of judgement in laying his suit at the feet of Hester Verney: he cast a long and rueful look at the seat beneath the cherry tree that was the locus of that disaster, and wondered if there was ill-omen in this. But the Commissioners, who had just had a convivial lunch, were glad to be relieved of the trouble of seeking out a man for the job, by a man seeking them out instead: an enormously fat florid farmer in a diamond-pinned cravat declared it made a change in these days, when nobody wanted to work, and then nodded off; Farmer Mather recommended Jonathan, and half an hour later he left the Spread Eagle entrusted with the job of running Hinching Fen's drainage mill, at the winter rate of twelve shillings a week, with the summer rate to be negotiated. Miller Eastholm he became – except that he disclaimed the formality of the surname, and was soon simply known to the denizens of Hinching Fen as Jonathan-up-at-the-mill.

Most of the fen windmills had been replaced by pumping-stations in recent years, and the Hinching Fen mill was provided with a steam-engine on the mill-house floor as an alternative source of power; but when the wind was fair, the traditional structure continued to do its traditional work, the thirty-foot sails operating the water-wheel which discharged the water from the dykes into the main drain, and preserved the safety of the fields of Hinching Fen. The mill luffed herself, the head turning into the wind by means of a fan-tail: Jonathan's job, in which he was coached at first by the mill-keeper of the adjoining fen, was to run the mill whenever there was a wind, keeping all the luffing-gear and striking-tackle oiled, and to stoke the boiler when it was necessary for the steam-engine to take over. Jed Gosling had taken to neglecting the mill unless the water in the drain were really high: Jonathan, anxious not to make the same mistake, was soon habituated to leaving his warm bed at the Surfleets' and tramping out to the mill at the first mutter of a rising wind.

Typically, Jonathan thought of the hardships and rewards of the job in terms that could only be called aesthetic. He found something satisfying to mind and heart in the mill just as he had in the lighters: mounting the five flights of stairs to the head with the oil-can, he dwelt with admiration on the symmetry of the gearing, the smooth movement of the great wooden cogs, the nice precision of the chain-hung weights which rose up and down to regulate the speed of the sails: the rhythmic revolutions of the great water-wheel impressed him with a sense of hypnotic fitness, like the figure in a Persian carpet. When he sat and rested a while with a pipe before the mill-house fire, the creakings and trundlings that echoed down the wind-shaft were like the comfortable stirrings of some large, benevolent animal. Jonathan began to love his work, and because he loved it he did it well.

There were long hours when there was little to do but be on hand, and these he filled with reading and thinking; but something – perhaps the tail-brass at the foot of the wind-shaft which gave a long reverberating organ-note when it needed oiling – put him in mind of music again, and set up the old longing for a tune, smothered during his recent troubles. He was still doing in-between work on the land, and had money to spare, so, with something of his former discomfiture at this weakness of his, he asked Rob Risby the tallyman whether he ever dealt in musical instruments.

'Oh! dear, yes,' sighed the tallyman. 'Any amount on 'em. Kit-fiddles, mouth-organs, banjoes, I'm carried 'em all in me time: "cornet, flute, harp, sackcloth, solitary, dulcimer and all kinds of music", as scripture has it.'

'D'you reckon you could lay your hands on a concertina?' Jonathan said.

'Say the word, miller, and it's done. A concertina you shall have – I shall bring it next week. If I'm spared,' Rob Risby said. 'Not that I can complain: my poor ole missis has got it wuss than me; and I'm not sure as the hoss ain't got it wuss than either on us.' The tallyman did not specify what 'it' was, but seemed to suggest that it was chronic, contagious and fatal.

The concertina the tallyman brought was of the piano-accordion type, much more impressive to the eye than Jonathan's old squeeze-box, and his fingers itched to play upon the gleaming keys; but he was too embarrassed to do so whilst Rob Risby was still there. 'Thass a handsome thing, miller,' Risby said. 'German, I shouldn't wonder, from that name on the side. All full of zeds and double-yews; and there's no one meks 'em better. I'm fond of a tune meself – it helps you forgit your troubles – for a little while any road,' he added with a graveyard cough. 'There's some people as don't seem to melt to music at all: as for me, the hairs are standing up on me arms the moment I hear it. There! it's such a pleasure to talk about with you, miller, that I almost hate to bring up the subject of a price. If it was just me, I'd let you have it cost; and if it was just my poor ole missis having to lay with her feet above her head, I'd hardly ask more; and even with my Nelly as she is, with her chest all bound up wi' brown paper till she can't sleep for the rustling, I'll only say three and six down, and ninepence a week, and I don't care if they do call me a fool for it.'

'Done,' said Jonathan, glad to be rid of him so that he might try the accordion out. He soon found, however, that the keyboard worked on a different principle to the studs, and he had a frustrating time of it, trying to conjure a melody from the instrument. Recalling Artie Gill, the old turf-digger who had played the fiddle at the Labour In Vain, Jonathan sought him out for advice as the only musical person he knew; though with little hope of success, as Artie Gill was known as a cantankerous fellow who would growl at his own shadow. But he found Artie flattered and delighted to be asked – there is a soft place in the flintiest man – and the old turf-digger went out of his way to call at the mill and instruct Jonathan in the rudiments of keys and chords; and thus two of the gruffest men on the fen could be found applying themselves to harmonising sentimental melodies, and mournfully declaring that o-ver rocks which are steep-est, lo-ove will find out the way.

Unexpectedly, Jonathan too found himself performing the role of a teacher of sorts – at first in spite of himself, and with no great faith in his abilities. Ever since Jonathan had helped him extricate the cow from the dyke, young Charlie Smeeth, Henry Wake's farm-boy, had regarded him in the light of an oracle, a prodigy, and a hero: during Jonathan's last hopeless days on his ruined smallholding, Charlie had come to offer his labour gratis whenever Henry Wake could spare him; and once Jonathan was established as mill-keeper, the lad was always turning up at the mill and asking if he could help.

Jonathan was often glad of a helping hand, especially when he had to run the engine: at busy times it was handy to have someone to mind the mill while he strode home to the Surfleets' for a meal or a wash; and Charlie Smeeth was so eager for this, that there was no question of taking advantage.

'Let me stoke the boiler, sir – goo on, do,' Charlie cried, 'I s'll mek a proper job on it, sir!'

'Well, thass a mucky job, Charlie, and I reckon you're done a day's work at Mr Wake's already. I don't want you overtaxing your strength.'

'I'm strong, sir – I'm like a Ox, reely!' said Charlie, exhibiting arms of approximately the girth of a walking-stick;

and proudly dug the shovel in the coal, and staggered with it to the stoke-hole, his face all red but gamely smiling.

But there were times when there was no work for Charlie to lend a hand with; and to Jonathan's perplexity, he would still remain there, looking up at Jonathan with his round eyes, and manfully trying not to be in the way, as if he could make his gangling limbs invisible by a mental effort of effacement. The comforts of the mill, besides the fire, comprised only a few square feet of swept floor, a mattress on which Jonathan snatched a little rest when he had to spend the night there, a shelf or two, and a couple of bentwood chairs, the rest of the space being occupied by the machinery. Charlie could never be persuaded to take a chair, but would prop himself against the wall, or squat on the floor, protesting against all the evidence of his bony and abraded joints, that he was as comfortable as anything. Jonathan was a man who could take any amount of companionable silence; but even he grew restive under Charlie's baleful gaze of humility.

'Won't your mam and dad be wondering where you are, Charlie?' Jonathan asked him.

'Ain't got a dad, sir,' Charlie said. 'Just me mam. And a uncle. Except he ain't,' he added, looking with great concentration into his cap. 'I know THAT.'

'Ah,' Jonathan said.

'They wun't be looking out for me, any road,' Charlie said simply. 'Me sister Edie might – but she knows I come the mill.'

'Won't there be no supper waiting for you?'

'Shouldn't think so, sir – not unless Edie's got summat in. It don't matter – Mr Wake give me some apples and a slice of waiting-cake when I come away from work today. He often slips me summat to eat, Mr Wake does – except I always have to mind and not tell Mrs Wake, he says – her being the way she is.'

'Don't sir me . . . I'm never seen Mrs Wake,' Jonathan said. 'I don't go to chapel, and that seems to be the only time she goes abroad. A bit severe, then, is she?'

Charlie twisted his cap as if he were wringing out a flannel, and said in a rush: 'I git all panicky when she comes near me

– she's so big, and she stares so and breathes through her nose – and her thumb bends all the way back – and there's all these hairs on her face, like on a peach, and I can't stop looking at 'em!'

'Calm down, boy. Think of a psalm like I told you.'

'Yes, sir.' Charlie gabbled The-Lord-is-my-shepherd under his breath.

'She don't treat you badly, does she?' Jonathan said when the boy had recovered.

'Oh! no. Thass a good job I'm got at Mr Wake's: he's very good to me, and she don't have much to do with me. It's just I'm a bit afeared on her – and sometimes I reckon Mr Wake is too – if she shouts for him from the house, when he's out in the field, he goes a-running – and once she come out to the yard, scattering the chuckies wi' her skirts, and her face all scowling like one of them gurgle-spouts on the church roof – and she lifted Mr Wake's hat off, and hit him 'cross the head wi' a cowcumber—'

'She did what?'

'Yes, sir – thass what she did, and she says "There's for you!", and then she marched back in – and Mr Wake put his hat back on all sad and mild-like, and he says to me, it'd perhaps be as well if I didn't mention what had just happened – and now I have – oh, 'ell!'

'Never mind, boy: I shan't tell anyone,' said Jonathan, mentally revising his opinion of Henry Wake.

'Thank you, sir. We never said no more about it; but a day or two after, when I was having a panic, and me heart were scuttering away like a rat in the hay-loft, Mr Wake says to me, take care of your heart, Charlie Smeeth – and never give it away careless-like, in case you come to regret it later.'

'Well . . . I dare say he's right there,' Jonathan said, frowning at the fire, and suddenly swept by a cloud of nameless emotions.

'Oh yes, sir. He's got all sorts of learning, Mr Wake – he reads in books when he don't have to, just like you do, sir – and he can read the words off a flour-sack without hardly looking at 'em.'

'Why, surely you can read, Charlie?'

'Well – I wouldn't go so far as to say I *can't* read, sir,' said Charlie dubiously, 'only it teks a lot out of me, I'm that slow – I reckon I told you it weren't a very good schooling I got.'

'I remember,' Jonathan said.

'Same wi' writing – it's so long since I learned how, and stopped doing it – thass like when you work the pump, and the prime goes.'

'Why, how old are you, Charlie?'

'Fifteen, sir – sixteen come Martinmas.'

'I'd thought you were younger.'

'Yes, sir – I'm all behind-hand wi' me growing, except uppards, and there ain't a hair on me face – and there's Mrs Wake all – oh, 'ell! I mustn't think of that!'

'Well, boy,' Jonathan said, 'I'll help you with your letters, if you like.' He thought it a pity that anyone should lose out on reading: even in the rural sphere of the fen, illiteracy would hinder the boy; and an occupation would at least divert Charlie's unnerving attentiveness. So the wall of the boiler became a blackboard, on which Jonathan chalked Biblical texts and other simple phrases in his own strong, unformed hand, Charlie doing his best to read and then copy them. Often, as he said, Charlie's 'head wouldn't go', and he got into a panic; but Jonathan's recent trials had revealed to him unsuspected reserves of patience, and what began as a chore became a pleasure. He wanted to help the boy get on: though he hardly knew it, this represented another stage in the breaking down of his aloof self-sufficiency, for his self of a year ago might well have disdained such an involvement with a harsh declaration that no one helped *him* when *he* was a lad. He guided Charlie through some elementary arithmetic too: remarking that this would all come in useful if he had his own farm some day.

'Coh! I should like that, sir,' Charlie said, contemplating a multiplication sum as if it were a work of art. 'I shouldn't want for nothing more, then. And I'd keep pigs, and ducks, and rabbits and all, them loppy-eared ones. Uncle won't let us keep rabbits, you see . . . Thirty-six. Is that right, sir?'

'Quite right.'

'I like the multiplying – it's the dividing that beats me down. Hester Vern.'

'What did you say?' exclaimed Jonathan.

'I'm reading what it says there – Hester Vern – thass right, ain't it, sir?'

Jonathan looked, and saw that he had chalked the name on the boiler wall – now when had he done that? – and had imperfectly rubbed it out. 'Yes – anyhow, that isn't anything,' said he, hastily erasing it. 'Well, stick at it, boy, and you may have your farm one day.'

'I'm always dreaming about it, sir,' Charlie said. 'Just a little holding like Mr Wake's – or like yours, sir – at least, yours as was – that were such a 'nation shame! And I should have Edie come to live wi' me, and keep house – 'cos she don't like it at home with Uncle there – which he ain't an uncle – nor an uncle wouldn't treat her the way he does – and she don't have to call him Uncle if she don't like, does she, sir?'

'No, Charlie, she don't,' Jonathan said firmly: remembering his stepfather and thinking he would have to meet this uncle some time.

Autumn approached the margin of winter gently and temperately: the water in the drain was seldom high, and Jonathan had plenty of time for casual work on the land. He took all he could get, for he still meant to revive his fortunes eventually; and the available work being strictly limited at this season, he was doubly interested in the piece of good news Charlie Smeeth brought him one day.

'Edie's got herself a place in service!' Charlie said breathlessly. 'Peggy Chettle saw there was boxes being carried into the big farm right over Upwood way – thass been empty half a year or more – and Edie went straight over yis'dy to find out if they wanted a servant-gal, and they were just starting to move in, and they says yes, and she starts next week!'

'You're pleased about that, eh?' Jonathan said – for Charlie's smile seemed to go right round to the back of his head.

'Not 'alf, sir! It's a good place, and she'll be free of Uncle, you see (which he ain't), and she'll be earning ten pound a year, all found, and she'll have a half-day every week, so I s'll be able to see her.'

'Well, I'm pleased for Edie, Charlie: I'm sure she'll do well. Farm over Upwood way, you say? Well, I dare say they might

261

be tekking on labour: I reckon I'll soodle over there and ask if there's any work going.'

Following Charlie's directions, Jonathan walked over late that afternoon to the western edge of the fen, coming to the farmhouse a little before sunset. The front door, which had steps going up to it, seemed a little grand for his errand: walking round the side of the building he came upon a broad yard flanked by brick stables. At the door of one of these he saw a fair-haired man crouching with his back to him, apparently working on a broken latch: at the same moment the figure of a woman appeared from a rear door of the house. Jonathan sprang back as if he had touched electricity; some instinct made him retreat a little round the corner chimney-breast of the house, where he could not be seen. Slightly short-sighted as he was, he knew the girl immediately – her very gait, swinging and supple, transfixed him with recognition. Half-way across the yard, the girl suddenly stopped and then began to tiptoe towards the crouching young man, who was plainly unaware of her approach: Jonathan saw her smile of mischief, white teeth touched by a tip of pink tongue. There was sawdust on the ground around the man, and the girl, swift and deft as a cat – yes, he remembered that! – bent down, scooped up a handful and, seizing the man's shirt collar, emptied it down his neck. The man started and leapt up – lithe as she, it seemed – made a grab and caught her to him, pantomimed raising a fist, whilst she reached up and tweaked his nose. All the time they were laughing. The girl put her arms around the man's neck, her face against his. Jonathan could see the curved, laughing shape of her mouth outlined on the man's cheek.

He turned, and walked back the way he had come. At the end of the drove he stopped to wipe his face, for though it was cold he found he was covered in sweat. A sort of blankness had taken possession of his mind, and it was only now that he bethought himself of why he had come. Well: that was out of the question.

He set out for home, trudging along the high road. It was empty as a trail crossing a steppe: in its straightness it seemed to unroll before him like the expression of some mysterious and intractable purpose. The wind was in the west, and blowing steadily, though the dead leaves at his feet whirled and scurried in cryptic little patterns, as if obedient to some other and discriminating force. The sharpness in the air was that of November, which while cutting enough is different in quality from that of February: the early winter retaining even within its desolation something of the foregoing season, as if it were the decayed corpse of the summer, whilst on the other side of the solstice there is an assertive rigour, which seems to have no conception of kinder days – the presence of cold rather than the absence of warmth. On the horizon the sun was momently disappearing, and profound layers of shadow were invading the land: at the very last a fiery cusp seemed to pause on the lip of the earth, and the shapes of objects near at hand appeared to start forward; the bare trees by the road revealing for a complex instant every twig of their tracery before coalescing in a soft blooming of blackness. In the sky above the sunset the eye was bewitched by a swift succession of colours, exhibited all in their tenderest, most opalescent forms, like the same note played on different instruments, until the last embers of orange were extinguished in a metallic afterglow: whilst at the same moment, from the opposite quarter of the firmament, the first stars sparked into life from a bed of harsh and remotest green. The wind freshened as if freed by the promise of night: it ran with a long dry whistle through every stalk of wintry vegetation that clothed the banks of the high road; it snatched the white vapour of Jonathan's breath and tossed it over his shoulder. He was wrapped in incomplete night, his footsteps here and there involved in pockets of pure black, and through the soles of his feet the bumps and concavities of the road's surface became magnified to his sense of touch, like the tiny ridges of the teeth when felt by the tongue.

All this presented itself to Jonathan's consciousness with utmost intensity, and yet with a certain disconnection, as if he were an infant seeing for the first time. All his mental processes seemed displaced by a large mass of emotion, which he could only apprehend, and try to feel his way around as he felt his way along the road. Minutes passed him like seconds, and when he beheld the distant cottage lights of Milney St Mary, and nearer at hand an angular patch in the darkness which must be the mill, he almost felt that he wanted to simply go on walking, on into the night, until his mind somehow freed itself of its burden.

At the mill he lit the lamp and climbed the stairs to the head to oil the luffing-gear. The slow creaking of the great machine sounded hollowly up the tower, and the wind sang through the sail-vanes. All was well here, and Jonathan, descending again, stood at the mill-house door, calculating the time from the stars, and thinking that Mrs Surfleet would have supper ready and he ought to go home.

All this time he had not allowed himself to think of the vignette he had seen at the farm: he had kept it at a distance. It seemed foolish to do so any longer. Hester was married; Hester was happy: these were simple facts that he must negotiate. Perhaps, he thought, it was fortunate that he had been confronted with them at last. He had been carrying his feeling for Hester around with him without ever strictly inquiring what it was, or what he expected from it: it was like some large, strange, unwieldy talisman that he could not let go of, useless as it was. Jonathan was severe on himself: he had suffered, he had expanded, but he would still sacrifice poetry on the altar of consistency, and believe that he was not doing violence to his nature. Mixed in with this was a sort of superstition, which suggested to him that fate had led him to the farm and prepared that paralysing dumb-show in order to administer a hard lesson that he had been too long evading. Out of a complexity of emotion he plucked a simple imperative: he leaned against the door-jamb and stared into the night, and an observer of his stillness would never have guessed that he was making a momentous decision – forcibly, violently – as if breaking the talisman over his knee.

He went home, ate supper, and then accompanied Andrew Surfleet to the Labour In Vain for a drop of beer. Inevitably, the news had reached the public house that Hester Verney, Saunders as she now was, had returned to Hinching Fen to live at the Upwood farm, and was the topic of much discussion.

'Done well for herself – this Mr Saunders' mother's the richest woman in Stokeley, so they say,' Jass Phelps said. 'There – I always said Hester Verney'd git on.'

'That you never,' growled Artie Gill. 'You always said she'd come to grief.'

'Well, I'm glad for her,' Henry Wake said. 'And it'll be nice to have someone local there – someone we know.'

'I don't know about that – she'll probably think herself too grand,' Jass Phelps said with malicious relish. 'Look down her nose at us – pretend she's never seen us afore – when *we* know what she's like, for all her airs. All red hat and no drawers, thass what some people say. Not that I'm saying owt against her, mind,' he added.

'No, no – Hester never looked down her nose at anyone!' Henry Wake said. 'I raise my glass to her – and her new husband; and I hope their married life will be as happy as – well –' he coughed – 'as can be expected.'

Jonathan raised his glass too: the company in the bar-parlour noticed nothing unusual in his demeanour. His decision had been made, the renunciation was complete, and he was determined to savour the serene pleasure of being heart-free. And yet that night he felt, in spite of himself, that a little of the glory had gone out of the world.

# Part Two
## 1899

# Chapter One

1

One morning in April found Hester at her butter-making in the dairy-shed of the Crooked House. This fanciful name for the place had become general on Hinching Fen; and it was never referred to as Saunders' farm.

The hour was early. The spring weather was exceptionally warm, and Hester had risen at dawn in order to do the butter-making before the mature heat of the day made it difficult. The rays of the climbing sun, obliquely penetrating the open door of the dairy, laid a bright triangle of gold on the brick floor: a few flies, prematurely roused by the early warmth, rotated drowsily with the light jewelling their wings. Hester turned the handle of the churn with a sure and practised hand – the training she had received at the Langtofts' had never left her – listening for the change in the sound of the squelching cream that indicated it had turned. From time to time she crooned a snatch of a song, though in a subdued voice, and with something more of wistfulness than gaiety. Just as her arm started to ache, and she began to think that the cream had gone to sleep, there was a soft satisfying thud within the churn: the butter had come. She gave it a turn or two more, then opened the lid to pour in cold water and wash out the buttermilk. At that moment the door of the house banged, and the farm-servant, Edie Smeeth, came galloping across the yard. Edie was fourteen: her height, which was mostly composed of leg, made her look older, as did the starveling thinness of her features; that, however, had been filling out since she had come to work at the Crooked House and eaten regular farm fare – so that altogether she was an odd mixture of childhood and womanhood. A neat black-curled head and bright black eyes gave her something of the look of an alert and pretty bird; and she had a quality of being intensely alive, her body containing a vitality sufficient for three or four persons if it were shared out; the energy required to shift a hundredweight of coal Edie put into closing a door, and she could not cross the yard without breaking into a galumphing run, embroidered with skips and hitch steps. She came bounding thus to Hester – who was fond of her and, being so recently a servant herself, found it practically impossible to act the mistress and order her about. The girl reminded her of herself too, as she was not so very long ago; and this made her both amused and sad.

'Ooh, missus, you're been a long while. Go to sleep, did it?' Edie cried, swinging her arms in unison back and forth, with a clap of her hands alternately fore and aft. 'D'you want any help?'

'No, I'm all right, thank you, Edie,' Hester said, lifting the shiny butter out and beginning to knead it.

'Don't it look a treat! Now, what did I come to say? Oh! ah. I'm give the horsekeeper his breakfast, thass it, and shall I put breakfast on for you, missus? There's them taters from yis'dy, what'll fry up wi' some bacon.'

'Oh! yes, please, Edie,' said Hester, who was mightily hungry. 'I could fancy that. Oh! wait a minute – is the master up yet?'

Edie shook her head, turning it through a hundred and eighty degrees, and most of her body with it. 'Still abed, missus.'

'Perhaps you'd better wait till he's up, then,' Hester said reluctantly. Her stomach protested at the delay, but it wasn't fair to make the girl cook twice over. 'Have you sorted the eggs, Edie? I shall be going to market today.'

'I'll do it now, missus. That little Dorking's been hiding 'em again – sly ain't it in it!' Turning to go, she whirled back again. 'I knew there was summat else – there's Billy Onyett turned up for wukk, and he says is he to go a-weeding of the wheat today, only master didn't say yea or nay, and there's a hoe all rusted through in the head, and he's mended it best he can, only thass going to bust like a twist of barley-sugar any day now.'

'Oh – I thought Lyle had . . . Well, anyhow – tell Billy to

do the best he can: and when I go to St Ives today I shall buy a new hoe.'

Left alone again, Hester finished the butter, making it up into pats and half-pats, and packing them up in muslin. She saved the buttermilk in a basin, and went to rinse her hands under the pump in the yard. The heads of four horses, protruding from their loose-boxes, watched her benevolently: two farm-horses and two ponies, one of which Lyle had purchased with the intention of training in carriage-work to sell at a profit, though he had not got round to it. The crazily leaning trees that surrounded the house resounded with the shriek of nesting birds. The horsekeeper appeared from the back kitchen door – stumbling and nearly falling down the two-foot drop from threshold to ground, which he never got used to – and Hester asked him to have the trap made ready.

Another hour had passed, during which she helped Edie in the kitchen, before Lyle came downstairs, yawning and amiably protesting that she should have woken him. They ate breakfast at the little table by the parlour window, Lyle picking at his bacon and finally abandoning it to bathe his lips again in tea.

'No letters for me?' he said.

'No, don't think so. Were you expecting one?'

'Oh! not really. Just to break the monotony, you know.' He rumpled his hair and yawned, looking at her with a foggy smile. 'By God, you do look healthy, love. You make me feel like something fished out of a well. How do you manage to get up so early?'

'Oh, the light wakes me, I think. You know the way it comes through your eyelids.'

'Not if you put your head under the blankets,' he laughed: then held his head. 'Ow! I don't know what they put in that beer at the Labour In Vain. I only had a couple last night. That'll teach me, won't it?'

'Oh, I shouldn't think so!' she said, with the quietest of laughs on her own part.

'Ah, is that Walt getting out the trap?' he said, glancing out of the window. 'I must have told him last night – damned if I remember doing it.'

'No – I asked him: I was going to take the butter and eggs to St Ives' market this morning.'

'Oh! that,' said Lyle vaguely, pouring more tea. 'Well – that'll wait, won't it?'

'But it's market-day, love.'

'Yes – I suppose. But the thing is, I wanted to take the trap today – to school that bay. You know.'

'Did you? Sorry.'

'I meant to tell you. Didn't I tell you? Oh.'

'I'm really got to go to market. The butter won't keep—'

'Yes, yes, I realise that.' Lyle dipped his spoon in his tea and toyed with it, watching the dribbles.

'Why don't you come to market with me?' Hester said after a moment. 'We could go together – and sort of make a day of it—'

'Oh! Lord, no – it would bore me to death,' Lyle said with a cross laugh. 'All those farmers talking shop.'

'You are a farmer, love,' she said lightly.

'Yes . . . but you know what I mean. Oh! well, in that case—'

'I shouldn't be back late,' Hester said, 'depending how busy it is—'

'Look, it doesn't matter,' Lyle said, pushing away his plate.

'Have you got a buyer for the bay?'

'Oh! no! Nothing like that. Probably won't get one, not at the price I was hoping. Bit of a pig in a poke, to be honest.' Lyle linked his hands behind his head and looked up at the ceiling. 'That's what comes of doing things half-measures. Can't really deal in horses properly here – no up-to-date equipment – no exercise ring . . . Hes, does this butter and eggs business really make much difference? You can't get much for them.'

'Shilling a pound for butter,' Hester said. 'It's a big help with the housekeeping.'

He looked at her with an expression in which the frown cancelled out the smile. 'You mean I don't give you enough?'

'No. It's not that, love. There's just so many little things that come up on a farm. Billy Onyett needs a new hoe—'

272

'Oh, that's what *he* says,' Lyle said. 'He's always got some complaint or other.'

'But he does need one – and he's got so much work to do, everything's so forward this year, there's thistles and charlock and poppies and all sorts choking up the wheat . . .'

'Just a few weeds, my dear.'

'Well, I know thass how it seems, love, but these are the things that matter on a farm – and if you just took a bit more interest—'

'Oh! all right,' said he breezily, 'don't keep banging on about it, my dear—' they were both employing that excessive number of endearments typical of a marital quarrel. 'I suppose we must be doing worse than I thought, if the butter and eggs are keeping us.'

'We're not doing badly, Lyle,' she said softly, 'are we?'

'Oh! how should I know?' He left the table, plucking up the newspaper and sinking into an armchair.

Hester went upstairs to change. She took off her apron and put on a powder-blue tailor-made jacket over her blouse and tied on her hat with a veil. On the dressing-table she noticed the jet earrings that Lyle had given her when she was Mrs Saunders' companion. She had not worn them since their honeymoon – how long ago it seemed!

Coming down again she found Lyle still in the armchair, one leg hooked over the side in his boneless way – one of those unconscious physical quirks that can make the heart stop with love more effectively than the most eloquently amorous speeches.

'You look very nice,' he said, putting out a hand to briefly caress hers.

'Lyle – are you sure you won't come with me?' she said.

'Oh! no,' he said, conning the newspaper, 'I don't suppose the farm can spare both of us.'

She stared down at his tousled head.

'Well, aren't you going?' he said, turning a page. 'After all that damn fuss about how you'd got to have the trap.'

Edie had carefully loaded the butter and eggs on to the back of the trap, and Walt had harnessed up the pony: and off Hester went. The long drove was dry, the air was warm, and the scene as the pony and trap rattled out on to the high-road was one of ripening beauty. The fens of Anglia can be incomparably bleak in winter, when uplands enjoy the advantage of undulation which may soften even the bareness of ploughed fields; but in a favourable spring the same fens are as richly green as a Wessex vale and, in the dazzlingly pure light of that almighty sky, would defy the brush of a Dutch master. The theme of green, set forth by the crops that extend in a carpet as far as the eye can see, is taken up by the wild growth that shoots up along drove, dykeside, and roadway, and elaborated in a thousand variations by grasses, by reeds and rushes, by wildflowers: and such was the view that met Hester, seated high up in the trap above the fields, whence it seemed that there was not a square inch of earth from horizon to horizon that was not giving forth leaf and bloom.

An observer might have judged the smart young woman in the trap, expertly gathering the reins in her gauntleted hands, as complementary to the beauty of the scene, and even surpassing it: for there was a certain maturity of expression about that well-shaped face beneath the veiled hat, a touch of shade about the youthful contours, which gave a finish lacking in the vernal landscape. In fact Hester was trying not to cry, and not entirely succeeding; so that the road before her often dissolved behind a watery film, and several times she had to trust to the straightness of the road and the sureness of the pony, while she fumbled to wipe and blink away the sporadic tears.

She was crying because of the quarrel with her husband, but the deep pain of it lay not so much in the incident, as in the general tendency of which it was a part. It would not have been so bad if she could have viewed it as an isolated outbreak – a bump in a reasonably smooth surface. But it was not so, and that was why she was troubled. The quarrel, such as it was, had been simply an intensification of the normal conditions of their married life: a downpour in a drizzly climate.

She had been naïve, she supposed, when she married Lyle seven months ago: if she had not exactly believed that love conquered all, she had at least held that the possession of it robbed the world of much of its power to hurt. And indeed in that she was not changed: when she woke in the morning she did not regard the face on the pillow beside her with hate or aversion; her love remained, and she cherished it still. It remained, but it seemed to be dissipated in a thousand trivial drops. The wings that had lifted her to such heights of promise beat in vain against the hard front of circumstance: and poor Hester, whose worldly aspirations extended little further than a full stomach and an intact roof, felt herself ground in the mill of the material.

Yet there was nothing, in reviewing her life since she had knelt beside Lyle in the church at Stokeley, that she could seize on as a separable cause of regret. She had married the man she loved; they had begun their life together on a fen farm, the environment she knew and loved best: she would change none of it. She laboured under a sense of grievance which she could not or would not shape: on the one hand she stoutly believed that there was nothing in her own conduct that merited serious reproach, but on the other she left a wide margin of allowance around Lyle's behaviour; and so she hovered in-between, in a limbo of doubt, the most oppressive to her straightforward spirit. For the first time Hester was hearing the eternal note of sadness, and recognising that its timbre, resounding from the soul, was different from that of sorrow or suffering; and she saw her self of a year ago, with a mixture of envy and pity, as a mere unreflecting animal living in a world of the simplest sensations.

The name of the Crooked House, which she and Lyle had coined in the first careless days, might have taken on a sinister meaning: it was tempting to see it fatalistically as a place where everything went awry. But, confused as she felt, Hester had not lost her practicality. They had taken on the farm in high hopes, and she saw nothing intrinsic in their situation that should dash them. She liked the house: though they had been able to furnish it only sparsely, there would be lots of time to improve it; and the holding of peat arable land, intensively farmed in the fen way, should support them with ease. She was used to hard work, and threw herself into it all the more willingly in the knowledge that it was for she and Lyle alone. Nothing could persuade her that the farm was a bad thing –

not even the belated revelation that Lyle had not really been able to afford it.

He had taken out a loan to make up the shortfall, a fact she only learned by chance on catching sight of a letter he had received from the bank. Her dismay at this he had shrugged off. 'Oh! it's not much,' he had said. 'That's what banks are for, after all. It'll be paid off eventually.'

'Oh but, Lyle – you never told me!' said she, with visions of bailiffs and bankruptcy courts.

'Why, I didn't want to bother you with it,' he said, with his cheerfullest smile: at the same time moving away a little restively, as if to tell her that she needn't look so reproachful. 'You wanted the farm, didn't you? No point in settling for some dingy cottage.'

'Well, yes – but if I'd known—'

'Well, you know now, love, and don't worry about it.' He remained good-humoured, but also seemed to suggest that he was being very forbearing in doing so.

Hester was left with a dual discomfort. The knowledge that the farm was not entirely theirs gave a new urgency to every task but, worse than that, her mind had laid hold of the horrible idea that she could not trust Lyle, before she could reason her way out of it. Reason hurriedly declared that he had not told her a lie – he had merely neglected to tell her some part of the truth, from the best of intentions: she was far too cut-and-dried about these things herself, and besides she ought to know that Lyle's was not a personality to be measured against a ruler – that was one of the things she loved about him . . . Still the unease could not be rooted out. And there was something else she knew he often omitted to tell her – his visits to his mother, and what prompted them.

She had never for a moment supposed that he would not continue to call on his family, and to try to make it up with Mrs Saunders – it was only natural. But when they had married, she had earnestly sought assurance from him that if the estrangement should prove permanent (which it showed every sign of being – Mrs Saunders was unyielding), then he would accept that as a fair price to pay. He had given that assurance freely – of course he accepted that! But now she began to see that Lyle had never really believed he would have to pay that price. He had once told her, jokingly, that that old chestnut about not being able to have your cake and eat it was nonsense – he had been doing it all his life. Now Hester feared that it was more than a joke. It seemed that at each fresh rebuff from his mother, Lyle – instead of cutting his losses – redoubled his efforts to win her round. He no longer spoke laughingly of his charm working on her in the end: he seldom spoke directly about the matter at all. It had become a grim struggle. And what chiefly oppressed her about it was the fact that Lyle would go to a great deal more trouble in trying to find a way back to his mother's favour than he would in working the farm. Hester was well-placed to understand such a perverse misdirection of effort: it was a habit of mind she had been prone to herself – but now it dismayed her to observe it in Lyle. She knew he was dissatisfied with the farm, and that he could not begin to be satisfied with it while half his mind was still fixed – in spite of his denials – on the more substantial prospects of the family business.

It was for the same reason, she supposed, that he was so ineffably careless about money. They had enough to live on, if they did not throw it about: but it was precisely because of that vague hope of his mother which he never relinquished that Lyle did throw it about; and thus a comfortable competence became a deficiency. Had he accepted that there would never be any more, he might have lived within his means – instead he tried to live as if that phantom inheritance were already in the bank, and chafed when confronted with the more modest reality. It was in this way that life with Lyle – one of the attractions of which had promised to be a freedom from niggling mundanity – was full of fretting about money. The words of Mrs Saunders' prediction echoed in Hester's ears like a curse.

And yet she loved him; and to quarrel with him cut her like a slow razor. Indeed perhaps it was now, rather than during the idyll of their courtship, that she beheld the full magnitude of her love: what smote most sorely on her heart was the perception that Lyle was not happy, when she longed to make him so, and felt she would do anything to that end.

Hester wiped her face, and sat up more smartly: a cart

was coming the other way. Along with sadness she had discovered pride, and she would sooner have walked on fiery coals than permit her distress to be seen. After all, she told herself, flicking the reins, this wasn't like her – wittling and cry-babying. Hadn't she always been down-to-earth and realistic – and wasn't marriage to be viewed in that light too? Wasn't it natural that it should have its troubles and disappointments? (Even as she strove thus to be mentally bracing, Mrs Saunders' words mocked her: *How long do you suppose that fairy-tale will last?*) She could not reproach herself with having gone into marriage blind: her far from sheltered upbringing had led her to anticipate at least as much shade as light across any tract of experience. Complexity was a condition of life, and she supposed that included what the Chapel called the life of the flesh. Well, she accepted that: perhaps it was unreasonable to expect the initial intensities of feeling to persist; the everyday was a fine diluter of passion. But still . . . Hester was not an outright sensualist: a sense of humour perhaps precluded it – she thought, for example, that the designer of the human libido and the designer of the human foot must have been working at cross-purposes; but her nature was warm and responsive, and she did not see why the physical celebrations of honeymoon should have subsided so swiftly to such a complete indifference. That bewildered and hurt her.

Of course there was the question of children – and with Lyle worrying about money as he was. . . How that took the edge off everything! It even made him irritable: he had seemed the least irritable of men before their marriage. Here lay something she had never expected to find, and she could not tell whether it was a common revelation of marriage or specific to their case – the fact that getting to know the person she had married was not a matter of penetrating further into known country, but of suddenly finding herself in unguessed-at and alien regions. That genial optimism which she had seen as the expression of Lyle's whole being turned out to be a somewhat thin and brittle crust on the surface of his character. The loss of a hen to a stoat, heavy rain making the drove impassable, the cost of a broken window: such small things seemed to gnaw at him, and pointing out that they were small made it worse. 'God! it's all so damn trivial,' he had said, 'that's what gets me. Like being eaten alive by gnats.'

Often – increasingly often – he escaped by going down to the Labour In Vain. Hester recoiled from an image of herself as the waiting, disapproving wife of the music-hall joke – but still she wished he would not do it so often. Of course, she had known he liked a drink when she married him, hadn't she? – at Mrs Saunders' he had been a frequent patron of the Nag's Head. And yet this seemed different – a retreat, an evasion.

No, Hester could not accuse Lyle of fostering any illusions about himself: that was why she shrank from acknowledging her own discontent, and why she flinched with a sort of guilt from the idea that instead of the broad open sunlit spaces which she had associated with her husband's character, there were dark airless tunnels, and redoubling mazes that led nowhere.

Well, something was amiss with their life: so much was definite, and she could no longer deny that at least. She wished Lyle had come with her – but in a way it was good to be alone like this, and think it out. If something was wrong, then she would have to put it right. There was no alternative, unless to admit that her marriage had been a mistake – the thought was like a cloud passing across the sun, chilling her before she could dismiss it – no, that was nonsense! Once she would have said that the best way of dealing with problems was to ignore them and hope they would go away: even now a trace of that attitude remained to her (Hester's flippancy was just as sincere as other people's solemnity); but in this case she must not turn her face away – as it seemed Lyle was all too liable to. If they quarrelled again, she decided, she would not draw back from the brink: she must openly confront what was wrong, confront even her great fear – that Lyle felt trapped, and that he might begin to blame her for it.

Hester arrived at her destination less dejected, at least, than when she had set out: it seemed to her that that stifled feeling that had long oppressed her was a direct result of pretending that nothing was wrong, and while the ache of tears lingered, she breathed more freely. The approach to St Ives was picturesque enough to lighten the heaviest heart. The road in revealed a broad prospect of river meadows, where spindly lambs darted among the sheep like another species, and it seemed impossible that they should ever become such thick solidities as their elders: the little town was enisled in greenness and sparkling water, with the two church spires hoisting aloft like twin masts. Hester's was not the only vehicle crossing the venerable bridge with the stone chapel built on it, for St Ives – the place of the man with seven wives – had once been a great trading centre, and still boasted a market more substantial than the modest scale of the town might suggest. Before the bow-fronts of comfortable houses, as quietly handsome as a country parson's daughters, a busy drama of commerce was enacted. Livestock, which on this southern edge of the fens were more common, huddled together in pens, and trembled singly on the backboards of waggons; early vegetables, still with the coldness of earth on them, toppled from wicker baskets and rolled off the trestles; bowler-hatted farmers weighed grain and seed on their grooved palms, and shook their heads and stroked their side-whiskers despairingly, as if their trade were sheer agony to them, and they would rather do anything else.

Here Hester, going about her marketing, was strongly conscious of being a farmer's wife (a young and pretty one), and enjoying it. It suited her well. You were an agent in your own right, instead of subsisting in your husband's background, like poor old Uncle Bevis's wife. Most pleasing to her, it was not an 'uppity' position, which set limits to who you could mix with: at the Crooked House she had re-forged her links with Lizzie Gosling and other old friends – though there had been no reconciliation with the Langtofts, and she was thankful that their farms were on opposite sides of the fen. Even as Mrs Saunders' companion, she had had to stand within the circle of that lady's dignity: here she was on her own ground. If only she didn't feel that Lyle was pursuing this life on sufferance! She knew that he could make a success of it: he had energy and resource enough for anything, if they could be rolled into one lump, and not dissipated in fitfulness – and if he were not always mentally looking over his shoulder for that elusive side-road that somehow got there quicker.

Hester counted up her butter-money, and ruefully reflected that she was doing the very thing she had always laughed at as the summit of futility – believing you might change your spouse once you had married him. But she did believe they could be happy: and somehow she must make him believe it.

She had various things to buy besides a hoe – salt, paraffin oil, soap, yeast, a roll of chicken-wire, things that Lyle never thought of – and after she had tipped the boy who had helped her load them into the trap, she returned to a stall that had caught her eye earlier. What attracted her were the sheaves of cut tulips. In recent years tulips had begun to be commercially cultivated in large numbers in the northern fens around Spalding: and thus a flower that had its origin in ancient Persia, and had bloomed on the Hanging Gardens of Babylon, pouted its exotic mouth among daffodils in a homely Anglian market town. For Hester their beauty was enhanced by association, for her mother had loved them; she had often been haunted of late by a strange longing wistfulness for her childhood, which formerly she had been glad to leave behind. Why this feeling of weakness? Wasn't love supposed to make you strong? But she could not resist the tulips; and she set out for home with two large bunches atop the rest of the goods in the back of the trap.

The day had begun to cloud over a little, but it was warm and still; when she came in sight of Hinching Fen mill she noticed that the sails were barely moving. The waters had been high after the spring thaw, and Jonathan must be running the pump a lot. On passing the mill Hester always freshened the pony's pace a little. When she had come to live at the Crooked House the presence of Jonathan Eastholm in the neighbourhood had first surprised and then made her a little uneasy. Of course that time on the lighters, and his strange, sudden and contemptuous proposal, were a good while ago, and so much had changed in her life that it all seemed to lie on the further side of a great gulf of sundering experience – even though, most curiously, there were still occasions when she woke up in bed and in the first hazy moments believed she was lying on the bunk in the lighter-cabin, with the river murmuring beside it. But spacious as the fen was, she was bound to see Jonathan Eastholm around from time to time, and when she did she had the disturbing feeling that he despised her.

Why this troubled her so she could not say. With the Langtofts, she had fallen out with them, and that was that. She was sorry it had to be that way, but she really didn't care what they thought of her – it was all in the past. But it was as if Jonathan saw her in some way which no one else could; and somehow it seemed that his contempt for her sprang from his contempt for himself, for his extraordinary lapse, as a man might regard the crazed ruins of a folly on which he had squandered a fortune. When she saw him she felt vulnerable; she seemed to stand in a ruthless beam of light. All this really made no sense, she told herself; and yet the feeling was as convincing as disquieting, like some unperceived colour in the spectrum of her emotions. And so it was with a double alarm that Hester heard a cracking sound from the left-side wheel, right opposite the drove leading to the mill.

A great jolt rattled her teeth, and before she could pull the pony up the trap had slewed to one side: some of her parcels went sliding off the backboard and fell in the road. Jumping down, she found to her dismay that a spoke of the wheel had snapped off at the socket; the metal wheel-rim was buckled, and the two adjacent spokes were bowing under the pressure. Another glance took in the scattered parcels, and, most melancholy, the tulips all over the road: and another, the sight of Jonathan Eastholm coming out from the mill, whence he must have plainly seen the accident.

'Bit of trouble, I think,' said he, frowning at the buckled wheel, whilst the pony peered over its shoulder, with an air of helpful attention.

Hester nodded in confusion, scarcely able to look at him; somehow it seemed the worst part of her distress that he should be the witness of it. 'I don't understand,' she said, 'the trap was perfectly all right – Walt greased the axles this morning . . .' All at once the memory of her quarrel with Lyle afflicted her; she had insisted on having the trap, and here it was broken! 'Oh! whatever will my husband say?' she murmured, before she could stop herself.

Jonathan looked at her with an expression of purest surprise. 'Why, it's not your fault,' he said.

'No . . .' How stupid she felt. 'Will I – will it bear up, do you suppose?'

'Well, I'm no wheelwright.' Jonathan bent to examine the wheel. 'Rusted—I shouldn't trust the other spokes. You'd best not ride any further; it wouldn't be safe with the weight. Try leading the pony – go very gently.' He looked down at the parcels. 'You'd best not load up again either. I'll carry these for you.'

'Oh, no – I can't let you do that – it doesn't matter.'

'Why, you can't leave them all over the road,' he said, in his short way, and began gathering them up in his arms.

She was reluctant to accept his help, but there seemed nothing else for it; and in her fear of Lyle's reaction to her bringing back the trap damaged, after that scene this morning, she found she could not think straight. 'Will the mill be all right?' she said feebly.

'She won't run away,' said Jonathan.

'Oh! don't trouble about them,' she said, as she saw him picking up the tulips out of the dust: but he ignored her, and such as were intact he laid in the crook of his arm.

It felt strange indeed to be leading the pony and the limping trap with Eastholm walking along beside her, the parcels tucked under his capacious arms. Once this might have tickled her, but she felt herself crushed between his silent disapproval and the prospect of more trouble with Lyle. Out of desperation she said the first thing that came into her head. 'Why do you call the mill "she"?'

It came out more pert and inconsequential than she intended. Jonathan, by his frown, certainly seemed to think it so; but he answered carefully: 'I don't know. Millers do, generally. I suppose it's the same as calling a boat she; and I suppose railwaymen do the same with an engine.'

'But you wouldn't call a house she,' said Hester, some part of her mind, in spite of herself, becoming interested in the question.

'No,' he said. 'But a mill, or a boat, seems to have a life of its own – and moods, too.'

'Ah, thass it. But men have moods just as much as women, it seems to me.'

'I wouldn't know,' said he.

Hester was silent. The coolness of the miller's manner depressed her. It was not that she expected to find the flattering jealousy of the rejected suitor: she had lost the coquettishness that might have looked for such a thing; and besides, Jonathan's suit itself had been so grudging and unloverlike that she suspected the only thing he now regretted was making it in the first place. No, what she felt was an acute form of that unease, which seemed all entangled with his opinion of her. Something made her long to say, straight out, 'You hate me very much, don't you?' But she could not; and chilled by a specific dread of Jonathan's perceiving her unhappiness – he of all people – she suddenly burst instead into rattling cheeriness. 'Well, ain't the spring being kind to us? You don't often get April days like this – course, the fields could do with a drop of rain – it'd be nice if we could just have the rain-showers at night, wouldn't it, and the sun all day – oh, I don't know though, I love the smell of rain on the land, you know, to stand at the door and sniff it, and you wouldn't get that if you were asleep . . .' She broke off. 'Look, Jonathan – it's been very kind of you – you needn't come any further, I don't want to take you out of your way . . .'

He stared down at her. 'Don't be a fool, missus,' he said. 'What's the point in bringing this stuff halfway?'

'Well, there's no need to snap at me!' she cried – wailed rather, more in wretchedness than anger. 'You always were terrible hard on me!'

His glance fell keenly on her, as if he saw much; he seemed to refrain from comment, and shook his head, saying: 'Well: never mind me. Come on, it's not far now.'

Hester was too perplexed by a sensation of having somehow given herself away, to say much more; and soon they reached the drove leading to the Crooked House. Edie Smeeth came flying out to them in the yard, and had to be pacified from a first impression that Hester had been flung from the trap into the ditch, and was walking wounded.

Jonathan gave Edie the parcels, and handed Hester the tulips. Holding the flowers in her arms, she suddenly thought to ask him whether he would like some of them, as a thank-you,

saw at once it was inappropriate, and said hesitantly: 'Jonathan
– I think there's some ale in the kitchen – would you like some
before you go?'

He looked at her with a fierce sort of astonishment. 'Why,
do you think I was just after a tip? What d'you think I am?'

'I'm sure I don't know,' said she, stung – for she had
intended no harm. 'I don't understand you at all – and I
reckon I never will!'

'I dare say: it doesn't matter,' he replied coolly, shrugging.
'I don't want no tip – thass all. Good day to you.'

In the kitchen Edie Smeeth, unwrapping the parcels as if she
were in a parcel-unwrapping race, said to Hester: 'Weren't it
lucky Jonathan-up-at-the-mill were around to help you, missus!
My brother Charlie says he'll always go out of his road for folk
– just like he did when Mr Wake's cow went in the dyke – and
he'll never tek no thanks for it. And they reckon the mill's much
better kept now he's there – and he does all manner of work on
the farms an' all, and never gits tired.'

'Why, he's never asked for work here,' said Hester. Did he
dislike her that much?

'No, missus,' agreed Edie, who (like many people) paid
to others' remarks about half the attention that she gave
to her own. 'And my brother Charlie said Mr Wake said
Jonathan-up-at-the-mill were quite an illegible bachelor, and
thass a wonder he don't git married; only he don't seem
interested, and just keeps hisself to hisself.'

'Well – probably he thinks just a shade too well of himself,'
Hester said, going to the kitchen door, and looking sombrely
out at the buckled wheel of the trap, while Walt unharnessed
the pony. Of course, as Jonathan had said, it wasn't her fault
. . . 'Where's Mr Saunders, Edie?' she said in a small voice.

'Not here, missus – he went into Stokeley. Got a lift on
Farmer Mather's cart.'

'Oh . . . did he?' And had he gone to renew the hopeless
siege of his mother's obduracy? She felt cold.

She helped Edie put supper on, and was in the parlour
mending a petticoat when she heard Lyle arrive home. A few
moments later the door opened, and she stared; a soldier stood
on the threshold.

'What—Lyle, wherever did you get that?'

Grinning, Lyle marched in. He was clad in a soldier's scarlet tunic, with gleaming buttons, which in the wainscoted farm parlour looked as outlandish as a sultan's cloak. He saluted smartly, clicked his heels, and bowed to kiss her hand.

'I've joined up, my dear. Taken the King's Shilling. Off to fight the dervishes, whatever they are. Oh! Hes, your face!' he said, laughing and falling onto the settle beside her. 'You really believed it for a moment there!'

'I never did,' said she, flushing, and slapping his knee. 'You gret fool – I was just a bit flummoxed for a second, thass all.'

'I'm sorry, love.' He put his arm round her and kissed her. 'I do wish I had a picture of your face just then, though. Well, how do you fancy me in uniform? I think I could rather take to it, you know. I reckon I look quite a Blade.'

'What does that make me, a battle-axe?' she said.

'Very cutting! Ow, we'd better stop these puns, hadn't we?'

'I think we had,' she said laughing. In fact his lean boyish figure did look well in the red coat. 'Where on earth did you get it?'

'At Balsam's – you know, the dyer in Stokeley. "Mourning Our Speciality".' He pulled a long face. 'He comes creeping out of the back of his shop with his head on his shoulder and says "Iss it a bereavement, ssir?" Anyway, that's my good news – I think I've sold him that bay pony. He's worth a mint of money, and he doesn't know a thing about horseflesh, so I ought to get a good price. That's a turn-up, isn't it? I knew today would be a lucky day. And when I was in the back of his shop, I saw these discarded tunics – he gets them for a song and uses the cloth – and he let me have one when I took a fancy to 'em.' Suddenly Lyle sprang up and strutted to the fireplace, tweaking an imaginary moustache. 'Couldn't you just see me at that great ball in Brussels before Waterloo, eh? With all those titled ladies in see-through frocks, admiring my regimentals – as it were.' He darted back and fell on one knee before her. 'Lady Montmowency, you are a wavishing angel. Your shoulders are like marble – all cold and veiny. Will you gwant me a single night of bliss, before I go off tomorrow and thwash Boney?'

'Oh! not tonight,' she said, 'I'm got the Duke of Wellington coming, and it takes him half the night to get his boots off. Oh! come here,' she said, kissing him warmly. 'Perhaps I'd better tell you while you're in a good mood. The left wheel of the trap's broken – a spoke came off and the wheel-rim buckled . . . I'm sorry.'

'Rusty, I should think. Did you manage to get home all right? Well, that can soon be fixed,' he said blithely. 'Oh! Hes, have you been worrying about that?'

'Well, a bit,' she said lamely; her relief must have shown in her face.

'Daft girl. Anybody would think I'm some sort of tyrant who takes a strap to you. What's that you're sewing at?'

'Just a petticoat of mine – it wants mending.'

'Pah!' said Lyle, 'chuck it away, my dear. No patched clothes for us. I reckon my selling that bay is just the first of a – well, it shows things are on the way up for us. Don't you think?'

'Yes, I suppose so . . .'

'Never mind suppose, wench. Of course they are – I never doubted it. Pessimist, that's your trouble.'

Hester did not propose to remind him of how different he had been that morning. She did not view married life as an exercise in scoring points, and at that moment she was happy just to have what she saw as the real Lyle back again.

'I wonder if I could mend that wheel?' he said.

'Oh, I don't think so, love. It wants somebody who really knows the job—'

'Pooh, I'll bet I can,' he said, getting up with energy. 'Just you see.'

But presently he was back, wiping his hands and shaking his head. 'No chance of that,' he said. 'Silly idea. Wants a wheelwright. That damned drove's in such a state, it's a wonder the trap's in one piece at all. Damn it, more expense. All these things just keep adding up . . . I don't see how we'll ever get out of the wood. It's like banging your head against the wall.' He sighed. 'Is it supper yet?'

After supper Lyle's brow cleared again. The night had turned chilly; he sat on the floor with his long legs stretched out to the fire – the floor was still his favourite seat – and leaned his head against Hester's knee. She stroked his hair, which sent him into a sort of cat-like trance; and at last she nerved herself to ask the question that had been in her mind all the time.

'In Stokeley today,' she said, very casually, 'did you go and see your mother?'

She could feel the muscles in his neck go tense, but he answered, quite as casually: 'Yes, I called in.'

'How is she?'

'Oh! still the same.' His fingers tapped a moment on her foot. 'Didn't get much of a welcome, as you can imagine.'

Hester licked her lips; her mouth had gone dry. 'Why do you go?' she said. She knew why he went, but it had to be said.

Lyle's neck was like the skin of a drum. She saw his jaws working in the firelight; but at last he said lightly: 'Don't know, really.'

'I mean,' she said with care, 'there's no pleasure in just being ignored, is there?'

'None at all.'

'When you never get any welcome . . . It would serve her right if you just stopped bothering.'

He half turned to her. 'You think I should?'

'I know it seems hard,' she said, with a feeling of walking along a tightrope, 'but it would save you the – the disappointment each time.'

He reached up for her hand. 'All right,' he said. 'Whatever you say, my dear. Whatever you say.'


2


Jonathan had been suffering from a cold. On his constitution this had rather less than the effect of a tick-bite on a bull, but he had unwisely mentioned it to the Surfleets, with whom he still lodged, and so it had got round to Peggy Chettle.

She visited him at the mill, arriving on the bicycle in which she had newly invested. These machines were a novel sight in the fens, and children ran out of cottages to watch Mrs Chettle go pedalling hardily by – looking, in her ample divided skirt and leg-of-mutton sleeves, like a genial balloon on wheels. 'It

288

cost me a pretty penny,' she confided to Jonathan, 'but in my line o' work you need to be mobile, what wi' laying-ins coming at all hours, and laying-outs, well, not that they're in any hurry, God rest 'em, but best not to delay when the warm weather sets in. Now then, dear boy, Mrs Surfleet happened to mention as you weren't at the top of your form, so I thought I'd come and look you over, neighbourly-like.'

Jonathan attempted to protest, with thanks, that he was quite all right.

'Oh! I know you young men, you reckon nothing short of a thunderbolt'll lay you low, but there's nothing worse than a spring chill if you don't cosset it. It'll go down in your lungs and lay there till you sound like Jass Phelps' donkey – ain't that right, boy?' Mrs Chettle added to Charlie Smeeth, who was visiting the mill as usual.

'Coh! I should know, Mrs Chettle,' said Charlie, who was one of those people who offer their ill-health as a matter for modest congratulation, 'I git 'em in spring and summer and all, I do. They mek me ears go all clogged – I were deaf as a post once for a dozen weeks together, I was, till I ran up to the hay-loft one day and they unpopped, and Mr Wake said it was because of the alti-chewed.'

'Now look here,' Mrs Chettle said, taking Jonathan's hand in her own pink scrubbed one, and pressing a jar into it, 'thass goose-grease, and you want to rub that all across your chest, well, p'rhaps not all across, my word, you'd need a bigger jar than that, but any road, rub it in well and then cover it with brown paper cut out in the shape of a heart – ah, I know that sounds a bit daft, but never mind – it may not be scientific but it works, like when I cured Chettle's little trouble with a piece o' lint and a clothes-peg. Now mind you use it, dear boy. Charlie Smeeth, you'll see he looks after hisself, won't you?'

'I will, Mrs Chettle.'

'Well, Charlie, and how do you go on? I declare you're more of a long drink o' water than ever. When are you going to grow outards a bit, instead of uppards?'

'I dunno, Mrs Chettle,' said Charlie, mournfully throttling his cap. 'I keep trying, but I don't git no thicker – Mr Wake says if I was a plant he'd train me on a trellis.'

'You'll be better when you git to twenty-one – third cycle of seven,' said Mrs Chettle. 'Well, I must be leaving you, I'm got to see poor ole Mrs Miles who should have delivered a week ago, and her with her busts sticking out like chapel hat-pegs and enough milk for a school-treat, still, it'll come, you git one like that sometimes, they stay up there and it's like trying to pull a football through a knot-hole – just tek hold of my iron steed, will you, Charlie, while I climb on, I'm all right once I'm got going but it's mounting up thass the trouble, that reminds me of a joke but it's not for your young ears, cheer-o, both!'

Charlie was deeply impressed by the responsibility of seeing that Jonathan looked after himself: and insisted on going up to the head with the oil-can, and doing the rounds himself, whilst Jonathan sat by the fire.

'This is nonsense, boy,' Jonathan said. 'All because of a little sniffle!'

'Oh, but let me, sir – goo on – you know I like doing it!' Charlie said.

'Well, if it'll mek you happy. And don't sir me.' Inactivity irked Jonathan, but he was in a brooding mood which had something of the Old Goblin about it, and by the time Charlie had come down again he had fallen into a deep abstraction from which he was only roused by the sight of the boy examining his own reflection in the opaque mill-house window.

'What's the matter, Charlie?'

'Oh! it's my beard, sir. My beard what I ain't got, I mean. It's like Mrs Chettle said – I don't seem to be growing proper at all.'

'Rubbish, boy. I was no different from you when I was your age.' In fact one of the reasons Jonathan kept so completely clean-shaven was that he did not have a very strong beard, and it had used to worry him just as it did Charlie.

'Weren't you really, sir?' said Charlie, with an expression that showed he longed to believe, but was forced to doubt.

'Thinner, if anything,' Jonathan said, with a hyperbole more kind than credible, for Charlie had scarcely more breadth of body than a folded umbrella.

'But there's me ears, sir,' said Charlie, in renewed despair, 'sticking out like anything! Oh, 'ell!'

'Calm down, boy. Say your psalm. We're all made different, Charlie: thass what it is,' Jonathan said, raking the fire and staring into the embers. 'There's some things we can change about ourselves, but some we can't no matter how hard we try – because we're made that way. We're all got our little peculiarities, see: and when these chaps stand up in their wing collars and high hats, and tell us we all ought to work harder, or we ought to be good and not have so many children, or we ought to stop drinking and go to church, just remember they're got their little peculiarities too, though they're trying so powerful hard to mek out they haven't got a single one; and when somebody reckons he never had a doubt, or a secret, or a weak moment – why, he's a liar, and no less. See your own little peculiarities, and you'll look different on other people's.' To a less appreciative ear than Charlie's, there would have been nothing remarkable in this philosophy – but it was remarkable in that it was quite new to Jonathan Eastholm, the harshly judgemental waterman who needed no one. A year or two ago he would have brusquely shied away from such ideas, and even now he groped at their incomplete form through a prickly mesh of self. 'Any road,' he said, hoping to turn the boy's thoughts to a more hopeful channel, 'you're got plenty of growing yet. Tek your sister Edie – I saw her just the other day – look how she's filled out, and coloured up, in just six months.'

'Oh, ah, sir, thass the best thing that ever happened,' Charlie said, cheering up at once. 'Edie loves it at the Crooked House: no more Uncle (which he ain't), and the way he – well, the way he used to behave; and all the grub she can eat. And she says young Mrs Saunders is nice as pie with her, and don't frighten her at all – not like Mrs Wake do me – oh, 'ell! And she says Mrs Saunders is allus giving her presents, bits o' clothes and the like, though she don't hardly ever have anything for herself.'

'Don't she, Charlie?' Jonathan said, his eyes on the fire. 'Aren't they well off?'

'Well, Edie reckons Mr Lyle Saunders put just about everything he'd got into that farm – but now he don't seem to want to mek a proper fist at it, and Mrs Saunders does all the work while he does all the spending – thass what Edie says – and when he's not riding about on his ponies, all fligged up to the nines, he's down the Labour In Vain – and he's always in a funny mood about summat or other, all strung up, like a dog that ain't had a walk all day – thass what Edie says. And there's Mrs Saunders doing her best, and Mr Saunders not caring about nothing, and Edie says they're allus quarrelling about it—'

'Charlie, don't tell me any more,' Jonathan said.

'Oh, sir – I didn't mean to tell tales,' said Charlie in alarm. 'Nor didn't Edie!'

'No, boy, I know. Still, best to keep them things to yourself, eh?' Jonathan looked at his turnip watch, without really noticing the time. 'Reckon you'd better be off home to your supper now.'

Charlie who, whatever his naïvety, had a tactful sense of when he was superfluous, quietly left. Jonathan climbed up to the mill-head and went over all the luffing-gear with rag and broom – the boy was always too liberal with the oil, though Jonathan chose not to tell him. At last he closed the boiler flues, scattered the ashes on the fire and, locking the mill-house door, set off home to the Surfleets.

He hoped he had not been short with the boy, but there was such a volume of thoughts pouring into his mind, and he needed to be alone to pump them out. When he had met Hester (how could he think of her as Mrs Saunders?) the other day, he had thought her greatly changed; but he had wondered then if he were seeing merely a reflection of change in himself. Now Charlie's words brought that scene back to the foreground of his mind from which he had consciously banished it, and forced him to consider what he had dismissed – that Hester had looked an unhappy woman. Both halves of that epithet were significant of transformation, for he had never conceived her being unhappy and he had never thought of her as a woman, rather than a girl. And that she most assuredly was now. The most strange and compelling symptom of her unhappiness, it seemed to him, lay in her beauty – and that was a word he would never have applied to her before: a beauty unaware of itself, and as far from mere prettiness as a night prospect of bare trees against snow. That slightly indrawn lower lip, and those slanting eyebrows, which had formerly seemed emblematic of sheer fun, had gained in subtle expression what they had lost in gaiety. Even in her voice he had detected a new timbre, a faint throb of disturbance which had not been there before.

His reactions to this ran a swift relay, from surprise to perplexity to confusion. Much had happened, of course, in the year since their ill-fated rendezvous at the Spread Eagle, but still that Hester should have changed so much seemed to Jonathan as untoward as if the mill had got up and walked about the fen; and he had had great difficulty in behaving normally when he had carried home her parcels. If she appeared to have entered new and sombre dimensions of emotion, his own feelings were more obscure. He had solemnly abjured all remnants of love for her on her marriage: half a year had passed, in which this conscious resolution had settled into a fixed habit of mind; and he supposed he was feeling something like the tugging unease of a person who has lost his faith, on revisiting a church. Her married state, and the apparent prosperity of large farm, pony-and-trap, and fine clothes, had emphasised the wide separation between them – they seldom met, and it was effectively as if they had never known each other; and this had helped him to build up a strong protective earthwork of indifference, which he was not sure he wanted breached in any way. If Hester Saunders was unhappy, it was none of Jonathan Eastholm's business: that was the only way to look at it.

He was able to acquit himself, at least, of any sensation of vengeful triumph at this discovery; and this was not magnanimity, conscious or otherwise: he simply did not feel it. Indeed, that was part of the puzzle of his feelings, and that night Jonathan, who was normally asleep before the pillow was warm, lay wakeful.

The next morning was a Sunday. It dawned overcast, but Mrs Surfleet declared it would clear. 'There's enough blue to mek a sailor a pair of trousers,' she said as she got ready for chapel, tucking her thistledown hair into an ancient poke-bonnet crowned with ribbons faded to the colour of dead leaves. While the Surfleets pattered off to the chapel, Jonathan followed his usual custom and went the other way, to spend the morning by the river which ran along by the Stokeley road. He did not hanker for the lighters, but the river still drew him as a patch of sunlight draws a cat: he loved the peace of the water-meadows on a Sunday morning, when most of the inhabitants of Hinching Fen were in their pews – and as Jonathan was if anything a pantheist, these open-air rambles could be seen as his equivalent of religious observance. This morning, however, on approaching his favourite spot where he would stretch himself out on the grass with a book or his thoughts, he found a party of children – the annual Sunday School treat. The Sunday School helpers were laying out picnic cloths and baskets, whilst the children ran about the buttercup-strewn meadow with squeals of release.

Jonathan drew himself off to a distance, and sat down by a clump of pollard willows to watch: childhood he found rather a wistful spectacle, his own having been terminated so prematurely; but his mild interest was suddenly sharpened by the sight of Lyle Saunders there, amongst the children. He knew that Lyle was not a chapelgoer, and it soon became clear that he had volunteered to come along and help amuse the children, because he simply enjoyed it. He had thrown off his jacket, and was giving the children piggy-backs, pretending to run right to the river edge, swerving at the last moment, and laughing as hard as they. Jonathan, watching, had to admire his patience: Lyle did not mind playing over again the same game which, in the manner of children, they wanted endlessly repeated: he submitted, with satisfying howls, when the smaller ones pummelled him and thrust grass down his collar; he drew the shyer ones into a game of blind-man's-buff, going first with the blindfold himself, and clowning by catching hold of a tree and pretending it was a person. Several little girls presented him with daisy-chains, which he put on with appropriate solemnity, and did not take off when the children sat down at last to the picnic lunch.

When Jonathan got up and left it was time for the sweets, which were distributed by being thrown and scattered in the grass, the children running to pounce on them: and Lyle was running and laughing with them, his adult voice standing out from the sound of their shrill ones by its finished quality, like a chord amongst random notes.

Jonathan made his way back to the Surfleets – but on impulse

294

carried on past the cottage, and struck the field-paths towards the western edge of the fen, where the Crooked House was. Whilst he had done casual work on most of the farms in the area, he had avoided seeking it there – it seemed an unnecessary complication; but now he had a desire to see what the Saunders' fields were like. It was a compact holding, stretching from the main drain to the edge of the upland, which was clearly visible on the horizon, the peat giving way to the purple-tinged ribs of clay. A glance was enough to show him that the Saunders acres were not well kept. The young green wheat was struggling for room with weeds: the fields had not been tilled right up to the dyke-edge – a tempting omission given the risk of the plough-team going into the dyke, but terribly wasteful on rich fen land; and the dykes themselves were choked with reeds and scum, and could hardly be doing their job at all.

Well, after all, it was none of his business. About Lyle Saunders Jonathan had striven to make no judgement, or at least postpone it; but the fact was, from what he knew of him, he thought him a worthless hound. However, he would have thought that in any case, whether he were Hester's husband or not. And he could not deny the man's charm – he supposed they were well suited.

Jonathan trudged home. The sun had come out with a flourish, but his mood was dark. This marriage was a fool's game, he said to himself, and grimly he embraced his old self-possession – his mind darted to it like a fish released back into water. 'Mind when you git married, boy,' he said abruptly to Charlie Smeeth at the mill that night, 'it's a fool's game—' surprising the boy, who had been thinking of nothing more romantic than whether to eat the apple-core in his pocket, or save it till later.


3


Jass Phelps, the landlord of the Labour In Vain, had found a comfortable increase in his profits of late. There was Mr Lyle Saunders, who (as Henry Wake put it) frequently favoured the establishment with his custom, and thought nothing of standing drinks all round for his neighbours. (The mistrust aroused by his slightly dandified clothes and waggish humour was quite overcome by this friendliness, and he was pronounced a fine fellow.) More surprisingly, the pub had a new regular in the shape of Chad Langtoft. Formerly Chad had been a rare visitor: not only his chapel upbringing but the tepid caution that marked all his habits had made him one of the most temperate men on the fen; but now he was sometimes the first to arrive, often the last to leave, and usually went home very far from sober.

This of course did not go unnoticed or unremarked. When he was not there, the explanation for this change in him was discussed among the company, and the blame was generally assigned to his domestic situation.

'Two women in one kitchen – ooh! dear,' Sunny Daintree said. 'I always said no good would come o' that.' For Chad had married Mary-Ann Cole with no separate home to take his bride to, and they were living at his parents' farm.

'Well, it needn't be, you know – depends on the nature of the parties,' said Henry Wake. 'But I'm afraid Bess Langtoft's not the sort of woman to tek kindly to anybody else having a say in the household. Still – connubial bliss, they say, but it's not all bliss,' he added with suppressed feeling, studying his tankard, 'not all bliss by any means.'

'And there's Mary-Ann a bit of a spitfire when she's crossed,' Sunny said. 'Ooh! she's got a voice in her. I were moling one day in Wag Langtoft's field when she come out to call the boys in – you could hear her from Dan to Beer-sheba. I wouldn't be a bit surprised if Chad's smelt her fist by now.'

'Some people might say he rushed into that wedding,' Jass Phelps said. 'There was hardly any courting-time. Almost seemed like a forced job – you know. Not that *I'm* saying that.'

'That don't matter how quick it is, if she's the right one,' said Andrew Surfleet. 'I'd only been walking out wi' my ole gel four weeks when we got wed. Mind you – her sister-in-law were my brother-in-law's second cousin, so that were different.'

'All the same, I can't help thinking Chad was a bit hasty,'

Henry Wake said. 'Took it into his head that he wanted to git married willy-nilly, and he's mebbe regretting it.'

'Why, he'll mek things no better coming down here every night,' said Jonathan, who had noticed what a truculent glare Chad could have in his cups, and who tended to sympathise with his wife. The girl that Chad had precipitately wooed and married was a healthy, broad-browed, wide-lipped creature who struck Jonathan as no more discontented than she was entitled to be. Occasionally, going at night back and forth to the mill, he would come across Mary-Ann waiting, white-aproned and sturdy, at the end of the Langtofts' drove.

'Not seen that husband of mine, have you, miller?' she said. 'Tell him he's got a wife waiting at home, in case he's forgot, if you do.' She would laugh: it was a mainstay of country jokes, of course; but looking at Chad drinking himself to a trance in the corner of the bar-parlour – Chad retreated to the corners as naturally as a trapped animal – Jonathan felt far from amused, and weighed in his mind some heavy thoughts about marriage, and what a fool's game it was.

Jonathan was one of the less frequent patrons of the Labour In Vain, with his time circumscribed by care of the mill, and when he did go it was usually later on in the evening: when he walked over one night in April he found that Chad Langtoft was already up to his ears in beer. He was slumped forward across the table in a doze, his head resting on his forearms. Jonathan sat down by Andrew Surfleet, who made his one mug of hot beer last all night, so that it seemed to diminish as much by evaporation as potation. 'Third night running he's been like that,' Andrew whispered, with a nod at Chad. 'And not even a crust of supper in him to mop it up – dear-oh-Lor!'

Jonathan was considering whether to wake Chad up – the young man was so prickly in his cups, and he wanted no quarrel – when the door was flung open, and conversation died away at the swaggering entrance of a young soldier, whose red tunic and brass buttons had the startling effect of a drawn sword in the dim smoky parlour. The soldier, his peaked cap pulled down low on his brow, a short cane under his arm, stepped smartly up to the bar and with a sweep of his hand across his glossy moustache ordered a pint of mixed. Jass Phelps, more snub-nosed and staring than ever, served him and said: 'A fine night out, is it, sir?'

'Misty, my good man,' said the soldier gruffly into his beer. 'I dare say it often is in these parts.'

'Were you perhaps looking for anywhere in particular, I wonder, by any chance?' Jass Phelps said in his most insinuating way, like a man peeping under a curtain.

'Nowhere in particular,' the soldier said, dabbing with excessive care at the froth on his moustache. 'I'm recruiting around here, you know: I wonder if any of these stout fellows would care to join the colours and defend our flag against the followers of the Mad Mahdi?' He turned to survey the company, his eyes invisible beneath the peaked cap, and suddenly pointed with his cane at Sunny Daintree. 'What about you, my good fellow?'

'Ooh! no,' Sunny said. 'You'd not git me near no Mardies. I couldn't abide the heat of them places, for a start-off. I knew a chap once as had a son jined up and went out to India – he fell down dead in a swelter the moment he stepped off the boat.'

'I doubt you'll do much recruiting around here, sergeant,' Henry Wake said affably. 'Fen-folk don't go for soldiers, as a rule.'

'Not since Oliver Crumble's time, any road,' Andrew Surfleet said. 'They marched to ole Noll's drum, all right.'

The soldier's well-made lips began to curve beneath the moustache. Jonathan knew there was something wrong with that moustache – it was too dark and smooth: it suddenly occurred to him what it reminded him of – a woman's hair. At the same moment Sunny Daintree's eyebrows rose like twin caterpillars to the peak of his bald head, and he exclaimed, 'Why, thass Mr Saunders, or I'm a Dutchman!'

Lyle Saunders pushed back his cap and gave a peal of laughter. 'Damn it all, I knew this moustache wasn't good enough. Took me an age to paste it on, as well. Still, it worked for a while, didn't it?'

After a moment there was a general round of laughter at the joke, and Lyle ordered drinks for everyone. 'Not a bad disguise at all, neighbour,' Henry Wake said. 'I hate to say it, but I'm afraid I saw through it straight away – I didn't say anything, not to spoil the fun, like.'

Lyle began to tell them the story of how he had come by the tunic, when his glance fell on Chad, dozing in the corner. Suddenly he stopped, pulled down his cap again with a grin and, signalling silence with a finger at his lips, marched across to Chad and shook him by the shoulder.

'Now then, lad,' he said, deepening his light voice to great effect, 'look alive there!'

Chad's pale, sleep-creased face came slowly up, and he blinked with fuddled astonishment at the military figure confronting him.

'What happened to you today, then, my lad?' Lyle said, drawing himself up tall and tucking the cane under his arm. 'You never reported to me at Huntingdon barracks this morning, and I have to come looking for you. What's it all about, eh?'

Chad licked dry, liquor-parched lips. 'Eh?' he said. 'What d'you mean? I don't know what you're on about.'

'Come! Never mind that, my lad,' intoned Lyle. 'You'll be telling me next you've never seen me afore. You'll be telling me next you don't remember what you did in this very public-house last night, in front of all this company. You'll be telling me next you don't remember taking the King's Shilling off me, and joining Her Majesty's army, as a private in the Huntingdonshires.'

Chad stared as if mesmerised by the scarlet and the glinting brass that filled his view. 'I don't know what you mean,' he haltingly murmured. 'I never did nothing like that—'

'Stow that, lad,' said Lyle. 'You may have had a drop to drink at the time – in fact I'd go so far as to say you were half-seas over; but you perked up when I came in here recruiting last night, and you stepped forward and said you'd join up to serve your country – swearing to it like a good 'un – and you gave me your signature on the papers; I've got 'em here—' Lyle patted his breast pocket. 'So come along, lad: your kit's waiting for you at the barracks: we're off to fight the dervishes, who've been insulting of our Queen!'

Chad started to his feet with a clatter. His face was pasty

and damp as a new mushroom. 'Here,' he stammered, 'this ain't right – I don't remember nothing o' this! You can't do nothing to me – it ain't right—'

'Why, many a chap's joined up when he was in his cups, and never regretted it afterwards,' Lyle said. 'You'll feel better when you get your uniform on.'

Chad, jammed against the wall, cast a wild and sweating glance around at the others, who were silent. Jonathan, finding something unpleasant in the atmosphere, was about to speak when Lyle threw off his cap and yanked away the moustache, wincing even as he laughed. 'Ouch! that hurt – serves me right, I suppose. Well, Chad, don't you know me now?'

Chad stared as if fearing he was the victim of some new trick. 'Whass going on?'

'Only a joke, Chad,' Lyle said, offering his hand. 'I just played the same one on the others, didn't I, neighbours?'

'Aye, aye, he did that,' several voices replied, a little hesitantly.

Chad did not take the proffered hand. 'Well,' Lyle said, undismayed, 'you're a damn good sport, anyway – let me buy you a drink on it.'

There was a heavy silence for some moments, while Chad continued to gaze at Lyle's cheerfully smiling face. 'You rotten bugger,' he said at last in a tight voice, flushing a flaming, painful red. 'You rotten stinking bugger.'

'Oh! well, I deserved that,' Lyle said. 'Have a drink on it anyway.'

His smile refused to fade: Chad's tortured expression, with his lower lip drawn down to expose clenched teeth, was like a horribly distorted reflection of it.

'I wun't tek a drink off you – you rotten sliving bugger!' Chad cried, edging round the table.

'Well, all right then: I'm sorry – you always seemed the sort to take a joke in the right spirit,' Lyle said blandly, putting his hands in his pockets.

Chad's eyes, transparent as glass above his burning cheeks, travelled swiftly over all the watching faces: there was a suppressed snigger, which Jonathan recognised as coming from Jass Phelps.

'You think you're so bloody clever,' Chad said, seemingly unable to look at Lyle any more, 'well you ain't – you ain't, see—' All at once he barged and blundered his way out, as he did so knocking over a glass which by some chance did not break but rolled round the floor in curious frantic circles.

'Well! I must make a better sergeant than I imagined,' Lyle said, picking up the glass. 'Perhaps I missed my vocation – perhaps it's *me* who should join up – what do you think, neighbours?'

Lyle did not stay long after that: after a couple of drinks he said laughingly that he had a sergeant-major of his own at home, who would have him on kitchen fatigues if he wasn't careful, and wished them all goodnight. When he had gone the hum of conversation rose like the noise of a stirred beehive.

'Coh, if that don't beat everything since Coggy Onyett laid hisself down on top of Squire Hardwick's tomb all covered wi' flour and clasping his hands, and the gleaners coming home through the churchyard thought he were a statue till he upped and shrieked at 'em!' said Sunny Daintree. 'And I'll bet their faces weren't half such an object as Chad's were just now.'

'I thought for sure Chad was going to flare-up, like, and poke him one in the eye,' Jass Phelps said with relish: adding piously: 'Not that I allow that sort of thing in my pub, mind.'

'Pah! no – not Chad,' grunted Artie Gill, who habitually threw dust in the face of any speculation. 'He's not the one to use his fists: he don't have the guts.'

'A good joke – a good joke, I suppose,' Andrew Surfleet said uncertainly. 'I'm known such things happen real, mind. There was a Stokeley chap took the shilling in his harvest-drunk, and he were in the Crimea looking down the Roosian guns before his head had cleared.'

'A good joke,' Henry Wake said, 'but Chad's not perhaps the appropriate individual to play it on, you know. He don't tek to being laughed at. I'll not say anything against Mr Saunders, him being a neighbour and all, and a very open-handed gentleman – but still, you know . . .' He glanced at Jonathan for corroboration.

'I'm glad he didn't try that trick on *me*,' was all Jonathan said by way of reply, shortly.

301

Edie Smeeth had been dreaming of the hooky-man: Hester could tell that from the marks under her eyes, like thumb-prints of charcoal. They were clearing out one of the bedrooms of the Crooked House, which was full of decaying lumber left behind by the previous occupants: it was a job Hester had long been putting off. Edie showed other signs of having had a sleepless night – she was only moving about twice as fast as the average person, for one – and at last gave herself away by dropping a box of bottles, for she was normally the most deft-handed of girls.

'I dunno what I'm doing!' she cried. 'I'll pick 'em up – I'll pay for what's broke!'

'Don't be daft, Edie,' Hester said. 'They're just a lot of dusty old bottles that we were throwing out anyway. What strange things people keep! And you needn't pick them up, either – I'll do it – you sit down on that stool and rest a bit.'

'I can't do that, missus – it's the middle of the day!' Edie said.

'Yes, you can. Sit down and keep me company. I can tell you're tired. Have you been having bad dreams again?'

Edie nodded, subsiding reluctantly on to the stool. 'It didn't start as a bad 'un,' she said, making a cat's-cradle of her fingers. 'I dreamt I was picking flowers down by the but-dyke – gret armfuls of 'em, jonquils and hen-and-chickens and Bess-in-her-braveries – it was a lovely dream really – and then up comes the ole hooky-man all of a sudden out o' the dyke, and grabs hold o' me leg – and I woke up sweating like a hoss, and I couldn't go back to sleep again. Oh! it sounds daft in the daylight, don't it?'

'Nightmares often do,' said Hester. 'But that don't make them any better in the dark.'

The hooky-man was a bogeyman with a practical purpose. Many unwary children had drowned in the numerous dykes of the fenland: mothers reinforced their warnings not to play by the dykeside with chilling references to the hooky-man, who would rise up and hook you in. That a girl of Edie's age, with a nature as clear as a vessel of rain-water, should still be having bad dreams about him, had puzzled Hester at first. But as she had gathered an idea of what Edie's home life had been like, with her mother's lodger or 'Uncle', she began to suspect that the hooky-man was the lingering expression of some less supernatural fear. It was encouraging that the dream was diminishing in frequency the longer Edie lived at the Crooked House; but Hester took care to ensure that Edie did not need to go home for anything, such as clothes and washing, and that her wages went into her own pockets and did not find their way to those of Uncle; and she had a large heavy warming-pan at the ready with which she was going to greet this uncle if he ever came round to object.

'Why, you don't have bad dreams, do you, missus?' Edie said.

'Well . . . sometimes,' Hester said. Her rest had been disturbed of late, but not by anything she could picture or name: the thoughts of her waking life seemed to persist through her sleep in subterranean distortions which left her with an oppressed, unquiet feeling.

'My brother Charlie don't – but then he sleeps so hard, after wukking at Mr Wake's, and then helping the miller, there ain't room for dreams.'

'You see Charlie on your days off, don't you, Edie?' Hester said.

'Always, missus. We go to Stokeley together, if it's fine.'

'Well if you ever get a wet day, and you want to meet Charlie, tell him he's welcome to come here – any time.'

'Lor, really? Thank you, missus!' Edie, forgetting her injunction to rest, wriggled down from the stool and picked up the red soldier's tunic which Lyle, tiring of it, had thrown in here. 'What's to be done with this, missus? Don't Mr Saunders want it?'

'I don't think so. We may as well keep it – something could be made out of the cloth. Lay it in the rag-box, Edie.'

'Handsome, ain't it?' Edie said, holding up the coat to the sunlight which streamed in through the dormer window, producing that warm peppery atmosphere of closed-up rooms.

303

'Billy Onyett says everybody was fooled when Mr Saunders went down the Labour In Vain in it last week – and Chad Langtoft made a right fool of hisself about it, they reckon.'

'How made a fool of himself, Edie?' Hester said, pausing.

'Oh! I dunno – Billy Onyett weren't there hisself. I don't listen to his tales. It's summat as they're all talking about, any road.'

After a few moments Hester went down in search of Lyle. She found him outside at the stables, the only part of the farm in which he took an habitual interest, hammering a cross-beam on a rotten loose-box door.

'Just a bodge,' he said as Hester came up. 'Planks are like matchwood. One frisky kick and the door'll be down.'

'Stubby don't kick, though, does he . . . Lyle,' Hester said, resting her hand on his shirt-sleeved shoulder, 'when you went down the Labour In Vain dressed in that soldier's coat – what happened?'

'Why, I told you. I walked in and fooled 'em into thinking I was a soldier, like I said I would: you let me cut a bit of your hair to make the moustache.'

'Yes . . .' She could not suppress a smile at the thought of it; yet she was troubled. 'But what exactly happened?' she said.

'This damn hinge is rusted through as well – I don't know how it's holding. Is there any part of this place that's not falling apart?'

'Lyle, what happened at the Labour In Vain – to do with Chad Langtoft?'

'What's this, training for the Inquisition?' Lyle said, straightening up and shrugging off her hand in doing so. 'It was a bit of fun, that's all, like I said: God knows I need it.'

'What sort of fun?' said she, soberly.

'How many sorts are there?' Lyle frowned at the hinges, picking off flakes of rust with his thumb. 'I swear you're getting to be quite a prig, Hes. You used to like a joke and a bit of fun. I never thought I was marrying a maunge-gut . . . I wonder if there are any stronger nails in the tool-shed.' He dusted his hands and walked away from her.

Strange how it was always with the coolest, lightest, most offhand words that he could hurt her most! Hester stood still

304

where she was for a moment, as if to bite down the pain of them; yet she felt it more than ever imperative that she should know what had happened. The memory of her own trouble with Chad over the turf-digging was more rueful than sore – after all, she had suffered for that; but there was something alarming in the thought that her husband had made a dupe of him, if that was what had happened: she feared that Chad was all too likely to see a pattern of persecution.

She must find out the plain faithful truth of what had gone on at the Labour In Vain that night; and instinctively her thoughts, seeking truth, flew to Jonathan Eastholm. Arming herself with an excuse that she wanted to seek Charlie Smeeth anyway, to tell him he should feel free to visit his sister at the Crooked House, Hester walked over to the mill that afternoon.

The sails were turning, with their long, creaking, communing notes, as if wood and iron were breaking into voice; and she found Jonathan leaning on the parapet above the mill-drain, watching the revolutions of the water-wheel. There was a curiously attractive smell here, compounded of timber, weed, fish, and the moss which depended in rank clumps from the paddles, like herbage from the mouth of a chewing cow; and always the air about the splashing wheel, seeded with infinitesimal water-droplets, seemed a degree or two cooler than everywhere else.

'Hullo there,' Jonathan said, drawing back from the parapet, 'what can I do for you?'

Hester said something about looking for Charlie Smeeth who, as she had half-expected, was not there: then herself turning to look at the churning water, she said, 'Jonathan – there was something I wanted to ask you – do you mind?'

'What is it?' Jonathan said, folding his arms across his chest.

She rested her hands on the rough brick of the parapet, having taken off her gloves first: Lyle had got her into the habit of wearing them when she went out, telling her she wasn't a servant any more and should remember her position, but she didn't like them – you couldn't feel the textures of things – it was like being half-blind. 'It's just something I heard,' she said, 'a sort of rumour – you know how you do; and I wondered if perhaps you could tell me the truth of it.'

'Well, go on,' said he.

'I should think you know Ly – my husband went down the Labour In Vain the other night in a soldier's coat – he'd got hold of this coat and he thought it would be fun to see if anybody recognised him in it . . .' How foolish it sounded, put like that!

'Yes: I was there that night,' said Jonathan.

'Were you?' Hester said, turning to him. 'What happened, Jonathan? I don't want to – to bother my husband about it, he's very busy,' she added lamely. 'Only – was there something to do with Chad Langtoft?'

After a moment's silence, Jonathan said yes, and told her in a few plain words of the trick Lyle had played on Chad. As she listened she stared into the evanescent rainbow that the sun drew around the water-wheel, and her heart sank.

'Well – of course, he didn't mean no harm, but – tell me,' she said, conscious that she had come here seeking truth, and was now seeking advice, 'you were there – do you think I ought to apologise to Chad?'

Jonathan, with folded arms, as straight and unmoving as the engine chimney-stack behind him, said promptly: 'No, missus. I think the whole thing's best forgot. Folk do worse things every day; and Chad's pickled half the time lately anyway.' Then, as she was feeling a touch of guilty relief, he added in a sharper tone: 'Besides that, if it's a matter of apologising, I don't reckon it's your job: your husband should do it.'

She glared at him: she remembered that tone of lofty arrogance. 'Well – that ain't none of your business,' she said – needled because deep down she had felt the same thing herself. 'Thass between me and him.'

'So it is,' Jonathan said without heat, 'and none of this is my business, but you asked me.'

'Well – what I mean is, you shouldn't speak against him to me – I won't hear it,' she said, further irritated. She might have added that she would not hear herself speak against Lyle either: her loyal reaction to the slightest imputation against him was so excessive because she feared it might put the spark to the tindery doubts in her own heart.

'All right then: but besides that, I still think it'd be better if you didn't speak to Chad.'

'Why?'

'Because I understand he once had a taking for you,' Jonathan said with great, though quiet, distinctness, 'and that complicates things: so it's best left alone.'

He seemed set on articulating all the things she did not want to think of; and in a sort of provoked flurry she replied airily, 'Oh, pooh – why – that's a long time ago – and I'm married, and so is Chad, and – well, after all, you had a taking for me once, or you thought you did: but you don't mind me.'

It was the first mention of it between them, and only her confusedly fluttered state could have brought her to allude to it; but Jonathan said readily, 'Yes: so I did, or I thought I did, as you say: and I don't mind you. But I'm not Chad Langtoft.'

This cool echo of her words afflicted Hester with a peculiar bleakness but, already troubled as she was, the feeling had no clearer identity than a darker patch in a clouded sky. 'Oh! I don't know what to do for the best,' said she, giving way to her vexation, then recovering herself and adding, 'I mean – it's such a trifling thing, it hardly seems worth all this trouble . . .'

'Leave it alone, then,' said Jonathan. 'It'll be soon forgot.'

'Even by Chad?' she said, raising her eyes to him.

'Well, I can't answer for him; but he's such a thin-skinned article, always fancying an insult, and teks you up on the slightest thing – so he's always got some grievance or other. I've no love for the man at all; but I still think it was a poor trick your husband played – a poor trick.'

'Well – I never asked your opinion about that,' said Hester, her defences going up again.

'Thass nonsense,' said Jonathan bluntly. 'You asked me what I thought, and I'm told you. Now, like you say, it's a trifling thing, and if you'll pardon me, Mrs Saunders, I'm got work to do.'

He left her, and went into the mill. Hester lingered irresolutely by the mill-drain, half-inclined to ask Jonathan something more, but feeling that she had already gone too far in revealing her private troubles to him, and chafed besides by some indefinable resentment of him; and at last she turned and set out for home.

All day she was gnawed at by indecision. She knew Jonathan's advice was sound – she knew, in spite of her annoyance, that he gave it disinterestedly, and was not a man to simply tell you what you wanted to hear: she knew indeed that he was right. And yet it was impossible that he should fully understand her own case. She had once done wrong by Chad Langtoft, even if the moral colour of that episode had been far more pepper-and-salt than black and white; and though she had never considered that she owed Chad anything, lately a new, half-superstitious feeling had begun to assert itself within her. It was a feeling that something had gone wrong in her life (much had gone wrong, said a desolate heart-whisper, much had gone terribly wrong) – and that somehow she must make atonement. She could not trace any logical path that led from her own unhappiness to her sensation of guilt towards Chad – only felt, with an intuitive conviction, that she must apologise to him. Of course, it would appear to Jonathan that she had acted contrary to his advice from mere perversity – but she did not propose that Jonathan, or Lyle, or anybody, should know about it. She would see Chad alone, apologise to him for what her husband had done, and thus in some way propitiate the gods.

The problem of how to see Chad alone was easily solved: the turf-digging season had begun, and she knew that Chad had begun digging a plot in the turf-fen. He went there at dawn, to get in a morning's digging before working the rest of the day on his father's farm; and Hester was always up at first light, three or sometimes four hours before Lyle. She did not delay once her mind was made up; and so the next morning she set out, whilst Edie was still yawning over the range in the kitchen and Lyle was buried beneath the blankets as oblivious as a winter root.

It was a morning of thick mist, which lay low across the fields, thinning to a dank white sky above and resolving to a heavy dew underfoot, so that the whole world seemed to be made of varying compounds of moisture, and the very shapes of the trees appeared as denser patches in a general texture of fog. The newly risen sun was a circular blob of filmy, clammy yellow, like an uncooked egg, and gave off no more heat than a live coal wrapped in a fleece. The sound of a horse-keeper calling to his team afield came to Hester's ears through the inspissated air like a spirit voice; and in keeping with this suspended, uncanny atmosphere, blackbirds and thrushes ran across Hester's path within inches of her skirts, pausing with the suddenness of enchanted things, and exhibiting that mixture of boldness and wary attention indicative of young in the nest.

Hester arrived at the drove leading to the turf-fen, which she could distinguish by the long walls of stacked cesses, like the uncovered ruins of an ancient town. There was no movement there, and she elected to wait for Chad up on the high road: she turned her face away from the turf-pit, more disturbed by the memories it raised than she had anticipated. Time seemed to be swallowed up too in the featurelessness of the mist, and she did not know how long she waited there, though her hair and dress were soon as wet as if she stood in a rainstorm. When a figure, bearing a spade and shovel at the slope, at last materialised, Hester started forward and began walking towards it, with a sudden idea that it would be better if it seemed a chance meeting in passing.

'Morning, Chad,' she called as they approached each other. 'You're at work early.'

Chad, after a silent moment of recognition, grunted and said, 'Have to be.'

'This fog's a nuisance, ain't it?'

'I don't mind it,' he said in his colourless way. He had slowed his pace momentarily, but now seemed about to proceed past her, and she was forced to stop and say, 'Chad – I'm glad I saw you, there's – there's something I wanted to say.'

Chad hesitated, and regarded her with a sort of half-averted face, like a dog pulling at the leash. His pale hair was flat and dun-coloured with the moisture. 'Whass that then?'

'Well – it's silly, really, but—' No, no, that was wrong, it wasn't silly. 'It's just that I heard about my husband playing one of his jokes the other night and, well, some people don't like that sort of thing, and I quite understand that, and so I wanted to say sorry to you – for what happened.'

Chad still did not look straight at her. The drink he was putting away had not fattened him: he seemed slighter and more angular than ever, his pinched mouth and nostrils like slashes in the taut skin of his face.

'It didn't bother me,' he said at last, with a boy's casualness.

'No . . . well, any road – he didn't mean no harm, but I wanted to say sorry.'

Chad shrugged, a sharp neural twitch of the shoulders. 'Didn't bother me,' he said.

It was a mistake, she thought, to meet him so near to the turf-fen: the air teemed with unspoken recollection. Uncomfortably she said: 'Well – if you say so . . . thass all right then. I just thought—'

'I don't care about him anyway,' said Chad. 'I couldn't give a tinker's damn for your husband.' His voice was flat, but his breast rose and fell with the swift palpitation of an injured animal. 'He thinks he's so clever, but it don't bother me.'

'All right then,' she said, beginning to move past him. She had done what she set out to do: she wanted no quarrel. But Chad had not finished. Pointing a stiff finger as she passed him he said, 'I don't care – I could tell you a thing or two about *him* if I wanted.'

She hurried on: she would not rise to that: it was a little flourish of vengeful bravado, that was all. You could only apologise to people – you couldn't make them accept your apology. She got home, boiled up a copper of taters for the pigs, cleaned out the hen-coop, and swilled out the dairy-shed, singing as she did so. When she came in to find Lyle sitting at the breakfast-table blearily studying a letter, she flung her arms round his neck and covered him with kisses.

'By the left, this is a bit much for a Thursday morning, isn't it?' he said in surprise. He put his hand to her cheek, looking into her eyes. 'Hes? What's up?'

'Oh! nothing,' she said, hiding her face in his neck with a broken laugh. 'Just glad to see you – thass all.'

5

On the first of May Jonathan had his quarterly appointment
with the Drainage Commissioners in Stokeley, at which he told
them of any problems at the mill, rendered his accounts for
coal, oil and other necessaries, and received his wage. Having
prepared himself for the formality of the occasion by putting
on a clean neckerchief and combing out his hair after his bath
till it shone the colour of a conker, he set out to walk to the
town with ample time, vaguely wondering whether to indulge
himself with a visit to the bookstall in Infirmarer's Street. He
could not dwell on this with complete satisfaction, however,
for he was troubled in his mind by the meeting with Hester
the other day. Had he, he asked himself, said the wrong thing
after all? He had tried to be honest. He had no time for Chad
Langtoft, as he had said: in his stern way he thought him a
self-pitying fellow, with something covert about him that he
could never trust. It had been handsome of Hester to think
of apologising to him; and in his disapproval of her husband,
Jonathan had perhaps not conveyed that. Had he not, rather,
seemed to put the blame on her side? He didn't know: he
wished he had never allowed himself to get involved in the
business. Never get involved, that was the golden rule: he
must stick by it.

Passing by the Langtofts' farm, he saw Wag Langtoft, Chad,
and the two younger boys at work digging out a black oak from
the field by the high road. As he was in no hurry, he went down
to see if he could help.

'I'm been putting off gitting this beggaring ole root out for
years, Jonathan bor,' Mr Langtoft said. 'I dunno why, 'cos it's
broke ploughs enough, and wishing wun't mek it disappear.'

The black oaks, or bog-oaks, which lay buried under the
fen fields were the remains of giant trees, felled by some
natural catastrophe thousands of years ago, and preserved in
the peat; the shrinkage of which brought them gradually nearer
the cultivated surface, to the despair of farmers. Jonathan, in
whose soul practicality and romanticism were intertwined like

311

the red and white of a barber's-shop pole, took up a spade to help dig round the 'beggaring ole root', at the same time marvelling at the sight of the great black trunk with all its gnarled grooves and vermiculations as clear to the eye as when the tree had stood flourishing in the sunlight an inconceivable age ago. Acorns were sometimes found alongside these venerable hulks, perfectly formed and soft as putty until they were dried: Andrew Surfleet had a tinful of them at home, and whenever Jonathan took them on his palm he always thought with excitement of the moment when those acorns had pattered to the ground, when the fen had been a forest roamed by strange beasts. Jonathan was like that: he had never forgotten once setting his foot upon a Roman causeway that had been unearthed in a potato-field, and how the sheer thought of it had made his heart race – though he would have been embarrassed to tell anyone of this. The black trunk that was protruding from Mr Langtoft's field was more than fifty feet long: one end had been dug completely clear of the peat, and Mr Langtoft and Chad, by means of great labour with axes, wedges and sledgehammers, at last succeeded in cutting off a ten-foot length and hitching it up with rope to the waiting plough-team to be dragged off to the yard and there broken up or burned. 'Twouldn't be so bad if there were some use to the awkud ole stuff,' Mr Langtoft said, before leading the horses away. 'Must be the only thing as comes out of the ground thass no use to anybody – but there, I suppose the Almighty must ha' known what he was doing, though I'm beggared if I can see it.'

Jonathan, with the Langtoft sons, continued digging round the remainder of the black oak, and became absorbed with speculations on what primeval disaster of climate, wind or wave could have felled all the trees. He was roused by the sound of swift wheels, and looked up to see Lyle Saunders pulling up his pony-and-trap on the high-road above. He was dressed for leisure, in a Norfolk jacket with a light bowler: he raised his gloved hand to them affably and said, 'Morning, morning, how's everybody? Chad, about that business at the Labour In Vain. I hope we're still friends. No hard feelings – eh?'

Chad, suspending his spade, looked at Lyle for some time

before answering, 'Your wife's already said sorry about that, as it happens.'

'Did she?' Lyle said. 'Well, anyway, accept my apologies too.'

'I wun't tek nothing from you,' Chad said.

Lyle's eyebrows lifted a little. 'Please yourself.'

'And here – I'll tell you another thing,' Chad said cumbrously. Jonathan wished he would stop; it was folly: to see him glowering up at Lyle Saunders was like seeing some dull and sullen dog barking at a canny cat high on a fence. 'I tell you – you don't deserve the wife you're got.'

'Ha, ha! Well, Chad,' Lyle said lightly, 'I dare say you deserve *yours*.'

The flush on Chad's face was terrible to see. 'You want to watch it,' he cried, lifting his spade slightly, 'you'll be just a bit too clever one of these days!'

'Well, there's no danger of that in your case,' Lyle said, laughing and flicking the reins.

'You watch it!' Chad called as the trap rattled away, brandishing the spade. Jonathan put a restraining hand on his arm. 'Steady,' Jonathan said. 'No call for that.'

Chad shook him off with a resentful stare. 'It's nowt to do with you,' he said. 'It ain't your business.' He turned and resumed his digging, energetically, with tight mouth and blank eyes.

Jonathan shrugged, said good-day to the two boys and continued on his way to Stokeley: it was, as Chad had said, none of his business. In the town, after meeting the Drainage Commissioners, he hurried down Infirmarer's Street with his wages dancing in his pocket – telling himself that one second-hand book wouldn't break him, and that his patched shirt would last a while yet. After a long combing of the bookstall he settled on Kingsley's *Hereward the Wake*; and he was looking into it as he took a short cut down a narrow alley that led to the High Street. The alley, bounded by fragments of ancient wall, opened at one point to a double yard: on one side belonging to the Hand and Heart public house, on the other to a firm dealing in agricultural implements. There was no fence or wall dividing the two premises, and the ploughs and harrows seemed to defend their half of the yard with a display of bared iron teeth. On the pub side there were several carts and light carriages; and Jonathan, looking up from his book, caught sight of Lyle Saunders, beside his pony and trap. He was with a girl – they were both patting the pony, and smiling – and the girl was not Hester.

Jonathan was past the mouth of the yard almost before this had sunk in. He wavered – he experienced a moment of hatred for himself, but it was no good – he had to step back, and look again. Lyle was helping the girl up into the trap. She was young, pretty, smartly dressed in a tailor-made costume with broad lapels and flared skirts. As she climbed up Lyle darted a kiss at her hand: she drew it back with mock reproach, and they both laughed.

Jonathan went quickly on his way, fumbling his book into his pocket, and bumping into several people in his haste. Not until he was past the Abbey ruins, and striking the high-road out to Hinching Fen, did he slow his pace: and then he sternly tackled himself for his reaction. He had seen Lyle, at the least, flirting: what then? Wasn't that, too, none of his business? But he could not dismiss it: he felt sick and shaken as if he had seen someone run down in the street.

Lyle hadn't seemed to care – somehow that was the awful thing. It wasn't furtive – there they were in broad daylight in the little town of Stokeley, where anyone might see. Had others seen such things, and told them? Rumour blew about the fen like dandelion-seed.

Jonathan felt himself to be up against something for which he had no ready responses. Perhaps he was a prig – perhaps other folk would laugh. And part of him went down like a bull's horns, saying: reject it; forget it; live to yourself, and let these people get all mired and entangled if they want, and thank the stars you're out of it – it just shows what a fool's game it all is. Yet what he had seen demanded more of him – his heart demanded more of him than this.

'She must never hear of it,' he said to himself with decision; 'and she shall never hear it from me.' For there was the memory of a treasured vision to which he still owed a loyal duty, if nothing more.

# Chapter Two

1

It was so unusual for Hester and Lyle to do anything together nowadays that when he came shopping with her in St Ives one May afternoon the occasion seemed to her to wear something of the aspect of a holiday. Once in the town, he left her to go and see a man who had a pony for sale – though there was one in the stables at home that he had bought to train and still not sold; but she would not allow herself to protest. It had dawned on her the other day that she might be worsening the strain between them by becoming a nag: moreover those stupid parting words of Chad's – *I could tell you a thing or two about* him – had stayed with her, and she felt that she must not give in to the malicious poison of them by seeming to reproach or mistrust her husband in any way. It was a sadly subdued and chastened condition that Hester thus found herself in, and she could not help but be conscious of the change in herself, from the carefree girl who had gaily gone away to the sea with her new husband last year: but the weather was warm, Lyle was in a good mood, and she was managing to shoe-horn her mind into a moderately cheerful groove as she returned down the High Street to meet Lyle with the trap, when she saw Westerby, the seedsman, hailing her from the door of his shop.

'Quite unseasonably warm, ain't it, Mrs Saunders?' Mr Westerby said, scooping a fat finger under his stiff collar. 'I'm glad I happened to catch you – I wouldn't dream of mentioning it under normal circumstances, but if I might just draw your attention to something – my bill, in short.'

'Oh!' Hester said.

'As I say, I wouldn't normally mention it – not so public-like

– only it's outstanding, you see – it's outstanding something alarming; and Mr Saunders wrote me some time ago that he'd be coming to see me about it.'

'And hasn't he?' Hester said.

'. . . No, Mrs Saunders,' the seedsman said, after a painful pause, in which he seemed to search desperately for some gentler word. 'I'm afraid not – and I'm really going to have to insist, you know. I'm got four mouths to feed, and they don't get any smaller, or less liable to munching; and I just can't afford to give unlimited credit. Would you be so good as to mention it to Mr Saunders – and say I shall be sending another bill directly? The fifth, I'm afraid –' he winced delicately – 'the fifth, Mrs Saunders.'

Hester said she would see to it that the bill was paid: and went on to find Lyle waiting for her with the trap in Spread Eagle Yard, quaffing a glass of beer. 'Devil of a thirst,' he said. 'All done?'

They set out for home, Hester taking the reins. It was still and humid, and the sunlight, though bright, had a tarnished look about it; and there was a sullen haziness about the horizons which seemed to presage an unsettled end to the long fine spell. Hester waited until they were out on the high-road, and then told Lyle what the seedsman had said.

'That was a bit of a cheek, catching you in the street like that,' Lyle said.

'Is he right, though, Lyle?'

'Eh? Oh! he might be – to be honest, I thought I'd paid that bill. We'll have to look when we get home. It won't hurt him to wait a bit longer, anyhow – he's not short of a few bob.'

'But—' Hester bit her tongue, and applied herself to her driving. Lyle enjoyed having his own coachwoman, he said, but as usual when they came to the main drain he took over the reins. The sleeper-bridge over the main drain, which was wide and deep as a small river, was narrow and unfenced, and though Hester had been over it umpteen times on her own, Lyle never quite trusted her steering just here.

'Those huge Belgian horses would never do in these parts,' Lyle said as they rumbled across. 'I reckon they'd go through these little bridges like matchwood.' His mind had been running on Belgium lately; and when they got home she had to remind him about the seedsman's bills.

'Oh! yes,' he said, and extricated a wad of unsorted papers from the old roll-top desk in the parlour. Humming a waltz, he went through them. 'Ta-da, ta-da, ta-yom-pom-pom – what is that one? Is it "Wine, Women and Song", or "Vienna Blood"? Ah, my apologies to Westerby – here it is. Well, I could have sworn I'd paid that in. Oh! well, I'll pay it next week.'

'He did say it was urgent,' Hester said timidly.

'They always do, my dear. Ah, there's that letter from Mr Dielman. Wants to know when he'll see me in Brussels again. God! it would be good to have a holiday. I don't see why I can't manage it . . . You'd love Brussels, Hes.'

'Yes,' she murmured; but at that moment she felt anything but yes. Who said she would love Brussels? She hated being simply told she would love something like that. She retrieved the seedsman's bill from where he had pushed it aside. It was more than she thought.

Lyle was absently arranging the papers into a fan shape. 'I don't see why we shouldn't go after the harvest. And Ostend, it's very smart there . . .'

Suddenly Hester had a terrible dizzying feeling of looking down a precipice. Her husband was an arm's length away, and yet a chasm lay between them. Here they were with not even the seedsman's bills from months ago paid – and, she guessed, without the wherewithal to pay them – and Lyle was talking about jaunts to Belgium! The realisation entered her, like a burning lance, that she and the man she loved, in that sun-smelling wainscoted room, were dwellers in two different worlds: that while she stood close enough to him to feel the emanated warmth of his flesh, his mind and hers were moving in such widely separated orbits that it seemed impossible they should ever touch. She recoiled from the horror of it; and in recoiling grew angry.

'And there's Ghent – absolute fairy-tale of a place – God! it'll be good to get away,' Lyle was saying dreamily. Hester snatched up the bills, and carrying them away said curtly: 'Perhaps you should take Mr Westerby with you – in lieu of paying his bill.'

As she stalked away there was a moment of surprised silence behind her, followed by a gust of laughter.

Later that evening she saw Lyle looking at the latest letter from the bank, and presently he said, impatiently crumpling it up, 'Well, it doesn't look as if there's any chance of a holiday this year, anyhow.'

Repenting a little of her sharpness, she said, 'We could manage a break nearer home perhaps, Lyle: down to Bournemouth again – or the east coast, Cromer or somewhere—'

He gave a loud mirthless chuckle. 'Hardly worth it. From one cage to another.' He glanced at his watch. 'Think I'll go over to the Labour In Vain for a spell.' He had slipped out, in his limber way, before she could answer.

He was not yet back when she went to bed and lay, with the covers thrown back for coolness, staring at the dormer-slope above her. While she felt still her severance from Lyle, and bleakly contemplated the way their inclinations seemed to face away from each other like two plants opening to two different suns, yet as she stretched out in the sultry darkness she longed, almost with an ache of amputation, to have him beside her. She could no more cease to give love than a spring cease to give water; and a single gesture of love from him would have been like a word spoken in a canyon, echoing back manifold in a joyous shout. She had sunk into a doze when she heard the iron bed creak and felt Lyle climbing in beside her: stirring, she turned over and put her arms round him, fitting herself to his slender, hipless body.

After a few moments he twitched, and said over his shoulder: 'Hes, I can't sleep when you maul me about like that.'

She disengaged herself, and resumed her staring at the lowering roof above.

The next morning Lyle was away early with the trap, taking the new pony he had bought and groomed: there was a possible buyer for it in Huntingdon, he told her. Something about his manner suggested that he was going to see his mother; but the morning was so airless and oppressive, with May-time thunderiness, that Hester had not the spirit to challenge him. Listlessly she went about her tasks, baking a batch of bread, feeding the hens and the pigs, mucking out the stables; and when she was returning to the house across the yard she saw the first stroke of lightning arc across the swollen sky above her head, clear as a vein in a clenched arm. Within the house it was as dark as dusk. Hester swept the hearth and tidied the parlour, listening to the thunder rolling around the horizons. Carefully she dusted the china cat which stood on the mantelpiece. It was a thing she loved: Lyle had bought it for her on their honeymoon, when it had seemed to catch her eye through the shop window with its artful expression; something about it always made her feel happy and amused. As she was gathering up her brushes and dusters Edie Smeeth came bouncing in and said in her best parlour-maid voice: 'Here's some chap to see you, missus – I dunno who.'

It was a little stout stooped man with a few strands of hair scraped over a liver-spotted scalp. 'How do, missus,' he said, briefly showing tobacco-brown teeth. 'Cresswell's the name. It's Mr Lyle Saunders I'm after – is he about?'

'No, he's out,' Hester said. 'Can I help?'

'Know when he'll be back?'

'No.'

'Well, I'll have to wait, then – I'll not be put off now,' grunted the man, glancing around the parlour.

'What's it about?'

'It's about a bay pony – thass what. A bay pony what I sold to Mr Lyle Saunders.'

'Oh! that one. But that was a long while ago – Lyle sold it to someone in Stokeley.'

'Did he indeed! Well he'd no right, missus: he still ain't paid me for it – thass what.'

'I don't understand—'

'It's plain enough,' the man said, breathing stertorously through his nose, and continuing to look all round him. 'Mr Lyle Saunders paid a deposit down, with an engagement to pay the rest later. Which he ain't done – and I'm been trying to track him down for long enough – thass what. I ain't going to be put off now – I want my money, and I shan't go away without it. I'll wait here while he turns up, if it's all the same to you.'

'No, it ain't all the same to me,' Hester said, more disquieted than she cared to show. 'I don't know when he'll be back – and I'm got work to do—'

'I can't help that, missus,' said Cresswell. 'I'll not be diddled any more. Your husband's got to come home some time, and I'll wait while bull's noon if I have to – I reckon it's the only way I'll get hold of him. He's a slippery one – it's like trying to git hold of a Eel – thass what!'

'It must be a mistake. I can't believe Lyle didn't mean to pay you the money,' Hester said; but she knew she was lying.

'I don't know nothink about that. All I know is my money's in his pocket, and I ain't going home till I'm seen him. I'm sorry, missus: you needn't think of fetching somebody to put me out, as I ain't in the mood to be put out. I shan't git in your way, but I shan't go neither.'

Hester stared at him a moment. There was no doubting he meant it. 'You'd better sit down then,' she faintly said.

'Shall I tek your 'at?' said Edie; but Cresswell tucked his bowler carefully under his arm. 'No, ta, gel,' he said, lowering himself on to the edge of a chair. 'I'll keep it by me: it ain't that I don't trust you, but I'm been robbed enough – thass what.'

Hester answered Edie's questioning gaze with a slight shrug. 'You'd best start dinner, Edie,' she said. 'I'll be along to help you soon. If our visitor don't object.'

Thunder sounded above the house, like a hammering at awful gates, and almost immediately following it came the lightning, filling the parlour with an instant of unhealthy light and throwing a spindly black shadow behind every stick of furniture. The sky at the window was the colour of a damson, but there was no sign of rain yet, and the low-ceilinged house was so stifling that even the carved settles and Windsor-chairs seemed to exhibit a sheen of sweat. Cresswell sat stolidly, nursing his bowler hat, and trying to ignore the perspiration that trickled down his temples, as if even that might be a ruse to deflect him from his purpose.

'Mr Saunders never owes him money like he says – never!' hissed Edie in the kitchen, her crisp curls, in the electrified atmosphere, seeming to bristle with indignation.

Hester glanced down the passage at Cresswell. 'Well, I don't know him – but I dare say there's – I dare say there's some explanation.' She felt like a traitor, for instinctively she believed the man: instinctively she knew Lyle owed him money; and though she hated him for coming here like this, it was mainly because he had thus revealed to her what she tried to deny – that she could not and did not trust Lyle.

The sky palpitated with hot thunder. The heavy charged air lay like a suffocating sheepskin across the fen. Hester went outside to shut away the agitated hens, and found Cresswell following her. 'No offence, missus,' he said. 'But I can't let you out of my sight. You're my only link to that there Eel.' He flinched as there was a crack overhead as if a giant vault had been blasted open, and a sulphurous flourish of lightning seemed to scrawl down from the highest heavens to within an inch of the stable roof. 'I'd advise you to go in, missus, any road.'

'Well, I don't know – I'm got work to do out here,' said Hester, with devilment, seeing he was frightened. But a moment later the first raindrops, fat as falling fruit, hit the cobbles of the yard, and she was forced to run in.

Dinner was on, and the house sweltered. In the parlour Hester tried to settle to some mending, whilst Cresswell perspired and fidgeted on the chair opposite her. The pounding of the rain drowned out the heavy tick of the old Dutch clock, and at the window nothing could be seen but a glistening screen of water, as if it must be descending in some more voluminous form than mere raindrops. The air had scarcely cooled, and Hester's sensation of oppression, of being hardly able to breathe, mounted into a more specific feeling of resentment. Trapped – that was what she was – trapped here, watched over as if by a policeman, whilst Lyle – well, what was Lyle doing? Dancing attendance on his mother, trying to wheedle his way back into her good books, the very thing he had said he wouldn't do? Furiously she flung down the sewing and went to throw open the window, not caring whether the rain came in, desperate for a breath of air. As she did so she saw the trap coming up the drive.

'That's him, is it?' Cresswell said, and hurried to meet him in the hall.

Hester stayed where she was. She heard them arguing for some time, Lyle's voice at first light and cordial and evasive, until it sharpened at last. 'All right . . . damn it, you'll get it, I tell you, you'll get it!' There was the sound of the door being opened, Cresswell shouting 'Ten days, mind! Else I'll tek it to law—' and then a slam. It was faintly echoed by a last dying growl of thunder in the distance. A few minutes later Lyle came in, having run upstairs to change out of his wet clothes, rubbing his hair with a towel.

'That's all I need,' he said, 'that silly old fool dunning me just when I get home soaked to the skin. Why didn't you get rid of him?'

'I couldn't,' she said.

'You shouldn't let these people in – that's the trick of it. It's when you let 'em past the door that the trouble starts. If—'

'You do owe him that money then?'

He looked at her for the first time, alerted by her tone: then resumed his towelling. 'He's a daft old beggar. He'll get it eventually. He's not a professional, that's his trouble – just does a bit of horse-dealing on the side—'

'Unlike you,' Hester said, 'who do a bit of farming on the side.'

Lyle's eyebrows went up. 'Who rattled your cage this morning, Hes?'

'Nobody. I just don't like feeling like a prisoner in my own home.' She was going to cause a scene: she couldn't help it; she was smarting so, with frustration and indignation and sheer weariness at the way their life was going. 'And finding out from a stranger how much we're in debt. While you're out as usual doing God knows what – while you just let the farm and everything we planned for go to pot, never thinking of how we're going to manage . . . I want this place to work, but I can't do it all on my own – it just seems you don't even want to try, your mind's never here at all—'

'Leave off, for God's sake, Hes,' Lyle said, 'I've had enough damn discouragement for one day.'

He began violently to brush his hair, tugging at the tangles.

'You're been to your mother's, haven't you?' she said quietly.

'Oh! if you say so. You seem to know so much about me.'

'You have, Lyle – haven't you?'

'All right,' he snapped. 'I've been to my mother's. Not a crime, is it?'

'You didn't tell me,' she said. Her heart, racing a moment ago, seemed to have slowed to a sluggish labouring. 'Did you see her?'

'No, I didn't, as a matter of fact,' Lyle said, with a sort of stubborn neutrality. 'She wouldn't see me.'

'When you married me,' Hester said carefully, 'you said it didn't matter about your mother – it was me you wanted and it didn't matter if she cut you off. And now you wear yourself thin trying week after week to win her round, while I keep this place going . . . And she *still* won't see you. Don't you see, Lyle – you'll never do it! You can't beat her – she meant what she said. You burnt your bridges. Why won't you accept that?'

'Well, by God, you needn't sound so pleased about it,' said Lyle in a pinched voice. 'I swear you're glad you separated me from my own family!'

'I did?' she breathed.

'Yes, who else?' With a chill briskness Lyle marched over to examine his reflection in the mirror over the mantelpiece. 'You're always going on at me not to go there. You seem to get some odd pleasure out of splitting us up. It was you who rushed things – pestering me to marry you before I could work Mother round to the idea. You were determined to drive a wedge between us. Well, I hope you're satisfied, my dear, because it's your doing. If I'm in a mess, it's your doing.'

A quiver ran through her: she felt the injustice like a physical assault; but more horribly and profoundly, in that moment, she had seemed to see the image of Gideon in the figure of Lyle standing stiffly before the mirror – had seemed to see, in a ghastly flash like the lightning that had passed, an incarnation of self looking at self, obsessed with self, able to see nothing but endless self. She felt paralysed; and all the words she could pronounce were those that flared like a firework in her mind: 'It's almost as if you wish you'd never married me!'

Lyle gave her a sardonic glance. 'Never mind the *almost*, my dear,' he said.

Hester fled. She ran from the parlour, but still the walls of the Crooked House seemed to crowd in on her, like a tightening ring of hostile presences; and, gasping with distress, she flung open the door and ran out into the rain.

The storm was over, and the weird coppery light had been replaced by a uniform murk of sombre cloud fitted over the fen like an upturned bowl. The drove down which Hester ran was pitted with wheel-ruts, and was turning momently to a cocoa-coloured ooze. On all sides the further fields could barely be seen for the rippling distortion of the rain, which fell bouncing in the dyke like coins dropped on a table-top, and formed before Hester's eyes a shimmering mass, shaken here and there by stirring currents of breeze, so that serpentine shapes seemed to writhe for an instant through the corridors of water. Hester had run out just as she was in her day-dress and apron; as she came to the end of the drove and splashed out on to the high-road her mud-soaked skirts were as heavy as mail, and her hair was clinging in thick tendrils to her face. She was crying without being properly aware of it – crying as though she would never know content again; and just as the tears were indistinguishable from the rain on her cheeks, she could scarcely tell what it was she was feeling. She stumbled along the road in a sort of trance, in which existence and wretchedness seemed conterminous, and her body had detached itself from her will.

At last a pothole tripped her, and she nearly fell, just saving herself with her hands: the jolt awakened her a little, and though the thought of returning to the Crooked House was unbearable, some renascent voice of rationality protested at the miserable drenching, and urged her to shelter. The prospect was bare but for a large, solitary elm tree beside the road up ahead, and ducking her head she began to run to it.

A tree in the fens, often standing utterly single and alone in a low flat expanse, its outline sharply delineated, retains thus something of the primal potency it bore for our ancestors, for whom its shape might express a giant, a transformed mortal, or a god. To Hester's eyes, streaming and half-blinded, the spreading branches of the tree gave a strong impression of generous, protective arms waiting to receive her: sobbing violently, and at the end of her breath, she staggered beneath the dripping canopy of leaves and flung herself against the thick trunk, half embracing it, feeling the ridged bark like a great hide beneath her hands. Looking up, she found herself completely roofed-in by foliage which, immature as it was, kept the ground immediately at her feet as dry as a sanded floor. As she gazed higher, her distress was riven for a moment by the sight of those leaves, bright spring green and tender, springing forth from the aged tree: in the bole and limbs was all the gnarled solidity of age, with great lumps and knots that on a human body would have appeared as the most hideous abscesses – yet this ugliness, every year through long lifetimes, yielded at its finger-ends the feathery freshness of a sapling. She was momentarily transfixed by a disconnected and childlike sense of wonder; and then she heard for the first time her own stuttering sobs, again like a child, that grows weary of crying. She tried to wipe her eyes on her sleeve, and through blurred lashes saw all at once that she was not alone.

On the other side of the tree-bole stood Jonathan, sheltering from the rain: that she had not seen him was accounted for not only by her blinding distress but by his extreme stillness, a stillness scarcely less deep and rooted than that of the ancient tree. There was a reason for it: for as Hester met his gaze, he said quietly, 'Don't move,' and signalled with his eyes to a spot a few feet away.

'Oh!' she said, involuntarily drawing back her skirts – for an adder was moving noiselessly through the grass, a spade's-length from her feet.

'Keep still – it's all right,' Jonathan said in the same calm and soothing voice. Adders were quite common in the fens, turf-diggers coming across them daily, but Hester greatly feared them, and her breath died in her throat. Jonathan, seeming to sense this, reached out and gently gripped her upper arm, which his large hand entirely enclosed so that middle finger and thumb touched, holding her still until the snake had slipped away into the field below.

Jonathan's hand left her arm, and then was back again, proffering a handkerchief. He was silent while Hester wiped her face: she could not look at him. The rain fell in a steady hiss, deepening to a papery, drumming sound on the layers of leaves above them.

'Is there something I can do?' Jonathan said at length.

Hester shook her head, and her sobs burst out afresh. She didn't know what sort of spectacle she must present, or what Jonathan must be thinking; but obviously he could see much was amiss.

'It isn't anything,' she stammered, muffled in his handkerchief. 'It's just – it's just sometimes . . .'

'Yes, I know,' said he gravely, as if she had said something eminently coherent and reasonable.

'I – must seem – a terrible fool,' she gasped, trying to control herself.

'No.'

'I don't know – what it is. Sometimes – things . . .' But she did know what it was: she felt at that moment as if innocence had died from the world for ever.

'It's all right,' Jonathan said; and again his voice, deep as a cello, seemed to instil a great calm. All at once she abandoned trying to explain things away: she felt with relief that he did not demand it, any more than the great unquestioning presence of the tree did.

'It's clearing,' he said. 'Look.'

He pointed to where a corner of the sky was pierced by a diagonal rod of pale light, like a ray through a chink in curtains. Just then such a naked emblem of hope seemed more mocking than genuine, but she nodded, and forced herself to take a deep breath, inhaling the bracing scent of earth quickened by rain. 'Yes,' she said, leaning against the bole of the tree, 'it's clearing.'

Jonathan looked at her and hesitated. 'Shall I leave you?' he said.

She nodded, her lips pressed together. 'I – I'll stay out here a while.'

'All right.' He paused. 'You're soaked. Don't take cold – go in soon.'

326

'I will . . . Jonathan!' she cried as he started to go.

'Yes?'

'You won't tell anyone you – saw me like this – will you?' Pride was all that remained to her: somehow he was the only person she could bear having been a witness to her distress. 'Please – I don't want anyone to . . .'

'I won't say a word,' Jonathan said. 'On my honour.' This strange phrase seemed natural coming from his lips. 'I'll leave you now.'

She stayed for some time after he had gone, her face against the bark of the tree, until the rain had stopped, and the sun, gilding the dispersing clouds, threw brilliant reflections of its handiwork into the broad puddles on the high-road. When at last she pushed back her wet hair and began the walk back to the Crooked House, it seemed to her like a new journey to a strange place – for she could not think of it as a return to home.

Half an hour after he had left her, Jonathan went back to the elm tree by the roadside: he had a misgiving, having seen the state she was in, that she might still be there in those drenched clothes, and he was relieved to find she had gone. He paused a while to contemplate the site of that meeting: for here he had felt a great temptation. As he beheld Hester's tear-stained face, and her throat pulsing like that of a singing bird, he had suddenly thought of asking her: was it worth it? It was plain whence her unhappiness came: did she know what her husband was up to? He had seemed to see in her the first painful tearing of the veil of illusion, and a savage wish had gone through him to rip it apart completely.

Jonathan had scaled down his own hopes and desires, which had been as strong as unexpressed, and this violent impulse had alarmed him – it threatened the temperate detachment which he had made his refuge. Fortunately, his sense of honour towards Hester had prevented him speaking out; fortunately, he had felt the influence of nothing more than that: and the thing he did not want reawakened slept on, a sleep indistinguishable from death.

2

In the Crooked House Hester knew how it felt to be a ghost – to haunt with longing frustration the scenes of former happiness.

Superficially there was no need for this. In the aftermath of their quarrel she and Lyle settled down to normal life together just as they had done before. He was not cruel to her – not even unpleasant: he was not short or snide with her, or continually harking back to what had been said. He was airily casual and easy as ever. There was nothing to mark this off from any other passage in their married life, except for the kernel of conviction, at the centre of Hester's consciousness, that her husband hated her.

His resentment seemed to her to fill the rooms like a noxious vapour, which she inhaled on first waking, and which lingered in her nostrils even as she drifted into sleep at night. There was nothing she could do to dispel it; nothing she could say to him that would not come out as reproaches, and provoke in its turn the utterly unjust and yet utterly unanswerable reproach that she had trapped him into a life he found insupportable.

Nothing to be done here; but in Stokeley, it seemed to her, there was something she could do – one lone and difficult chance that, after three intolerable days of terrible, seething calm, she knew she must take. She would go and see Mrs Saunders, whose long shadow fell blightingly on their marriage – see her, and set things straight once and for all. She would confront her with a choice – forgive Lyle and make it up with him, or signal to him as she had yet failed to do that he had nothing to hope from her. The cat-and-mouse game she was playing was futile: it was doing nothing but poisoning their marriage at its roots; and Hester could still not believe – refused to believe – that such was what Mrs Saunders single-mindedly and maliciously sought.

She walked across the fields to Stokeley at mid-morning. Looking up at the Saunders' house before she knocked, she remembered her days here as a companion-help – remote as schooldays they seemed now – and she wondered that it had never occurred to her then just how grim and aloof this house was, with its louring eaves, massive stanchions, and high narrow windows, so heavily curtained they gave an impression of eyes blindfolded for some sinister purpose.

'OH dear,' Judy exclaimed on seeing Hester, 'I'm not sure as the mistress can SEE you I'm sure but I'll INQUIRE if you'd be so GOOD as to wait, ahem!'

There was a smell of paint in the hall, and dust-covers on the furniture. Judy returning led Hester through to the dining-room, where she found decorators at work, and Mrs Saunders hovering watchfully about their stepladders, as if even the painting of picture-rails could not go forward without some subtle plan to cheat her manifesting itself sooner or later.

'What do you want here, gel?' Mrs Saunders said, betraying no surprise even if she felt it.

'I want to speak to you, please, Mrs Saunders,' Hester said. Mrs Saunders – her own name – how mad it was!

'Do you!' Mrs Saunders glanced round at the decorators. 'Oh, well. Judy, you keep an eye on 'em. I shan't be long. Come in here.'

Mrs Saunders led Hester through to the adjoining room – the winter parlour, a small room that was seldom used. This too was all emptied, sheeted and stripped for redecoration: and Hester remembered long afterwards the way her mother-in-law had received her in a blank room, without so much as a chair.

'High time we had this place redecorated,' Mrs Saunders said. 'Not that I shall pay what these chaps are asking – they needn't think I will.. Well, what is it?'

Hester looked at the long sallow mask of a face. Had the lines grown deeper and harsher, or was that her own doubts deceiving her?

'I don't rightly know how to say it – straight out,' Hester began.

'Can't be worth saying, then, I reckon,' snapped Mrs Saunders. 'Something to do with Lyle, is it? Here –' suddenly there was a flash of vulnerability – 'there's nothing up with him, is there?'

'No – well, yes, there is. That's what I come to see you about.

Lyle ain't right, he ain't right at all, because of the way things are – between us and you, Mrs Saunders.'

'Us?' she said heavily, sour again now.

'The way things are,' Hester said, trying to stay composed. 'He ain't right because of – well, because of falling out with you.'

'I told him,' Mrs Saunders said with contempt. 'I told him what would happen – he wouldn't listen. That's all.'

Hester ignored this. 'He wants to make it up with you, Mrs Saunders. He wants it more than anything, I know. I want that too, because . . . Mrs Saunders, I'm come to ask you – look, I'm begging you – make it up with Lyle, please. All right, he went against your will, and he's suffered for it – we both have – so please, forgive and forget. Be friends again, for God's sake.'

'That's what you've come to ask, is it?' Mrs Saunders said.

'Not just that. Something else. If you can't forgive and forget, then say so. Finish it, and let us lead our own lives. Don't keep him hanging on all the time – forever looking for a way back that ain't there. I know you can't like me – but you must love Lyle – and he ain't happy, and surely, surely, that's not what you want.'

Her words had the curious distinct flatness of wrenchingly deep feeling: they seemed to exhaust her.

'That's it, is it?' Mrs Saunders said crisply. 'Well, you've got sense, gel, because, like you say, there's no way back for that boy of mine. And if he doesn't know that – if he doesn't know me well enough by now – then it's no good me telling him. You tell him, gel.' Her eyes had the bright pitiless gleam of broken glass. 'He's yours now. It's your job to tell him he's got nothing to hope for but that piddling farm and your face looking at him over the bread-and-seam. Tell him, and see how he likes it. See who he blames.'

'You don't love him,' breathed Hester. 'You really don't love your son at all, do you?'

'Love, love, that's all you folk ever think about, spooning and slobbering and canoodling!' cried Mrs Saunders, flaring up for the first time. 'It doesn't mean a thing! I always thought

Lyle realised that – till you came along, spoiling it all! And see what it's got you!'

Hester turned away; and found herself saying, as if the protest was torn from her not against the stubborn old woman but against the tyranny of fate: 'I always meant well – always!'

Mrs Saunders opened the door. 'You needn't bother coming again,' she said. 'You know your way out.'

Hester stared into her mother-in-law's face: stared, in the last hope of detecting some flicker of hesitation, of doubt, of remorse. But she was the first to drop her eyes – it was like staring at a portrait. She opened her mouth to speak, then closed it with a snap and swept past her.

She was walking blind when she wrenched open the front door, and in the porch she collided with Gideon, just coming in.

'What the devil are you doing here?' he said, patting down his cravat as if she had spoiled it.

'God knows,' she said. He smelt of whisky, and his eyes were bloodshot. He looked drawn and irritable – more ground-down than ever, in fact – and it struck Hester that since Lyle's leaving, Gideon had probably come in for much of Mrs Saunders' resentment and bitterness. His next remark confirmed that.

'Well, don't expect me to give you a welcome,' he said. 'You've caused enough trouble here already.'

She brushed past him. His little eyes followed her, and as she reached the gate he said, 'Didn't last long anyway, did it? – I suppose you know Lyle's been carrying on with any little piece that catches his eye. I saw him in Huntingdon with a girl just the other day – he didn't even bother to hide it.'

'Well, they're in no danger from *you*, that's for sure,' she said venomously, and stalked away down the street without looking back.

The answer seemed to have risen to her lips quite independently of her mind, which was reeling groggily back from the blow. Her body too was working like an automaton, and it had taken her briskly across the fields half-way home before she came to herself.

She stood still a moment on the field-path. On all sides the green fen was empty. The wind boomed and mumbled in her ears, the wind that blew from a far continent across great tracts of naked land and yet seemed to bring its muttered secrets to her solitary consciousness alone. As she recovered from the shock, a little faint-heart voice within her was advising: forget it – ignore it. Just Gideon's spite. And what Chad had hinted too – coincidence. Pretend you never heard it, and stay sane.

But she would not be convinced, for the plain reason that as soon as Gideon had spoken, she had believed, and though her heart cried out in anguish at her mind's betrayal, she believed still. She could not deny the truthfulness of her own nature though she wanted to, and in the same way she could not deny that her trust in Lyle was gone. And yet in the same instant she knew – with a sort of despair in the knowledge – that her love for Lyle persisted, not one whit the less: indeed the terrible insinuation seemed to drive her love for him deeper into the aching vitals of her self, like a dagger thrust deeper into flesh.

'Oh Lyle!' Involuntarily she spoke aloud. She looked up, and was almost tempted to cry her pain to the skies; but instead she breathed deeply and carried on walking. In Hester a seam of adamant existed deep beneath the layers of easy pliability; and she had struck its tough face now, in a conscious refusal to bow to fate. The faint-heart voice had told her to be passive, to hide, to go under, but Hester walked hardily on to the Crooked House, nourished by a determination to do none of those things, and to save her marriage. Lyle, she knew now, was the sort to yield when things did not go well: all right, she accepted that; she would have to do it alone.

And she would have to confront him. She dreaded it, but she dreaded delay even more, and she hardly knew what to do with herself when she found he was not home. At last she made herself sit, quite still, in the parlour, with her hands in her lap, and thus she waited until in the late afternoon she heard the sound of the trap in the yard, and Lyle came in.

'Hullo, love. Wait till you see what I've got. Picked it up for a song,' he said. He had a parcel under his arm, which he unwrapped before her, revealing a framed print – a Regency horse-rider taking a fence. 'Nice thing, isn't it? Worth what

I paid just for the frame.' He began holding it up at various places around the parlour and examining the effect. 'How about here?'

'Yes.'

He glanced round at her. 'You're quiet,' he said. 'Had a hard day?'

'Yes, in a way.' She clenched her hands together. 'I went to see your mother this morning.'

He froze: with his back to her he said, 'You did what?'

'I went to Stokeley to see your mother.'

He turned round: his cheeks had gone pink. 'What the hell did you do that for?'

'I went to try and sort things out,' she said, forcing herself to look him full in the face. 'Because we can't go on the way things are, with you and her. It's ruining everything—'

'You bloody little fool!' stormed Lyle, putting the print down with shaking hands: Hester flinched. 'How dare you go interfering between me and my mother!'

'You're married to me – not her,' she said, keeping her voice level. 'And as long as you're being pulled both ways there's no hope for us. That's why I went to see her – to ask her to settle it one way or the other.'

Lyle put his knuckles on his hips and stared down at her. 'So, you've finally done your best to turn my mother against me, have you, Hes? Get what you've always wanted.'

'That ain't fair—'

'Don't you ever go there again, do you hear me? Not ever.' Lyle's voice had gone as thin and tindery as the crackling of brushwood.

'I won't,' she said, her breast heaving even as she gripped the arms of the chair and tried to hold on to the calm she had instilled in herself. 'Not because you say so – because she treated me like muck.'

'What did you expect?' Lyle snapped. He paced over to the mirror, glared a moment at his burning reflection, then turned edgily round to her, punching his clenched hands into his pockets. 'Well, that little contribution of yours must have just about finished my prospects. You've pretty well wrecked my life, you know, Hes,' he said, in a ghastly echo of a conversational tone. 'This marriage. Oh, I'm not saying it wouldn't have been a viable proposition, later on, if we'd waited. But you wouldn't wait, you pushed me into it. I had smart prospects, I had a future – but you pushed me into losing the lot.'

Even at this she somehow clung on to her calm, and her voice was as steady as her gaze into his smoke-blue eyes as she said, 'I never pushed you into meeting other girls, though.'

Lyle was still, his head on one side like a listening cat. 'What's that supposed to mean?'

'Gideon told me. Something about you and a girl, in Huntingdon.' She swallowed down a monstrous indignation that rose in her throat like acid. 'Is it true?'

'So you believe Gideon's word rather than mine, is that it?' Lyle said.

'I just want to know the truth.'

Lyle shrugged and moved restively away. 'What shall I say? I dare say he did see me with a girl. I'm trying to sell her that pony I bought. She rides, she's got money. She needs buttering up a bit. It doesn't mean anything. It's nothing serious. I'm not a serious person, Hes. That's the way it is. You knew that when you married me. You just have to take me as I am. You didn't suppose you were getting some hymn-singing model of virtue, did you? Isn't it enough that you've got me here in this damn cage? My God, I need to break out of it sometimes, and remember what it's like to enjoy myself.'

Hester stared at her husband, with the hallucinatory feeling that he was simply not seeing her – that she was really not there at all – that she was melting into vapour. Struggling still to be practical, to outface the crisis, she said: 'Tell me you won't see that girl again.'

Lyle did not answer: he walked to the door.

'Where are you going?' she said.

'Out.'

'Lyle – tell me you won't see her!'

'Eh? Don't be ridiculous,' he said casually.

'Please – Lyle, don't go like that – wait,' she cried, springing up and running to him. Tears were trickling down her face: for all at once poor Hester had lost the fight with herself. The pride that had sustained her had crumbled in a terrible instant of dread at the idea of Lyle's withdrawing his love: she had seen all that she cherished, all that she valued about to disappear into the abyss; and her dignity and self-respect were simply torn away by the passionate desperation that whipped through her, so that she found herself clinging to Lyle's arm and sobbing out: 'Wait, Lyle – just say you love me best – please, Lyle, say you love me best!' At that moment she could no more feel shame at this abasement than a tree broken and humbled in the blast of a gale.

Lyle's face expressed the mild distaste he reserved for the display of strong emotions. 'Don't start the water-works, Hes,' he said. 'Now I'm going out.'

'Where?' she said, her hands still on his arm.

'Huntingdon maybe. Or St Ives, or Stokeley. Anywhere I can have a little fun. Remember that? It's what we don't have any more.'

He disengaged himself from her hands, and opened the door. Gasping and paralysed, she watched him walk out into the hall.

'You're hateful,' she said in a choked, mechanical voice to his back. 'You're hateful.'

He went out. Leaning her forearm on the door-jamb, covering her eyes, she heard him talking to one of the ponies as he harnessed up the trap: then at last the clatter of hooves and the rattling away of wheels. Stiffly, like a person rising from a fever-bed, she turned back into the parlour. The friendly eyes of the china cat on the mantelpiece met hers. She picked it up, with an instinctive, child-like groping for comfort. But the comfort the child within her sought, the china cat could not supply to the adult woman. She did not know whether it was because of this that she suddenly drew back her arm and, hurling the ornament against the wall, smashed it to fragments. It seemed some deeper response prompted her to thus destroy by her own hand what she loved – as if defiantly to rob the fates of their power to hurt her more, by doing it herself.

The crash brought Edie running from the kitchen. 'Oh, missus – thass that sweet little cat all broke!' she cried, flinging herself down on her knees amid the pieces. 'Can we glue it together?'

'I don't think so, Edie,' Hester said. 'I don't think it can be mended.'

The recent rain had left the turf-fen as wet as a marsh, and Chad Langtoft had had a wretched muddy time of it digging in his pit early that morning. It started the day off badly. The cesses would take longer to dry now; but what chiefly irritated Chad was the fact that it made the stacks all messy, for he was a man who liked things neat. His white duck trousers were caked in slub when he went out to his father's fields for the rest of the day, and he did not like that either. Then when his dinner was barely settled in his belly he had to go out again to help with digging out the last of that stubborn bog-oak. The end of the trunk seemed to go right down to the level of the buttery clay, which made him more of a muck than ever; and it was early dusk before they had freed the oak sufficiently to begin hauling it away. It was about then that Chad looked up at the high-road above the field to see Lyle Saunders go speeding by in his pony-and-trap, all dashing and dandy in his sporty bowler and jacket, with his characteristic air of knowing not a care in the world.

'Ah! Off on the skylark again,' grunted Mr Langtoft, in his mild way, watching Lyle whisk by.

'All right for some,' said Chad, for whom the sight was like a final emphatic underlining of all his reasons for discontent. It was dark when at last they trudged back to the house, where Mary-Ann welcomed him by shooing him out of the kitchen.

'Git away wi' them boots – gret lumps of mud dropping all over the floor – I'm been on my knees scrubbing that this morning! Honestly, Chad, what shall I do wi' you – you are a yawnucks sometimes!' she said, bundling him away. There was more of affection in this than Chad was prepared in his present mood to see: perhaps too there was a certain insecurity in Mary-Ann's insistence on the floor that she had cleaned, for she was seldom allowed to feel she had any stake in a household of which Mrs Langtoft remained firmly the mistress. All Chad saw at that moment was his young wife giving him a dressing-down again; and the evening seemed to hold out no other prospect than more of the same, with Mary-Ann pecking on at him about when they were going to get a place of their own. Her argument was that they could afford to do so sooner if he spent less money at the Labour In Vain: but if she didn't go on at him so, he wouldn't need to, was his obscurely felt rejoinder; and nothing would stop him getting his beer tonight, after the day he had had. He told her if he couldn't come into his own home in his boots, he'd go elsewhere; and set out for Milney St Mary with a growl in his stomach at having had no supper.

The Labour In Vain beamed its welcome to him as ever: though he could not get a corner seat, and this further annoyed him. A steady succession of tankards of beer, which Jass Phelps kept strong, dark and heady, did their accustomed work on Chad, floating his mind away like a boat lifted from a strand by incoming tide; and bringing him to a secure conviction, which always seemed darkly to elude him in sobriety, that he was in the right, and misunderstood. He was just about to order another pint when he heard the sound of wheels outside, and a moment later Lyle Saunders came in, cheerfully calling out greetings, and declaring his mouth felt like burnt paper.

Chad got up and slipped out, the blood thumping in his head. He refused to stay with Saunders there: that was that. Outside he saw Saunders' trap, the pony tied to the railings beside the pub, which indicated that he would probably not be staying long. But still, Chad would not go back. It ruined his drinking when Saunders was around. It ruined everything.

Chad swore – an unusual thing for him – and began to walk unsteadily down the village street. It was a deep blue starlit night, the cool air laced with fresh and sappy scents of spring which under darkness seemed more potent and more acidic. As he walked Chad's resentment mounted. He had just fancied one more pint, and being robbed of that one seemed to him to cancel out the effect of all the others. His day had finished as badly as it had begun, thanks to Saunders.

He struck the empty high-road. He began to gnaw on an idea that Saunders, seeing him slinking away when he arrived, must think him a weakling. He had after all let Saunders insult him and make a fool of him, and never shown any fight at all. Fenmen were supposed to have a reputation for standing up for themselves; and Chad laboured under a smarting feeling that Saunders must be laughing up his sleeve, and thinking he was a poor sort of fenman, with no guts at all. He swore again.

He came in sight of the sleeper-bridge that crossed the main drain. This was where he normally turned to take the field-paths over to his father's farm, but instead he stopped. An accumulation of frustration throbbed at his temples. When he got home there would be the usual wigging from Mary-Ann, and meanwhile Lyle Saunders would be confirmed in his opinion of him. He resolved, or the liquor in his veins resolved, that he would salvage something out of his miserable day, and teach Mr Lyle Saunders not to laugh at him. He would wait for him, and give him what for – it was high time. He had never in his life felt so utterly ready for a scrap – it seemed the only possible thing that could equal in satisfaction that last pint he had missed.

Whenever Saunders came, he would have to cross the bridge over the drain, and there, on the far side, Chad composed himself to wait for him. Not that he reckoned Saunders knew how to use his fists, anyway – it was him who was the weakling, leaving his own wife to go and apologise for that trick he had played. Chad began to brood on that; and finding himself more weary than he thought, sat himself down on the edge of the sleeper-bridge. He stared woozily at the stars reflected in the brimming drain below, and lost track of time; and came to himself with a start, gripping the beams of the bridge with his hands as he saw how close he had come to nodding over the edge – and a fuddled moment later realising that the sound of hooves and wheels in his ears was what had roused him.

He saw the white blaze on the approaching pony's face, and the white too of Saunders' dandy collar: typically, confidently, Saunders was coming at the bridge at quite a lick – it would be just like him to speed by and frustrate him again, thought Chad; and as the hooves and wheels came with a hollow thundering on to the bridge, Chad leapt up and forward shouting: 'Hoy, you – stop, I want you, you bastard—'

With a whinny so shrill it was almost a shriek, the pony shied at the yelling figure springing up in its path: iron-shod hooves hammering on the wooden bridge, it reared and side-stepped in a dainty dance of alarm. 'What the hell—?' Lyle cried, standing up in the trap and wrestling with the reins: his exclamation was cut short by a fearful grinding squeal – the backward thrusts of the pony in the shafts had driven the right-side wheel over the edge of the narrow bridge; and before Chad's eyes the trap tilted, overbalanced, and plunged down into the drain, hitting the water with Lyle underneath it, and dragging the screaming and plunging pony after.

A spray of cold dyke-water covered Chad's face, blinding him for a moment: he blinked and wiped it away, but when he opened his eyes again the scene was unchanged – the pony bucking and struggling in the water below, and the sinking shafts of the overturned trap, and the thrashing spume sparkling in the starlight. He stared, hardly able to connect what he saw with the normal world of a handful of moments ago: his legs would not move – seemed indeed barely able to hold him up, as if there were no bone within the flesh. All at once his mind broke free of the numb clutch of shock, was lucid for a moment, and then careered into a blank wall of panic. With a rambling cry he turned and ran. He ran with his soft, low, furtive gait, across the field-paths towards his home; and he did not slow his pace until he had left the scene far behind him, and could begin the task, necessary and terrible, of persuading himself that he never saw it at all.

Jonathan had been over to the adjoining fen, to consult with the old miller there about a problem he was having with the boiler-engine, and on the way home he dropped in late at the Labour In Vain for a half. When he left, in company with Henry Wake and Artie Gill, it was a clear still night the beauty of which all three men fell silent to appreciate.

'Is that a voice I hear?' Henry Wake said at last.

They stopped and listened. The sound came again, carrying far over the flat, empty distances.

'A hoss,' Jonathan said.

'That must be a hoss gone in the dyke somewheres,' Artie Gill said. 'That way – hark at it!'

339

Without another word they began to run: all were accustomed to dropping everything and running across the fields to help when a neighbour's plough-team or carthorse went into the dyke. Jonathan's long stride soon left the other two behind; and when Henry and Artie came to the bridge over the main drain, Jonathan was already slithering down the bank where the pony, half-drowned, had somehow – with that invincible will to survive – dragged its front legs out of the water and was feebly struggling there like a great eel, covered in mud.

'Have a care, Jonathan – it's deep – she'll thrash you down with her!' cried Henry from the bridge; but Jonathan had already plunged into the chill dark water and was sawing at the leather traces with his clasp-knife to free the pony from the shafts.

'Dear God, thass Mr Saunders' rig,' Henry breathed, as Jonathan came clambering back up the bank.

'She can't get to the top – need a rope – shift the trap – at the mill,' Jonathan gasped; and set off immediately at a run, following the bank of the drain, which would take him directly to the mill. He had the ability to still completely the workings of his mind at moments when critical action was called for, and he had never been so grateful for it as now. He did not know how many minutes elapsed in his furious sprint to the mill, where he grabbed a coil of rope and a storm-lamp: that was one of the things he did not think of. When he came pounding back to the bridge he found someone else there – a young farmhand passing along the road – who had thrown off his jacket and was swimming along the reedy edge of the drain, sweeping and feeling with his hands.

It was a long business, nightmarishly long and laborious and nightmarishly lit by the swaying beams of the lamp – hauling the pony out of the way and tying the rope to the shafts of the overturned trap and dragging it round and across to the bank. The leather seat came heeling up, puffed and glistening in the lamplight, like some robust and grotesque water-creature.

'He mebbe got out – further down – mebbe he crawled out further down,' Henry Wake was saying, over and over, as he held the head of the shivering pony.

It was the young farmhand, tirelessly swimming, who found

him. Jonathan joined him, and together they dragged the slight and waterlogged form on to the bank, where Artie Gill straddled it and began to thump with his huge thick hands.

Jonathan stood back, reeling a little: for the first time in his life he felt himself near the end of his strength. The young farmhand was stretched out on the grass, exhausted. Jonathan watched the hunchings of Artie Gill's square shoulders: he could not bring himself to look down at the pale face, with the weed intricately tangled in its crown of curly hair.

Artie stopped: sat slowly back on his haunches, and rubbed his hand across his face.

'Artie,' Jonathan said, 'what's—Try again, Artie!' His voice rose. 'Damn it, try again!'

Artie got to his feet, shaking his head. 'No, no,' he said softly, patting Jonathan's arm and turning away. 'No, no.'

# Chapter Three

1

Summer came like the unfurling of a banner after a chequered spring. On Hinching Fen, where folk lived in as close relation to the sun as pears on a wall, there was a swift ripening of complexions in the ever-lengthening days – the light of evening persisting so long and the light of morning appearing so early that they seemed almost to meet, leaving only the thinnest sliver of true night between them. In the fields bare arms and throats grew ruddy, moderately fair men turned Viking blond, and young girls pulled their sunbonnets low, and despaired of their pink noses being put right even by buttermilk. And yet Hester was as pale as any duchess in a closed carriage: she saw no more of the sun than a grub under a stone, and as little sought it.

She remembered as a girl hearing stories of the old queen as the Widow of Windsor, and how silly she had thought her, shutting herself away like that. Now in her own widowhood she embraced a similar seclusion – insofar as conscious will could be said to be involved, for she shrank from the world as a wound closes against infection. For the first time in her life, Hester failed in courage – an attribute she had not even known she possessed until it deserted her.

Lizzie Gosling had come to stay with her for the first week after Lyle's death, unasked, in an instinctive movement of solidarity. Her sturdy capable presence had shown itself indispensable at that time: quietly doing things that had to be done, quietly rousing Hester to do the things only she could do. Lizzie offered to stay longer, but with the same instinct perceived that she was not wanted – that beyond a certain point her bluff practicality was no more effective than a candle-flame in a cavern. Hester struggled to express both her gratitude and her need to be left alone – struggled, for all the channels of feeling within her seemed to be dammed, choked, and locked to an everlasting confinement – and she could only hope that Lizzie understood.

The Crooked House was her keep and fastness, guarded by Edie Smeeth, who alone could Hester bear to have continually by her. Young Edie protected Hester from the world's incursions with the doughty resource of a mother bird guarding a nest of young. She revealed a great deal of tact along the way: for Hester, desolately imprisoned within herself, could not convey, and the neighbours could not at first understand, that their kindly attentions seemed like invasions of a last redoubt of selfhood remaining to her. And the people of the fen, though they would have rejected as self-admiring and sentimental any Cockneyish claims to a familial community, had a ready sympathy with loneliness. They came one by one to the Crooked House to offer whatever help they could. Peggy Chettle brought a tonic wine, which she admitted was more wine than tonic, but if it made you feel better then God meant you to have it was her motto; Andrew Surfleet, looking about as brawny as an ancient pixie, came to say if there was any heavy work wanted doing, he was the man. Most distressing of all to Hester were the frequent visits of Henry Wake – distressing because she hated to seem ungrateful to a man who had shown her the most delicate kindness. It was Henry who had taken on himself the job, that night in May, of bringing her the news of Lyle's fatal accident; Henry who had shown, in the way he broke that news to her, that a sometimes conceited and absurd little man bore within him a selfless gentleness and grace. She longed to let him know how profoundly she appreciated that, but could not; longed to see a time, however distant, when she would be heart-whole enough to say it – but could not. Impenetrable shades had closed in upon her view, beyond which the most familiar and comforting figures were the merest wraiths, and the future a dark vale of doubtful contours. She could only listlessly register the names of callers that Edie brought her – Jonathan Eastholm's was the only one that did not occur – and hope that they would not think badly of her for withdrawing from a sympathy that would flay what it meant tenderly to touch.

From one potential source of commiseration – and that surely the most natural – she had nothing to fear: her late husband's family. No gesture in recognition of common suffering came her way from Mrs Saunders; there was to be none of the union in grief that Hester had heard about in stories. At the funeral, which had taken place in Stokeley, Mrs Saunders had not spoken one word to her: none, Hester supposed, had been needed; eloquently enough came the message that if Lyle had not married her, he would still be alive. She remembered very little of the funeral except that Phoebe Purefoy had been extremely kind to her, and that when the coffin was lowered there had been a brilliant flash from the brass plate in the sunlight, as if Lyle's own mercurial gaiety had sparked out for the last time. There had been no more communication between her and Mrs Saunders, and the extent of the old woman's jealous resentment, thus revealed, only failed to wound Hester because she was already numbed beyond the power of further pain. No help was forthcoming with the legal matters consequent on Lyle's death, except when Gideon accompanied her once to the solicitor's in Huntingdon – and this, Hester guessed, because Phoebe had made him do so.

The dealings with the solicitor were the only ventures Hester made outside her self-enclosure. The property which devolved on her from her late husband was encumbered with debts, some of which she knew about, others of which were new to her; and the solicitor was at pains to point out to her, as discreetly as possible, that material stresses were soon likely to be added to the sorrows of widowhood, unless she applied herself to her affairs. This had no closer effect on Hester than if he had informed her that the sun would cool down in a million years' time. While the busiest season of the year for the farm approached, Hester scarcely glanced at the grain ripening in the fields, and the eggs and the milk went off, or were given away. When old Walt the horsekeeper, or Billy Onyett the daysman came to her to ask for instructions, she could only tell them to do as they thought best; and if she was not properly aware that young Edie Smeeth was not only keeping the house but seeing to the pigs and fowls and the two milch-cows and dealing with tradesmen as well, it was because Edie kept it hidden from her: the young girl proving thus, unwitnessed, that the greatest acts of heroism are not necessarily performed with swords and standards, nor recorded on any monument.

Immured in the Crooked House, Hester ignored the broadening, flourishing summer outside: indeed she obscurely felt it all to be an illusion; for she was still mentally stuck fast in that cool spring night when Lyle had walked out of the house and out of life, and she could not move forward from it. His death had been no more nor less than a tragic accident: certainly he had been at the Labour In Vain and had a drink or two, very probably he had been driving too fast as usual, but the dykes and drains had been the scene of so many drownings, and so many vehicles had come to grief by not getting their wheels straight on the sleeper-bridges, that there was nothing unusual to protest about in this random stroke of fate. The trap that had pinned him underneath it had been taken away and broken up, the pony sold at market – Lizzie Gosling had quietly seen to those things; and Hester's inevitable self-reproaches that she should have somehow stopped him driving so fast and drinking so freely did not last long – Lyle would not have been Lyle without those ways. No, she felt that she might eventually reconcile herself to the fact of his death, were it not for another, more elusive fact that made it unbearable: a fact that only she could appreciate as such – that there had been a death twice over. Something had died between them before that night, and it was because of that knowledge that Hester was trapped within a dry stony vault of grief, and breathed its vitiated air in a suffocation of self-loathing. The hideous, insuperable obstacle cutting her off from consolation – cutting her off even from ordinary healing tears – was the image of Lyle walking out of the house to his death with words of hate ringing between them. *You're hateful*, she had said to him; and, worst of all, she knew that at that moment she had meant it. Worst of all? – was there not a further refinement of torture: the knowledge at last that Lyle had simply ceased to care whether she loved or hated him anyhow? No: there was no worst of all, for all was tangled in an agonising knot of sorrow and guilt and regret, like some convolution of throbbing veins at her heart, and it seemed she could not unravel it without tearing herself in twain.

Much as she had always disliked mourning-weeds, she wore her black – she would scarcely have noticed if she had been clad in rags, and a mute obedience to the conventions helped her efface herself from the world. The colour did not suit her: her whole situation, viewed from an exterior perspective, did not suit her. Trial had given to Hester's young, truthful-natured womanhood a distinctive dignity, but it was not of a tragic sort, any more than a meadow-flower resembles an orchid; and there was no nobly elevated beauty in the pale face she saw in the glass. It was a measure of how deeply Hester was suffering that she looked drawn, shapeless, and plain – and not a trivial measure: for Hester the soul and body could no more be disjoined than the power of vision and the eyes. When Edie Smeeth sometimes helped her to put up her hair, the two reflected faces in the mirror might have been separated by fifteen years instead of half a dozen. Equally new to her, though not so much foreign to her nature as a forced development of it, was the deep introspection in which she passed her days. Hester felt that she had never till now known what silence was: how it was not mere absence of sound but had a positive quality of its own, like heat or light; how silence, through the long waning of an afternoon, could seem in its accumulated weight and profundity to be on the verge of an utterance. Never before had she spoken so little: when she did speak her voice came hoarse and hesitant, as if she hardly knew how to frame her words. And never before had she truly known what thought was – how it could be as absorbing, exacting and exhausting as labour. It was not really a matter of thinking *about* anything: her mind simply had locked horns with the awesome thing that happened to her, in a static grappling. Memories of Lyle, memories of that last night, speculations about what he was thinking or feeling as he left her, who he had gone to see when he left her, longings to undo what had been done, suspicions that nothing could have been done – these were but recurrent motifs in a ceaseless mental jangling. While Hester sat in motionless silence, there was a deafening cacophony in her head, a rough-music that came to no resolution – as utterly fragmented as the beautiful dream of love that had begun a year ago, which was now in so many jagged pieces that nothing, not even the merest consoling memento, could be salvaged from it.

Just occasionally she forced herself to go out of the house for air: she slipped out at night when there would be no one around. In the lingering dusks of midsummer she walked briefly about the field-paths, a gliding black figure as insubstantial as the stretched shadows: whilst all about her the flat world brimmed with light like honey in a comb. For the first time in her life, Hester felt herself dissociated from her environment. The fields, waters and skies of her Anglian homeland, which had always borne as personal and intimate a relation to her consciousness as the shape of her own hands, blankly met her gaze as if they had no more to do with her than polar ice or alpine steeps. The power of the landscape to interact with human feeling seemed lost: there was nothing of hope or even mocking irony in the growing richness of the season; it all seemed to her to be going on behind a thick pane of glass. Returning home, she saw the trees that surrounded the Crooked House, their twisted roots exposed by the shrunken soil, with an unutterable sensation of strangeness; and looking up at the roosting birds, which formed soft blots among the leaves, she had the impression that if she were to shout and clap at them or even pelt them with stones they would not be disturbed, or acknowledge her existence by so much as the stir of a feather.

She knew what it was that made her think, dimly, that she ought to begin to break this sterile circle – it was the sight of Edie one morning, through the kitchen window, crossing the yard with an empty pail and breaking into a skip as she did so. Edie had doted on Lyle – girls did, Hester was able to say to herself without bitterness – and had mourned him deeply, but in that unconscious skip was revealed the unconquerable urge towards happiness, the assertiveness of life, as uncompromising in its way as death. Hester perceived this too at one remove, as if through glass – it was apt that she saw it as a tableau through a window; but she strained to apply it to herself. 'I ought to be glad I'm alive,' she murmured. 'I ought to feel – feel *something*.' All her human faculties seemed to have shrunk inward, as if she were undergoing a slow turning to stone: she saw at that moment that she was *willing* the process; and feebly, without conviction, she sought to wrest her will another way. 'I must do something,' she told herself; and an opportunity seemed to present itself very soon.

Henry Wake, making one of his regular calls to ask after her, mentioned that he was going in his dog-cart to Peterborough – 'Mrs Wake requiring sundry purchases not to be got at in the immediate vicinity' – said what a treat the weather was, and invited Hester, without much hope of success, to accompany him. Hester flinched at the prospect: but, desperately grasping at that resolve she had formed before it withered away completely, she forced herself to accept. While Henry waited in the yard, urbanely chaffing Edie, she dressed herself to go out – this feeling as bizarre to her as putting on armour. Pinning on her straw hat, she suddenly noticed the trimming of little crêpe flowers circling the crown – she had always liked them: now they struck her as an emblem of innocence lost, of a vanished gaiety and freedom from care as irrecoverable as Eden: all at once she convulsively clawed at them, whimpering like a creature in pain as she plucked them off and threw them to the floor.

'I can't go – I can't,' cried she, standing amidst the torn petals, and covering her face with her hands. For some minutes she remained thus, staring into the dancing blackness of her closed lids; until, the sound of Henry Wake's voice filtering through to her from the yard below, she wrenched her hands away, took a deep breath, and went downstairs.

'Morning – morning – glad you could come – splendid day for it,' Henry Wake said, nodding approval as she came out, and exhibiting a cheerful determination not to notice anything at all about her appearance. 'I said to Mrs Wake this morning, I must ask Mrs Saunders if she'd care to accompany me, seeing as I'm got the conveyance out, and it's so fine – not a chance of rain – no clouds anywhere – there'll be no rain.'

As they set out Henry repeated several times his assurances that it would not rain; and indeed the sky was that piercing and rarefied blue that makes all other colours seem drab, while the warm air was like an exhalation from the sweetened summer earth. Henry beamed so appreciatively at the unrolling scene, as if with perfect confidence in its recuperative powers upon Hester, that she found herself consciously turning her head about and looking at everything – the green crops, the trees with their deep furbelows of shade, the sheep in the rich wash-meadows, even the cow-parsley along the roadside – her motions, in their absence of spontaneity, sadly resembling those of a clockwork toy. 'Lovely day,' Henry said several times, 'splendid day,' and finally, glancing at her sitting stiffly beside him: 'Any little purchases you'd like to make in Peterborough, I wonder?'

Numbly she tried to think of something they needed at the Crooked House. She had no idea: she had left it all to Edie; she struggled as if she had been asked some teasingly difficult question. 'No – I don't know – I don't think so . . .'

'Oh! not to worry – just wondered. The ride will do you good, any road.' As if this were too naked a reference to her situation, he went on hurriedly: 'Mrs Wake's very particular about who she buys from – very loyal in her custom is Mrs Wake. I remember we bought our tea from a different supplier once, and we'll never do that again. It turned the teacups green. Which *can't* be right.'

In Peterborough they left the dog-cart at one of the many old inns which still gave the cathedral city, girded with railways and brickyards, a Pickwickian air at its gabled core; and Henry Wake gave her his arm with his peculiar bowler-hatted chivalry. It was very long since she had been amongst so many people: she found herself staring into their faces – rudely, she supposed, but she could not rid herself of a feeling that she was somehow invisible to them. 'Tell me if you're tired, now,' Henry said as they went about the shops, 'just say the word, and we'll have a rest.' But she was not tired: she was trying to somehow bring into focus the busy scene, the golden stone of old buildings, the bright colours of market awnings, the sight of a little dog tied to a lamppost – to convert her random thoughts about these things – 'That's nice – that's interesting – that's sad' – into some genuine currency of feeling. This effort continued when, shopping done, they took a walk through the cathedral close, through the brilliant flower-beds of the Bishop's Garden, and then down to the river-embankment. Everything seemed to be striving to charm her eye: the running sparkle on the water, the massy trees bending to wash their gorgeous reflections, the sails of little pleasure-craft flinging back tenfold the white rays of the sun. And her eye was charmed – dazzled – whilst her mind stood back from it, like a patient parent to whom the things that are enrapturing its child have long been commonplace.

'Ah, that's a handsome sight – I never git tired of that,' Henry said, turning to look at the long profile of the cathedral, rising like a walled city in itself above the trees. 'That reminds me – Milney St Mary church is to be closed – did you know? Oh! not permanent. It's all to be restored – practically rebuilt from inside out, Sunny Daintree says. Not that that will greatly concern us chapel folk, but it'll mean no place in the parish licensed for christenings and weddings, and such, which is a bit awk'ud.'

He had nearly said *and funerals*, Hester perceived, but had adroitly covered it up. She wished she could tell him that she didn't mind if he mentioned the funeral, Lyle, any of it: at least that seemed to have some reality. For the worst part of her failure to respond to the pageant of sublime and homely sights that he had prepared for her was just that: it seemed simply a pageant – as flat as a stage set, with nothing behind it.

They rode back to Hinching Fen. Hester felt tired – not from the unaccustomed exercise, but from the continual effort to convince Henry, with a show of animation, that his kindly plan to take her out of herself had been effective. It appeared she succeeded: he nodded with satisfaction at her very weariness, and said there was nothing like fresh air; and when he dropped her at the Crooked House, he genially shook her hand and said, 'Well, now – that was a rare nice day. Next time I mek that trip I shall tek the liberty of calling again – no, it's no trouble to me – not a bit of it.'

She thanked him as warmly as she could; and fled into the house with a sort of smothered horror at the thought of doing it again. She hid in her room, burying her face in the bed-clothes. She seemed to have come to a new and terrible knowledge,

350

which her young frame could hardly bear to have thrust upon it – that the human capacity for pleasure was finite, while its capacity for suffering was limitless.

Edie did not disturb her; and at long last she raised her head to look at the tin clock by the bedside, and then at the window, where the sky was suffused with a subdued radiance, like light seen through fine china. She went to throw back the curtains, and looked out at a landscape still at eleven o'clock seething with rose-pink shadows; and for the first time she remembered that today was the longest day of the year.

2

It was a couple of weeks after her outing with Henry Wake, and Hester was taking one of her evening walks about the farm. She was dully watching the turning sails of the mill in the distance when Edie Smeeth came calling for her in distress.

'Missus! Oh, missus, come quick – in the yard – it's old Rusty – he's gone funny, I dunno what to do!'

Hester hurried after her to the yard, where she found Rusty, the oldest and most reliable of the two farm-horses, lying on his side outside the stables. His belly was swollen, and his great chestnut flank heaved like a bellows.

'Oh! whatever happened to him?' cried Hester.

'I dunno, missus – I come out here and found him just like that. Walt's gone home, missus – who shall I run for? Mr Wake, mebbe?'

'Wait a moment,' Hester said: she had just noticed that the barn door was standing open. With a heavy heart she went in to find her fears realised. Rusty, being the most docile of horses, was often left to amble at will about the yard, which was bounded by the house, the stable-block and the barn, with a stout gate leading to the stack-yard beyond: on this occasion the barn door had been left open, the corn-bin left uncovered, and Rusty had obviously wandered in and helped himself. 'He's got at the wheat,' Hester said to Edie, who had followed her. 'It'll kill him if he's drunk water on top of it.'

They ran across the yard to the water-butt; and looking into it Edie moaned and clutched her pinafore to her lips. 'Oh! missus,' she said, her round black eyes liquid, 'that were near full this afternoon – I know it.'

A deep groan from the prostrate horse confirmed the grim diagnosis. Hester knelt down beside him and gently touched her hand to his heaving, hardened side.

'Can't we do nothing?' said Edie in a hushed voice.

'No, Edie,' Hester said. She had lived long enough on farms to know that nothing could be done for a wheat-blown horse once it had drunk. All at once the tears that had been aridly sealed within her for so long sprang to her eyes: her heart seemed to unlock at last – through pity for something other than herself. 'Oh! the poor thing,' she cried, as her tears dropped on to the chestnut coat, 'poor thing – suffering so,' and she continued tenderly to stroke the old horse, until within a mercifully few moments he stretched out his neck and died.

Hester rose to her feet, wiping her face; and became aware that somewhere in the trees a blackbird was singing, in pellucid, endless roulades, as if there were nothing but joy in the world.

'Thass my fault,' said Edie, bleakly. 'I should ha' seen the barn door was open – I'll bet it was me who left it like that—'

'No, no,' Hester said. 'It's not your fault, Edie. It's my fault. You and Walt can't be expected to do everything: it's not fair on either on you. It wouldn't have happened if I'd been doing my share – if I'd stopped feeling sorry for myself and – and got up out of my bloody pit before now.'

She spoke harshly: Edie gazing at her said, 'Oh, missus!' in mingled reproach and surprise.

'It's true, Edie: it's true. And the knacker shan't have poor old Rusty: it was my fault, and it'd be an even worse shame if I got so much as a penny from it; we shall bury him tomorrow, over in the paddock corner,' said Hester. 'I want you to wake me very early tomorrow, Edie – I mustn't lie abed in the mornings any more: I'm got to – to change my ways.'

Hester shed more tears when she went to bed that night: but, wretched and self-accusing as she felt, there was tremendous relief too, relief from the long barren ache that had threatened to become a permanent paralysis of the senses. She did wonder whether the morning might see her sunk once again in a slough of apathy, but she woke in the same freshened mood: poor Rusty's death had effected what summer flowers had failed to do, forcibly wrenching her from an inward absorption that had become a sheer self-embrace. Compelled thus to sympathy with something outside herself, she swiftly advanced to the logical next step – realising how much she owed to the loyalty of Edie and Walt who had kept the farm going while she languished: and it was the first thing she said to Edie when she came down next morning.

'I'm never given you a word of thanks for all the extra things you're had to do, Edie,' she said. 'I'm not sure how to say it even now – I should probably start roaring again: and I'm done enough of that. I reckon the best way for me to show how much I appreciate everything you're done is to start doing a few things for myself, and take the weight off your shoulders: and I'm starting now.'

After she had done the morning chores, and sadly watched Billy Onyett and Walt digging a grave for faithful old Rusty, Hester told Edie to come upstairs with her and help sort out the master's things. In the bedroom she flung open the closet and the drawers, and stood contemplating Lyle's many clothes – untouched since his death, and seeming still to await his return.

'What you going to do with 'em all, missus?' Edie said from the doorway.

'I don't know – I don't know what to do,' Hester said, touching with a tremor the empty sleeve of a jacket. 'I'm been trying not to think about these. I can't just hang on to them for ever while the moths get them – but it seems so hard to throw them out . . .' Impetuously she seized an armful of the hanging clothes and piled them on the bed. 'No – I'm got to do it now, else I never shall – I can't hide any more. There's poor folk on the fen desperate for warm clothes come winter – they'll be glad of 'em – and they're doing no good hanging here. I know the vicar's wife distributes such things – I shall pass them on to her.'

The only way to perform such a painful task was to do

it quickly, and within minutes she had filled several boxes. Suddenly she hesitated and looked up at Edie.

'You don't think I'm hard, do you, Edie?' she said plaintively.

'I think you're right brave, missus,' Edie said.

'No . . . I ain't brave . . . But I'm going to have to be. It's the only way.'

Somehow she got through the sorting of Lyle's possessions. Refusing to allow herself to dwell on what she had done, she next addressed herself to the state of the farm, and made a tour of the fields. Being on the edge of the upland, they had hay-fields, which she saw were late in being cut: the wheat looked well but the root crops needed thinning. The dykes were in a terrible condition and could hardly be draining at all: how had they ever got like that? Returning to the house, she got out the accounts – telling the tale, in their scrappy disorder, of Lyle's loss of interest – and presently called Edie and asked her to fetch old Walt and Billy Onyett.

It was wages day: Lyle had used to pay the workpeople through the open window, but Hester brought them in to the parlour, and after she had given them their money asked if they would stay a moment.

'I wanted to say thank you for all the work you're been doing these past weeks,' she said, standing by the bureau with the accounts, and feeling highly self-conscious in this role of chatelaine. 'And I'm sorry I'm not been more help, and you're hardly known where you are or what you're meant to be doing – thass done with now, I promise you. That is, if you still want to go on working for me.'

'Ah, we ain't gooing anywhere, are we, Walt?' said Billy Onyett, a long-shanked stork of a man with a wry comic mouth and a complaisant temper.

'Not I,' Walt said.

'Well, I'm glad,' Hester said. 'I'm got to – I'm got to make a fist at working this farm on my own, and keeping it going somehow. You may as well know that my – my husband left a few debts: and now with poor Rusty gone we shall need another draught-horse . . . So all in all it ain't going to be easy to manage, and I can't offer you no more than the standard wage you're been getting, even with the busy time coming up – but I hope you'll each take this extra five shilling now, just as a thank-you from me for keeping the farm going. Now the next thing,' she hurried on before they could embarrass her with thanks, 'is to see about getting more labour. We're late starting on the hay – I know you couldn't help that – and there's corn-harvest and root-lifting not far off, and even with me pulling my weight again, we shall want more workers. Do you know of anybody who's available straight away?'

'There's most folk been took on while harvest already, missus,' Billy Onyett said. 'At Farmer Mather's and such. I tell you what though – there's Jonathan-up-at-the-mill. Summer months he has buckets of time, and does all manner of casual work, where it's wanted, and you wun't find more brawn on a ox.'

'Ah – he's the very man,' said old Walt, who never advanced an independent opinion, but functioned as a comfortable echo to whatever was proposed.

'Oh! yes – Jonathan-up-at-the-mill,' said Edie, 'ask him, missus.'

'Well – I don't know – he's never come near me all this time,' Hester said in a small voice. 'He's perhaps busy . . .'

'Jonathan never turns down wukk,' said Billy Onyett, 'and there's no one sets in more willing, missus.'

Hester's thoughts had, indeed, instinctively turned to Jonathan; but he had always held himself aloof from the farm, more so since her widowhood it seemed, and she felt timid of asking him. Seeing her hesitation, Edie said: 'My brother Charlie sees him every day at the mill, missus – how about if Charlie was to ask him?'

Hester agreed readily to that: and she concluded her first day out of the pit with a concentrated assault on the backlog of letters, bills and invoices that Lyle had dealt with by stuffing them behind the clock on the mantel-shelf. The resulting piles of paid and unpaid bills showed an unpromising disproportion, and it was as much as Hester could do to let them lie and tentatively plan a trip to market, bank and solicitor's in one go. There was nothing so calm as acceptance in this new mood of hers: it was the fruit of a decision made against despair rather than for anything positive, and it required a constant effort of grim application to maintain it. She was trying to render herself as impervious to thought or feeling as a labouring ant; but still when she went to bed that night, the emptied cupboards seemed to reproach her for seeking to live on.

3

The coal-dray was making a delivery to the mill when Charlie Smeeth arrived. Jonathan, hoisting a sack of coal on to his back, gave Charlie a cheery greeting, but was firm when Charlie proposed shouldering a sack of his own – it would be like a grasshopper trying to lift a brick. 'Go in and open the coal-hole for me, Charlie, if you will,' he said, 'and then we'll have a pinch of tea.'

That young Charlie had something of moment to communicate to him was obvious from the way the boy twined himself into knots, and did everything with his cap but put it on his head before finally bursting out: 'I'm got a message for you, sir – from Edie – not from Edie though – from the missus at the Crooked House.'

'Ah?' said Jonathan, pausing in brushing off the coal dust from his shirt.

'Mrs Saunders has got to see to the running of the farm herself – she ain't been up to it, Edie says, but now she's setting her mind to it proper,' Charlie said. 'And seeing as she wants a good worker, Edie said you're the man – was that all right, sir?'

'Eh? Oh! yes . . . that was very good of Edie.'

'And so the missus says to ask you whether you're very busy at the moment, and would you think about going to work at the farm if you're not. Thass the message, sir.'

'I see.' Jonathan, after unsuccessfully craning round to get the dust off his back, pulled off his shirt and shook it at the door; then stood in thought, forgetful of his uncovered state, whilst Charlie suffered a lowering of spirits, and sorrowfully counted his own ribs. 'How are things there, Charlie?' Jonathan said at last. 'Difficult?'

'Missus ain't got much money, Edie says, and she'll have her work cut out to manage, all on her own. Except she ain't quite, because Edie's sticking by her.'

Jonathan had fallen into his peculiar poised stillness, the light falling through the open door making of him a parti-coloured creature, with cream breast and copper back. All at once he threw on his shirt and declared: 'I'm afraid I can't tek that work, Charlie: will you pass the message on, and say thank you for the offer, but – but I'm afraid I can't. Will you do that for me?'

Charlie, about to protest something, stopped at the sight of Jonathan's deep inward frown, which was like the pulling down of a vizor. 'All right, sir,' he said. 'I'll tell Edie.'

Jonathan had lately moved out of the Surfleets', where space had been so restricted, and moved into a rented cottage of his own: it was part of an old T-shaped stone house at the end of Milney St Mary, which Farmer Mather had divided into three small dwellings. Thither Jonathan returned that night, and in his lamplit house-place, amongst oak furniture as smooth as glass with age, applied himself to mending his shirts and stockings – his long-established solitariness making him as adept at this as a seaman, and as little self-conscious about it. But he was far from at peace with himself, as an observer looking in at the domestic vignette through the latticed window might have supposed. It was foreign to him to dwell on a decision once it was made – but he could not simply dismiss the one he had made today. Ever since he had seen Lyle Saunders' drowned body stretched out on the drain bank, the stout keystone of Jonathan's life had been a determination not to intrude on the widow's grief. Even before the fruitless visits of Henry Wake and others had revealed that Hester needed to be left alone, an instinctive feeling, a fundamental identification with the needs of the embattled soul, had kept Jonathan at a discreet distance. He had called at the Crooked House often – daily at first – but always very early in the morning, asking Edie if there was anything he might do, and extracting a promise

357

from Edie that she would not bother her mistress by telling her of his visits. Just as Jonathan for all his physical size and strength was very light on his feet, so the large blunt profile of his emotions was offset by a peculiar refinement. His own jealously guarded individuality had given him a horror of crudely imposing on that of others. The effect of his pity and sympathy for Hester, profound as they were, was to make him draw a large ring around her, beyond which he did not wish to trespass, especially as her widowed position was so fraught with delicacy. It was because of this that he had made that unhesitating refusal today.

He was so accustomed to referring to his sense of honour as the supreme tribunal that he did not know why he should be aware of a small pocket of dissatisfaction within him. He went to bed convinced that he had made the honourable choice; and so he could not place the demurring voice that disturbed his rest – could not tell whether it was his conscience, or his inmost heart, that accused him of cloaking craven self-preservation with the name of honour, and pretending not to hear a call for help.


4


It had been a July day of brazen heat, and an exhausting one for Hester, who had been to the bank and the solicitor's in Huntingdon and then to see a farmer on Tick Fen who had a carthorse for sale. With the trap gone she had to make these trips in an old farm wagon, which she supposed made her seem even more eccentric: already she was a conspicuous figure, a lone young woman going about business in those unwelcoming panelled offices, which were as dourly masculine as pipe-smoke. The necessary expense of the horse had been grudgingly conceded by the bank, and Hester's nerve was feeling fragile again when she got home; Jonathan Eastholm's cool refusal to take a job with her had dismayed her and was preying on her mind; but she resisted the temptation to hide, snail-like, inside the house. Billy Onyett had begun the delayed cutting of the hay, and she took him out a jar of home-brewed ale. Her skirts trailed a long train of shadow as she crossed the field in the bright afternoon: the upright figure of Billy, standing in his cleared swathe, cast a shade as clear as a sun-dial.

'Ah! thass a good drop of ale out your cellar, missus,' Billy Onyett said. 'Reckon I could drink enough of that to be sorry for it. Now who's that coming over from Will's mother's? There's only Jonathan-up-at-the-mill I know as sits atop a pair o' legs like that.'

Hester shaded her eyes with her hand. With the sun behind him, crowning his head with a ruddy aureole, Jonathan was striding towards them, ploughing like a wader through the uncut hay. 'Yes – it's Jonathan,' she murmured – startled: there was something larger than life in the way he had suddenly appeared out of the sun, and at that moment his onward progress through the waist-high grass seemed somehow to suggest the advance of an irresistible force.

'Day to you, miller,' Billy called.

'How do, Billy.' Jonathan came right up to where Hester stood clasping the empty jar, and put up a hand to push back his sweat-damp hair, with a vestige of doffing of the hat in the gesture.

'Mrs Saunders,' he said. 'I'm come to work for you, if you still want me.'

She was glad to be called Mrs Saunders – so many people went out of their way not to say it, as if Lyle had never existed at all; but her chief emotion was a relief overpowering in its intensity. To her burdened mind, Jonathan's great-shouldered figure seemed an incarnate challenge to all the difficulties that beset her; and for a moment she could not speak.

'I'm sorry I haven't come before,' Jonathan said.

'No, no,' said she. 'You're here now, and – well – when can you start?'

'This very moment,' Jonathan said promptly. 'I'll set in with Billy here, if you've another scythe.'

'Come up to the farm,' she said, 'there's one in the tool-shed.'

He walked beside her, across the fields to the Crooked House.

359

'I can pay you the going rate,' she said. 'Of course there's the mill – I mustn't take you from that—'

'Don't worry about that – this is the slack time, I'm hardly having to pump at all. I can be here morning to dusk: every day, if you want.'

As he said this the melting relief within her almost reached the point of tears; and stopping in her tracks she said reproachfully, unable to meet his eyes: 'Oh, Jonathan – I thought you were ignoring me or something – when you turned the work down, I didn't know what to think . . .'

'I'm sorry, Mrs Saunders,' said he. 'That must have seemed churlish of me.'

'Perhaps I should have come to see you myself – instead of sending a message by Charlie Smeeth – but—'

'No, no.' He seemed to wish to close the subject, and walking on said, 'They're a nice pair, them young Smeeths.'

'Oh, I couldn't do without Edie,' Hester said.

'Charlie's a big help to me at the mill. I give him a few bob, though I have a job to make him take it. I just hope that uncle of his don't git his hands on it.'

'You've heard about Uncle too,' Hester said. 'Have you ever seen him?'

'No – he lives over on New Fen. I wouldn't mind seeing him, though,' he added grimly.

'Well, if you ever do, send him on to me when you're finished with him,' she said, and they exchanged a smile.

'Your crops look well,' Jonathan said as they came to the yard. 'It should be a good harvest this year.'

'I don't know . . . I'm afraid the fields haven't been – well, properly attended to,' she said, opening the tool-shed. 'Billy Onyett's done his best, but it's been too much work for him really.'

Jonathan surprised her by breaking into a broad smile. 'Don't you worry,' he said, shouldering a scythe, and seeming to radiate strength at every pore. 'It'll all be safely gathered in.'

Jonathan threw himself into the work of the farm. He was afield before the sun had cleared the horizon, and even on wages day he was late in coming to the house for his money, arriving at last from the hay-meadows when Hester was despondently looking over the accounts once more.

'Should have it all cut by Monday,' Jonathan said, pocketing his money.

'I wish I could have all these debts paid by then,' Hester said, adding an unpleasant letter from the draper to the pile.

Jonathan hesitated, then said: 'Bad?'

'Oh! just a lot of little things – but they all add up. I suppose lots of people run up these bills, but . . .'

'I hate being in debt myself, no matter how much,' Jonathan said. 'You never feel easy.'

'Thass just it,' she said gratefully: she was glad he did not think her priggish – it was simply that her honesty chafed at these things which Lyle had always shrugged off. 'When I go into Stokeley I feel like I ought to go creeping down the back alleys . . . Silly, ain't it?'

'Not really. You know, Mrs Saunders, if it would help, you could pay my wage at the end of the month – or even when the harvest's in.'

'Oh, I couldn't do that!' she said, looking up at him in surprise.

'Well, I get my pay for minding the mill, you know; and if you're struggling —'

'Well, it's just a few bills . . .'

'But you hate having them outstanding. I understand that. Now what would make you feel easier in your mind? – I mean, what's your first priority?'

'Well . . .' She nodded. 'To get these bills paid off.'

'Then thass what you should do. Instead of paying me by the week, put that money to settling the bills: and then when the harvest's in we can see where we stand.'

The prospect of being free of these oppressive debts, which were undermining her still frail resolve, was very attractive; but she did not want to seem to be taking advantage of her own vulnerability, playing on folk's sympathy to get concessions. Yet Jonathan spoke straightforwardly, with no pitying overtones.

'It's a very kind offer, Jonathan,' she said. 'But I don't

think these bills will break me, you know – and I'd have to be absolutely sure you can manage.'

'I reckon I can manage – if I don't, I shall have to ask you for a little sub,' he said with a slight smile, 'but I reckon it'll work. Suppose you draw up an account each wage day, putting my wage into the bill fund, like this—' She passed him a blank sheet of paper. 'Pardon me –' he wiped his hands – 'I'm all of a sweat from the field – now suppose you draw up a plan, setting all these little bills in order, and giving yourself a particular target every week or fortnight, say, so you can cross 'em off one by one. You'll feel better seeing the list gitting less and less.'

'Yes – thass what I need – to feel I'm getting somewhere – at the moment I just seem to be banging my head against a wall,' she said. 'Well, I'll do it this way, then, Jonathan: it's very generous of you.'

'Practical, thass all,' he said, with the slight smile again.

'I ought to make some sacrifices of my own – I ought to start thinking of some little economies—'

'Write them down too,' he said. 'Then you can see 'em add up. Sort of make a challenge of it. You can work it, Mrs Saunders: I'm sure of it.' He took the money she had given him from his pocket and placed it on the bureau. 'And there's a start. See you tomorrer.'

He was gone, leaving behind a faint odour of sun-soaked labour, and seeming too to leave with her a little of his overflowing strength.

It stayed with her, indeed, for a couple of days in which she was refreshed and heartened, and set about her work with a will; but then she was cruelly set back by a visit from Cresswell, the ugly little man who had virtually imprisoned her in the house that stormy day when he had come dunning for the money Lyle owed him. To have those memories revived was bad enough: worse was Cresswell's cold-blooded insistence that he didn't give a fig whether her husband was alive or dead – he was still owed money. Her self-command was barely intact by the time she had got rid of him, promising him a banker's draft on the first of next month. She had not the heart to get out the accounts and place another figure on the debit side; nor at that moment could she bear to be in the house. Though she had

362

given his clothes to the needy and put away his small personal effects, there were still times when Lyle's presence seemed intensely, intolerably strong in the Crooked House, and this was one of them. Hester's spirits were dangerously low, and she had to force herself with a grim effort of will to go out to the hayfields, the last of which was being cut by Jonathan, and do the raking.

Jonathan just paused in his mowing, holding his scythe in the back-stroke a moment to nod a greeting to her, and then sweeping it forward again with his long easy motion. His swing was as fluid as a dance, seeming to have nothing strenuous about it at all, as if he could go on mowing for ever. About half the field was already cut. Hester picked up the hay-rake and began to turn the bleaching rows of cut grass with their little wreaths of wild flowers. The heat of the afternoon pressed down on the field, shadeless but for a couple of pollard willows in one corner. Sharp flecks of light flew from Jonathan's swinging scythe, leaving a jagged dazzle on her retinas whenever she looked up. On all sides the horizons simmered, and there was no sound but the rustling of her rake and the soft swish of Jonathan's scythe as he advanced through the hay, leaving behind him a neat wake of symmetrical swathes.

The idleness of those long weeks when she had shut herself away had caught up with her: she felt exhausted. As she straightened up and wiped her brow the field seemed to swim dizzily around her. It was as if all the vitality which she had once had in such abundance had come to an end, for ever. Jonathan, pausing to take his whetstone from his belt, saw her wilting.

'You'd best stop a minute,' he said, coming over.

'Oh, I can't,' she said. 'We're late as it is.'

'Just for a minute,' he said.

She had brought out a basket with some ale and buttermilk and a few girdle-scones. They stood in the shade of the willows and drank, and Jonathan urged her to eat.

'You'll feel better,' he said.

'Oh, I don't see how I can feel better just now,' she said, sounding peevish, for her heart was in blackest shadow. 'I may as well just work – at least then I can't think.'

363

'Is there something new?' he said after a moment. 'To do with money, I mean?'

She nodded. 'Not much – just one more . . . Oh, I can't manage it,' she said, feeling herself yielding to despair, letting go, unable to control herself. 'I can't manage this place alone, I know I can't. I just ain't got the heart.' Strangely, it was the first real mention of her situation that there had been between them. She had not meant to say it to him: the words burst from her. 'I don't know what to do. I just don't see how I can go on.'

'You can,' Jonathan said, calmly tilting the jar of ale on his forearm and taking a long drink. 'I'm not just saying that to be comforting or anything like that. What I mean is, you're got an established farm, planted, working. You know farming. I know it don't seem like it, but thass a head start. It won't go under unless you do. I suppose it's odd me saying this, when I lost my own little place – but thass the point. I was starting from scratch when I had that little farm, I hadn't even thought properly about it, just jumped into it – I was tekking a big risk and it didn't come off—'

'Oh! Jonathan – don't reproach me,' she said, with fresh distress at this reminder of how he had once overturned his life because of her. 'I can't bear it if you reproach me.'

'I'm not,' said he, 'truly: thass not what I meant. The thing is, I lost that farm because of bad luck – a fen-blow. I used to think it was somehow my fault, that I'd failed because I hadn't tried enough. I thought that for a long time. But now I know it was just bad luck: I'm stopped accusing myself. I worked at that place as hard as I could, and thass a satisfaction in itself. Believe me, it is.'

'I'm not afraid of the work,' she said, though feebly. 'It's just – it's just that I can't see any point in it.'

'Well, I know the farm mebbe doesn't seem worth much at the moment – mebbe seems nothing more than a pile of bricks, a few fields of black muck. But even if you can't think of it as anything more than that, still it's worth working. There's salvation in work, Mrs Saunders – making that earth yield – making your own *self* yield.'

'Is there really, Jonathan?' she said. She longed to be convinced, though the demon of doubt held her fast.

'I know it. And I'm not just handing you second-hand saws from the old grannies.' With his eyes fixed on the quivering hot distance, Jonathan went on: 'When I was a lad my father died and my mother married again. My stepfather didn't want a boy into the bargain and he – well, he let me know it. There's more than one way of being cruel . . . Anyway he got me out, and so I was on my own. I felt the world hated me. Folk talk a lot of blather about being carefree when you're young, being able to bounce back . . . all I know is I never want to know such darkness as that again. I was down at the bottom of the well and I couldn't see any way out. But it was work that got me out, in the end. Not quickly; and I don't reckon I was even aware of the moment when I got into the light again. But work did it: it made me whole again.'

The singing stillness of summer flowed back as Jonathan paused. Hester became aware of the hum of bees, like a furry tingle in the warm air, passing among the grass-twined flowers. Something in the way Jonathan spoke, both tentative and distinct, gave her the feeling that he was telling something long hidden, telling it perhaps for the first time.

'You're got the farm,' he said. 'Work at it. Mebbe there'll be no satisfaction in it at first, but it'll stop you going mad – I swear to that. There's enough waste in the world already, Mrs Saunders, enough cruel waste to make a man shake his fist at the heavens for pity – you know that too well, I'm afraid. It'd be a shame to see this farm thrown in the dust: I don't want to see that.'

'Neither do I, I suppose,' said she listlessly. 'I just wish I could *care* more.'

Jonathan fixed her with a hard attentive look. 'You can't love life now,' he said. 'I know that. I dare say you can't see a time when you ever will love life again. All right: but you can fight it instead. Fight it, and throw it. With hate, if you like.'

'Was that how it was for you?' she said. His tale of his youth had called forth a glint of curiosity, at least: she stepped outside her brooding self for a moment.

'Yes,' he said; and added after a hesitation, 'Too much hate perhaps.' He stoppered the jar of ale and picked up his scythe.

'You look worn out,' he said in quite a different voice. 'I can manage here. You mustn't go making yourself ill.'

He returned to his mowing. Hester lingered beneath the willows, watching him, sipping the last of the buttermilk, and scarcely seeming to have the energy to brush away the teasing flies. At last she picked up the rake and, half sulkily, but with a sort of subdued determination like a reef beneath still water, resumed her work.

Hester kept on: somehow, as the summer deepened, she made herself go on. If there was no alteration within her, there was a visible difference to her appearance; the long days she spent at hay-turning swiftly brought colour back to her skin, and she no longer looked like the papery and bloodless ghost that had haunted the field-paths at eventide. She adhered to the plan she had formed with Jonathan of paying off the backlog of bills, and the fact that he was prepared to postpone his wages to help the farm put a little iron into her own soul. She set her mind dourly to the task of economy, yoked it and drove it, permitting herself to think of nothing but survival: she was as narrowly absorbed as the most obsessive old miser. She so forced herself to think of this as an end in itself that she was unprepared for the sense of satisfaction when, on successive wages days, she found herself crossing off the debts one by one.

Jonathan always came to the house last on wages day – they had agreed on this lest the others find out he was receiving no money and think it might be expected of them; and she took a pleasure in showing him the diminishing pile of bills. Always she sought a definite assurance that he was managing: always he told her, 'I'm gitting by, Mrs Saunders – don't worry about that.' Always, too, he was quick to be away once he had congratulated her on the latest little success and she had noted down his week's work; he never lingered to chew the fat as did Walt or Billy Onyett. Indeed it was notable that he always placed himself carefully on the opposite side of the table on which she wrote, as if to emphasise the distance between them. This perplexed her – perplexed her more as the little triumphs gradually put to flight the worst shadows of despair, and enabled her to appreciate his efforts. The very perplexity was an indication that she was beginning, however painfully and gradually, to lift her head and raise her eyes from the earth. Another indication was her noticing for the first time that Edie Smeeth had an admirer.

Rob Risby, the tallyman, had recently taken on a boy to help him with his rounds: a stocky youth of peeled and gingery aspect, with a sprouting growth of hair in the middle of his chin like the base of an onion. Though they never bought anything from the tallyman, Risby's boy habitually got down from the cart at the end of the drove and came up to the Crooked House, and hanging his face and hands over the top bar of the yard gate like a man in the stocks, inquired, 'Anythink today?'

Edie was always quick to reply: 'No thank you very much!', with shrill emphasis, but Risby's boy lingered at the gate, wrinkling his brows and following Edie with his eyes, like a recumbent dog that hopes against hope for a walk. All the time Edie marched briskly about, her face as serene as a madonna, and expressed by means of severe sweepings and pumpings and pig-feedings, her utter unawareness that any such a thing as a tallyman's boy existed anywhere under the sun; occasionally stopping short, and noticing the mournful face with a tremendous start of surprise, and an exclamation of 'Not today thank you!' It was notable, however, that she always found something to do in the yard when Risby's boy was there; and when the moony face disappeared at last, she always ran to the gate and watched the youth's departure as attentively as she had ignored his presence.

One hot morning Hester was witness to a startling development in this intrigue. She returned from the hay-field, where the carting had just finished, to find Risby's boy in his usual place, and to hear him solemnly declare to Edie: 'I like yer 'air.'

Edie, fastening the barn door, stopped and looked all the way around her. 'Are you addressing me?'

'I like yer 'air,' said Risby's boy again, as if this were a gambit compelling enough to bear repetition.

'Git away wi' you!' cried Edie, giving her curls an unconscious shake. 'Passing remarks on a person's Hair indeed!'

'Well,' said the youth, after an enormous pause, during

which Edie locked and unlocked the barn door numerous times, 'I do.'

'Oh! can't a person git no peace!' said Edie. 'Ain't you got no work to do, 'stead of bothering a person to distraction?' And she sailed into the house, examining the bunch of keys as if keys were the one thing she found most fascinating in all the world.

'Well, Edie,' Hester said soon afterwards, as together they lifted the heavy iron tray of new bread out of the range, 'it looks like you're made a conquest.'

'Oh him!' said Edie, with the greatest unconcern, as they set the tray down: then covered her mouth with her apron and gave a shriek of laughter. 'The gret yawnucks!'

'Don't you like him?' Hester said smiling.

'Him! huh!' Edie said with another shriek, and then, 'He's all right.'

'You weren't very nice to him.'

'Pooh – show 'em any encouragement and they start sticking to you tight as the miller's shirt when he's mowing. *I'll* manage that 'un, missus.' Edie gave a little chuckle to herself, then looked up at Hester with a sudden apprehension. 'Oh! you don't mind him hanging around like that, do you, missus? It's only fun, but – I mean, I just thought, if it meks you feel sad about things, seeing us – oh! I'll send him away, missus. I feel awful now – I never thought—'

'No, no, Edie,' said Hester, quieting her with a gentle hand on her shoulder. 'I don't mind a bit; it don't make me feel sad. I know life's got to go on. I can't expect nobody ever to have any fun because of me – and I don't want that now, though a while ago I'm afraid I probably did. I was selfish then; I suppose I didn't think it right that life should go on, and young folk fall in love, and flirt and have fun – but of course it's right.'

'Well, you're young yourself, missus,' said Edie earnestly.

'I suppose so,' Hester said, kneeling down to rake out the oven. 'I suppose I am . . . But not in that way, Edie. All that's finished for me, now. I shan't ever have them young feelings. It's a pity, but I don't regret it really – I don't want that back again. I'd rather just look on. That's the best way.'

\* \* \*

Harvest began a fortnight into August. On the land of larger proprietors like Farmer Mather the horse-drawn reaping-machine could be seen whirling its spindly arms, but around the Crooked House (which was now slowly becoming known as Mrs Saunders' Farm) the work went ahead with scythe and rake just as it had when villeins had tilled the estates of Stokeley Abbey. Harvest was when every hand was needed and every hand did all it could, and the work of Jonathan, Billy Onyett and Walt was supplemented on a casual basis by many of Hester's old friends on Hinching Fen. Sunny Daintree, his bald head the colour of a flower-pot beneath the hot sun, came from time to time; so did Artie Gill, who, singularly, declined the ale that Hester supplied to the reapers, saying it made him heady, and refreshing himself instead with frogskin-wine – dyke-water – which he scooped up in his hat. Even old Andrew Surfleet, who was past wielding a scythe, did a little raking, whilst Hester herself and sometimes Edie followed behind, making the bonds and tying the sheaves. In their manner towards Hester there was a quiet curiosity, veiled by respect. She could understand that; for here at last in full view was the hermit-like widow of the Crooked House, who had hidden herself away from their solicitude. Often, indeed, when she looked up from gathering in her arms a spiky, lolloping sheaf, and saw the people working around her, their movements conforming to immemorial patterns, yet each stamped with the idiosyncrasy of the individual, she was moved by an extraordinary gratitude for their presence, which even as she felt it she saw no way of expressing.

Resting a moment in the shade beside Andrew Surfleet, she remarked how hale and brown he was looking.

'Well, thass funny, gel,' Andrew said – using a local mode of address, perfectly polite, for any female under sixty, 'I'm not got no browner, the last ten years, I reckon; just git topped up to the same level of brownness every summer, like.' He contemplated his forearms, on which the walnut-coloured skin appeared as loose as a cat's nape. 'And yet you'd think you'd goo on gitting browner all the time, and be dark as a black-bloke by the time you git to my age. I can tek any amount of sun, meself – not like my ole missus. The sun meks her sneeze, you know, and thass another thing I'm never understood, how the sunlight can git up your nose and mek it sneeze.'

'Is Mrs Surfleet's rheumatiz better, Andrew? – I'm not seen her for ages.'

'Ah, she's diddling, gel, she's diddling: excepting when this sun meks her sneeze, as it happens – not that there'd be any hurt in that, but she wun't let a sneeze come out, my ole missus – she's such a tidy body: "I wun't have no splashing, Dad," says she, and she holds 'em in so, I'm afraid sometimes she's gooing to go pop like a bottle of beer.'

It was then that Hester wanted to say something in acknowledgement of Mrs Surfleet's kindness in sending her some tender beans from their garden, in those weeks when she had been shut away; but she found she could not. Somehow it seemed inadequate, nothing more than a belated and dutiful thank-you note.

It was Jonathan at last whom she asked about this: it was Jonathan who drove the harvest forward like a great untiring engine, and in whom the springs of resilient life, towards which she was slowly groping, flowed most forcefully. They were reaping one day in the Popple Field, so named for the magnificent row of poplars, regular as street-lamps, that bounded it on one side, and when Jonathan sat down in the shade to eat his dockey she took her question to him.

'Folk were so kind to me – and I couldn't properly appreciate it at the time,' she said. 'And now I can appreciate it, but I can't say it properly.'

'They'll not be offended – they understand,' said Jonathan. 'You're showing your appreciation just by the way you are. I felt something similar, you know, when I lost my own place, and folk pulled round to help me stay on my feet. I felt uncomfortable about it – like they were putting me under an obligation. It took me a while to realise it weren't like that – and that they don't offer help expecting anything back. I don't think fen-folk like a lot of fuss and ompolodge. They're reserved. Like when they meet they never say "How are you?" and all that – but it don't mean they're not interested if you're sick or sorry.'

'I remember when I worked for old Mrs Saunders, and the

posh customers used to come in for tea, and it was all "How are you?" "How are *you*?", and I used to think how daft it was,' she said smiling: and suddenly realising that she had calmly brought out, without pain, this reference to a time she had hitherto found unbearable to recollect. If Jonathan recognised this he made no sign; only smiled too and, finishing his dockey, took an ear of wheat and threshed it in his cupped hands, blowing out the chaff and showing her the ripe grains on his palms.

'That's good wheat,' he said. 'Your own crop. That's fine, isn't it?'

She nodded; it did feel fine: fine, too, was the sight of the line of poplars like stiff torches against the sky. The green beauty of them touched Hester a fraction before the guilt. The old guilt, the feeling that she was being a traitor to the dead by finding things to enjoy in life – would it ever leave her? But the guilt had come tardily: for a moment her soul had responded like a sun-opened flower to the beauty of the trees. She felt torn: it was sweet to rediscover the desire for life, even fleetingly, but should she not crush it and deny it?

'Jonathan,' she said suddenly, 'that was a sad story you told me a while ago. About when you were a boy, and your stepfather. Did you – were you never friends?'

'Never,' Jonathan said. 'He tried to make it up once, but I wouldn't have it.'

'Do you ever wish that you had, after all?' she said; and as he was silent she added, 'I'm sorry – I'm being nosy.'

'No, no,' he said. 'I'm trying to think of an honest answer. I was very bitter for a long time: mebbe that weren't a good thing.'

'You're not bitter any more?'

Stretching out his great legs, Jonathan said, 'It's funny – I suppose I'm not, now, but I couldn't have told you when it stopped – it's like when you're got a headache, and suddenly you realise it's gone, but you couldn't have pinned down the moment when it left you.'

'Just time, I suppose.'

'Just time.'

Time, and work: they formed the medium in which the

shape of Hester's grief and shock was gradually moulded, until presently that grief and shock coexisted with normal life instead of monstrously displacing it. In the harvest fields the sun blazed, the wheat toppled, thick and dark as reeds, and Hester, stretching her arms around the sheaves, felt the old give and bend in her young body like the flex of a sapling, and undressing at night saw the familiar dimplings and cross-hatchings on her bare forearms where the ears of wheat had scratched her. These things, true and valid in themselves, could exist alongside the terrible thing that had happened: accepting them for the good in them did not mean accepting or forgetting the other. Instead of a uniform grey there was light against a background of dark. And a day of bright light came at the end of August, when after paying her workers their wage she reckoned up her accounts, and was able to cross off the last of the bills left behind by Lyle.

She was just solvent for now – no more; but a good harvest should see her able in the next quarter to meet the long-term advance from the bank, and breathe freely. It was an achievement; her undeniable pleasure in it was fused with gratitude to Jonathan for his help both in setting it before her and in reaching it, and when he came in from the field she had a tankard of ale waiting for him.

'Here, Jonathan,' she said. 'Drink a toast to debts paid off.'

'That I will!' he said. 'Thass fine news, Mrs Saunders. I knew you could do it.'

He drained the tankard, and seemed about to take his leave when she said: 'And now, now I'm out of the wood – won't you take this?', taking a pile of shillings from the table.

'Well, I reckon we might as well go on as we started, and settle up when the harvest's in,' Jonathan said. 'Oh – unless it's more convenient for you like this.'

'Well . . . no, I suppose.' She had meant him to take a gift, as a mark of friendship; but his punctiliousness was discouraging.

'Right then. Now I'd best be off, Mrs Saunders.'

Instinctively she had wanted to share her feeling of mild celebration, and his coolness dismayed her. 'You're always running away from me, Jonathan,' she said, half laughing. 'I feel as if I'm got something catching.'

'I'm sorry, Mrs Saunders,' he said. 'I didn't mean to seem rude.'

'No – it's me who's been rude,' she said, regretting the way she had spoken, and yet feeling she must be frank. 'It's just – I wanted to say how I appreciated the way you've helped keep the farm going. You're done so much – so generously – I can't just speak to you like boss to workman after all you're done. And yet at first you wouldn't come to work for me at all . . . I don't understand.'

Jonathan frowned and licked his lips. 'Well, Mrs Saunders, I'll tell you,' he said. He glanced into the passage: Edie was singing in the kitchen. 'Come outside, if you will.'

Mystified, Hester followed him out, and they walked round the south side of the house, where the skewed trees threw their addled shadows, towards the paddock.

'Have I seemed distant with you?' he said.

'Well . . . sometimes.'

He bent his gaze to the ground, and spoke carefully. 'After your husband died, I didn't want to intrude. That was my first thought. And then there was your reputation. It's best that we be business-like, because people will talk. A widow's in a vulnerable position, and it don't take much malice – it don't take much more than curiosity – for people to start saying how Miller Eastholm's taking advantage, and trading on your situation. Just gossip,' he hurried on, as she was about to speak, 'and ridiculous, I know: but there it is. I wanted to spare you all that – you're got quite enough on your plate without that sort of nonsense coming to your ears. I don't know whether you're gitting any peace of mind yet – if you are, it's been hard-won, and it's too precious to spoil. Thass what it is, Mrs Saunders: I never meant to offend.'

'Oh, no, you didn't offend, Jonathan – and I do understand,' she said earnestly. Her surprise was great, for she had not even thought of such things; and momentarily she was profoundly touched by this disinterested protectiveness which she had not guessed at. She shook the moment away, however, for a bewildered indignation rose up as she said: 'But can't folk

373

ever think of anything else? Don't they realise that that's all over for me?' She stopped beneath the apple trees, where a cloud of gnats hung like a thick mesh stirring in the sulky air. 'Yes, I'm got a little peace of mind, Jonathan: not much, not all the time, but it's there, and you helped me to it . . . But that don't mean I can – I can ever be like I was before. Or ever want to be – thass the thing. I'm learnt my lesson – with love you think you'll get the moon and stars in a basket, but really there's nothing but pain and heartache to be got.'

'I understand why you feel like that,' he said. 'When such a terrible thing happens—'

'No,' she said, 'no, I don't just mean – I don't just mean Lyle's death. Oh, that sounds awful – I know there *couldn't* be anything more terrible – what I'm trying to say is, it all comes to heartache one way or another – whichever way it ends . . .' She looked at him very soberly. 'I can say this to you because – well, you remember that day of the storm, when you saw me under the tree?'

He nodded.

'That's what I mean. You couldn't help but see the way I was. The way Lyle and me were – there's no point in hiding it, I suppose it was common knowledge on the fen. That's what makes it all seem so fiendish and empty. It wouldn't be so bad, maybe, if you felt that you'd at least made that person happy—'

'Mrs Saunders, you don't have to say this—'

'No,' she insisted, 'I need to say it – I'm so needed to say it to someone who understands. Because I couldn't feel I'd made that person happy: that was the worst part. That it had all been a waste, a waste of life and heart. And that's why it seems almost like a sickness, what I'm had, and won't have again.'

Jonathan had leaned his arm against the tree-bole and was gazing concentratedly upon her; but when he spoke it was in an abstracted tone, as if to himself. 'A fool's game,' he said softly. 'All a fool's game.'

'Yes,' she said. 'I knew you'd understand.'

Stirring, he looked up into the foliage, sticky-green as if varnished. 'No fruiting on this one?' he said.

'No, it's sterile,' she said. 'Jonathan – it's very good of you to be – well, to think of my reputation like that. But I don't want to see a good friendship spoiled by talk. Like you say, there's some things too precious. One thing I'm learnt now is to value what's true and real and honest. I didn't think I would be able to care about the farm, and working at it to make it pay – but it has been worth it, just like you said. When you told me there was salvation in work I must admit I only half believed you.'

'But you stuck at it,' he said smiling. 'And the credit's yourn.'

'Well. If you say so.' They walked on, round to the rear of the house. 'And you really won't take that money, Jonathan – as a friend?'

'As a friend,' he said, 'I can say no. We'll stick to our plan, eh? And wait till this stack-yard's all brimming with wheat ready for the threshing. And now I really must be going.' Just as he was about to turn, however, they saw Edie Smeeth go bouncing across the yard, skirts flapping, clucking in imitation of the hens. They both smiled at the sight, and Jonathan said: 'Charlie tells me Edie's got a beau.'

'Rob Risby's boy,' Hester said. 'She's as sharp as glissy-needles with him – I don't know how he puts up with it – but he moons after her all the more. And he can't bring himself to say he likes her, and if she likes him, she don't give none of it away.'

'Aye,' Jonathan said, shaking his head, and then lifting his hand in farewell. 'A fool's game.'


5


Jonathan woke suddenly in his cottage bedroom some hours before dawn. Since he had become a miller his sleep had grown as light as a wild animal's, and the slightest shift in wind or weather would interrupt it. He lay for a few moments staring into the darkness, his senses bristling. The air that touched his face was cool. The broad backdrop of sustained sound behind the silence of the room was not the wind, as he had first thought: it was raining in a steady torrent.

Jonathan slipped into corduroy trousers and a shirt and padded downstairs. Lighting a lamp, he swallowed a mouthful of cold tea and pulled on his boots, whilst the stray kitten that had lately adopted him blinked crossly at him from his chair. Jonathan remembered that the kitten had been repeatedly washing behind its ears last night, which was supposed to presage heavy rain; and recalled too the arrow-wiggles that had invaded the house-place from cracks in the walls. All this past week August had been dying in humid fits of thunder, interspersed with downpours which cleared to freshness only to cloud over again; but he had thought yesterday that they were entering a fine and settled spell. Now when he threw open the door his lamp cast its light upon a glistening barrier of rain, which beat down upon the wide village street in a furious drumming, and chattered in piccolo tricklings from every sill and roof-eave.

Putting on his cap and throwing an old oilcloth over his shoulders, Jonathan set out for the mill. Milney St Mary's street was awash, and he was soaked up to the knees in a few moments. As he struck the plashy path alongside the main drain, he could hear the pounding hiss of the rain upon the drain-water, which was already high from those summer storms, and when he got to the mill he was drenched by the solid spouts that were coursing off the motionless sails. He paused only to light a lamp before plunging into the stoke-hole to fire the boilers; and within a few minutes of waking, with not a crumb of breakfast inside him, Jonathan was working like a galley-slave.

By the time the boilers were fired, and the pump working, the light of the oil-lamp had died in the light of dawn like a spent moon. The noise of the engine-beam and the water-wheel had obscured any sound outside, and for a moment Jonathan thought the rain had stopped, but a glance out at the mill-drain showed that it was still descending in a breezeless deluge from a stone-coloured sky: the underbelly of cloud seemed no higher than the cap of the mill or the sodden tops of the trees. Jonathan watched the water-wheel doing its work, and thought of the harvest still half-gathered in the fields.

Old Andrew Surfleet came pottering along the high-road, and passed the time of day with Jonathan as was his custom.

'Reckon this'll clear today, Andrew?'

'I wouldn't wait for it 'less I was sitting comfy,' Andrew said, with water pouring from the brim of his hat all the way round so that he seemed to be wearing a bee-keeper's veil. 'It must have come down in pails and tubs last night. Stokeley Drain's all full to the lip, they reckon. The corn'll want fetching in quick if it keeps up. I'm glad we're got you manning the pump, Jonathan bor.'

'I'd best git back to it then, Andrew.'

He stoked the boilers till dinner-time, stripping off his shirt in the heat of them, and emerging with his skin coated in oil and coal-dust, so that Charlie Smeeth, running over to see him from Henry Wake's, was startled by his swarthy appearance and flashing eyes.

'Coh, sir, you'll be worn to a shade at this rate!' cried Charlie.

'Got to keep the pump going, Charlie – never git much wind with heavy rain like this.'

'Let me do a bit o' stoking, sir – I can manage it.'

'No, boy: you'll bust a gut with willingness one of these days . . . I tell you what though – it'd help if you could step down Mrs Saunders' drove on your way back. You know I'm been harvesting for her, but I can't leave the mill while the dykes are filling like this. Give her my apologies, will you – and tell her I shall try and come afield later – just as soon as I can.'

'I'll do it, sir!' said Charlie, setting off like a hare, and unerringly succeeding in treading in all the deepest puddles as he went, with a groan of surprise at each one.

The weather did not clear that afternoon: it was like a detached piece of greyest November thrust into the hot summer. The pumping-engine throbbed, the water-wheel thrashed, and Jonathan shovelled coal until the sooty sweat ran down his wrists; whilst all the time his mind dwelt on Hester's nearly-reaped fields. The wheat would need cutting, carting and stacking as soon as possible, unless the weather improved dramatically: wet wheat might grow in the ear, and roots might soon be drowned. He remembered tales of wet years when the harvest had to be gathered in by boat. It wasn't that bad . . . but still he was haunted by images of those fine crisp sheaves which Hester had tied, standing inch-deep in muddy water. It seemed to him that a failed harvest now would cost her more than just financial security: it was plain that making a success of the farm had done much to lift her from the stagnation of despair, and it would be the cruellest blow to her delicately poised equilibrium – a waste doubly destructive. Too much waste in the world, as he had said to her.

Late in the afternoon Jonathan stoked up as high as she would go, touched the feed-pipe to make sure she wasn't overheating, and set out across the waterlogged fields to Mrs Saunders' farm. He had had nothing to eat all day but some hard-tack and bungo – ship's biscuit and rock-like cheese that he kept in a tin in the mill for just such an emergency – and he had to rely on the still torrential rain to give him an impromptu wash, which it did very imperfectly, so that he arrived at Hester's harvest-fields resembling a half-drowned chimney-sweep.

Billy Onyett was there, still mowing: and there was Hester, in the old fen-woman's padded bonnet and a dripping shawl, raking the heavy damp wheat. She looked up in astonishment at the great blackened figure jogging up to her, and then gave a cry of relief.

'Oh! Jonathan, it is you – Charlie gave me your message. What a sight I must look!'

'No picture myself, I'm afraid, Mrs Saunders,' Jonathan said, roping back his hair, which was as wet as a swimmer's.

'Folk must think we're mad reaping in this weather,' Hester said, 'but if it's going to keep up, I thought we ought to get on with it and not waste a minute.'

'You did right,' Jonathan said, picking up a scythe. 'I'm sorry I couldn't come before – but I can put in a couple of hours now.'

'Jonathan, have you been running the engine all day?' Hester said. 'You must be so tired already – haven't you had any dinner?'

'I'm had a bite,' Jonathan said. 'Let's git this wheat finished,

378

eh?' He was swinging the scythe before he had finished speaking.

At supper-time Billy Onyett, looking more than ever like a bedraggled wading-bird, took himself off home; but Jonathan and Hester laboured on, the only moving things beneath the tent of cloud, with all about them the vivid percussive sound of rain on standing wheat, like the endless applause of a vast crowd. They did not speak: they did not even look up until Edie Smeeth came out to them from the house with an umbrella.

'Ain't you coming in, missus? It'll be dark any minute,' she said – holding the umbrella over Hester, as if she were not already so drenched that she inhabited a pool of water within her clothes. 'I'm put some good soup on – you could smell it from here if the rain weren't in the way.'

Hester pressed her hands to the small of her back as she straightened. 'Ow! I suppose I'd better come in. Jonathan, won't you have some soup? – I'm sure you could do with something.'

'Much obliged, Mrs Saunders,' Jonathan said, 'but I'm got to git back to the mill – the engine'll want firing.'

'Shall you have to be there all night?' Hester said. 'How will you sleep?'

'I'll tek a cat-nap once she's all stoked up,' said Jonathan. He looked about him, where a corner of the field like the hem of a handkerchief remained to be mown. 'I'll be here as soon as I can tomorrer.'

'Make sure you get some sleep,' she said. 'And Jonathan – thank you—' but already he was jogging back in the direction of the mill.

The rain did not stop that night. Jonathan ran the pump continually, until the mill-house sweltered and the steam ran down the walls, but still the water in the drain, bearing the burden of the Hinching Fen dykes, brimmed at the banks. Some time before dawn he snatched a doze on his mattress on the floor, but anxiety about the pump kept starting him awake with galvanic jerks, and always in his mind he was either shovelling coal or scything wheat. In the morning he dipped his head in a bowl of cold water to freshen him, swallowed some tea and hard-tack, and after stoking again ran over to put in a couple of hours' work on the harvest. He succeeded in getting the last of the wheat cut, and before he had to go back to the mill he stood a minute with Hester looking at the fields under their curtain of steady rain. Already the heads of the stooks, which had stood up like golden shaving-brushes, were draggled and drooping.

'It's like the summer's gone all wrong,' Hester said, leaning on her rake.

'I remember a downpour like this in '80,' said Jonathan. 'Best get the wheat carted as soon as you can.'

He meant to get back to the farm late that afternoon, but he was delayed when he found a boiler overheating: the feed-pipe was blocked and he had to dismantle it and clean it before he felt the engine was safe to leave for a while. It was early evening when he finally got over to the fields, and after a short remission it was raining again. Old Walt, after a day's carting, was getting ready to go home: his joints played him up in the wet. Billy Onyett stayed until it began to fall dark, but after that there was only Jonathan and Hester.

'Do you want to go in, Mrs Saunders?' Jonathan said.

'No – if you can stay a bit longer, Jonathan, I'll carry on,' she said. 'I'll fetch a storm-lamp: and I can go up on the cart.'

He hesitated. 'It's heavy work – are you sure . . . ?'

'I reckon I'm as strong as old Walt, and I can handle a hoss. Give me a budge up.'

Jonathan lifted her on to the cart; and they worked on into darkness. At last, returning to the stack-yard with the laden cart, Jonathan walking beside the horse's head saw Hester slumping over the reins.

'You're half asleep,' he said as she got down. 'This had better be the lot. Throw a rick-cloth over the load for tonight.'

'I am weary now,' she said, wiping an open hand across her face, child-like as one is when deeply tired. 'We're done well, though, haven't we?'

'Safely gathered in,' he said with a smile. 'Git going again early tomorrow. Shall I see to the hoss for you?'

'No, I can do that, Jonathan – you're done enough, you'll want your sleep. You will be able to get home for a proper rest tonight, won't you?'

'I should think so,' he said. 'Good night.'

But there was little chance of that. There was still scarcely a breath of wind to ripple the unrelenting rain, and he had to run the pump at the mill all night. Once, sitting down for a moment to rest, he fell asleep in the chair with his head against the wall, and woke sweating from a dream in which the boiler was about to explode and he was locked in the mill. He went outside to clear his head, and found that the rain had stopped. A few stars were reflected in the swollen drain.

'Now stay like that,' Jonathan said.

He went in, slept a good sleep on his mattress, and rose to find battalions of cloud re-forming, and the rain coming down.

All morning as he fed the boilers he chafed at the thought of the wet stooks in Hester's fields. If only Charlie Smeeth could mind the mill for him – but the boy would have his hands full at Henry Wake's, getting in the harvest there . . . At three o'clock he piled on coal, then flung on his jacket and left the pump working. The mill would have to manage by itself for a while – that was all there was to it.

Again he worked at carting till it was dark, and again he and Hester were the last, labouring on by lamplight. Once she raised her face to the sky and shook her fist. 'Oh, stop your damn everlasting rain!' she cried. 'Why d'you have to be so cruel?'

'I'm often done that myself,' Jonathan said. 'But I'm never got an answer.'

'D'you believe there's anyone up there to hear, Jonathan?' she asked him.

'I don't know. Sometimes I do. But whoever it is, I don't reckon he's the listening sort.'

'Neither do I,' said she. 'I'm glad I'm not the only one. And folk think you're wicked for that, don't they? As if you can choose not to believe.'

'You can choose not to give in,' Jonathan said. 'Thass what we're doing.'

'Yes.' She mopped back her dripping hair, then bent again to lift the unwieldy sheaves. 'I shan't give in.'

When he got back to the mill at ten, not having seen his

home for three days, he was startled to find a light within. Charlie Smeeth appeared, black with coal-dust.

'There you are, sir – hope you didn't mind – I come to see you and I lifted the latch and found the mill empty and the boilers had nearly gone out, so I stoked up – was that all right, sir?'

'Gone out?' said Jonathan with alarm.

'All but cold, sir – I got 'em going again.'

'You're a fine fellow, Charlie – you'll make a better miller than I some day,' Jonathan said. 'Run home to your bed now – you're earned it.'

When Charlie had gone Jonathan set about replenishing the boilers with an agitated mind. The consciousness of having neglected his duty, even briefly, was bitterest gall to him: the knowledge that most millers had their lax moments was no consolation to a nature which was both exacting and tinged with arrogance – that was well enough for *them*, but *he* should have known better. He set his face against any sleep that night. He was down beneath the floorboards oiling the pumps when there was a great hammering at the mill-house door, and he opened it to find Chad Langtoft there.

'Come quick, Miller,' Chad said. 'Milney Bank's busted – a gret crack big as a field-gate – Sunny Daintree and Henry Wake and me were bank-watching when we saw it. There's folk there trying to stem it but we s'll have a job.'

'I'll come,' Jonathan said, throwing on his jacket. 'God above, Milney Bank? The whole fen'll be drowned.'

'We're been watching it every night – Milney Drain's been full to the brim these three days. You got anything here we can tek to put in the breach?'

'Damn, not a thing,' Jonathan said. 'And raining still.'

They spoke little as they hurried along the path by the drain. Chad Langtoft seemed to have been trying to change his ways, and not drink so much: the change was since about the time of Lyle Saunders' death, and perhaps that was what had made him stop feeling sorry for himself and pull himself together, folk said – but instead he drank deeply of an intolerant brew of religion, which caused sudden outbursts about sin, and he took you up sharper than ever; so Jonathan had as few words with him as possible. His mind, moreover, was caught up at that moment with troubled thoughts of the harvest, and the precious root crops still unlifted.

He found a swarm of people at the breach in the drain bank, all talking at once – cursing, lamenting, suggesting, and arguing with each other in their alarm. A couple of horses and carts had been brought up, and all manner of miscellaneous material was being heaped into the breach like a barricade. Jonathan found himself shifting bags of cement, gate-posts, an old mattress, a gunning-boat, and numerous iron hurdles with which to shore the whole mess up, whilst Henry Wake ran round and round on his short legs, telling everybody to put everything everywhere else. But when someone finally illumined the shadowy scene, by lighting paraffin in a brazier so that a great white flare went up, Jonathan saw how feeble and how pathetic had been their efforts – the sad pile of homely goods from house and yard looking so childish, and presenting an eloquent image of the puniness of man's efforts against nature, once she decided to flex even indolently her muscles. Whilst the rain still poured from the sky, it was difficult to tell where the general wetness ended and the flow of flood-water began; but old Andrew Surfleet, standing beside Jonathan as he rested a moment, lifted the end of his stick with a fragment of weed sticking to it. 'No,' he said, shaking his head with the resignation of a lifelong war with flood, 'there wun't be a happy end to this one, Jonathan bor. You'd best jack your furniture up on bricks, and lay a plank for the puss-cat.'

Hester heard that Milney Bank had blown some time before dawn, when Billy Onyett called at the Crooked House on his way to the breach to pass on the news. Within a few minutes she was dressed and hurrying over there to see if there was anything to be done. There was a greyness in the sky, more like a weakening of darkness than the positive coming of light, when she arrived at the scene. A few people were still there, struggling to shore up the barricade in the crumbling bank-earth, but most had gone home to look to their own affairs as the water crept up. 'We shall be awash, missus,' Artie Gill said, at her inquiring look, 'thass the breadth of it – awash.'

383

Hester's mind flew to her hard-won harvest, with an almost maternal intensity of feeling. All that work gone to waste? All that labour, in which she had invested her bruised self and found some redemption, come to nothing? Suddenly she saw Jonathan, still striving to heap up the motley barrier, and called his name.

'Ain't there nothing to be done, Jonathan?'

'Not now she's blown,' Jonathan said. 'I reckon that late frost we had must have cracked the bank-earth. Well, no point in worrying about the mill now. I'll just have to shut down the engine till we get word from the Drainage Commissioners – can't pump into a breached drain – you're just pumping straight on to the fields.' He presented to her a grim smile. 'He didn't listen, did he? We were right.'

'At least we're got most of the wheat in,' Hester said. 'Oh, but all the taters, all the roots—' Potatoes were an increasingly precious fenland crop, and the loss of hers would be the most telling blow to her precarious solvency.

'Only one thing to do,' Jonathan said. 'Lift 'em all now, before they're quite ruined.'

She looked solemnly at him: she saw how his eyes had the raw stare of fatigue. 'Can we do it?' she said.

'I'm ready,' he said. 'I'm ready now.'

He walked back to the farm with her. He trudged slowly and, concerned at his tiredness, she suggested he go home and get some sleep first; but he would not hear of it, and by the time they reached the Crooked House, his stride had lengthened again, as if he had somehow tapped a fresh vein of vitality within him.

Walt, Billy Onyett, and a couple of day-men got on with the carting of the remainder of the wheat, and the mounting of the stacks on high staddles out of the wet, whilst Jonathan and Hester repaired to the root-fields.

The potato-fields, which had been a mass of purple flower in early summer, presented a bleak sight. The flooding of the fen was both dramatic and coolly impersonal. In the creeping up of the dun waters there was a dreadful and soul-blighting reversal, for those who had tilled the drowning fields with hope and sinew – but it was also, with harsh irony, a reversal to normality: the water was simply claiming its own. Across this colourless wash of landscape Hester and Jonathan moved with bent backs, grubbing up the cold potatoes from the mud, urgent and unthinking – fighting the hostile earth for food quite as elementally as if their sodden clothes were skins and furs, and their tools of bone and horn.

Hester learnt that day that discomfort, whilst never becoming anything more than discomfort, could yet be as afflicting as actual pain. She was up to her ankles in water; water still drizzled from the sky, running down her neck and back and breast and trickling from her very eyebrows; water chapped her hands, so that she could barely feel the haft of her fork. Whenever she straightened up to look round at the dreary scene about her, with the water steadily rising to the tops of the rows, there was a feeling in her lower back of taut threads being terribly tightened; and when she trudged back to the house for something to eat, the mud pulled at her boots with grotesque suckings, as if the earth begrudged her even the facility of walking.

Jonathan stayed out in the field, working on. She took him out a pork dumpling and new bread and hot tea and made him eat.

'You can't go on without food,' she said, finding what shelter there was under a thorn bush. 'Rest a while.'

Jonathan ate mechanically, occasionally putting out an upturned hand to feel the rain. 'Fighting on two fronts, thass the trouble,' he said. 'I reckon we'll git most of 'em up, though – if we just stick at it.'

'The house is all right, any road,' Hester said. 'That's one good thing about it standing up proud of the peat – the floors are higher than the flood. Oh! Jonathan – your cottage – won't the water come in?'

'A bit, mebbe,' he said. 'It won't hurt – the floor's loose brick, just made for floods, and there's no furniture that ain't got its feet wet before.' He bolted the last of his food. 'Thank you for that, Mrs Saunders. I'll set in again now.'

Back at the house Hester sat down for a few moments, pulling off her boots and stockings. Her feet and calves were as cold, wet and white as the new-dug potatoes. She leaned back, closed her eyes, and felt soft plumes of indifference caressing her and cajoling her to let go and give in. Her life, since her resolution to go on, had been a series of stepping-stones – each day of work, of managing and striving and succeeding, leading on to the next; but now as she stretched out her aching limbs, it seemed to her that she had come to the end of the stepping-stones, and the end of her capacity to care.

'Coh! missus, you look right trampled,' said Edie coming in. 'I'll fetch you some clean stockings. Walt says they'll git the last cart of corn in and stacked before sundown, don't you worry . . . Is the miller still in the tater-field, missus?'

'Yes, Edie.' Against her will, the vision of Jonathan's long-backed figure stooping along the flooded rows appeared on her closed lids. It was he who had roused her to wrestle with the farm, and set out a plan of salvation: was it up to him alone to carry it through to the end?

She sat up, put on the stockings that Edie brought her, and pulled on her boots. 'Back to work, Edie,' she said.

Billy Onyett joined them in the potato-field that afternoon, carting away the lifted roots to clamp, and later Edie came too, hopping along the rows in her white apron like a bright wagtail. Just before dusk the rain stopped, quite suddenly, and the day ended with a brief coda of streaky sunshine.

'It's a bit late for that, you ole beggar,' Hester said to the sky. 'Jonathan, you're done wonders, but you ought to go home. You can only do so much – we're got a fair few up.'

Jonathan glanced blankly round at her. His fatigue made him look bleached, as if he had been bled. 'I'll carry on a while,' he said. 'Water's still rising – these'll be drowned soon.'

He stayed out there after darkness fell, working by lamplight. Hester, after a bite of supper, sent Edie to bed – even her energy was exhausted – and then went round the stack-yard and looked at the tall covered ricks, the mound of roots. It was true: he had done wonders. The harvest, scrambled and part-spoiled as it was, had been got in, as much as was humanly possible. He could do no more.

She found him in the mangold-field. He did not know she was there until she touched his shoulder, and he started.

'Enough, Jonathan,' she said. 'Please. You're only flesh and blood—' As she said the word *blood* she looked down at his hands. The days of stoking the engines and labouring in the waterlogged field had left them rubbed raw. 'Oh! Jonathan – your hands – I didn't know . . . Come on. You must put something on them. I'm got some goose-grease in the house.'

Still crouched over the rows, Jonathan said, 'But these mangolds – and there's the turnips—'

'The stack-yard's nearly full,' Hester said. 'We're done it – I'll survive – truly. Come on . . . What is it?'

Jonathan winced and shook his head. 'I can't straighten up,' he said. 'Dear God – I shall be walking about like poor ole Andrew Surfleet.'

'It's the wet that's done it,' she said. Wet-harvesting, stooping for hours at a time in cold water, could send crippling pains shooting through the back and loins: she remembered Mr Langtoft saying he had once wept like a child with it. 'You must get dry. Come on – lean on me. Lean on my shoulder.'

He hesitated. 'I'm no feather, Mrs Saunders—'

'Well, I'm no weakling neither,' said she smiling. 'You're got to lean on someone every now and then, Jonathan – you can't always stand alone.'

Slowly they made their way back to the house, Jonathan hunched and hobbling, and in spite of his protests that he'd be off home in a minute she made him sit in the kitchen before the range, which was still hot, while she smeared the goose-grease on to his large cracked hands.

'First time I'm ever been waited on,' he said.

'It won't hurt you for once . . . Is it very bad – your back?' she said anxiously, seeing the sharp line between his brows.

'It – I'm known nicer feelings,' he said through clenched teeth.

'Mr Langtoft reckoned horse-oils made him feel easier. I know Walt keeps some. Could you bear to be treated like a hoss, d'you think?'

'Nay,' he said. He was in that gripping, startling pain which somehow squeezes the mind into a feeble flippancy. 'Well – if you don't mind . . .'

She found the horse-oils and, peeling up his shirt, rubbed the glistening stuff with her fingers into the skin of Jonathan's lower back. To the eye this smooth and well-shaped physique seemed scarcely susceptible to pain, and only the way the muscles twanged beneath her hands like tortured wires showed what he was suffering. The sight of him, so indomitably strong, reduced like this, and the knowledge that it was on her behalf, touched her with almost unbearable keenness; and she wished that her soul might speak out at her fingertips and soothe as deeply as she felt.

'Any better?' she said at length.

He nodded. 'Thank you . . . You're very kind.'

'It's me who should be thanking you, Jonathan – but it's like we were saying the other week: I just can't say my thanks any way equal to what I feel . . . As long as you know it. Now, drink this,' she said, mixing him a hot toddy of rum. 'I shan't forgive myself if you're gone and ruined yourself clawing up my harvest.'

'Right as rain in a while,' he said, swallowing the drink. 'Well – not rain.'

'No – definitely not rain,' she laughed. 'What an end to the summer . . . There'll be lots of crops spoiled on the fen, won't there? What will the Drainage Commissioners do?'

'They'll have to get some contractors to repair the breach in the bank properly. No good pumping till then – just have to wait for the water to go down.' Jonathan consulted his turnip watch. 'I'd better be moving.' He levered himself out of the chair, and by a great effort of will stood almost upright.

'Jonathan, are you sure? I mean – will you be all right?'

'I reckon so, Mrs Saunders. The horse-oils worked a treat. I ought to git home for once – my poor ole cat'll be hungry – 'less he's caught a fish in the street.'

She smiled. 'Well, don't come early tomorrow – d'you hear? This is me being sharp with you. And when you do come, I shall give you them wages at last – and you shan't turn 'em down this time. And if there should be a bonus there you'll take it – as a friend – like we said. D'you hear?'

'Right you are.' He walked stiffly to the door, then on the threshold turned, with a smile that was for the moment clear of pain. 'All safely gathered in, eh? Good night, Mrs Saunders.'

# Chapter Four

1

Within the barn behind the Crooked House, above a dozen people were gathering in a kindly October dusk. On the lintel above the door were fixed sheaves of wheat, signifying the harvest supper, or as it was known in the fens, the horkey.

This was a special horkey. The idea for it had grown in Hester's mind out of her increasing desire to do something to say thank you to all the people who had helped her in the first stricken months of her widowhood; and the generally gloomy state of Hinching Fen following the flood offered another motive. If it had been a bad year, then she reasoned – with an echo of her old gaiety of spirit – that there was all the more need for a little junketing; and her harvest had been better than most. And so all the friends who had worked for her or helped or offered to help or had simply been consoling landmarks in a waste of despair were invited to the farm to eat and drink as hugely as they might at the long trestle tables in the lamplit barn, which was the only place big enough to hold them.

Hester and Edie had been busy all day preparing the feast, and Lizzie Gosling had come over in the afternoon to lend a hand. Working beside her in the kitchen, Lizzie had paused and taken Hester by the elbow and held her at arm's length.

'Let's have a look at you, then,' Lizzie said. 'Let's see how the land lies.'

Hester smiled at Lizzie's dark, clever, tolerant face. 'What d'you see then?'

'Well, I see a human – thass summat,' said Lizzie.

'Didn't you before, then?' Hester said, smiling, but soberly. Lizzie shook her head. 'Not really. Midsummer I was frit to see you . . . You was like a shadow what had been torn away from the person it belonged to.'

'Was I? I suppose that's how I felt,' Hester said. 'I didn't think I'd ever climb up. I did – but not on my own . . . I'm not frit any more, Lizzie – not always sort of flinching at life. It's like a skin's grown back somewhere. There's still a sort of hollow feeling, right deep inside, and I don't reckon that can ever change. But I know I'm going to go on – and that there's years ahead, waiting to be dealt with, and I'm not afraid of 'em.'

So it was: she had climbed up, most of all out of the clinging entrapment of self, and it was a great satisfaction to her to see the company sit down at the trestle tables, and attack the eatables with a flattering lack of ceremony. The food was all set out along the centre, between vases of flowers sprigged with corn-ears, and the idea was that if there was something you could not reach, you hollered for it to be passed down to you: thus Hester and Edie could sit down with the rest, and did not have to wait on them. Hams and legs of cold roast pork formed the mainstay of the supper, but there were pork pies, bowls of boiled eggs, pickled onions jostling to the lip of the jar, potatoes speckled with mint, new bread and new butter like two extremes of gold, apple and plum pies and tarts as deep as tubs, and an abundance of ale still with the cold sweat of the Crooked House's peaty cellar on the jars. Hester sat at the head, with Edie and Charlie Smeeth on either side; Henry Wake had characteristically appropriated the other end of the table (Mrs Wake remaining as usual incommunicado) and was ostentatiously carving for Peggy Chettle, who had left her bicycle in the stable just as if it were a beast of the manger, and whose great teeth crunched upon onions with a noise like breaking brushwood. Artie Gill had brought his fiddle, but was not drunk enough yet to play it, and was grumpily denying to Sunny Daintree that he was going to play at all; Andrew Surfleet and Mrs Surfleet gnawed diminutively, like two hoary squirrels, and reminisced with old Walt through a long backward succession of horkeys; Lizzie Gosling and her brother Jack came in for all Billy Onyett's broadest, cheesiest jokes.

Only Jonathan was not there. He had sent word that he might be delayed, having been called to a special meeting of the Drainage Commissioners in Stokeley. Since the repair of Milney Bank he had been almost continually occupied at the mill, running the pump to clear the last of the flood waters. His absence could not be helped; yet it seemed to Hester that a harvest supper at the Crooked House – after those labours of his for which the word heroic was alone appropriate – was sadly incomplete without him.

'How did Jonathan go to Stokeley, do you know, Charlie – on the carrier?' Hester asked Charlie Smeeth.

'I dunno, missus – I doubt it – anythink less'n ten mile he goes on his legs. He had his best clo'es on the smorning, any road – I went to show him mine – and he said my blue gansy was an out-and-outer, he did!' concluded Charlie, with a modest reference to his neckerchief.

'Best blue gansy and a hole in his trews,' Edie said, with sisterly disesteem. 'Honestly, Charlie Smeeth, what an item you are wi' that gret tater sticking out your knee.'

'I couldn't help it – I tunnied over on the way here.'

'I dunno,' Edie said. 'Only you could fall over on a flat road in broad daylight. I dunno what you'd do if you lived where there was hills!'

'I should think I should fall over like fun,' said Charlie, with equal humility and logic.

'You were hurrying to get here, I should think, Charlie,' Hester said. 'And I take that as a very nice compliment.'

'Thass a pity the lad's so awk'ud in his limbs, though,' Sunny Daintree said. 'Ooh! dear. I wouldn't be a bit surprised if he's outgrowing his strength. I knew a lad like that once, as had to tek to his bed when he turned sixteen, and lay there like a gret daddy-long-legs for a whull year, waiting for his strength to catch up, and tekking his meals through a straw.'

'I'm strong – I am,' said Charlie. 'It's just me feet go on too long.'

'And one's bigger than tother,' Edie said.

'That wun't hurt,' said Andrew Surfleet. 'It gives a body a bit o' character. "Fearfully and wonderfully made", thass what the psalm says we are – fearfully and wonderfully made. Why, one of my legs goes up higher than tother, at the top: I can't recall which one it is, just on the tip o' the moment, but I know it's one on 'em – and it don't seem to go no further down, but it surely goes up higher than tother one at the top – don't it, gel?' he said to his wife.

'Andrew,' Mrs Surfleet said, affrontedly, 'don't talk Sauce.'

'They're mebbe giving Miller a bonus, for all the work he's put in,' said Billy Onyett.

'Ah! he belongs to git a bit of recognition,' Andrew Surfleet said. 'A boon – thass what he's been. Not as I weren't a bit frit of him at fust – the way he used to frown down at you from atop o' them gret shoulders; but thass more manner than meaning.'

'Well, I'm a married woman,' Peggy Chettle said, 'and I'd not trade Chettle, even with his little trouble: but if I was a few dark hairs younger, and bare-fingered, and forward with it – why, wouldn't I give that miller a buss! – and never mind cheeks neither!'

The barn was, at least in part, considerably older than the Crooked House itself. The far stone wall was pierced by high narrow ogive windows, through which the late sunlight was syringed in honey-coloured concentration, revealing lofty and massive roof-beams hung with immemorial cobwebs as heavy as tapestry. The great door stood open to the quiet evening, and from time to time a sparrow would flit in and out, as casually as if it were passing beneath a canopy of trees. The smooth floor of the barn standing well proud of the earth, the feasters within bore an air of being slightly larger than life, and uplifted above the mortal – an impression reinforced by a general haze and bloom of straw-dust which, teeming in the orange light, seemed to make their every gesture magnified and deliberate, as in a half-way house between men and gods. There was no doubt that, after the ache and fret of the wet harvest, and with the pinch of winter lying ahead, all felt their present situation at the convivial table could scarcely be more desirable; and Billy Onyett declared that if he didn't eat his length in rashers, he'd never trust his teeth more.

'A sad sight to see, Milney St Mary church all closed and boarded as it is,' Sunny Daintree said. 'It's all to be turned innards-out, vicar says: restoration they call it. I know the screen were like a lace-hankercher wi' worm.'

'It's hard for church-folk,' said Henry Wake, resplendent in a high and roomy starched collar into which his head periodically sank up to the eyebrows. 'Us chapel-folk can go to church if we will, but church-folk can't be doing with chapel – rather like a cat can't follow a mouse through a mousehole, though the mouse can go through the cat-flap. Thass what you call a similitude, you know.'

'I call it stuff,' grunted Artie Gill. 'Cats and mice, indeed!' He was tetchy because no one had asked him to play his fiddle lately, and given him the pleasure of refusing.

'Ah, thass a heathenish thing to lack a church, even if you don't go to it,' Sunny Daintree said. 'What we could do with is that there floating church coming down our river.'

'Why, whass that then?' said Andrew Surfleet, open-mouthed.

'Thass a barge, bor, all roofed over like, where they hold church services,' Sunny said, forking up a vast slice of ham and chewing it in like a goat eating a newspaper. 'Vicar over Ely way had it built, reckoning as a lot of folk out on the lone fen weren't gitting benefit of clergy; and he sails it from place to place, and fetches folk aboard, to top 'em up wi' religion. I'm seen it moored at Pondersbridge – the Fenland Ark they call it. Pews and all, and a little organ sounding off the note, just like a real one.'

'Well, I don't know about that,' said Andrew, with a glance of wonderment at his wife. 'That can't be right. A church has got to be on consecrated ground, don't it? Thass not on any ground!'

'Well, there's pews,' Sunny said. 'I can answer for the pews; and thass church enough for me.'

'The water's consecrated, I dare say,' said Henry Wake comfortably. 'I think you'll find thass what they'd do – consecrate the waters.'

'Why, holy water's Popish, ain't it?' said Andrew, alarmed. 'Chaps in night-shirts, sprinkling it out of salt-cellars – I'm seen it in a book. No, no – none of that for me: old Oliver Grumble'd squirm in his casket.'

'I should like to see that there Ark,' Charlie Smeeth said

with energy. 'I never do see things somehow – like when a balloon went over, from Pete'borough Fair, and I missed it on account of just when I were looking up, a little fly flew right in my eye, and the balloon had gone over by the time I come un-blind again.'

'Ah – it's wicked when a fly goes in your eye like that,' said Andrew. 'You just see it coming before it plunges in – and it's almost like it's aiming for you!'

'Terrible queer case for the fly, an' all,' Sunny said. 'Meeting its end in a gret eye. Ooh! dear – just think on it – with the gret lashes flapping round you . . . I shall likely have a bad dream about that tonight,' he added to himself, 'I wouldn't be a bit surprised.'

'Well, now, neighbours,' Henry Wake said, loudly clearing his throat and getting to his feet, which brought him about level with Peggy Chettle sitting down, 'I hope you're all got a drop in your mugs: I reckon a toast's in order. I'm not a man of many words meself, but if I might just say a very few—'

'You might,' said Artie Gill in an undertone, 'but I bet you won't.'

'I'm sure we'd all like to raise our sups to Mrs Saunders, for laying on such a do,' Henry continued, 'all the better for coming after a poor ole time what we'll none of us be sorry to see the tail of, not to mention a particular sad time for one among us, which we won't allude to, which is to say except with sincerest respect, which we all feel, which I'm sure of.' Becoming rather entangled in whiches, Henry coughed and disappeared into his collar for a moment. Surfacing again, he went on: 'And I'm sure there's a lesson to us all, laid out in this here tasteful spread, and the hospitality of neighbours, what we'll all lay to our souls . . .' Billy Onyett chose this moment to launch a sulphurous belch, as a suave hint that Henry was somewhat losing his audience; and Henry concluded at the gallop: 'Which I mean to convey as it were, a toast to Mrs Hester Saunders, and good health to her!'

They cheered and drank. Hester, profoundly moved, found herself rigid with unaccustomed shyness; and at last was only able to stammer out, half laughing, 'Oh – you're very kind, and thank you – and I can't think what to say except thank you again – and have another drink, do – and – won't you play your fiddle when you're ready, Artie?'

Amid the general laughter and the commotion as Artie Gill at last struck up a tune, Hester was able surreptitiously to wipe her eyes – she still had a strange dread of being seen in tears – and to present a tolerably composed face when Edie asked her in a whisper, 'Shall I clear all these here broken meats, missus?'

'No, leave them, Edie,' Hester said. 'Folk'll mebbe get a second appetite after a few dances. You can fetch some more ale, though: it'll all soon get sweated out, and we want plenty for Jonathan when he comes.'

There was space at the end of the barn for dancing, on what had been the threshing-floor, and here Artie Gill mounted on an upturned bran-tub and poured forth jigs and reels. Lizzie Gosling, laughing with her eyes though not her lips, footed it with Billy Onyett, in his tipsiness as limber as an eel; Lizzie's brother Jack danced with Edie, who seemed to be on springs; the ancient Surfleets slowly trod some decorous measure of their own, which might have been danced in powdered perukes and face-patches, and which gave the venerable couple the appearance of the little mechanical figures that come beetling out of twin doors on clock-faces to strike the hour; whilst Peggy Chettle and Henry Wake stood up together, after a brief discussion as to its propriety. 'Bless you, dear man, two old married bodies like us, who're known each other practically since Ballyclava,' said Mrs Chettle, 'not to mention my trade, where I'm seen more britches down than up, and it don't mean no more to me than the sight of a dabbling duck – why, it's as innocent as lambs,' and she proceeded to engulf Henry's hands in her own, and fling him about like someone shaking out a feather pillow. Charlie Smeeth, with the uneasy aloofness of his years at such an occasion, looked on at a distance; and perceiving this, Hester engaged him in conversation, accepting that her own place now was as an onlooker, with quietude, and with a certain wistfulness that she was glad to find was not bitter.

At length Artie Gill paused in his fiddling to take a long pull of ale. 'A pity Miller's not here with his squeeze-box,' said Andrew Surfleet. 'He used to be shy as a man having his teeth drawn about it, but he'll play now, if you ask him.'

Hester consulted the watch at her waistband. Where was Jonathan? It wasn't fair if those old buffers were keeping him at the Commissioners' meeting all this time.

All at once there was a cheer as Billy Onyett appeared holding aloft a broomstick he had fetched from the yard. 'Show us, Sunny,' he said, handing the broomstick to Sunny Daintree, who shook his head and groaned from the very depths of his soul, 'give us the broomstick dance!'

'Ooh! I don't know,' Sunny sighed, as the others joined their voices in calling for the broomstick dance. 'I ain't done that since the ole Queen's last jubilee, and I swore then I wouldn't never do it again, not if she asked me herself with her crown on.'

'Goo on, Mr Daintree,' Charlie Smeeth said, 'I'm never seen it – I missed the jubilee being laid up wi' the chicken-pox and all I had was a paper flag on the bed-post – goo on, do.'

'Well, if I'm got to,' said Sunny, ambling with the broomstick on to the threshing-floor, as Artie Gill struck up a fast jig. 'Ooh! I'm too old for this game – I shall rue it – I shall never bend to me mole-traps in the morning—' Abruptly Sunny ceased his moans, and sprang into an astonishing dance: grasping the handle of the broomstick with the besom resting on the floor before him, and executing a series of hops, throwing first one leg and then the other over the broom, and going faster and faster as the onlookers clapped in time, until his capering legs were almost a blur – all the time wearing the expression of a man performing some humdrum and slightly distasteful task which he will be glad to get over with. It was doubtful who would weaken first, Artie fiddling or Sunny dancing, but at the last it was Artie, breaking off the music with a despairing cadence, whilst Sunny went on to execute a few final unaccompanied leaps before dropping the broomstick and retiring with gloomy head-shakings to his seat amid the applause.

'No,' he said, sipping his ale, 'I tole you I couldn't do it.'

While the others resumed the dancing, Hester looked at her watch again and spoke to Edie. 'It's funny Jonathan not being here yet,' she said: happy as she was that the horkey was going so well, she missed his presence sharply. 'I wonder if he's all right.'

'D'you want me to run and see if he's home yet, missus?' said Edie. 'I can be there and back in two shakes.'

'No – it's all right, Edie – I reckon I'll slip down to the village myself. I'm got an idea he might not like to turn up so late – you know how particular he can be about such things. Everything's all right here,' she said, looking at the pounding dancers. 'Make sure everyone's got enough to drink, Edie – I won't be long.'

Hester stepped into the house to put on her hat, and walked across the stubble-fields, soaked in the autumn afterglow, to Milney St Mary. At Jonathan's cottage, before knocking, she glanced in at the window. He was there; seated in his hard chair before the cold hearth, staring intently into the middle distance, with his shirt-sleeved elbows upon his knees, and his pipe loosely held in his cupped hands. Immediately she had a sensation of being flung back in time – the scene reminded her so forcibly of the very first time she had ever seen Jonathan, through the smoke of that waterside inn to which her wanderings had brought her. What a strange, foolish, long-ago creature she saw in herself then! Hard on the heels of this impression came another – that Jonathan had been home some time, and had ignored her invitation to the horkey. This idea hurt her, and she stood in hesitation a moment immobilised by the pain of it, undecided whether to knock after all. But something odd about the way he was sitting there by the ashes turned the question for her. He answered her knock after a few moments: he looked more preoccupied than surprised.

'Mrs Saunders.'

'Hullo, Jonathan. I – we wondered where you were.'

'Ah. Of course. Will you come in?'

She entered the spartan house-place, all softened with dusky shadows. A kitten came to her, and she picked it up and gave it her finger to bite.

'Will you have a seat?' Jonathan said.

'It's all right, Jonathan – I'm just come to ask if you won't come along to the horkey. I know it's a bit late, but it don't matter – everybody's still kicking up their heels, and there's lots of ale—'

'I'm sorry, Mrs Saunders – I should have sent a message.' Jonathan drew away from her and leaned his arm on the mantelshelf. 'I'm had a bit of a day of it, to tell the truth.'

'Oh, did you have a long meeting with the Commissioners? We were just saying, at the horkey, how you might be getting a bonus for all your extra work—'

'Nothing like that,' he said, with a twitch of a smile. 'I'm afraid I shan't be miller for Hinching Fen no more: they give me the sack.'

For a second she thought he must be joking. 'Jonathan . . . No! Why? How can they?'

'Oh . . .' Jonathan worked his hand through his hair, shrugged, and seemed about to dismiss it. 'Something and nothing.'

'But they must have a reason!'

Frowning down at the floor, Jonathan said: 'Failing in your duty's what they call it. It was the time of that downpour – before the bank broke. Somebody came to the mill when I weren't there – when I'd left it unattended: whether it was one of the Commissioners, or just a busybody, I don't know. It don't matter: it got back to 'em that I were neglecting the mill just at the worst time, with the drain filling – and so I'm to be dismissed.'

'Thass ridiculous. You all but broke your back keeping that mill going – anybody round here'll say so—' She stopped and bit her lip. 'Oh! Jonathan – it was when you were helping me. It was when you were getting my harvest in – that must have been it – oh, I feel awful . . . Jonathan, I'm so sorry . . .'

'No, no,' said he shortly, shaking his head, avoiding her eyes. 'It don't matter – it can't be helped.'

'But your job . . . Anybody on Hinching Fen'll vouch for you: I will. Yes, can't I go to the Commissioners—?'

'It's no good, Mrs Saunders. Fact is, I reckon the whole situation was ripe for a scapegoat. Milney Bank should never have bust like it did: it seems likely the Commissioners weren't seeing to the upkeep of the banks like they should have, and

398

I reckon they knew it. Just bad luck my head has to roll. In any case, once they had me up on the carpet like that . . . well, let's just say I was damned if I were going to beg and plead at 'em for the job,' he said with harsh pride.

'Quite right too!' Hester said. 'It's a terrible pity – I know how you liked that job . . . but any road, it's their loss. You know you don't have to worry about a living while I'm got the farm – at least I know a good man when I see one: and now I'm got set on my feet, we can think about you being a proper farm bailiff, and—'

'No, Mrs Saunders, I'm sorry,' Jonathan said quickly. 'I can't do that. I was going to tell you – I can't work for you any more.'

'Have you got another job?' she said, putting down the kitten.

'No, not yet, but I'll find one of some sort.' He took a spill from the mantelshelf and toyed with it.

Hester regarded him steadily: still he would not look at her. 'It's because you lost your miller's job on my account,' she said. 'I see that – I feel terrible about it, Jonathan, really—'

'No, it ain't that,' he said. 'Honestly, it ain't that at all.'

'Then what is it?' she said, taking a step closer to him.

'I just think it's best I don't go on working for you, Mrs Saunders,' Jonathan said, drawing himself up stiffly. 'I'm glad the farm's all secure now – and I was glad to do what I could to help set it up. And now you're all right, I reckon I'll look for work elsewhere.'

His coolness was utterly dismaying to her. It seemed to thrust her backwards – back towards the dry, empty, self-imprisoned days which she thought she had left behind; and all the small, healing triumphs she had made appeared suddenly hollow. She could hardly believe that the man who had shown such a discreet and delicate touch upon her flinchingly sore feelings should now turn about and hurt her in this way. She struggled to speak.

'Jonathan, I don't understand – I thought you were my friend . . . I really thought you were my friend.'

Jonathan snapped the spill between his fingers. 'No offence, Mrs Saunders,' he said, speaking briskly and yet looking everywhere but at her. 'I'm grateful for all the work you give me, and truly there's no bad feeling towards you over me losing the mill job – I would have done exactly the same if I'd known that was going to happen. But I really think it's best for all concerned if I git work elsewhere from now on. I'm happy you're got things on an even keel, and I hope they stay so – I'm sure they will. Sorry about the horkey, but I'm a bit weary-limbed.' The frown and the lowering of his heavy lids seemed to make his eyes physically withdraw, as if in token of his greater withdrawal from her.

She did not understand; and the coldness seemed all the sharper after the warm and genial feelings of that day. 'Well,' she said quietly. 'If you say so.' Her dismay was too great even to allow her to challenge him, and something – perhaps maturity – inhibited her from wantonly throwing back the darts of pain from her own breast. The room had passed from dusk to darkness as they talked, and she fumbled blind for the door-latch. 'Goodbye, then,' she said, and stumbled out before she could hear his reply.

## 2

Gentle autumn gave birth to a stern, gaunt, thrustful winter, who howled in chill winds through the broken slates and decayed window-frames of the Crooked House, and reminded Hester that she must begin to turn her mind to the state of the buildings, now that the farm as an economic concern was moderately secure. She was far from approaching a condition of luxury – there were no fortunes to be made with wheat twenty-six shillings a quarter – but neither was she in debt; and at the banker's and solicitor's she noted some raising of grizzled eyebrows at the way she had put through a programme of retrenchment and brought the farm round to solvency so smartly. What, she wondered, had these men expected? Did they suppose she would squander herself bankrupt on frocks and hats as soon as she was out of six months' mourning? It was a pleasure to feel the rebirth of this feisty scepticism within her: she found that, imperceptibly, she had ceased to be intimidated by the panelled offices and wing-collars – and it must have shown, for now a clerk was always despatched respectfully to conduct her out to the little spring-cart in which she had invested.

She had bought that for a song, too, having successfully beaten down the farmer who sold it to her; the thriftiness which had been a life-sustaining challenge was now a habit. Unhappily, she no longer found the same satisfaction in it. She had left behind the dark valleys of bereaved and helpless grief, and now found herself on a plateau of neutral acceptance, featureless to the view, and leading nowhere in particular – a prospect comfortably without threat, but seeming to offer nothing to engage the powers of her reviving soul. The work of the farm went on in the cold and overcast days – ploughing and drilling, all the potatoes to be riddled and the wheat threshed – there was always enough to do to keep her busy twenty hours a day if she chose; and at first she thought the tang of weariness was nothing new. Only gradually did she come to see that this sensation of being utterly alone, of forever feeling the yoke of life pressing down on her sole shoulders, was not a continuation of the helplessness of her bereavement: that had been left behind, and this was something new. Only gradually did she come to realise how acutely the loss of Jonathan's friendship affected her, and in the process to perceive the strengths of that friendship, which at the time had been as the stout unseen keel of a buoyant ship.

And it was in working the farm that she missed it most: in work – demanding, satisfying, undertaken side by side – their friendship had struck roots. On Jonathan she had relied without depending; in him she had confided, with no furtive feeling of thrusting secrets on an unwilling ear, and she had been rewarded with a reciprocal confidence, as natural as the earth they tilled together. It was this unforced and organic quality about their friendship that made the absence of it so disorientating, and caused her mind to worry at it like a tongue probing the gap of a missing tooth; and left her pensively puzzling over Jonathan's decision, and how it was that he so coolly accepted a withdrawal which was to her a disabling wrench.

The explanation that occurred most insistently to her was Jonathan's pride. If she was to believe his assertion that he did not blame her for the loss of his miller's job – and to imagine Jonathan lying was like imagining the stars being made of tinsel – then the most plausible reason for his refusing to work for her was that he was simply too proud; that to continue taking work from her, once the crisis was over, would seem to him like taking charity – and their friendship would make the situation all the more uncomfortable. This accorded well with what she knew was a sternly, sometimes bleakly honourable nature; and yet it did not quite fit. He must know that she needed labour, that Billy Onyett was more well-meaning than reliable, and that there would be quite as much commonsense as gratitude in her employing the man who had almost single-handedly saved her harvest. Surely he must see that.

She was troubled too by thoughts of how Jonathan was managing without his steady miller's wage. There was much sympathy and good feeling towards him on Hinching Fen, and the new miller, a droopy object who had come over from Norfolk where they all had chalk for brains, was poorly thought of; but it was the lean season, and work was thin on the ground. In December Sunny Daintree, who acted as the local rat-catcher, came to rat the stack-yard at the Crooked House, and Hester took the opportunity to ask him what Jonathan was doing.

'Turns his hand to whatever's going, I reckon, missus,' said Sunny. 'A while ago he did blackbelly-picking for that chap as comes down from Wisbech wi' the baskets and pays you by the pound – starve-gut sort of work: but he's been on the land as well, stone-picking here, digging gault there. Ooh! they're narrow sort of times, these, missus: I'm not sure as we shall ever squeeze through 'em. And now chaps going off to fight these here Boo-ers over tother side of the world – don't ask me why – there's enough battles near at hand without going looking for 'em. Old Gladstone would never have allowed it. Ooh! dear. If there's better coming, it's on tother side of a pile of worst.'

Even allowing for Sunny's habit of looking on the dark side, this was a discouraging report of Jonathan. Its shadow touched an otherwise convivial Christmas that Hester kept at the Crooked House with Lizzie and Jack Gosling, and it lingered into a freezing, flint-hearted new year, until a chance remark one day galvanised her, and set her quiescent emotions on end like hackles.

The steam threshing-tackle was making its tour of the farms, and benevolently signalling its progress by flattening out the rutted, ankle-turning surface of the winter droves. While the machine was at Henry Wake's, Hester went over to see the engineer and fix the date when he should come to the Crooked House for the threshing of her wheat. This engineer was a coaly, sinewy, taciturn man, who worked as hard as he drank; and Edie Smeeth informed Hester later that day that he had been thrown out of the Labour In Vain the other night.

'Too drunk, was he?' Hester said.

'Oh! no,' Edie said, 'he couldn't git drunk enough – thass what it was – he reckoned Jass Phelps were watering the beer, 'cause he'd had six pints and he couldn't feel no difference – so there was a bit of name-calling, and he were turfed out. I don't know whether it's true about the beer, but they reckon Jass Phelps can't afford to lose custom like that, what wi' Chad Langtoft mending his ways and going all funny and religious instead of supping, and then the miller-as-was refusing to set foot in the place any more.'

'Jonathan? Why's that, Edie?'

'Oh!' Edie suddenly flushed from nape to scalp. 'It were – it were just a quarrel – I dunno.'

'Jonathan quarrelling?' Hester said. 'No, I don't believe it. Edie . . . come on, tell me.'

'Oh – I don't like to say, missus.' Edie swallowed, as visibly as a frog. 'It was just . . . well, they reckon Jass Phelps – you know what he's like – said summat about how Jonathan seemed to be keeping his distance nowadays from – from that pretty widow at the Crooked House, and how it was about time too, and it looked like he wasn't going to get his legs under her table after all. Thass Jass Phelps saying it, not me, missus! And they reckon Jonathan didn't say nothing, just got hold of Jass Phelps by his neckercher, and picked him right up till his boots weren't touching the floor – and then it was as though he

403

thought better of it, and let him go like a sack of taters, and he walked out and won't go back there no more . . . I'm sorry, I didn't want to say it, missus . . .'

'Well, I did ask you, Edie,' Hester said gently.

But she wished she had not: or at least, wished that she had not heard, or . . . She did not know what to think. How mean and stupid people could be! She remembered how careful Jonathan had been of her reputation before. No wonder he had half throttled Jass Phelps: she felt like it herself. The tale certainly threw some light on why Jonathan had elected not to work for her any more . . . but the substance of her reaction to it was a sad disgust at the friendship she had valued being chewed and mangled in gossiping mouths. It seemed more than ever a pitiable waste of what was good and true.

It was the chill middle of February, the time of the year that most closely corresponds to the small hours of the night, when all the faculties of life are at their lowest ebb, and the merest pulsebeat differentiates the sleeper in darkness from death: thus it was with the earth, frozen beneath an overpowering leaden sky. This sky, plainly stored with snow, yet remained obstinately dry, as if even to release the flakes would be a relenting – an adulteration of pure winter. In the stack-yard of the Crooked House the steam-engine that ran the thresher throbbed and rumbled, throwing out sparks that hissed upon the frosted cobblestones, and Hester, pulling on her gloves and pinning a muffler round her throat preparatory to going out, watched Billy Onyett and Walt begin feeding the first sheaves into the machine. Billy, looking unsteady on the vibrating platform, did not care for this work: what a pity Jonathan was not here – how he would sail through it as if it were nothing! Yet she had resolved that her feeling of loyalty towards Jonathan would not be wasted in regrets: if he would not work for her, then she would help him to other work – extend to him a supporting hand, as he had disinterestedly done to her, even if she could only do so by proxy. She had recently learned that Lyle could have served as a Drainage Commissioner for Hinching Fen, as the farm was of the required acreage. Characteristically, he had not bothered; but as the property was now hers, she had a right to attend the Commissioners' meetings (even though there would surely be resistance to a woman being actually sworn in as a Commissioner) and take part in their decisions. And amongst those decisions was who should run the Hinching Fen mill.

So she drove the little spring-cart to Stokeley, and sat down with the Commissioners in a private room at the Spread Eagle; and in spite of their efforts to asphyxiate her with pipe-smoke, and drown her out with jingling watch-chains, and generally put paid to her with a great parade of velvet-waistcoated, round-bellied, patronising masculinity, she patiently persisted in raising the matter of Jonathan Eastholm's dismissal from the post of miller, and stating why she believed it to be a mistake. She referred for testimony to the many small proprietors of Hinching Fen, and drew attention to the deficiencies of the new miller; and she found an ally in Farmer Mather, who said he had always opposed the decision. An old buffer who sported a huge bristly moustache, as if he were inhaling a hedgehog, began to come round to her way of thinking, though it seemed he was impressed more by her pretty ankles than her arguments; and the meeting adjourned with an agreement to inspect thoroughly the work of the new miller, and if he was found to be unsatisfactory, to consider reinstating Jonathan Eastholm in the post.

This was vague enough, but solid enough too: Hester had regained enough of her old self-belief to be convinced that she could completely settle the matter at the next meeting, with a combination of advocacy and ankle-work; and she was so pleased with her success that she decided to take the news at once to Jonathan herself. She knew that he was currently doing casual labour for the masons who were restoring Milney St Mary church, and so from Stokeley she drove straight to the village, descending from the spring-cart at the churchyard gate, and hitching the pony to the yew-tree fence.

She saw Jonathan at once on entering the churchyard. He was engaged in sawing up into disposable pieces a section of the old removed screen, which he had propped upon two ancient gravestones a few feet apart, as if on a workbench. Other broken and disjointed fragments of the church interior littered the churchyard: in this energetic destruction of ecclesiastical ornament there would have been much to please the eye of Cromwell's soldiers, who in this very corner of Anglia had done the very same thing for different reasons, two hundred and fifty years since. Everything around Jonathan was bleached and colourless – the white splintered heart of the timber he sawed, the weathered tombstones, the gravel and grass all gripped by profound frost, even his own soda-white shirt; yet the tan of summer harvesting seemed scarcely to have faded from him at all, and the skin of his bare forearms was as smooth and brown as a hen's egg. So pleased was she to see him in that so typical posture of tensile yet graceful labour – the freshness of his colour like a memory of summer made flesh – that she called out 'Jonathan!', suddenly and involuntarily, making him start.

'Oh! I'm sorry,' she said, drawing near, 'what a fool – I might have made you cut your finger off.'

'How do, Mrs Saunders,' he said, suspending the saw. 'Were you looking for someone?'

'Yes, you,' she said.

'Ah?'

She scarcely noticed his wary tone. 'Jonathan, I'm got some good news for you – any road, I think it's good news, though perhaps I shouldn't count my chickens . . .' She told him of her meeting with the Drainage Commissioners, and her efforts to get the miller's job back for him. 'Of course, they're got to stroke their whiskers and hum and haw about it for a while, because they don't like to admit they were wrong. But I reckon the ole beggars have learnt their lesson – and come the next meeting I wouldn't be a bit surprised, as Sunny says, if they made a decision to ask you to be miller again.'

Jonathan was silent for some moments, brushing sawdust from his hands. 'Well, it's very good of you, I'm sure,' he said at last.

He did not sound glad: he sounded almost surly. 'Don't you – don't you want your old job back?' she said.

'Oh! I dare say.'

His face was dark and set. Surprised, she said, 'I thought you'd be pleased.'

'Like I say, it's very good of you . . . I'm sure you meant

406

well,' Jonathan said curtly. He picked up the saw again, as if to resume his work – as if to dismiss her. For a moment, crestfallen and bewildered as she was, she was speechless.

'What am I done wrong?' she said finally. 'Jonathan—' All at once the sight of his broad back made her angry. 'Jonathan, will you please stop ignoring me? I just don't understand you. Tell me, if I'm done the wrong thing. I only meant to—'

'Don't you see?' he said, turning on her. 'Don't you see how this will seem? Don't you realise what folk are going to say about me taking favours from you? Think how folk will talk about you. Think, Mrs Saunders.'

'I don't care what folk say,' she said quite calmly. 'That don't matter a bean to me, Jonathan. I told you before.' As he made a brusque gesture she went on: 'Why should it matter? There's things that are so much more important. Like being true to a true friend. Jonathan, you half crippled yourself helping me get my harvest in – you did everything for me so selflessly – how can I just forget that? I wanted to help you in return and now I'm found a way. How can there be anything wrong with that?'

Jonathan did not speak, but leaned his arms upon the broken screen, his eyes lowered.

Hester's disappointment was complete; but now she was determined to speak out. The chill of these long months since he had so bafflingly withdrawn from her – she could bear it no longer. 'I know you're a proud sort of man,' she said. 'But this ain't a question of favours. I felt so glad about maybe getting you your old job back. Same as I did about you carrying on working at the farm. I still don't understand the way you – well, the way you turned so cold and hard on me. All this time I'm thought about that. It was almost as if you wanted to hurt me.'

'No, no,' he said quickly. 'No, not that.'

'Well, I'm glad,' she said. 'But it seemed that way . . . It still does. Why?'

All at once Jonathan gave a deep bass sigh, and surprised her with a gentle smile. 'Life can be a wry business sometimes,' he said. 'The very person you don't want to hurt is the one you end up hurting . . . I'm sorry if that's the impression I gave

407

you: though in a way I'm not, because that's the impression I wanted to give, I suppose . . . but I shall have to say it now. The thing is, you see – all that time when I helped you at the farm, I wanted it to be absolutely plain that this was a practical arrangement – no strings, like. I couldn't bear it to seem like I was – well, taking advantage. Looking out for what I could get . . . It didn't seem that way, did it?' he said with sudden appeal, his brows puckered.

'Why, no,' she said earnestly. 'Never.'

'Well, that's it, you see,' Jonathan said. 'I had to stop working for you – being with you – when I realised I couldn't be disinterested any more. You said about me acting selflessly; but I knew I weren't being selfless any more. It couldn't be a matter of business because – because I'd started to feel more. Much more. I never meant it to happen: I tried to deny it to myself; but there was no help for it. That night of the horkey when you came to my house, and you said you thought I was your friend . . . Friend!' he said fiercely. 'As if that were all I felt for you! As if I wouldn't roll up this whole fen like a carpet, or catch the east wind in a net, if you asked me to!'

The white steam of his breath whirled about in the bitter air as he spoke these words, whilst Hester's mind whirled too: giddily she snatched at a multitude of fugitive emotions that flew upon her like dead leaves before the blast.

'I'm sorry,' he said, dully. 'That's why, you see. That's why I had to keep away. There was you being so kind to me, confiding, trusting – I felt like a traitor, feeling for you the way I do.'

Unsteadily she put out a hand to touch the mossy marble of a headstone. It was as cold as ice. 'Oh, Jonathan – why didn't you tell me this before?' she said. Light was breaking in: much of the recent past was swiftly becoming clear. 'I didn't know – that night of the horkey . . . Why didn't you say?'

'How could I?' said he softly. 'How could I do that – when there was you, just beginning to get a grip on life – just beginning to smile a little again? I loved to see your smile coming back, like seeing the first buds on the trees . . . How could I go and destroy that smile, by telling you something that – well, that could only be unwelcome to you? You'd had burdens enough. It's not that I don't cherish your friendship. God, no. Nothing on earth could have made me break that – except one thing: knowing that what I felt wasn't just friendship . . . that it had gone beyond that . . . Well! like I say, I'm sorry. I'm had to say it in the end. So you won't think I'm cold and ungrateful. That's the last thing I am – the very last.'

Hester turned her face from him, trying to think clearly; but she groped in mists of astonishment and self-reproach. Of course she should have seen: but how could she have seen what he had so scrupulously guarded against her seeing? For the moment her own predicament presented itself less vividly to her than Jonathan's, which her heart ached to behold. What a torment it must have been to him! A momentary recollection of that night of the wet-harvesting – her hands massaging his naked back – made her cheeks sting, and she hurriedly thrust it away. She must say something to him. He was looking steadily at her, as if readying himself for some harsh response, and she owed it to him to show the same respect for his feelings that he had shown for hers. But she struggled in vain to speak.

'There,' he said. 'It's happened – just what I was afraid of. That shadow's come back to your face. Look, try and forget what I said—'

'I can't do that,' she said. 'How can I?'

'No . . .' He was sombre. 'I suppose not.'

'But it's not that I – I mean, I can't blame you for saying it, Jonathan – it's right that you did. I'm only sorry you're had to bottle it up so long. Now that I see, now that I see how blundering I'm been, I feel awful about it—'

'Don't,' he said emphatically. 'Don't feel awful. You did nothing wrong: you couldn't have been expected to know.'

The truth of these words seemed to her an incomplete truth: she still felt herself impaled on a sharp point of conscience. 'I should have known,' she murmured. 'But I never imagined . . . Whatever you once felt for me, I thought that was long, long dead.'

Jonathan seemed to weigh his thoughts carefully, his chin lowered, his hands thrust in his pockets. 'So did I,' he said at length. 'And in truth I think it was. The man I was then and the man I am now seem to me like two different people

– made of the same clay, mebbe, but no more. When I came to work at your farm I thought I came heart-whole – I would never have come otherwise. I didn't want none of them tangling feelings that break your rest and turn you into a fool. But they came in spite of me. When I looked in your face for that smile, I found it wasn't just that I wanted you to be happy: I wanted that smile for myself. So the game was up. I'm sorry.'

'I'm sorry, too, Jonathan,' she said. There were tears on her lashes which she wished he might not see – she did not want him to reproach himself with having made her unhappy. 'Sorry because – it seems so cruel and wicked that what you feel for me should be wasted . . . It's a bitter world where something as true and good as that can go to waste . . . But you know that's all over for me, Jonathan: you know I'm finished with all that.' These words had become so automatic with her that she spoke them without thinking, her mind moving ahead of them.

'Aye, I know,' he said.

'But even though I haven't got a heart to give, I'm got a heart to feel grateful – flattered – oh, everything except hurt by what you've said. Truly, Jonathan. Do you believe me?'

'Yes,' he said, straightening with a smile. 'I believe you.'

'I'm got to go away now – but I can't go if you're believing, deep down, that I think badly of you – promise, now, that that's not what you believe,' she said, with a desperate sort of lightness.

'I promise,' he said.

'And there was me going on about your mill job . . . I feel a fool about that – yet I don't, because you deserve it, and I shall always want the best for you. I just wish . . . Oh! goodbye,' she said brokenly, unable to restrain her tears any longer. She turned and picked a path through the gravestones, her boots imprinting crisp dimples in the frosted grass.

Jonathan went on with his work. He was supposed to have all this timber disposed of today, and the master-mason was a bit of a tartar. It went hard with him to yes-sir and no-sir for the few shillings this job paid, but there was no help for it – it was the only practical course. It was perhaps odd that Jonathan could feel he was being practical when he shunned good work and struggled to get by on bad, simply because of the unruly longings of the heart; but Jonathan's practicality was another man's romanticism. He laboured on now, in flat contradiction of an opposite urge, very powerful within him, to give it up and hide his head in a dark place.

He had told her: in a way he still wished he hadn't, but it was done now. Yes, love was a fool's game, but he was a fool and that was all there was to it. On the night of the horkey he had known he must break away from Hester or he was lost, but in truth he had been lost some time before that. Stealthily and relentlessly had the infection taken hold: the blind god needed no ambience of candlelight and silk – in harvest-fields, quiet comradeship, labour, even pain, he could work his disturbing magic. A number of layers had covered Jonathan's feeling: a chivalrous protectiveness; a growing admiration for the way Hester's spirit rose to grapple with adversity; a friendship characterised by unhurried confidence. Each was true in its way, but his heart's-truth pierced them all.

And he had seen the tears, just now, that she had tried to conceal – seen the tears he had caused! A wry world, as he had said: a wry world, and a dark. Not even the Old Goblin, it turned out, had known how dark.


3


Hester reached home in the early afternoon. The steam-thresher was still there, and the first stack had diminished. Billy Onyett was complaining of frost-bite in his hands: he couldn't untie the sheaves wearing gloves, he said. Mechanically Hester told Edie to make him some beef-tea: mechanically, still in her veil-tied hat and cape, she wandered out to the paddock, where they had recently begun clearing the great tangle of thorn and elderberry that bounded it. The dry, black and knotted growth, scarred by fagging-hook and mattock, looked in the wintry light as lifeless as wire, and no more liable to leaf and flower than an iron railing.

She found herself walking away from the farm, taking the field-paths on to the upland, where the ploughed clay stood forth in jagged clots. The cold intensified momently, a congealing cold, as if the world were slowly setting like starch. She did not notice it: the brisk rhythm of walking not only warmed her but soothed the jangling perplexity of her mind, and she wanted just to go on, away from everyone, the earth her only companion.

A wry world, Jonathan had said: that it was! Had her sense of humour been working, she might have laughed at the memory of her old vain self, and how she would have relished men falling in love with her. But there was no place for humour here: it was fearfully serious. Jonathan's revelation had thrown everything out of joint – there was not a corner or crevice of her life that was unaltered by it. Her peace of mind was cleft to its foundations. (But had it really been peace of mind? Or a dull, cottony muffling of the emotions?) And protest as she might about the disruption, she could not wish his declaration unsaid; for in that there would be a hiding, a retreat, as life-destroying in its way as her grieving self-imprisonment in the Crooked House last year.

Ahead of her rose that most unusual sight in this part of Anglia – a hill. It was Oxey Hill, an ancient earthwork, the ramparts of which still appeared in sinuous contour in spite of the smoothings of grass and time, like the muscles of some half-tamed but powerful creature. Love had suddenly bulked too into the flat terrain of her life, but not tempered and softened as was this work of perished hands: it pressed urgently, dismayingly upon her. She had not sought Jonathan's love: she could not have wished it upon him, for love was pain – did she not know that? – and she could not wish such pain upon anyone, least of all Jonathan, for whom she deeply cared. This whole winter had been a lesson in how deeply she did care for him. And now he had walked into that dark thicket of pain, of poison and thorns!

She climbed a footworn track up the slope of Oxey Hill: silent starlings waddled and hopped out of her path, as if they had no more power of flight than chickens. She passionately wished there was something she might have said to Jonathan today, something that would have helped him – something that would not have left him stricken, hopeless, and surely regretting that he had ever spoken at all. It seemed to her that as it was, she would never know a moment's rest again after that meeting.

Of course there was something she could have said. Something which was as simple as earth or air – and yet which to her mind was a treacherously complex labyrinth, which even to think of was to shun. No, no: as she had told him before, that was all over, that was not for her, not any more – that part of her self was consigned to as permanent an oblivion as the dark side of the moon. She knew it to be so, and was glad of it. The kernel of dissent within her, which murmured that it was a pity, was not to be trusted.

From the summit of the earthwork she looked out across the fens. The sun, which had been no more than a faintly shining mark like the trail of a slug upon the surface of smothering snow-cloud, had drawn clear as it neared the horizon, and now the red disc scattered the embers of the short day over the western fields, whilst to the east the land died into smoke-coloured shadow, traced with a cobweb pattern of dykes. Hester, standing with tingling cheeks and steaming breath on the top of the hill, was the sole human being within sight: the high-road that crossed the landscape was deserted, the nearest cottage as insubstantial as a relic in the consuming dusk. She saw it all, the miles of encircling space, with a keen eye – turning herself slowly about so as to take in the whole panorama – while yet her mind's eye conned the expanse of her past life, and beheld a wasteland strewn with wrong decisions. She gave a sort of groaning sigh: the great stretch of ancient and indifferent fen seemed to thrust upon her small figure the whole burden of consciousness. How much easier to be like the unfeeling earth! Wasn't that the best way to live?

Yet as she thought of Jonathan, and cast her mind back over the past year, a sort of tender wonder stole over her as his every action fell into place. In everything he had done he had thought solely of her – sought her good but sought no return. His rugged devotion he had refined to a delicacy of conduct which she had only just begun tremulously to grasp. It was true that she had been shut up within herself . . . it was not true, after all, that she had been alone.

The sun was on the horizon: Hester began to descend the

slope. Somewhere out there was Jonathan – just such a vital pinprick of identity as she. She wondered what he was doing at this moment. Out of the blur of her confusion and perplexity, one hard fact appeared to her. If she were to be consistent with what she had said today, then she ought not to see him any more: that was only fair to him, for anything else would be to torment him.

Yet that was a hard fact indeed: it gripped her bleakly, more bleakly than was in the power of the cruellest winter that ever denied the inevitable spring.

4

For a couple of days the cold loosened its bonds sufficiently to allow a few sporadic showers of snow to fall, settling in powdery fichus on the dykeside only to freeze again. The steam threshing-tackle had developed a fault in the boiler, and had only just begun working again on the day Charlie Smeeth came to the Crooked House: it was Edie's half-day, and they were going together to Stokeley. Hester met him in the kitchen, where he greeted her with a paroxysm of coughing.

'That sounds like a bad chill, Charlie,' she said.

'Oh! it's about the usual for this time o' year, missus,' Charlie said. 'I reckon me tubes git froz, and won't shift – like the shutters of the mill-sails in the frost. They're stuck fast now.'

'I didn't know you still went to the mill, Charlie,' Hester said.

'Not usually – but Mr Eastholm's there this morning, so I went to see him.'

'Mr Eastholm?' she said in surprise.

'Yis – oh, he's just giving a word of advice to that poor ole Norfolk dumpling they're got wukking there now, who ain't got no more brains than a pig's got pockets. Mr Eastholm's finished his job at the church, and I suppose you're got to tek pity on this new miller. Not that *I'd* call him a miller,' Charlie said loftily.

Hardly knowing what she did, Hester gave Edie and Charlie a baked apple and a pastry each, and stood at the window staring out. Abruptly she said: 'Charlie – Edie – on your way, would you stop off at the mill and ask Jonathan if he'll step over here when he's got a minute? I'm got some news for him – business.'

'All right missus – cheer-oo.'

After the Smeeths had gone, Hester remained where she was, repeatedly smoothing her apron and gazing out at the threshing going on in the yard. Still she had the curious feeling of hardly knowing what she was doing: something had impelled her to summon Jonathan, something demanded that she must see him, but beyond that she came up against a blank wall within herself. At length she returned to the parlour, where she had begun her campaign of renovation by tearing down the worm-eaten panelling that she disliked; but she had scarcely mounted the rickety stepladder before there was a knock at the back door. She went to open it.

'Jonathan,' she said, 'I'm glad you could come – I hope I'm not took you away from anything, only I'm got some news, from the Commissioners . . . Come in.'

There was a fresh smell of outdoors about him as he stepped into the kitchen. He looked both puzzled and guarded, as if he were determined to betray no expression.

'Charlie tells me you're finished at the church,' she said, folding and refolding some linen.

'Yes, it was only temporary work,' he said.

'Oh – well – what I wanted to tell you was, Farmer Mather called the other day, and – he thinks the Commissioners might soon come round to our way of thinking – and if not, he's heard that the miller over on New Fen might soon be retiring – and so there's another possibility for you there. I thought you'd – I thought you'd like to know.'

'Thank you,' he said. 'Matter of fact, I'm got a proper job lined up. I went over yesterday to a small brickyard over Yaxley way to see if there was owt going: I start next week.'

'Oh! that's good. At least . . . Is it? I mean, is it what you want?'

'It'll pay the rent for the time being,' he said.

She folded the linen again. This was madness. An impulse had told her, with the force of a command, that she must speak to him, that all was dangerously incomplete between them and she must face him again, but the impulse had not told her what to say. God knew what he must think of her.

He rescued her: glancing out of the window at the yard he said, 'Why, what a cobble Billy's making of feeding that thresher!'

'Oh, I know,' she said joining him. 'I have a job to get him to do it. He don't trust the machine at all – he says it makes his teeth rattle.' She laughed nervously.

'You want another man feeding,' Jonathan said, in his slightly arrogant way, 'thass what. And have Billy taking the sheaves down. It'll take for ever at this rate.'

Hester hesitated, not looking at him. 'I hardly dare ask,' she said.

'What – if I'll do it?'

'Oh, I do understand if you don't want to, Jonathan: I would have asked you before, but—'

'Do you want me to do it?' said he plainly.

She nodded. A smile came and went on his face.

'I will, then,' he said.

Within minutes Jonathan was in place on the platform of the thresher, and the work was going on apace: the very engine seemed to throb with new vigour. Later Hester herself joined the team, untying the bonds of the sheaves to hand them to Jonathan: the rhythm was swift, and the stack was soon down to the staddles; she felt once more the satisfaction of the old companionable toil of the harvest-field. Harmony succeeded to the nagging discord of her thoughts. Whatever it was she had meant to say to him, she simply let it go like the chaff on the breeze: an enigma that had been compelling became, in his presence, merely dispensable. It was just so good to have him at the farm again: there was a sense of rightness that extinguished the haggard questionings and ambiguities as the sun extinguishes the moon.

'Tomorrow?' he said to her when the day's work was done.

'If you could . . . we've got on so much better,' she said. 'But have you things to do . . . ?'

'Job doesn't start for a week,' he said. 'This work'll fill in nicely.'

She could not tell what he was thinking; but she found she could not reproach herself for irresponsibility, for selfishness, for allowing things to go on unresolved. It was as if a moral shutter had come down. She slept well that night, and woke in the morning feeling more alive than she had done for months. She worked on the thresher beside Jonathan until dinner-time, and in the afternoon attacked the parlour panelling again with cheerful gusto: when she went out to see the men on the thresher, she was covered in dust and flakes of plaster.

'You needn't have got yourself all dressed up,' said Jonathan from the platform.

She grinned up at him and blew a smut from the tip of her nose. 'Now you can tell folk what Mrs Saunders does in the afternoon,' she said. 'She gets plastered.'

That evening she found her nerves all a-jangle: she could not sit down. She went on tearing at the panelling until bedtime, and even when she lay in bed her fingers seemed to itch to attack it again. At last she uneasily slept, and dreamt that someone had replaced all the panelling just as it was. This ghostly, formless figure stood admiring its handiwork, while she shouted at it: 'You can't put the past back, you know! You can't – it's done with!'

The next morning she did not join the men on the threshing-machine: she went feverishly back to the panelling as if it were the most important thing in the world. She was still absorbed in this at noon when Edie called, 'Here's Mr Eastholm, missus.'

Jonathan stood in the parlour doorway. 'We're all finished, Mrs Saunders – it's all threshed.'

'Already?' she cried – in such a strange, plaintive tone that she startled herself, and Jonathan gave her a quizzical look.

'The engineer's getting ready to go,' he said.

'I'd best settle up with him then.' She dusted her hands, and looked at the chaos of the parlour. 'Oh! damn. It seemed like a good idea at the time.'

'Are you leaving that side intact?'

'No – I can't prise it off – I feel like setting light to it!'

'Let me have a go,' he said, taking up the crowbar. 'It'll make a change from bashing churches.'

She went out to pay the engineer, and when she came back

417

into the house a great ripping and screeching noise confirmed that Jonathan was doughtily at work. There was a great crash and a cloud of plaster as she entered the parlour: Jonathan smiled out at her from the choking midst of it, coated in dust.

'That's shifted it!' he said.

'Oh, Jonathan,' she laughed, 'you're always getting in a mess for me. Here—' She handed him a clothes-brush.

'I shall be in a worse muck than this at the brickyard, I should think,' he said.

'Of course, the brickyard . . . I can't imagine you there somehow.'

'I shall get along. I'm done so many jobs. Milling, digging, building . . .' He tilted his head forward and ran his hand rapidly through his hair to get the dust off: Hester stared, transfixed by a sharply revived memory that for a moment she could not place. Then it came to her – the day she had left his lighters, on the towpath below Saunders' horse-yard; blossoms had fallen on to his hair and he had shaken them off with just that gesture. Something about it made her heart seem to expand to the tips of her breasts.

'And boating,' she said.

'And boating.' He smiled, but without ease.

'D'you ever think about the old lighters?' she said.

'Oh, often.' Jonathan studied the splintered panelling still intact above the cornice: as he lifted his head she saw there was a little dust on the bare skin of his throat where it emerged, smooth and rounded as a column, from the collar of his striped shirt. 'I think about it . . . but it's all in the past. Gone. You know.'

'Yes,' she said. 'I know.'

Jonathan stretched up, long-bodied as a cat, to touch the cornice. 'No,' he said, 'need the stepladder – even I can't reach that.'

'It must be lovely to be that tall,' she said.

He looked at her in surprise as he opened out the stepladder. 'D'you think so? It's funny, you know – when I was a lad I hated it, I thought I was too tall – I wanted to be like everyone else.'

'Oh! but it looks right on you,' she said. 'You wouldn't be you without your height. It's part of you . . .'

All at once Hester found she could not look at him. She was crushed by a sense of her self of the last couple of days as an alien, unfathomable being. When did the change begin – was it when she had stood in the graveyard with Jonathan? And who was she now? What was she doing?

'Jonathan,' she said huskily. 'I . . . I don't know what you must think of me . . .'

He was silent, his long brown hand poised on the stepladder.

'I'm been meaning to – to say something, truly, after – after the other day . . .'

'That's forgotten,' he said quickly. 'Don't think of it.'

'But it was awful the way I sort of ran away,' she said, 'I didn't answer you properly, and now it must seem like I – like I'm ignoring it . . .'

'Hush,' he said. 'That's best.'

She shook her head in distress. 'No, it isn't.'

'Yes it is.' He smiled faintly. 'You always were a contrary one . . . I wouldn't have stayed if I thought that – well, it was upsetting you – and I'll be off now, if it is. Is it?'

'No,' she said, smiling in return.

He turned his face quickly from her. 'Let's finish this job,' he said, pounding up the creaking stepladder, which swayed perilously.

'Oh dear, be careful!' she said, gripping the stepladder and wedging her foot against it. 'I don't trust this thing – it squeals like an old sow in farrow. How much do you weigh?'

'I'm got no idea,' he said, ripping at the panelling.

'How tall are you?'

'I don't know that either,' he said, and suddenly they were both laughing.

'You gret yawnucks!' she said. 'We shall have to measure you. You'll be saying next you don't know how old you are – except I do – you must be near twenty-seven, because I remember you telling me – except you were twenty-five then – so I'm added it on, you see.'

'Oh, I see,' Jonathan said, mockingly grave; then gave a great

419

wrench at the last panel, almost losing his balance. 'Look out below!'

The panel crashed down. Jonathan came pounding back down the ladder, no-hands. 'Mind!' Hester said, holding on to the wobbling structure. 'Honestly, Jonathan, you ain't safe . . .' As his waist came level with her eyes she had a sickly feeling as if a heavy plumb-line had dropped from her throat right down through her body. Jonathan stepped down to the floor, and without a word Hester put her arms around him and with closed eyes pressed her face against his chest. She inhaled the scent of him for the space of two deep heartbeats, throbbing at her ear, before his own arms encircled her, and they clung together, entwined like one creature, amidst the broken timber, plaster and dust.

'This is why I wished I was a bit taller,' she whispered, reaching up to kiss him.

Releasing her lips at last, he shook his head, studying her so intently that she seemed to feel the focus of his brown eyes like a palpable caress about the curves of her face. 'No,' he said, 'don't change a thing – not a thing.'

She smiled, and moved her arms to clasp him more closely: her fingertips meeting between his shoulder-blades, her whole body was as tightly moulded to his as the rind upon a fruit. But suddenly she could not look at him, for she remembered the untruth that had led to this wonderful moment, and a bat's-wing of superstition brushed her. She buried her face in his neck, and said, half sobbing: 'Oh, Jonathan, I lied . . . when I asked you here the other day, and said I had news for you, about the Commissioners and everything – I didn't have any news at all really, I just pretended because – I wanted so to see you . . . and so I'm started off with a lie . . . I'm sorry . . .'

Slowly she became aware of a sort of tremor, passing from his body directly to hers. He was tenderly laughing, deep in his chest.

'That's a white lie, my dear,' he said, turning her face to his with one firm finger. 'If ever I heard one – that's a white one.'

\* \* \*

Snow had begun falling: the large slow flakes spoke softly at the parlour window. With the imperviousness of lovers to discomfort, Hester and Jonathan had only slowly disengaged themselves from their embrace in the centre of the littered room, and now he was sitting on the oak settle and she upon his knee. Her arm was around his shoulders, which felt as warm as a sunned wall, and her other hand was engaged in a long tactile examination of the contours of his face, which now and then she interrupted to convulsively press her lips to it, with a feeling as if her heart were being pulled up at the roots.

The prospect of Edie coming in was one of the many things which did not seem to matter.

'Are you—' said Jonathan, 'did you—'

'What?'

His teeth playfully closed on her thumb for a moment. 'I forgot what I was going to say,' he said. 'I was just trying to work it out . . . It's a mystery, ain't it? Here, I mean—' pointing to his heart.

'It is,' said she. 'I'll never understand it.' Their mood, mutually reflected, was curiously both light and solemn. 'Let me feel that heart,' she said, placing her hand on his chest.

'Is it going?'

She nodded. 'Nineteen to the dozen.'

He laughed, a boy's laugh, slightly hushed. 'That's how I feel,' he said. As her hand still rested on his heart he said, 'It's yours. Will you have it?'

'Yes. Yes, please.' She ran her fingers across his chest and round his neck. 'Fearfully and wonderfully made – that's from a psalm, ole Andrew says. That's what you are, Jonathan – fearfully and wonderfully made . . . Oh! dear – I should have thought you'd have hated me, instead of loving me.'

'Now how d'you work that out?'

'Well – I don't know . . . When you told me the other day – I just ran away; ran away inside my head as well. I wouldn't face it. A coward. All this time I'm been so cold and closed-up and afraid—'

'You're just going to have to get used to being loved,' he said, 'because I'm not going to stop it.'

421

'How much do you love me, then?' she said, with an air of curiosity.

For answer he made a huge expansive gesture with his arms, before enfolding her in them again.

'It's the same for me,' she said. 'More. From here to the sea – from here to the stars – that's how much I love you, Jonathan.'

He gazed raptly on her, like a knight before the grail, as if his very soul would brim out at his eyes; and for a moment neither was able to speak.

'If only—' she said.

'What?'

She looked down at his hand upon her hip, which seemed to fit together like lock and key. 'I was just thinking – that time at the Spread Eagle yard, long ago, when you proposed to me . . . if only I'd said yes then – if only an angel or something could have come down and told me what to do!'

'Ah, who knows?' he said. 'I wonder if it would have been right then, somehow: I don't know whether I could have given you all the love you deserve – all the love I want to give you now.' He breathed out a long breath and shook his head. 'And that's all I can give you, Hester! Then I had a farm of my own – and now I'm got nothing. Can you take me as I am?'

'I'll take you as you are, Jonathan,' she said. 'Nothing else will do. I seem to have been running in the wrong direction for half my life – I shall make sure I go the right way, this time.' She buried her lips in his hair, and her glance fell for the first time on the window, which was framed like a cameo with white. 'Oh, look – it's snowing!'

'Drifting, too, by the look of it,' he said.

'Oh, well – we're safe here, ain't we?'

He wrapped his arms around her. 'Yes,' he said. 'Safely gathered in.'

# Chapter Five

The end of February, the shortest and longest month of the year, brought not gleams of spring but snow. The sky imprisoning the fen was a sombre steel-grey, darkening almost to black in places, so that it seemed impossible that such whiteness should fall from it, and the spiralling flakes might have been plausibly expected to be the colour of soot. On the flat fields the layer of snow was as smooth as linen, folded into blue shadow only on the marge of dyke and hedge, and frozen and re-frozen to a crystalline consistency, so that the spiky footprints of birds were preserved on its spangled surface like etchings of beautiful delicacy. Within the dykes and drains the crust of ice thickened nightly, with strange, creaking, protesting sounds in the emptiness, as if the water were not merely freezing but undergoing an agonising and irreversible transformation into solid. The snowfalls gave place only to a bitter north-easter, which scourged the fettered landscape as if with an almighty Cossack whip: its pagan whoops resounded between the high drain banks, and the snow upon every rush and reed was frozen as it blew, so that each assumed the appearance of a tiny white pennant forever fixed in the instant of its unfurling.

On just such a bleakly sparkling evening, Hester and Lizzie Gosling walked together down the wide street of Milney St Mary, which the cold moon illumined like a streetlamp to the tip of every last pendant icicle. Their caped and gloved forms had a large bloom-like softness in this angular world of ice, and they were laughing.

'They got Artie Gill to do it last year,' Lizzie said, 'and he got so drunk he fell asleep with his costume still on, and woke up in the morning all covered with weals like he'd been horsewhipped.'

'Well, I'm never seen Jonathan drunk,' Hester said. 'He seems to swallow it down without it hurting him.'

'Ah! you wait till you're wed – you'll mebbe learn all sorts about him.'

'Lizzie Gosling,' Hester said, 'I swear you're getting more cynical than ever!'

Lizzie grinned sidelong at her. 'You don't want to tek no notice of me,' she said, 'and I know you ain't anyway – you're got such a shine in your eyes as I never saw.'

'Am I really?' said Hester. 'I know that's how I feel – except it's more like a sort of shine all over. Daft, ain't it!'

'Dear oh lor – you *have* got it bad,' said Lizzie. She gave Hester a devilishly searching look. 'A shine all over, eh? Whatever are you pair gitting up to – and with the banns not even called yet!'

'Git away with you,' Hester said, aware of a blush conveniently hidden by the general tingle of her cheeks in the cold air, and unable to repress a secret and involuntary smile. 'Lizzie – serious, though – you do think it's a good thing, don't you? Me and Jonathan?'

'Why, what's it matter what anyone thinks?' Lizzie said.

'You're not just anyone – you're my friend,' said Hester.

Lizzie gave her one of her brisk, abrupt squeezes. 'If your looks are anything to go by, it's the best thing as ever happened,' she said. 'And the miller's looks too – he seems two inches taller, if thass possible. Oh! I shall have to get used to not thinking of him as the miller – unless he's taking that job back, is he?'

'It might well be offered to him,' Hester said, 'but I don't think he'll do it. We'll have the farm, you know – and I want him with me: if he was milling I shouldn't hardly see him from one day to the next!'

'Or one night to the next,' Lizzie said. 'No, you don't want a husband who's always off to oil the luffing-gear . . . you want him at home oiling yours.'

'Lizzie!' reproached Hester, choking on her laughter.

'And stoking your boiler . . . Well, it's good to see you laugh,' Lizzie said, with one of her sudden swerves from saltiness to affection. 'That does my heart good. And Jonathan too – you seem to have brought that out in him. Softened the edges a bit. And in turn I reckon he'll just steady you – you always did need a bit of ballast. There, I'm sounding like a regular old gipsy-granny!'

'That's all right,' Hester said. 'A gipsy once told me something true – he said I'd wait for gold; and I have, and now it's come. I thought I knew what love was like before . . . but I dunno. I didn't know this was love until I found I was deep in – over my head. It wasn't really a question of will. I'm joined to Jonathan, fixed – like a magnet to north.'

To forestall the inevitable gossip, Hester and Jonathan had swiftly decided to let it be known, informally to their friends on Hinching Fen, that they were engaged, and planned to be married some time in the spring. Hester's feelings were such that she would have been happy to shout it from the rooftops, but a word to Peggy Chettle performed the same function. In the meantime Jonathan came every day to work at the farm, though she was afraid very little got done . . . How could you spend a whole morning just gazing at someone? Quite easily, was the answer. Even as she talked and laughed with Lizzie, she kept falling into deep pockets of abstraction in which the memory of the touch of his fingers upon her cheek was so vividly present to her that she had to give it her whole attention, and she came to herself with a sensation of waking from a doze.

They reached their destination at the end of the village – Jonathan's cottage, which was brightly lit within, and full of people. They knocked, and Charlie Smeeth flung open the door with an excited greeting. 'He's ready!' Charlie cried. 'It took us ages, though – I reckon we'll pick somebody shorter next year – we must have used a barnful of straw!'

In the house-place, and filling it to the sills, were Billy Onyett, Lizzie's brother Jack Gosling, and Artie Gill; and a strange apparition, a towering creature seemingly made entirely of oat-straw – Jonathan, dressed in the traditional costume of the Straw Bear. He came forward and gravely kissed Hester's hand.

'Evening, my dear,' he said. 'You're just caught me trying on my wedding clothes.'

'Oh, Jonathan, we'll clash – there was me going to wear a grass skirt and a hay-bale on my head,' she said, going off into a scream of laughter.

'Took us ages, but he looks a treat, don't he?' Billy Onyett said proudly. 'Thass summat *like* a bear. I remember the year Henry Wake did it – more like a straw cub, that was – we had to keep him out the way of the cows, in case they took him for a snack.'

'I don't know how I'm going to manage if nature calls,' Jonathan said, looking critically down at himself.

'You'd best bring along a pair o' scissors, Hester,' Lizzie said, to shouts of laughter. 'You know the spot!'

The Straw Bear was an ancient fen custom, possibly widespread once but now surviving only in Stokeley and, obstinately, in a few surrounding districts like Hinching Fen. Each year one of the menfolk of the fen was chosen by his fellows to represent the Straw Bear: the choice perhaps falling on Jonathan this year as a tribute to his engagement, with an element of the mock-ordeal that has always been inflicted on men soon to be married. On the appointed day the man chosen was dressed by the others from head to foot in clean straight lengths of oat-straw, which was plaited and bound to him with lengths of twine, and brought to a peak above his brow, so that only his face showed. Come nightfall this 'bear' was then led on a rope by his friends around the farms and cottages and pubs, garnering largesse with mock-threats and capers. The men had decided on this occasion that all offerings in the form of drink and eatables would go down their throats, whilst any money obtained would go towards the Gooding, the traditional winter collection made for the elderly poor women of the parish. Jonathan, who claimed that his dancing resembled a real bear's too closely, had rehearsed a song to the accompaniment of Artie Gill's fiddle. What might be the origins of the custom of the Straw Bear it was impossible to say: certainly it bore no relation to the Christian festivals of the agricultural year, and a darker world of propitiation and sacrifice might have been glimpsed behind its present jokey manifestation. Hester laughed to see her lover dressed in the quaint costume, but when at last they all set out from the cottage to begin the ritual tour, it struck her that Jonathan with his breadth and stature made an alarming figure to anyone not in the know; and when he turned to give her a peck on the cheek she said, 'Oo-er – I'm a bit frit of you like that.'

'Grr,' Jonathan said, in a tiny voice, with a grin.

People turned out at their cottage doors as the procession passed down the street, and children craned from upstairs windows to see: tumblers of hot sugared beer and toddy and trays of girdle-scones and baked apples and chestnuts were brought out, and one old woman produced some of the local home-made elderberry wine which, hot and spiced, hit the stomach and then the head like a firecracker. It all made a pleasant interruption to the dead season between Christmas and Easter, and presently a large knot of people were out in the street, wrapped up in mufflers, laughing and blowing on their hands and stamping on the frozen snow, which was barred with orange where the open cottage doors sent forth the glow of fire and lamp from within.

'Shall we be gooing to the Labour In Vain, sir?' Charlie Smeeth earnestly inquired of Jonathan. 'There'll be a lot of folk there, and they always expect the Straw Bear, you know.' There was doubt on this point, of course, because of Jonathan's quarrel with Jass Phelps the landlord, over those insinuations he had made. Privately, however, Jonathan had already agreed with Hester that they should let bygones be bygones; after all, as Hester remarked, Jass Phelps was only prophesying what was to come, if you looked at in a charitable light – and they were both in greatly charitable mood.

'Yes, Charlie – the Labour In Vain it shall be,' Jonathan said. 'And if ole Jass Phelps don't give us all drinks on the house, I shall sing at him, so help me!'

At the Labour In Vain old Andrew Surfleet had just arrived, and was lowering himself with infinite slowness into a seat beside Sunny Daintree. 'A bitter night – bitter! That wind blows right through you and buttons up at the back,' Andrew said. 'I wouldn't have ventured, meself, only I like to see Straw Bear Night: I could hear the procession up tother end of the village – they'll doubtless be here soon.'

'Well, now – unless the miller-as-was decides he don't care to come in here, where there was certain aspersions cast, and who could blame him,' said Henry Wake with measured severity.

'Don't look at me!' said Jass Phelps, his arms daintily folded atop his great balloon of a body. 'I'm sure I never meant no harm – not a grain of it. I were wishing the miller and Mrs Saunders well – thass what it was – not my fault if I git took up wrong.'

'I remember the year they picked me for the Straw Bear,' Sunny Daintree said. 'Ooh! dear. The straw brought me up in a red rash, and I had to lay in a salt bath, and Peggy Chettle made a joke about how in a week I'd be Cured, which I weren't in a way to appreciate.'

'I think you'll find Jonathan'll bear no grudge, you know,' Henry Wake said, 'and the procession'll come here. As for me, I was like a dog with two tails when I heard that news about Mrs Saunders and Jonathan's engagement – the best thing that could happen: me being one of the first to be told, as it happens, being a particular friend to those parties.'

'Ah! Cured – I see it,' said Andrew Surfleet with a chuckle. 'Thass a good one, that.'

In his habitual corner, Chad Langtoft slowly sipped his half-pint. He didn't intend staying for that Straw Bear business. It was heathen, he considered; and he was a God-fearing man. It was a pity, because he could just fancy another half – no more, he knew how to keep it within limits: but no, he was to be denied that simple pleasure, because of this heathen tomfoolery! It contributed in his mind to a general sense of unfairness, which proceeded from this engagement they were all talking about.

Chad had a vague but powerful feeling that that engagement was not right. After a long period of refusing to believe that there could possibly be any real blame attaching to him for Lyle Saunders' death nearly a year ago – a period in which he had hungrily embraced the religion which seemed to offer the self-vindication he craved – Chad had at last come round, with a sort of serenity, to a conviction that he had, in some measure, freed Hester from that Saunders one. It was as if Providence had worked through him – and Providence, after all, could not be guilty, could not be right or wrong: it just was. And yet here Hester was, enjoying the fruits of that Providence – deciding to marry again – whilst he was still stuck with the same grinding, put-upon life with Mary-Ann. It was a grim confirmation – not that he needed one – of the injustice of life towards him. And there was the miller worming his way into Hester Saunders' favour – what had he ever done for her? If anyone, it should have been he, Chad, moving in there, but the world had thwarted him at every turn: not that he wanted anything to do with her anyhow – there was nothing but trouble to be got from women; he should know, for one of them had trapped him good and proper. But it irked him to hear them all talking on as if everything were satisfactory; and when Henry Wake said something about wishing them happiness Chad burst out, with an irritable twitch of his shoulders, 'Why, who says they deserve to be happy? You can't just expect happiness to be given you on a plate – thass for the Almighty to decide.'

'I take your meaning, Chad,' Henry Wake said. 'But you wouldn't wish them unhappiness, would you? There's sufficient of that knocking about the place.'

'Man was born to suffer,' Chad said. 'Besides, who's to say they'll be any good for each other? Everybody knows what a disaster her and that Saunders one were. Who's to say this'll be any different? It's all a rum business, if you ask me.'

Henry Wake sighed. In the small fenland communities there was a great tolerance, even appreciation, of idiosyncrasy, but they were all rather weary of Chad's monotonous mistrust, interspersed with poison darts of scripture. 'Charity, Chad, remember charity,' Henry said.

'It's a funny thing – there's always somebody who can't bear other bodies to have a mite of happiness,' said Andrew Surfleet.

Chad subsided, hunched down in his seat, with a dully smouldering outrage. He couldn't even speak his mind, it seemed – they were all against him! Though he had always known that.

Henry Wake had opened the door. 'Ah! here they come,' he said. 'Watch this here bear don't get you, Jass.'

'The miller'll tek a drink on me, I hope,' Jass Phelps said, perspiring rather. 'We're good friends really, you know.'

Chad finished his half and was ready to go – he wanted none of it, it would make him sick to see them – but just as he stood up, in came the Straw Bear party, with Artie Gill playing his fiddle, Lizzie and Hester jigging – what right had she to jig? – and a whole crowd of folk from the village pouring in after, laughing and cheering at the tops of their voices. The crush was such that Chad could not get to the door: they treated him, he thought, as if he didn't exist!

'Evening, Mrs Saunders – evening, Miller,' Jass Phelps was saying, with a fixed and sweaty smile. 'A very fine Straw Bear you make, Miller – quite the best I'm seen; and congratulations on your engagement, by the by, and have a drink on it – have two drinks—'

'Oh! that'll do, Jass,' Jonathan said, laughing. 'Here, shake hands with a happy man.'

While Sunny Daintree was tossing some coppers into the hat, Chad began to edge his way round to the door – as best he could, with everyone trying to trap him in with this heathen rubbish. It was just typical of his luck that Billy Onyett should turn and see him at that moment.

'Here, Chad – no sneaking out without coughing up fust,' Billy said. 'C'mon – ha'penny'll do.'

Chad froze, the backs of his thighs jammed against a table. Jonathan loomed towards him, smiling and shaking the hat. She was there, smiling too, holding on to the rope: yes, she had roped him in good and proper, Chad thought blackly – soon be leading him a real dance. Such filth.

'Aye, come on, Chad – else I'll sing at you,' Jonathan said to a general laugh, waving the hat.

'You needn't come near me wi' that heathen muck,' Chad said, his eyes flicking from Jonathan to Hester and back again.

'Well – never mind that,' Jonathan said. 'A copper for the poor widows, eh?'

'You'd know all about helping widows!' Chad cried: they were all pressing round him and staring – with a sudden clawing movement he struck out at Jonathan. His fist glancingly connected. There was a gasp; but Jonathan scarcely flinched.

'Make it a shilling,' he said, with a deep fierce frown upon Chad, 'and I'll forget about that blow.'

Chad threw a wild glance round at the ring of faces. 'You're all agin me!' he burst out; and with a sudden twist of his body, seized the oil-lamp from the table behind him and dashed it with a sweeping movement against Jonathan's body. The glass globe smashed upon the floor, and the straw costume caught fire with an upward flourish of flame.

Hester could never remember whether her own voice figured amongst the screams that followed; she remembered only a series of bright, disjointed images – the blood dripping from her own pricked finger as she tore the brooch from her cape and flung the cape around Jonathan's legs to smother the flames; Chad hurling himself out at the door just as Billy Onyett made a grab at his collar; Henry Wake ineffectually throwing water from a jug on the bar on to the burning straw – before Sunny Daintree, moving with astonishing speed, came cannoning into Jonathan and bodily drove him outside, shouting, 'In the snow! Douse it in the snow!'

By the time she had fought her way outside with the rest – seconds that seemed like hours – Sunny had thrust Jonathan down upon the ground and was rolling him in the drifted snow before the door. Steam was hissing and rising in the bitter air. Hester flung herself down upon her knees beside Sunny, heaping snow with her hands on to Jonathan's body, little animal gasps coming from her throat. Sunny put his hand on her arm. 'It's all right, missus,' he said, 'it's out.'

Jonathan sat up, his eyes bleary with smoke and smuts. 'The damn fool,' he said. 'The poor damn fool.'

'Any hurts, bor?' Sunny said.

Jonathan shook his head and got to his feet, his hand on Sunny's shoulder. 'No harm done,' he said shakily. 'Don't ask me to be Straw Bear again, though, will you, neighbours?'

Hester gripped his hand and pressed it against her face, her eyes closed.

'A terrible thing nearly – terrible!' Henry Wake said. 'Where did Chad go?'

'Took to his heels,' Billy Onyett said. 'I tried to git a hold on him – he was away like an eel.'

431

'He mustn't get away with this – he ought to go before the law!' Henry Wake said. 'We all on us saw what he was about.'

'Come on, we'll catch him – he can't have got far,' said Billy Onyett. 'Who's wi' me?'

'I'll come!' cried Charlie Smeeth, in a voice of unaccustomed force.

In a moment Billy was off on his long legs, with Charlie Smeeth and Jack Gosling and Artie Gill following, and Henry Wake pattering along behind. Hester, with Sunny's help, began stripping off the damp, blackened straw. Jass Phelps, elbowing aside the clucking onlookers, handed Jonathan a large tot of rum. 'Get that down you quick,' he said.

'Gladly,' Jonathan said, draining it in one go and coughing. Presently the last of the straw was peeled off him, and he stood shivering slightly: the costume had been warm and he had worn no jacket underneath.

'You're damp,' Hester said, putting a hand to his shirt. 'Come in and get warm.'

'No,' he said. 'I reckon I ought to go after them fellows – Billy and Artie are hot-headed sorts – no knowing what they'll do.'

She regarded him steadily a moment. 'All right,' she said. 'I'll come too.'

They set out after the others, with Sunny Daintree carrying a storm-lamp from the pub, though there was a broad light from the moon. At the end of the village the tracks in the crusted snow led them on to the field-paths, and out into white sparkling openness that extended for miles on either hand.

'There – that long streak's Billy Onyett, I know,' cried Sunny, pointing. 'And Charlie along of him.' They ran along the dyke-side where the snow was thin, and drew level with Billy and Charlie close to the main drain.

'Lost him,' Billy said, clutching a stitch in his side and panting out white vapour. 'Artie and Jack went across the bridge to head him off—'

'Ahoy!' came a shout from the further extremity of the field behind them. Hester, whirling round, saw three figures – Chad Langtoft racing across the field, and Artie Gill and Jack Gosling advancing on him from opposite points of the compass. There was something weird and deliberate about all their movements that for a moment she could not understand: they seemed to be running as one runs in a dream, laboriously, with balletic slowness. Then she realised – with each step they were sinking almost up to their knees in the pure untouched snow that covered the field.

'We're got him – head him off,' Billy said. As he started to move Chad saw him, made a sudden hare-like swerve, and headed straight for the drain bank. He lurched clear of the deep snow a few yards ahead of his pursuers, scrambled up the bank like a spider, and tore away from them – running on the smooth frozen surface of the drain, which aimed at the horizon like a straight glassy road.

'That bastard!' Artie Gill grunted, struggling exhausted to the top of the bank. 'We shall never catch him now.' But within an instant of his speaking, there was a curious noise like the dropping of a load of slates, and a flat cry; and the stubby figure of Henry Wake, who had got himself lost, appeared in silhouette on the crest of the opposite bank, fifty yards further along, calling for help.

'Here – he's gone through the ice!'

Jonathan was the first to reach the spot along the bank opposite Henry. 'There!' Henry cried. 'See – where the reeds are . . .'

Close to the bank someone had made a dipping-hole in the ice to get water, which had then thinly frozen over again to a treacherous cat-ice, barely discernible but for a faint sugary glitter; and here a splintered hole gaped, the water beneath tilting and rippling and stippled with moonlight.

Hester clutched at Jonathan. 'Don't go down there, Jonathan,' she cried vehemently, and held him back, 'don't!'

The men formed a chain down the bank, gripping each other's belts, with Charlie Smeeth, the lightest, tentatively inching out on to the cracking ice. He groped an arm up to the shoulder into the water, but all was still and silent there.

'There ain't nothing,' Charlie said, shuddering at the numbing clutch of the water. 'He ain't here.'

'He's underneath the ice,' Artie said quietly.

More people had arrived from the village, some with lamps.

433

All began to roam up and down the banks of the drain, throwing the lamplight down upon the grooved and glinting sheet of ice below, shouting and pointing at every shadow and clump of reeds. Hester and Jonathan worked their way downstream, not speaking, until they were in sight of the mill, when there was another shout from Henry Wake on the other side of the drain. He had mounted the brick parapet surrounding the mill-pool, into which the drain led, and was pointing downward.

Hester ran up to the mill ahead of Jonathan. She peered sickly over the wall into the mill-pool. The great water-wheel was still, with a neat pan-pipe of icicles hanging from each paddle, but the water in the pool was only partly frozen, with clear patches that shone like black oil. Chad's drowned body lay amongst weed and slivers of ice, face down, his head buried in the crook of his left arm, as if he had sulkily turned his back on life.

# Chapter Six

A light two-wheeled cart came rattling into the yard of the Crooked House on a gusty morning in late May. Walt came out to hold the pony's head, and Henry Wake stepped down from the cart with a certain dash, short legs notwithstanding, that would have done credit to a silk-hatted gent in Rotten Row. He stopped to rearrange the flower in his buttonhole before glancing up and urbanely waving to Hester, who saw him from her bedroom window.

'Henry Wake's here,' she said, waving back. 'Go down and let him in, Edie. No – wait – are you sure I look all right?'

'Bless you, missus, of course you do!' said Edie. Taking Hester by the elbows, she guided her to the mirror. 'There,' she said looking over Hester's shoulder, 'not much wrong with *that* face!'

Hester gazed into her own brightly reflected eyes, and found herself smiling. 'You know, I reckon I *do* look all right,' she said gaily. 'Jonathan's a lucky fellow, really, ain't he? I hope he knows it.'

'He knows it, missus,' Edie said. 'Oh! 'ell, I'm just thought – what am I to call him when he comes back here – I mean, when he's here to live, like? Should I say mairster?'

'Oh, I think Jonathan wouldn't know where to look if you called him mairster!' Hester laughed. 'Anyway – don't count your chickens – he might have done a bunk at the altar.'

'Never!' Edie said with huge emphasis.

'Yes, he's a lucky man,' Hester said, smoothing the high-necked bodice of the pearl-grey frock, and regarding herself in the mirror, while Edie ran downstairs. 'And I'm a lucky woman . . .' She smiled again, gently. What else was there to say? She remembered Mrs Dawsmere, the housekeeper at the Saunders' yard, and how she would have crossed her fingers forebodingly to hear her say that. But you couldn't question your luck when it came to you, Hester thought: you just had to seize it and rejoice in it. Take the light: push back the dark. And, by God, so she would. Her luck was waiting for her now at the church: she must go and get him. She glanced round at the bedroom, to which she and her luck would be returning later. She had a suspicion that he might knock his head on that low beam . . . Oh, well, he wouldn't be walking about too much anyway – she'd see to that . . . She forced herself to stop smiling, and picked up her bouquet.

'I'm ready,' she said to her reflection.

Henry Wake was waiting for her in the parlour. His trousers fitted his legs like gloves, and there was so much macassar oil on his hair that his bowler hat kept sliding off. 'Well, now,' he said admiringly, on greeting Hester, 'I don't know as I'm ever seen anything finer in the illustrated papers – no, not in the *Sixpenny Gallery of the Fashionable Fair* – that's a monthly publication, you know, taken occasionally by Mrs Wake – who's indisposed today, I'm afraid, but sends her best. Now, shall we depart? You might not believe it, but I'm never been called upon to give a bride away before, though I'm performed quite a few responsible functions in my time, no good pretending I haven't . . .'

They climbed into the dog-cart and set off at an appropriately ceremonial pace, Hester seated beside Henry, with Edie sitting on the backboard with her legs swinging. The west wind was bowling the white clouds swiftly across the sky, so that giant stretches of shadow and sunlight continually alternated across the level fields, with an effect like the rolling and unrolling of vast carpets. They did not take the road to the village, for Milney St Mary church was still closed for restoration. They took the Stokeley road, which ran directly alongside the green river; and then followed a short turning, which led to the river itself, and a small landing-place for boats amongst a few hoary willows. Here a peculiar vessel was tied up at the bank: a long barge, roofed-over with timber and iron, from which, through the open doorway, came the reedy sound of a harmonium. It was the Fenland Ark – the floating church, which had come to Hinching Fen to serve the bereft parishioners.

Henry Wake hitched the pony to a tree, and very carefully handed Hester on to the boarding-plank. She was all right, though – she knew all about boarding barges . . . How strange, and appropriate, she thought, that she should be marrying Jonathan on a boat! Who could have foreseen it? The only certain thing about the future, it seemed, was that it was uncertain . . . The gipsy had said she'd wear an eelskin wedding-ring, and that was wrong – but also that she'd wait for gold, and that was right . . . The barge was swaying very gently as she advanced down the narrow planked aisle. Met on a boat – married on a boat: perhaps it was a good omen. Then she saw a large shoulder jutting out ahead of her – Jonathan's dark head turned, and he smiled at her, and somehow she knew that he had been thinking exactly the same thing. She smiled too as she drew level with him. That was the only omen she cared about . . .

'Oh! 'ell – thass Mr Wake's Chloe tied up there,' said Charlie Smeeth, as he, Sunny Daintree and the Surfleets turned off the high-road and approached the river. 'We're late for the wedding – we'll miss it – everybody else must be there – I told you!' All the way from the village he had been trying to get the other three to hurry, which was rather like attempting to hurl a feather.

'Calm yourself, bor,' said Sunny, 'the bride's likely only just this minute arrived, and the parson'll still be on about the brute beasts wi' no understanding, and the prosecution o' children. Ooh! it goes on for yards, that service. You could grow a beard before they git to the joining-together and putting-asunder, and whiskers to suit.'

'I ain't much of a boater – I hope I shan't git sea-sick,' Charlie said.

'Well, like I say, I'm never held with this idea of a floating church,' said Andrew Surfleet, stepping gingerly on to the boarding-plank. 'I still say it ain't on consecrated ground; and though Henry Wake explained it to me tother night, with a stack o' tall words, and made it sound straight enough, I'm still got me misdoubts. It meks you wonder if it's a bad omen for the pair, gitting wed this funny way: what do you reckon, Sunny?'

'Ooh! I don't know,' Sunny said, as they entered the church. 'I reckon they might be all right together, you know, this pair – I wouldn't be a bit surprised.'

# A selection of bestsellers from Headline

| | | | |
|---|---|---|---|
| THE GIRL FROM COTTON LANE | Harry Bowling | £5.99 | □ |
| MAYFIELD | Joy Chambers | £5.99 | □ |
| DANGEROUS LADY | Martina Cole | £4.99 | □ |
| DON'T CRY ALONE | Josephine Cox | £5.99 | □ |
| DIAMONDS IN DANBY WALK | Pamela Evans | £4.99 | □ |
| STARS | Kathryn Harvey | £5.99 | □ |
| THIS TIME NEXT YEAR | Evelyn Hood | £4.99 | □ |
| LOVE, COME NO MORE | Adam Kennedy | £5.99 | □ |
| AN IMPOSSIBLE WOMAN | James Mitchell | £5.99 | □ |
| FORBIDDEN FEELINGS | Una-Mary Parker | £5.99 | □ |
| A WOMAN POSSESSED | Malcolm Ross | £5.99 | □ |
| THE FEATHER AND THE STONE | Patricia Shaw | £4.99 | □ |
| WYCHWOOD | E V Thompson | £4.99 | □ |
| ADAM'S DAUGHTERS | Elizabeth Villars | £4.99 | □ |

*All Headline books are available at your local bookshop or newsagent, or can be ordered direct from the publisher. Just tick the titles you want and fill in the form below. Prices and availability subject to change without notice.*

Headline Book Publishing PLC, Cash Sales Department, Bookpoint, 39 Milton Park, Abingdon, OXON, OX14 4TD, UK. If you have a credit card you may order by telephone — 0235 831700.

Please enclose a cheque or postal order made payable to Bookpoint Ltd to the value of the cover price and allow the following for postage and packing:
UK & BFPO: £1.00 for the first book, 50p for the second book and 30p for each additional book ordered up to a maximum charge of £3.00.
OVERSEAS & EIRE: £2.00 for the first book, £1.00 for the second book and 50p for each additional book.

Name ................................................................................................

Address ............................................................................................

...........................................................................................................

...........................................................................................................

If you would prefer to pay by credit card, please complete:
Please debit my Visa/Access/Diner's Card/American Express (delete as applicable) card no:

| | | | | | | | | | | | | | | | |
|---|---|---|---|---|---|---|---|---|---|---|---|---|---|---|---|
| | | | | | | | | | | | | | | | |

Signature ...............................................................Expiry Date .......